PILLAR OF THE SUN

Exalted, Book 4

By Carl Bowen

Bear Fist jumped up and tore off the ruins of his shirt, then turned to the portcullis mechanism. He sent the wheel spinning and the counterweights whirring so that the portcullis retracted out of the way, then he smashed this mechanism like he'd done the other. That left the way open for his men, and not a moment too soon. No sooner had he heard the portcullis mechanism falling through the wall shaft to its demise when he heard the roars and battle cries of his first groups of beastmen and Arczeckhi raiders tearing across the field down from the rise and heading straight for the city's open front gate. At about the same time, alarms started ringing out all along the walls, while the guards in the watchtowers rang the enormous bronze bells that hung beneath their lookout posts. The sound carried from one corner of the city to the other, and men began to rush along the walls to man the catapults and heavy oyumi that alternated positions between the watchtowers.

"Too little, too late," Bear Fist said with a hard grin as he saw the men rushing around just outside the guard station. Many of his first-wave raiders were already inside effective catapult and oyumi range, rushing up the steps to engage the wall-top guards hand to hand. "Go ahead and do what you think you can, though," he said. "I'd be disappointed if you didn't put up a fight."

He emerged from the ruined guard station then, just as the guards he'd knocked down and scattered were rising to their feet. They looked at him with almost the proper amount of fear and reverence, and Bear Fist smiled like it was his naming day

It Is the Second Age of Man

Long ago, in the First Age, mortals became Exalted by the Unconquered Sun and other celestial gods. These demigods were Princes of the Earth and presided over a golden age of unparalleled wonder. But like all utopias, the age ended in tears and bloodshed.

The official histories say that the Solar Exalted went mad and had to be put down lest they destroy all Creation. Those who had been enlightened rulers became despots and anathema, and the First Age gave way to an era of chaos and warfare. This harsh time only ended with the rise of the Scarlet Empress, a powerful Dragon-Blood who fought back all enemies and founded a great empire. For a time, all was well—at least for those who toed the Empress's line.

But times are changing again. The Scarlet Empress has either gone missing or retreated into seclusion. The dark forces of the undead and the Fair Folk are stirring again. And, most cataclysmic of all, the Solar Exalted have returned. Across Creation, men and women find themselves imbued with the power of the Unconquered Sun and awaken to memories from a long-ago golden age.

The Sun-Children, the Anathema, have been reborn.

Among their kind is Dace. Before his Exaltation he was a grizzled mercenary, a veteran of the petty wars of the so-called Scavenger Lands—the region around the great trading city of Nexus. Now, empowered by the Sun with unparalleled combat skill, he leads his own mercenary force and has become one of Nexus's protectors. But the weight of destiny lies heavily on his shoulders, and he fears great struggles are ahead. Already he has faced grim agents of the Deathlords and invading demons.

There is little rest for the chosen of the Sun.

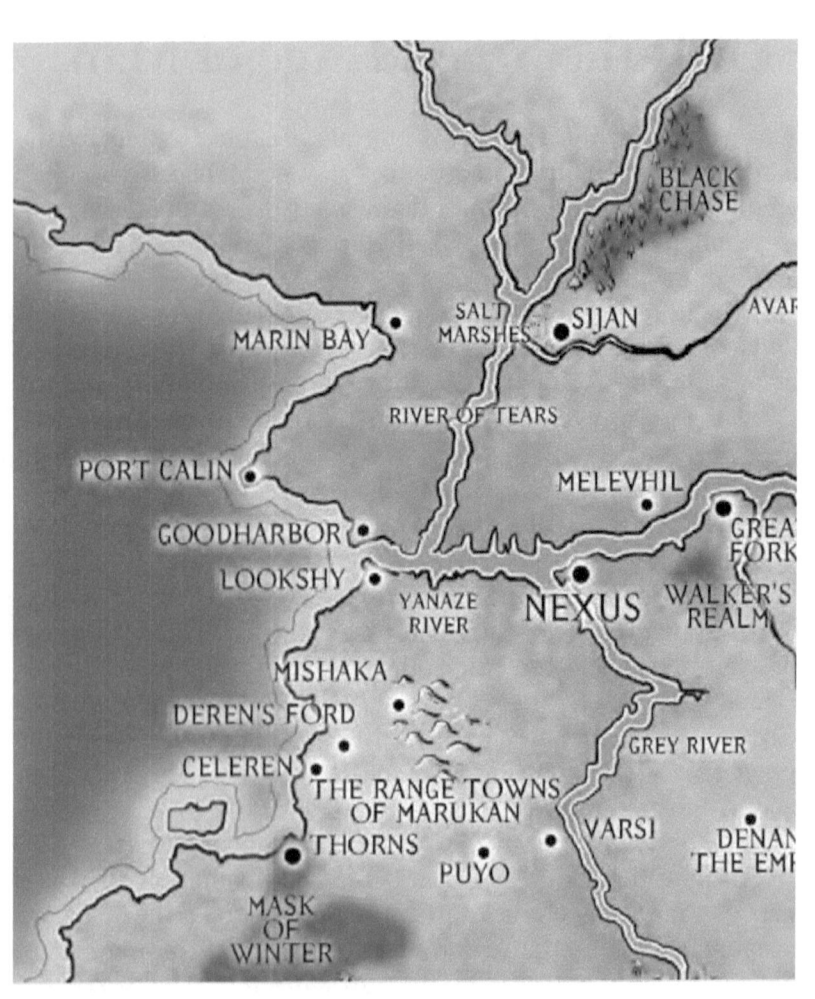

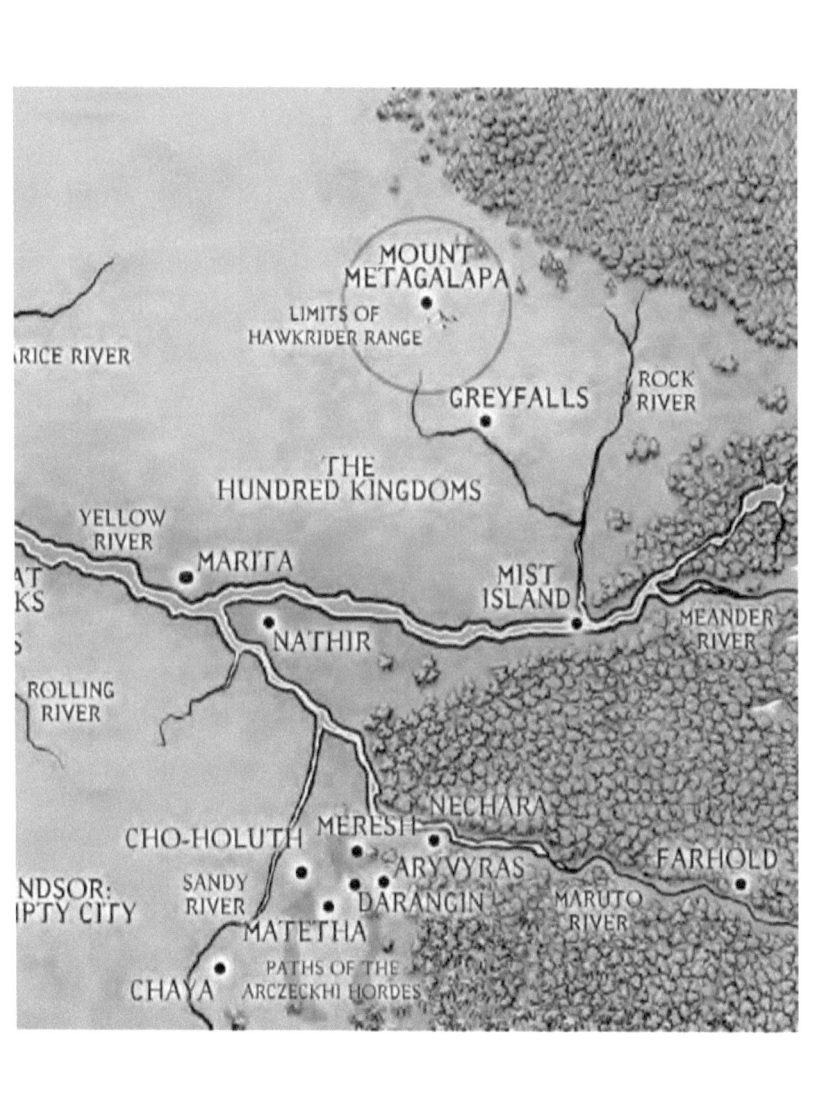

Prologue

In a place far from civilization near the Eastern edges of Creation, a line of thirteen beings walked in solemn procession, formulating silent plans for war. Light from the moon broke through patchy, scudding clouds only occasionally, but the being in the lead knew its exact position in the sky without looking, just as he knew that its face was full. He didn't have to be able to see it to know it, for this being was no man, but a demigod—one of the Chosen of Luna, the fickle, ever-changing goddess of the moon. This demigod had once been merely human and doomed to die in ignominious anonymity like the rest, but no longer. The light of the moon was in him now, and the quicksilver fire of its power burned in his blood. It made him strong and nigh immortal, and it gave divine meaning to a life he might once have wasted. His name was Bear Fist, and he was Exalted above mortal men and women.

That included the twelve men who followed him, though they were only men in the loosest sense. They walked upright on two legs, clutched weapons in five-fingered hands and peered about with sharp, clear eyes, but even in the intermittent darkness, it was obvious they weren't human. Coarse gray and white hair covered their bodies, and their long fingers ended in hard black claws. Their legs were coiled and bent like those of goats, and instead of feet, they had sturdy cloven hooves. But what made them stand apart most from humanity were their long, caprine muzzles and the straight, sharp horns on their heads. These goatmen weren't Exalted like their leader, but they were the offspring of Bear Fist's lord and master, who was also one of the Chosen of Luna. Their sire's name was Ma-Ha-Suchi, and they served him fanatically as his warriors and as the caretakers of his diminishing kingdom in the jungles of the East. They surged and thrived in the current of his will.

Ma-Ha-Suchi's will tonight for these twelve beastmen was that they accompany Bear Fist north through jungle, marsh and forest, across the Maruto and the Yellow Rivers to the fringes of the Hundred Kingdoms. When they reached their destination—which only Bear Fist knew—a holy work would begin, and through them all would Ma-Ha-Suchi begin his war upon human civilization. The time had come to raze everything that encroaching, usurping mankind had built and to take back for his people what had been lost an age ago. And through Bear Fist and these twelve followers would that righteous campaign be started. Bear Fist was young and recently Chosen—centuries Ma-Ha-Suchi's junior—but he was honorable, brave, strong and devout, and Ma-Ha-Suchi trusted him with this crucial early strategy in the all-out war to come. And who Ma-Ha-Suchi trusted, these twelve beastmen obeyed without question.

"We're here," Bear Fist sighed over his shoulder, as he pushed through a tangle of underbrush and disappeared. It was the first he'd spoken since the thirteen of them had set out from Ma-Ha-Suchi's nameless jungle lair. "What a mess. This is no way to honor a war god, no matter how insignificant."

The beastmen emerged from the dense forest in which they'd been marching into a quiet, perfectly circular clearing. Bear Fist stood just within, and a shaft of bright silver moonlight had pierced the cloud cover to illuminate it. A ring of roughly squared-off standing stones had once bounded this clearing, but they had long since fallen over and broken. Animal tracks and spoor marred the area inside the circle, and castoff animal bones littered the clearing as if some careless predator had once laired here. Or more likely, human hunters had once made camp here, and they'd chosen not to clean up after themselves. A smaller ring of scavenged stones around a long-unused fire pit near the center of the clearing confirmed that suspicion in Bear Fist's eyes. As the goatmen filed in behind him, Bear Fist paced the interior of the clearing and began to clean up the detritus that man and uncaring nature had left lying around.

"Set up the lamps, and give me some space," Bear Fist said,

picking up a gnawed deer rib and tossing it into the trees. "I don't like it, but this is going to have to do."

Quietly, reverently, the goatmen unslung hide bundles from their hairy shoulders and opened them to reveal pots of pungent oil rendered from bear fat, glass lamps, long wooden poles topped with iron hooks and metal censers full of a mix of skullweed roots and powdered horse dung. As Bear Fist sat down and crossed his legs, the others filled the oil lamps, hung them and the censers on the iron hooks and then staked the poles into the ground in a wide circle around the clearing. When they were finished, they lit the lamps and censers, and a heady aroma filled the clearing. When he was satisfied with these preparations, Bear Fist lifted his head and began to meditate, whispering silent prayers to Luna and promising Ma-Ha-Suchi that he would not fail.

He sat before the only unbroken and relatively intact icon that remained in this clearing. It was a thick, tall ironwood totem pole standing fifteen feet high and sunk securely in a bleached stone base. At the center of it was depicted Mokuu, the god to whom this clearing had once been dedicated. The god's eyes were wide and bright red, and his mouth was full of vicious fangs. Black hair and stylized war paint covered him from his bandy legs to the tips of his pointed ears. His long arms terminated in three-fingered hands with cruel, black talons. Time had dulled and scoured away much of the paint and the fine details carved into the totem pole, but Bear Fist could still make out the telltale characteristics that harked back to the Arczeckhi barbarian tribe among which Mokuu had lived before his death and subsequent deification.

Around the base of the pole were carved crude pictograms designed to convey the simple messages, "He is real," and, "Believe in him." Around the top of the pole were carved the faces of the bestial, vicious lesser gods Mokuu had worshiped in his mortal life, whose power the barbarian had used to unify his people and to become the greatest warlord the Arczeckhi people had ever known. Above that was a large, comfortable nest some enterprising bird had built atop the totem pole Luna only knew when. Bear Fist shook his head, sighed and closed his eyes to begin meditating in earnest. After the long day's march, he needed to gather his strength for what he was about to do.

He remained thus for another hour, and the goatmen waited with their heads bowed and their hands clasped. The aroma from the censers permeated the area, and gradually, even the sounds of the forest died away, until all was still and everything was ready. As Bear Fist meditated, his power welled up inside him until the mystical marks of his Exaltation began to glow with an excess of it. A milky-white circle of moonlight began to radiate on his forehead, and the looping, spiraling tattoos and patterns of raised dots his people had ritually marked him with began to incandesce as well. He lifted his head to the sky and opened his eyes, and the silvery iris of his left eye shimmered with reflected light. Only lamplight shone in his blue right eye.

"I'm ready," he said to the goatmen, staring up at Mokuu's totem pole. "Bring my weapons."

At his command, two goatmen approached him, each carrying a weapon fit only for an Exalted warrior. The weapons were called smashfists—wide, heavy blades and bracers affixed to the backs of a pair of leather gauntlets. Each was made of an alloy of steel, yellow jade and orichalcum, and the surface beneath the stout blade was fashioned in the shape of a ram's head with thick, curled horns and a red gemstone set in the ram's forehead. The ram's head was wide and long enough to protect the back of the user's hand and part of his wrist, and the thick, serrated blade extended several inches past the line of the knuckles. Ma-Ha-Suchi had given these weapons to Bear Fist, and they gleamed like gold in the flickering lamplight.

Bear Fist held out his hands, and the goatmen strapped the weapons around his wrists and cinched the buckles as tight as they would go. When they were finished, they stepped back again, and Bear Fist rose without acknowledging them. He had eyes only for the totem pole before him, and he approached it now, glowing from within. He lay the fingertips of his right hand against the rough-hewn ironwood for a moment, then drew his hand back across his body for a backhand blow. The flat circle on his forehead glowed just a bit more, as did the gemstone in the ram's forehead on his weapon, and he smashed the back of his hand almost as hard as he could against the side of the pole. A hollow boom rang out, startling birds into flight for a mile around.

"Mokuu!" he cried, lifting his voice to the heavens. "Open up! You and I have business!"

Nothing happened, so Bear Fist raised his fist again and smashed another blow into the side of the totem pole—harder this time. Another boom rang out, and the bird nest at the top of the pole disintegrated and rained down pine straw, twigs and bits of hair. Where this blow fell, a thin, short crack could now be seen in the ironwood surface.

"Now, Mokuu!" Bear Fist called out. "You know what I represent and what it's my right to do to you if you refuse me!"

Still nothing happened, so Bear Fist let fly two more powerful blows in quick succession. There was an audible crack this time near the base of the pole, and the entire thing shifted in its anchor of stone. Even the goatmen murmured in appreciation of their leader's might.

"I'll destroy it, you petty, half-real spirit!" the tattooed, glowing Chosen one yelled. "Now, open your sanctum to me, or risk my wrath!"

Bear Fist actually had to raise his fist for one more blow before Mokuu gave his answer. With a creak of ancient joints and a shower of dust and splinters, the totemic icon of Mokuu raised one long, gnarly fingered hand in supplication and pointed at the ground behind Bear Fist's feet. Bear Fist turned that way, and the ground parted silently to reveal a thin, stone stairway that appeared to lead down into the darkness of the earth. Where it actually went was to the tiny pocket dimension in which Mokuu dwelt when he wasn't walking up and down on the earth. The totem pole resumed its original form, and Bear Fist nodded in satisfaction.

"I'll be right back," he said as the goatmen gathered around the opening to Mokuu's sanctum. "If this takes me longer than five minutes, I'll kneel before Ma-Ha-Suchi and cut open my own stomach to redeem myself for the shame."

The goatmen huffed and chuckled at that, and one of them

stepped forward to accept Bear Fist's boots as he kicked them off. Another reached out to unbuckle Bear Fist's weapons, but Bear Fist shook his head. He flexed his fingers and ran the serrated blades against one another with a smile then said, "No, I'll keep these. Mokuu's a crafty one, and he might need some convincing." The goatman nodded and stepped back. The rest of them formed a semicircle around Bear Fist, and their leader stepped down into the sanctum's stairway. He descended out of sight, and all was quiet.

"Two minutes," a goatman named Scar Horn huffed a moment later to break the silence.

"Four," another, Bark Back, answered.

"One minute," Slate Knife, the warrior holding Bear Fist's boots, bleated. "Or else why did we even follow him all this way?"

"One?" a fourth, whose name was Red Leg, mused. "You want to lick those boots you're holding, too? I say two minutes."

"What about between minutes?" Bark Back asked.

"Up to thirty seconds goes to the last minute," Scar Horn said. "After that goes to the next."

"Is anyone counting?" Bark Back said.

Last Runner, the beastman who'd tried to take Bear Fist's smashfists, raised his hand, silently mouthing the count to himself.

Before anyone else could speak, a commotion broke out from within the sanctum, and two forms flopped up and out of the stairway to land awkwardly in front of the totem pole. The figure on top was Bear Fist, whose tattoos glowed white hot and could be seen through numerous tears in his clothing. The light from them ran up his thick, hairy arms and twisted into a stout braid of pure energy that coiled around the other figure's throat. The other figure was Bear Fist's height, though proportionately squat and bandy legged, but he was scrawny and mangy like a malnourished dog. He was covered in patches of curly hair, which tufted at the tips of his ears, and his eyes glowed a lurid cherry red in the faltering lamplight. He snapped at Bear Fist with sharp teeth, and he tore at the energy leash around his neck with the horny black claws at the end of his three-fingered hands. Yet, his struggles availed him nothing.

"Settle *down*, Mokuu," Bear Fist growled, slamming the god's head against the ground for emphasis. "You *will* listen to what I have to say."

Mokuu shoved Bear Fist back off him mightily, but the energy leash around his neck still prevented his escape. Bear Fist jerked the lead taut in his left hand, pulled Mokuu toward him and punched the god in the stomach. Mokuu's spirit flesh didn't bleed or spill his guts, but he doubled over and fell into a three-point crouch with an explosive gasp. The door to his sanctum closed in front of him, and when the god tried to reach out and reopen it, Bear Fist kicked him hard in the ribs for good measure. The blow lifted Mokuu off the ground, and Bear Fist flipped the god onto his back with a twist of the energy chain.

"Damn you, little god," Bear Fist hissed, "if you'd just listen to—"

Mokuu didn't listen. He jumped up and flung a handful of dirt at Bear Fist's face, then tried to close in and press his advantage. For the trouble, Bear Fist reached back with his right hand and backhanded Mokuu across the face before the god could land a blow. Mokuu's head rocked back, and a second, more powerful backhand with the same smashfist whipped Mokuu around and sent him staggering. Before the god could fall, Bear Fist hauled back on the leash, dug in his heels and swung Mokuu around by it as hard as he could. Mokuu's feet actually left the ground, and he flew in a half-circle around Bear Fist, sending goatmen diving out of the way. The god crashed into his own totem pole, back first, and the pole cracked in half and fell over. Mokuu tumbled over it and finally lay limp, making a sound somewhere between an ape's grunting and a human's crying.

"Look what you've done," the once-proud Arczeckhi chieftain turned minor war god whimpered, running his knobby fingers over the fearsome image of himself that lay before him. "Now who's going to remember? How can I be real now?"

"Shut it already," Bear Fist growled, shaking dirt off his face and gathering the slack in his glowing leash. "I could have explained to you what I actually *came here* to do if you hadn't jumped me. We could have done this an easier way."

"I don't care," Mokuu pouted, not looking up at his attacker. "Just let me fade away and disappear. I'm hardly real as it is."

"I said shut it," Bear Fist barked, rolling Mokuu over and forcing him to face the one who had beaten him. "I didn't come here to unravel you for your essence. I came to recruit you. There's a war starting, and your people are needed."

"What war?"

"My master has declared war against human civilization and means to take back the lands that once belonged to his kind. The lands your people conquered when you were alive can be yours again if you take our side."

"My people?" Mokuu snapped. "My people are beaten. Scattered. Three centuries have passed since my conquests terrorized the South and East. When I died, far from here at the hands of a Dragon-Blood, my people were broken."

"The time has come to change that," Bear Fist said, snarling at the mention of the Dragon-Blooded. "Your people survive to this day, and others still fear the Arczeckh horde. If they were unified, the Arczeckhi could trample this land flat and take what they wanted. The dream you had as a living man could come to life. Now that you're a god, you have the power to make it so. And you owe it to those of your people who still remember you and know that you're real."

Mokuu relaxed just a little, and a cunning gleam washed out some of the self-pity and skepticism in his eyes. "But how? I'm beaten myself—here at the door to my own sanctum."

"You will lead them to glory through me," Bear Fist said. "I'll go to your people with these men here, and you'll give me your blessing as I speak to them. I'll forge them into a weapon worthy of your legacy. You'll stay at my side to silence the nonbelievers, and through me, you'll reap worship and adoration from your people that you've never dreamed possible in all these centuries since you became a god."

"But you don't need me for that," the crafty god said. "If you're powerful enough to beat me, you're powerful enough to beat any Arczeckhi chieftain."

"I don't just need their obedience," Bear Fist said, "I need their faith. Some will fight me even with your endorsement, but many others won't if they see me as your instrument and their means to glory. And I won't need to put down as many good, strong, capable barbarian leaders this way."

"I see," Mokuu said. "But suppose I refuse and choose to rally people against you? What's it worth to your master that I don't do that?"

Bear Fist's eyes flashed, and the glowing circle on his forehead glared even brighter. He twisted the energy leash around his left wrist and lifted Mokuu off the ground by the throat. The shining blade on the back of his fist flattened the god's ear against his face.

"We aren't *negotiating*," the Chosen of Luna said as Mokuu struggled. "You will do this thing. If you refuse, you'll cease to be real right here and now, among these broken things in this forgotten place. If you go along now but try to turn against me later, I'll destroy you in front of your people, and my master's warriors will *end* the Arczeckh horde. Do you understand me?"

Mokuu's eyes goggled, but he nodded as he was able around Bear Fist's meaty fist.

"Good," Bear Fist said, lowering Mokuu once more and letting go of his throat. "Now come with me, and I'll tell you what you're going to do. You others make camp and get plenty of rest. We've got a long way to go tomorrow."

Bear Fist led Mokuu out of the clearing to speak with him privately, and the goatmen gathered to start making camp. They glanced in the direction that Bear Fist and Mokuu had gone, but none of them commented on what they'd just seen their leader do. For several long minutes they worked in silence until Scar Horn finally spoke up.

"So, how long was it?"

"One minute, twenty-two seconds," Last Runner said.

Slate Knife smiled and knocked heads with the other three who'd bet against him. He gave Red Leg an especially hard jolt before settling up with the other two.

"Like I said," Slate Knife said as Red Leg shook his head to clear it. "Why else would we follow him all this way if we had so little faith in him?"

Chapter One

After countless days of travel into the forested East, Panther's journey was coming to an end at last. He wasn't entirely certain how long he'd been walking, but he knew at least that the year had ended and Calibration had come and passed. He vaguely remembered the month of Ascending Water coming and going, though the chill of winter's heart hadn't touched him. It was early spring now, in the month of Resplendent Earth, and though he wore no coat or shirt over his thin, baggy pants, he was just as warm now as he'd been every day since his journey had begun. The light of the Unconquered Sun burned within him and kept him warm. There was so much inside him… so much that he had to make a conscious effort to contain it within himself, lest it consume him, or worse, flare out and let everyone for miles around know where he was and what he had become. The Unconquered Sun's power protected him, making exposure to the weather seem a vain concern, but it wasn't subtle. It was glorious and radiant, harking back to a time when ones like himself strode proud and defiant among the cowering mortals over whom they ruled in the sun god's name.

He had left the crowded, thriving metropolis of Nexus and walked away from his life. He'd followed the Yellow River east, shying away from human settlements that surrounded Nexus, dodging shadowlands and Great Forks entirely and skirting the boundaries of the Hundred Kingdoms as well, just to be safe. Never once had he stopped to sleep. Never once had he paused to eat or drink anything. The power he'd been given had sustained him thus far, but though he'd relied on it, he'd kept it hidden. The elite Dragon-Blooded of the imperial military hunted down ones such as himself, labeling them Anathema.

Panther knew now that the Dragon-Blood's dogma was based on ancient lies and treachery, but that made the scions of the Realm no less powerful. They believed that the Chosen of the Unconquered Sun were diabolical terrors given flesh, and although Panther didn't believe that, he had to stay away from them until he could figure out what he *did* believe.

He thought about that now as he had made his way deep into this forest far from human civilization. What had he become? What did the Unconquered Sun want with him? In fact, why had the most powerful god in Creation chosen *him* in the first place?

Granted, in the life he'd abandoned, he'd been famous. Perhaps his fame wasn't as world-spanning as that of the familial heads of the Realm's Great Houses, but his was one of the few names known (and more importantly, respected) throughout the Scavenger Lands. Anyone who knew enough to talk about the sport of pit fighting knew Panther's name and knew that he never lost, no matter what. They didn't know that the name Panther wasn't the one his mother had given him, but even he agreed that it suited him better than that other one. He'd been thrust into slavery after his mother's death, and the master who'd bought him had given him the name in honor of his size, ferocity and languid grace. Word of the same spread as he fought in arenas all around the Scavenger Lands until he was ready to compete in the main arena in Nexus itself. And the more he fought, the more he won, and the more he won, the more his fame grew. He might not ever have been a household name, but in pit-fighting circles, he was as well known and feared as any mortal gladiator from Arjuf to Great Forks and beyond.

Nonetheless, Panther doubted very much that his fame as a brawler and a warrior and a showman had attracted the Unconquered Sun's attention. With the power he'd been given, he could do things now that made his earlier prowess seem laughable in comparison. Nor could the divine calling have come as a result of Panther's fame and fortune. If the Unconquered Sun needed servants with those qualifications, there were plenty of better people in Nexus alone to choose from. Panther's erstwhile master, Maxus, had much more money and was known farther afield than Panther had ever been, for instance. A onetime patron of Panther's, Kerrek Deset, was even more widely recognized and even more affluent, and he didn't even traffic in human beings. Panther had neither man's money or recognition, but more to the point, he lacked the respect that he saw people had for those other men. People knew nothing about him except that he killed for money and the applause of a delighted crowd. That was all Panther had ever been; that was all there was to see of him. Could that possibly have been what the Unconquered Sun wanted of him?

As Panther walked and thought these thoughts, a path of branches and fallen leaves subtly wove itself in front of him. The trees here were thicker and darker and older, but they bent out of his way ever so slightly and spread their highest branches slightly to illuminate the path. The normal animal sounds of the forest hushed in reverence, and even the wind seemed to hold its breath in anticipation as he passed. He didn't notice these things among his swirling thoughts, but he followed the path, adhering to some ancient memory that clung to the divine essence that the Unconquered Sun had reincarnated within him. Instead of noticing the grandeur of nature all around him, he chose instead to relive the moment when his entire life had changed and the Unconquered Sun had named Panther as his own.

It had happened shortly after an arena match with a team of fighters who called themselves the Leather Sharks. The match had filled the Nexus arena to standing-room-only capacity, and though it hadn't turned out to be a fight to the death, it had been worth every dinar the attendees had coughed up. The night that followed had been a blur of parties and liquor and drugs and harlots, yet when the haze of celebration had ended, he'd woken up alone. He'd sat up in his empty, dirty bed with a hollow feeling like maybe the best part of his life was over and he had no more reason to exist. That thought had hit him like a hammer right between the eyes, and he'd just sat there, weak and nauseated, thinking *I can do nothing else in this life greater than what I've already done. What else is left for me but to die fighting in the pit?*

It was then that he'd first heard the voice, and he still remembered every word it had spoken to him. It echoed in his mind like the roar of an arena crowd, but it wasn't the bloodthirsty baying of the end of a match. It had sounded the way the crowd had sounded the day Panther had won his freedom.

"Go and see," it had said, compelling him to rise. "Look at the face that has chosen you." The power in those words had pulled him outside onto his balcony, right to the rail, and there, he'd stopped, staring up in awe at the blazing face of the summer sun at its zenith. It had blinded him with its glory and buffeted him with the essence of its power, filling him past overflowing, then adding even more.

"You who have no father," the voice of the Unconquered Sun had said, "I am your father now. You who shed blood and know not why, I give you a reason. In my anger, I turned my face from the world of men, but I shall do so no longer. Know you are among my chosen priests. Go, and make the world a righteous place as you know best. Take light into darkness, and know you act with my blessing."

The light had flared around Panther then, and it blazed from a golden circle of pure light on his forehead. The radiance had scoured the inside of his apartment as he'd stumbled back inside, and in a moment of purest enlightenment, he realized that everything he'd ever been told about the Anathema and the Dragon-Blooded was a lie. He'd been Exalted by the most powerful god in Creation, and he'd been given a mission. That very day, as soon as he was able to contain the power within him and subsume the radiance that emanated from him, he'd left his old life behind and begun the long walk eastward that had led him to this forest.

And now, reliving that moment, Panther broke through a ring of trees into a clearing dominated by the largest oak he'd ever seen. Crystal-clear water burbled up through the roots to form a mirrored pool. The shade in this place, this silent temple surrounded by tree pillars with a carpet of branches and fallen leaves, was cool but not nearly so dim as the rest of the forest had been. Panther's eyes widened when he saw the place, and he let out a long, tense breath. He hadn't realized how tired he'd become, and as he approached the temple oak, the weight of his long journey caught up with him all at once. He sat down at the base of the tree in a comfortable place between its roots and leaned back against it to think.

He would never forget that first time he'd seen the face of the Unconquered Sun and heard its voice, and the words that the god had spoken to him would ring in his ears for all time. Yet what troubled Panther most was that he didn't know what those words meant. All he knew how to do was kill and survive in a way that pleased a crowd. He'd never learned how to be a leader, nor had he ever cared to. He'd never addressed a crowd of more than a handful of people, and the only times he'd done even that had been to threaten or disparage an opponent he was about to kill for a select audience's amusement. He was no teacher either. In fact, he'd never considered himself any smarter than anyone else.

How, then, could the Unconquered Sun have chosen him to be a priest? The god had commanded him to go and make the world a righteous place as he knew best, but what did a former slave turned pit fighter know about righteousness? All he really knew was that he was nothing resembling a righteous man, and he never had been. So why had he been chosen? What had the Unconquered Sun seen in him that had made the god bless his body and end his normal life of lingering discontent? Could the Unconquered Sun have made a mistake? Was that even possible?

Panther sat beneath the enormous oak in its temple of silence, and he contemplated these things. He drank occasionally from the cool spring beside him, and he meditated for the first time in his life. The first thing he sought to do was to clear his mind of the fear and anxiety and insecurity that was giving these troublesome questions their frantic, spasmodic life. After that, he would have only to empty his mind and surrender himself to the will of the Unconquered Sun and hope that the god would speak to him again. When he'd finally readied himself and reached the proper mental state, Panther reasoned, the Unconquered Sun would explain everything so that Panther's work could begin. Whatever it might be.

So Panther relaxed and absorbed the silence that surrounded him. He found, however, that he could no more clear his mind than he could simply will his heart to stop beating. As he tried to ponder the motivations of the Unconquered Sun, memories of the life he'd led back in Nexus began to play themselves out before his mind's eye. They were memories he could neither escape nor undo, as much as he might wish to now, and they showed him all the reasons that the Unconquered Sun should never have turned to him in the first place...

Chapter Two

"You're not all going to win this," the grizzled old slave-trainer said as he limped in a circle around the knot of frightened young fighters who waited in a cramped, musty stall beneath the arena. "Some of you are going to lose. For some it's even going to be pretty quick." He glanced at the trembling reed of a slave at Panther's right, and Panther felt the fighter shiver. Panther didn't like that fighter, whom Maxus had named Javelin, but he didn't think the old man should try so hard to rattle his confidence right before the fight.

"Some of you are going to get hurt," Maxus went on, combing his fingers through his gnarled, gray whiskers. "It happens, and if you don't believe that, you're going to be the first person it happens to. I was a star here for years without so much as a scratch, but it happened to me. Believe me when I tell you."

Panther nodded, and he heard Javelin sniffle beside him. He wanted to feel sorry for the wiry beanpole, but he couldn't bring himself to. His attention was divided between Maxus and the older fighters such as Wolf, Boar Spear and Snow Tiger around him—the ones who had actual fighting experience. Maxus had trained them all like he'd trained Panther, but they weren't his slaves. They were indentured proteges who'd given up their freedom contractually and come to be honed into professional gladiators.

"Some of you," Maxus continued, "are even going to die. In fact, one of you is *definitely* going to die. This is a nonlethal competition bout, but we all know it's going to happen anyway. The other trainers and I already have a pool going about which of our boys it's going to be. Javelin, my jade's on you, just so you know."

Javelin's crotch turned instantly dark, and a rank, acrid smell assaulted Panther's nose. Everyone around Javelin took a step back as the tall fighter broke out in a couple of hitching, snorting sobs. Boar Spear and Snow Tiger elbowed each other and laughed out loud at their teammate.

"Gods, there's always a pisser," Maxus spat. "That ain't a diaper you're wearing, boy. You want to do that where your teammates are standing? You make me sick. Get up to the front of the formation, and you shut up that crying. I didn't buy you 'cause I bedded your mama. I bought you to fight."

Shaking and turning crimson in shame, Javelin nearly dropped his blunted short sword and buckler as he pushed through his fellow gladiators to the front of their spearhead formation. The musty stall in which they were waiting started to stink immediately, despite the best efforts of the hay and wood chips on the ground soaking up the boy's urine. The other fighters let him pass without argument. None of them was really willing to take the dangerous point position in the spearhead formation except Wolf, but he stepped back as Javelin pushed to the front.

"All right, tighten it up," Maxus said as Javelin took his place and the others reordered themselves. "There's nothing crying's going to do to save you. Some are going to lose, some are going to get hurt, and Javelin's probably going to die." Javelin flinched again, but Maxus' words produced no further outburst. "Now, you all better listen up because these are the rules. If any of you break the rules and the judges catch you, I'm selling you to an undercity miner I know who'd love to have you. He likes teaching little boys how to follow the rules, and none of you would be his first.

"First rule, this ain't no fight to the death. You're not going out there to kill my friends' and rivals' property. You're only going out there to beat 'em. None of you are worth killing yet, and neither are any of them. Boar Spear, Snow Tiger, what'd I just say?"

"Ain't no fight to the death, Master Maxus," the two fighters said in unison, smiling as they said it.

"No, I said *you* ain't worth it, you cockerels," Maxus said, rapping the side of Snow Tiger's bronze helmet with his stout walking stick. "It'll happen by accident, of course—Javelin—but I don't want any of you getting carried away out there." If Javelin was even listening to Maxus' words at this point, he gave no sign. He only stared at the stall door in front of him like a convicted criminal.

"Second, listen to the judges. If you get somebody down, or if somebody gets you down, you don't do anything else until the nearest judge makes a ruling. You hear me, Wolf? You got away with something last time, but they're going to be watching you closer than ever now."

"I'll keep it in mind," the scarred, stocky fighter behind Javelin said. He sounded like he was smiling, and that helped Panther relax.

"Third," Maxus went on, "don't touch the judges. I repeat, *don't touch the judges*. I'm not going to tell you why, though, because I kind of want to see what happens if one of you idiots thinks about trying it.

"Finally, don't touch the weapons on the racks until the judges give the signal. It's only sword-and-shield or sword-and-cestus for a while, so the fighting goes on longer. You guys are low-bill, so the arrangers are still filling seats, and they want to keep you going for as long as they can."

"When do we get to use the rack weapons, Master Maxus?" Panther asked.

Maxus limped over to glare through the slit in Panther's helmet. "When the judges say so, boy."

"It'll be when they let out the animals," Boar Spear said, tapping his sword against the mailed gauntlet on his other hand in anticipation. "The crowd loves it when we see 'em coming and start scrambling for the pikes and nets like cowards."

"Oh, I'm *sorry*," Maxus said, rounding on Boar Spear and jabbing him in the back with his walking stick. "I thought *I* was the master and trainer here. I guess *you* are instead. I didn't realize I had it all *backward*!" Each time he emphasized a word, he jabbed Boar Spear a little harder.

"Sorry, Master," Boar Spear said, sounding insincere.

"How many animals?" Panther asked. "And what kind?"

A quivering started in his bowels, and he realized how Javelin had probably felt just a few minutes ago. Sweat started soaking into the cloth his short sword's hilt was wrapped in.

"Don't know either way," Maxus said. "The arrangers said they wanted to surprise us and the crowd."

"But we… we can kill them, right?" Javelin asked. His voice was hollow and quiet, echoing eerily inside his helmet. "Whatever they are."

"If they don't get you first, boy," Maxus said, laughing. "But who are we kidding, right?"

"Just worry about the other teams first," Wolf rumbled. "They won't let any animals out until one whole team goes down."

"And when they do, it'll probably just be a pack of dogs or a starved, elderly bear," Snow Tiger said.

"Nothing we can't handle," Boar Spear said.

"Yeah, we'll see, boys," Maxus said. "We'll see. Just stick together when you see the signal and don't lose your heads. Now, remember the rules, and get ready to fight because they're about to open the gate. And remember too, if you can't make me proud, at least make me look good out there. If you can't do either, you're going to be sorry."

The fighters murmured at that, and Panther wasn't sure if he was supposed to be inspired or intimidated. All he felt for sure was uncomfortable, what with the late morning heat and the smell of Javelin's urine. Everything else was a cold sheen of mortal fear with an undercurrent of mounting excitement.

"Hey, Panther," Maxus whispered suddenly, squeezing Panther's shoulder. The sound was a raspy echo inside his sweltering helmet, but he doubted that the fighters within one step of him could hear what the old arena veteran was saying. "I want you to watch what Javelin does out there. I know fighters, boy, and that one's going to be a bolt of lightning now he's let out what was inside him. Smart money says he takes two fighters out of the game for good before he gets a scratch."

"I thought you said he was going to die, Master," Panther whispered, trying to keep his voice down inside his helmet, though it sounded like thunder to him.

"Die? Not today, boy. If anybody dies, it'll be Boar Spear. That cocky idiot's never been in a beast match before. Nah, Javelin ain't going to go. If he does... Hell, I'd set the lot of you free and quit this business for good."

Before Panther could respond to that, a shrill whistle went up from beyond the stall gate and a round of hoots, cheers and strained applause rose from the crowd in the arena. Everyone in the stall stiffened up immediately, and whispering broke out as a scrawny djala slave lifted the bar from in front of the stall door. A couple of fighters in the back pushed forward, ready to rush outside.

"Quiet, you panic monkeys," Maxus barked. "They'll open the doors from outside when it's time to start. Right now, the caller's just warming up the crowd." Panther could vaguely hear the rumble of an amplified voice over the murmur of the crowd, but his helmet rendered the words unintelligible. "Right now, he's going on about, 'Thank you for coming early, you won't be disappointed.' Now, he's describing the rules. Setting the betting limits... Wait, now what's he going on about?

A particularly long pause ensued, after which Maxus continued. "Oh... right. He's saying you're all reenacting some famous battle from a couple hundred years ago. Must be somebody important visiting from Lookshy today. Now, here comes some bullshit about warrior's pride... Honor between combatants... Ah, here we go. Get ready boys. He's just introduced the team owners... the rich bastards who supplied the animals... the smith who provided the weapons... and now, it's, 'Let's all cheer for our warrior athletes as they come out fighting! May they die well or not at all!'"

As Maxus mimicked the caller's final words, the door to the stall was jerked open, and the fighters rushed out. The excitement caught up the indentured fighters, and they hollered and raised their weapons like a barbarian raiding party, daring any of the opposing teams to get close enough to get hurt. The defiant shout came back just as loud from four other directions as four teams entered the arena at the same time from equidistant gates around the pit wall. Panther's team maintained a tight spearhead formation, while another marched slowly in a tighter fang-style formation like imperial foot soldiers. The other three of them just ran en masse like street gangs. The meager midday crowd applauded politely as the fighters took the field.

Ignoring the applause, Panther kept his eyes at the pit level and tried to come up with some kind of strategy that would keep him from harm and help his team win. A wooden weapon rack loomed tall and lonely like a brutal oasis in the desert of the pit's featureless sandy floor, and seven judges divided their attention between it and the fighters. Each judge wore ankle-length robes of black, white and green check despite the heat, and each carried a thin black baton with a spherical jade head. They kept well away from the oncoming fighters but never so far that they couldn't see them or get to their sides quickly. Each also had a handful of bright silk flags tucked under a bright red sash.

As for the other teams of fighters, they seemed little different from Panther's team. They were all young, tall and in good shape, and none of them were scarred, hardened veterans. They all wore helmets, sandals, gloves and either leather shorts or simple loincloths. All of them were armed with heavy, blunt short swords, and everyone either carried a buckler shield or wore a mailed cestus on his off hand. Each fighter on a team wore a rope belt that had been dyed a particular color so his teammates would recognize him in the heat of battle. Most wore theirs around their waists, but Maxus had told his fighters to wear theirs looped over one shoulder instead to set them apart better.

Panther's dreams of strategy withered on the vine, though, as soon as the opposing teams saw each other and the crowd's applause got to them. In the sudden rush of excitement of everyone shouting and running, the fighters abandoned strategy and just rushed into each other. Three places ahead of Panther, Javelin snarled an incoherent noise of pent-up rage and charged like a madman into a knot of fighters wearing blue belts. Half of the team behind him hustled to keep up and maintain the formation, but the rest—led by Boar Spear and Snow Tiger—took off toward the weapon rack in the center of the pit. They barreled into the flank of the fighters imitating an imperial fang, who were wearing red belts. That left Panther alone for a second, but after only a moment's hesitation, he joined Javelin, Wolf and the others.

He made it in among a handful of his teammates just as Javelin was laying out two orange-belted fighters with the edge of his shield. The first one stayed down and put a hand to the bloody gash over his eye, signaling to a nearby judge. The other kicked Javelin in the knee, driving him back toward Panther. His lanky teammate fell backward into his arms, but Javelin had no idea who'd caught him. He lashed out with a wild swing over his head that knocked Panther's helmet askew, then he kicked away like a wildcat fighting for its life. Panther let him go and staggered back with only a crazily skewed slit of light visible in front of him. He heard somebody coming and saw a shadow fall over him, and he knew that he was about to get seriously hurt, so he tore his helmet off with his free hand. No sooner had he done so than when he saw an orange-belted thug in a bronze helmet looming over him with a sword drawn back for what looked like a killing blow. Without even thinking, Panther pitched the helmet as hard as he could underhanded into the thug's stomach. The thug staggered and doubled over, falling to his knees and dropping his sword. Surprised that that had actually worked, Panther followed up with a left-handed punch with his cestus that laid the fighter out with a huge dent in his helmet's faceplate.

"Down!" a judge said, sweeping in front of Panther seemingly out of nowhere and holding up a silk flag with the glyph for surrender on it. Panther stepped back with a grin on his face and looked up to see the people in the crowd nearest that part of the arena laughing and clapping. Something was born inside him then, and any worry he might have felt before the match evaporated. The sun warmed his face as the crowd's applause warmed his heart, and he knew that, here in the ring, he could be happier than he'd ever been—as long as he kept fighting and making the crowd happy, anyway. He waited another moment for the nod from the judge then rejoined his teammates.

The next several long minutes were only a blur, and all

Panther would remember of them in the future would be the excitement and the faint sensation of the few bruises and cuts he got whenever he got careless. Between Wolf, Javelin and himself, his team managed to clear out the orange team members who hadn't already joined the melee in the center of the arena. They lost only two of their own to minor but painful wounds. When the area around them was clear, they raised their swords and voices to encourage the crowd then charged in to help their teammates at the central weapon rack.

The rack bristled with two each of spears, javelins, tridents, simple wooden staves and weighted nets. Some of the fighters around it hacked at each other with their bated swords, drawing blood or breaking bones with every solid hit. Others used their shields to shove foes into their teammates or even toward the weapon rack to see what would happen. Some of the bigger, older fighters had resorted to simple wrestling moves and were trying to use their size against smaller, more timid opponents. The ones who were already getting tired threw clumsy, careless punches with shields or cesti, putting their faith in dumb luck and raw determination. Of the ones who were resorting to that tactic, Boar Spear seemed the most effective and the one most enjoying himself.

Panther, Wolf and Javelin waded into this mess with a zeal that woke the crowd up a little. Panther ducked and wove between a couple of attacks and made his way to Snow Tiger, who was surrounded by two orange-belts, a red and three yellows. The six of them were mostly getting in each other's way, but they all seemed intent on taking down Snow Tiger, who was arguably the biggest member of Maxus' team. Panther disarmed one from behind and sent him crashing into two others. Another, the red-belt, jumped on his back and tried to brain him, but Panther whipped forward and drove the fighter's head into the ground. Something cracked as the fighter collapsed into the sand, but Panther pretended not to hear it as he jumped over the red-belt and kicked an orange square between the shoulder blades. Snow Tiger caught that one in a vicious clothesline with the edge of his shield, and for a moment, no one was left standing around them. They nodded to each other with matching wicked grins of delight as judges swept between them signaling which of the fallen fighters intended to stay down and which intended to keep fighting.

Suddenly, a roar went up around them, and Panther raised a hand in a gratified, self-confident salute. By the look on Snow Tiger's face, however, he realized that the crowd wasn't cheering for them, but rather for the part of the fight he had been dreading since before the match began. A quick look around confirmed it, as he saw three mangy, scrawny, white-maned, pale-eyed Southern lions coming out of their stalls into the arena for the first time. The beasts flinched at the bright light as the sun shone on them, but that was the only indication of their discomfort. They'd been bred for deafness so that the roar of the crowd, even the early, low-bill crowd, wouldn't frighten them. They'd also been nigh starved and abused for the last two weeks, fed only rare tidbits of criminals caught stealing in the Little Market. This treatment made them look awful and instilled in them a maddened bloodthirst that made for the best sport this early in the day. Despite his excitement and the thrill of making it this far into the event, Panther still had to gulp down his fear and prepare himself to face this new foe.

"The rack!" Snow Tiger called out, leaving Panther where he stood. "Panther, get to the rack!"

Pulling himself together, Panther took a couple of steps toward the center of the pit and then paused to take stock of the situation there. Every fighter who was still standing had rushed over there, and they were all tussling and shoving one another trying to get a hand on something with which to fend off the yowling, snarling lions that were headed their way. Even teammates were fighting one another, which the people in the crowd who were paying attention seemed to find hilarious. From this general mess, the standing members of the red team emerged first, carrying the tridents and one of the spears between them. They flanked the lion on the farthest right and drew it away from its brothers. Panther tried to get over to the rack in the space vacated by the red-belted fighters, but a fierce fight broke out between the last two yellow-belts, and he got tangled up in it. They slammed into him, knocking the three of them into a sprawl, and when he got to his knees, Panther could see that the shorter yellow-belt was completely panicked and willing to murder his teammate for standing between him and the weapon rack. The small fighter sat on his comrade's chest and pinned his arms with his legs, then pounded on the downed fighter's helmet with the butt of his sword until the pinned man wasn't moving anymore. The shorter one then flipped the short sword around in his hands, clearly meaning to plunge it into his teammate's chest or throat. Knowing he was wasting valuable time, Panther scooped up a handful of sand and threw it at the slit in the yellow-belt's helmet, making the short, enraged fighter lurch backward coughing. Panther then rose to his full height and lifted the short yellow-belted fighter off the ground with a tremendous uppercut. The punch sent the fighter flying off his dazed partner and right toward a judge who'd been rushing in to prevent the impassioned murder himself. The judge reached out with his jade-capped staff and touched it to airborne yellow-belt before the fighter could collide with him or hit the ground. A bolt of crackling green energy surrounded the unlucky fighter, and he collapsed to the ground twitching.

Panther heard the crowd react to his display, and he grinned over his shoulder at the people seated nearest him. Then, to add to the moment, he reached down and offered a hand to the dazed yellow-belted fighter whose life he'd just saved. The grateful fighter accepted the offered hand, but he wasn't expecting what happened when Panther pulled him up to his feet. Without letting go of the fighter's cestus, Panther twisted the man's arm up behind him and drove him back down to the ground, this time on his face. That earned him a laugh from the crowd and a concession of victory from the judge.

He got back up then and saw that the red-belted team had one of the lions cornered and was having little trouble putting it down. He was also surprised to find that Wolf was facing one down all by himself with nothing but a weighted net while Boar Spear, Snow Tiger and a blue-belted fighter came over to help him. That left only one beast, and it looked like it was giving the remaining fighters more trouble than the other two combined.

It was roaring and waving its big claws in the air, and it more or less cornered Javelin and the rest of the blue team between itself and the weapon rack in the middle of the arena. A miscast net lay on the ground behind it, and Javelin was trying to hold the beast at bay with the broken end of a wooden staff. The other blue-belted fighters each held a javelin in unsteady hands, but they were wielding them like spears rather than projectiles. They were all terrified, and none more so than Javelin, who had finally run out of the animating spark that had made him so ferocious all throughout the match thus far. Whatever Maxus had recognized in the boy had clearly run its course.

Panther froze for a moment. He glanced around at the bodies of the fallen to see that the beaten ones were carrying the injured ones off the field and the judges were standing vigil over the unconscious ones until the match was resolved. It looked like the red fighters had their lion under control and would bring it down any second, so Panther couldn't very well just run over there and pretend to help. They certainly wouldn't appreciate it, and when the beast fell, he'd be surrounded by fighters from a different team. Wolf, Boar Spear and Snow Tiger were closing in on their lion, but they were all the way on the other side of the arena by now. That left Javelin and the weapon-rack lion closest, so he hesitantly made his way over there.

Feeling a surge of power and insane energy, the kind that only blooms when one is doing something foolish to entertain strangers, Panther walked over in Javelin's direction banging his sword against his cestus and hollering at the top of his lungs. It didn't occur to him until he was almost at the weapon rack that the lion couldn't *hear* him, but he was big and he was moving, so fortunately, the lion did look up to gauge him as a threat. That gave one of the blue-team fighters a chance to actually throw his javelin, but fear took the strength out of it, and the weapon only scored a shallow gash across the underside of the beast's rib cage. The fighter fell back as the lion whipped around and roared at him, and he bolted in fear, which was probably the worst thing he could have done. The lion pounced on him and tore his back and legs open with one hard swipe. The crowd squealed with delight over that, and the blue fighter's teammate lost what was left of his nerve. He dropped his javelin in the dirt and started running in the opposite direction. The crowd nearby jeered and hissed at the coward, but a much louder cheer from across the way drowned it out, telling Panther that either someone else had died at one of the other lions' paws, or one of the lions had just been killed. Since the one that had killed the blue fighter was now rising from the laid-open carcass, however, Panther didn't look to find out.

"Gods preserve us, Panther," Javelin mewled, running over on shaky legs to stand beside and behind his teammate. He grabbed Panther's arm maniacally and shook it as he spoke. "That thing's going to kill us. We're the only two left, and we're going to—"

Kicking up bloody sand, the lion pounced at them before Javelin could even finish blubbering. Panther had to not only dive out of the way but shove Javelin in the opposite direction, and the beast's head and shoulders sent them sprawling. Luckily, the beast crashed into the lone, empty weapon rack and took a couple of seconds to regain its senses. Panther took the opportunity to back up and steel his courage, but Javelin didn't quite have the presence of mind to take so safe a course of action. He'd dropped his weapon, the broken-off length of wooden staff, but rather than retreating and looking for another one, he dove for it now even though doing so actually took him closer to the lion. He realized his mistake just as the beast was extricating itself from the wreckage of the weapon rack, and he found himself lying on his stomach, looking right up into the white lion's bloody maw. There were tears in his eyes, and all he could think to do was look back over his shoulder, sniveling.

"Panther," he gasped. "Help me."

Panther blinked, and the moment stretched to infinity. Javelin was going to die or at least be mauled so seriously he'd probably pray for death when it was all over. But that was only if Panther did nothing, and Panther knew that he could probably save Javelin right here and now. He could throw his sword, for one thing, and blind the beast or break its fangs or *something*. He could certainly hurt it. There was also a dropped javelin on the ground near him. He could probably snatch it up and hurl it before the lion did more than scratch Javelin's back up a little. Hell, even if he didn't have any weapons handy, he could still scoop up a handful of sand and throw it in the lion's face. That would at least give Javelin a chance to get out of there.

But Panther hesitated because of what Master Maxus had said just before the fight. He'd said that if Javelin died out here today, Panther and the other fighters could go free. All Panther had to do was stand right where he was and let it happen, and he'd be a free man. All for doing nothing. And would anybody be able to blame him? All he'd have to say was that he froze when the lion got the drop on his comrade.

"Panther!" Javelin squealed, but Panther still didn't move. He'd made his decision. He looked hard into Javelin's eyes and willed him to understand what was about to happen, and judging by the dawning horror that bleached the wiry beanpole's face and made his eyes shoot wide open, he understood perfectly. In the same moment, the scrawny white lion raised a bony paw and let out a hideous roar matched only by that raised by the crowd in response. Yet its fatal blow never fell on Javelin's back.

Before the lion could sink its claws into his downed teammate, Wolf suddenly plowed into the lion's ribcage, getting his head and shoulder under one foreleg and awkwardly knocking the beast onto its side. It thumped to the ground screeching, and it rolled all the way over, tangling Wolf up with it. The indentured pit fighter bashed the beast's legs and ribs with his sword, but it hissed and clawed and gave better than it got. The noise and the sudden interruption broke Panther from his paralysis, however, and he ran over to help at last. Thankfully, the lion ignored him, and it presented him with an opportunity when it next rolled on top of the fighter who'd attacked it. When its back was in the air, Panther lunged toward it and ran his short sword right between its ribs, through its lung and into its heart. The lion yelped out a sharp, wet gurgle, then it fell lifeless at his feet and rolled over on one side.

The midday crowd practically went insane cheering, and Panther raised his head for a long look around. He dared not believe it, but it seemed that they were actually cheering for him and him alone. That turned out to be partly correct, but Panther could see that the spectators were also cheering for the general end of the match. All three lions lay dead now, and what was better, Boar Spear and Snow Tiger were pointing long, wicked tridents at the downed forms of the last three members of the red-belted team. That meant that not only had he survived the fight without serious injury and not only had he not been taken down, but his team had actually won. And the crowd loved it.

Damn, Panther thought as the sun beat down on him and the judges came toward him. *Maybe I can be a free man* after *I get tired of this.* He raised a hand to the crowd, which politely upped the volume of its applause a little, then he turned back around to look at Javelin. The beanpole was still lying in the sand on his belly, but now he had his hands over his head and he sounded like he was crying again.

"Gods, what is it now, Javelin?" Panther sneered. "That thing never even touched you."

"It's not me, you bastard," Javelin said, not even bothering to raise his head. Instead he pointed toward the lion's dead body. "Look… *Look!*"

Panther looked down at where his comrade was pointing and saw that Wolf still lay bloody and tangled up beneath the white lion. Neither one of them was moving now. Neither one drew breath. Both were bleeding out. Both were dead. Panther stared, all but unable to comprehend what he was seeing.

"Wolf…" he whispered. "Why did you do that? I would have… I mean, I probably could have… Wolf?"

Chapter Three

As that memory ran its course, a numb, disgusted Panther sipped cool water in his peaceful arboreal temple and tried again to clear his mind. He opened himself to the wise counsel of the Unconquered Sun, but the lingering effects of that match crowded out everything else. That day, Maxus had offered Panther only faint praise for his skill and performance, while the trainer had clapped Javelin on the shoulder with somber respect, despite the abuse he'd heaped on the wiry fighter before the match. He'd even treated Boar Spear and Snow Tiger with gruff, weary affection. The loss of Wolf had hurt him, though, and there had been tears on his leathery face when the judges brought the young man's body to him. It was the weakest Panther had ever seen the grizzled old veteran, and his respect for Maxus had diminished. People died in the arena... surely the old man had seen it plenty of times. Surely he'd killed his share of men. What was there to cry about?

To make matters worse, Javelin had laid out the whole story, venting all the fear, anger and excitement that the near-disastrous match had kindled in him. The fact that Panther had made an effort to save the life of a fighter from a different team but not one of his own had only added fuel to the smoldering fire of Maxus' grief, and the old man had rounded on him, enraged. Panther had tried to smooth things over by reminding Maxus about what he had said before the match about everyone else going free if Javelin was killed, but that hadn't helped one bit. A horrified Javelin had slunk away, and the trainer had been so incensed at Panther's lack of judgment that he'd lost his temper and beaten Panther senseless right there in the arena's staging area. All Panther could do was roll with the old man's blows and curl in a ball on the ground while Maxus worked out rage and grief in the only way he understood. And when Maxus had finally come to his senses, the old man had sworn that Panther would be sold to the undercity miner the next day and never see the sun again.

But of course that hadn't happened. Panther had been dragged to the training field on Maxus' estate the very next day, and he'd been out there on the sandy battlefield with his teammates that next week. Panther had later learned that several of the other trainers and local team owners who made their money at the pit arena had come to Maxus and offered to buy Panther after the show he'd put on at the previous match. Despite himself, Maxus had realized the potential that lay yet untapped in Panther, so he'd stubbornly held onto him. He'd also realized that if the other trainers liked Panther, it was because not only was Panther talented and attractive, but there was something the crowds liked about him as well. When Panther showed off, the crowd responded; when the crowd responded, Panther picked up on it and gave them more of the same.

So, in the months and years that had followed, Maxus had given the crowds as much of Panther as they could stand. The old man had propped him up in Nexus' downtown arena every week, expecting his rivals' fighters to punish Panther where he himself would not. He'd placed Panther only in nonlethal, low-bill mass melee events at first, making it no secret that his teammates were under no obligation to help if Panther got into trouble. Javelin had taken especial glee in following his master's advice. Most of the fighters that Maxus owned or agreed to train wanted to be solo fighters anyway, though, so asking them not to help out one of their number was no hardship. Yet, despite this backhanded punishment, Panther had grown strong and quick and graceful quickly, and never once was he beaten or severely injured. And when it had become evident that Panther could fend for himself well enough and in a way that made the crowds remember him from week to week, Maxus had eventually grown bored with the punishment and let the whole matter drop. Javelin had gone out of his way to make the next few fights actually *harder* for Panther, but even he'd had to give up eventually. Life went on.

One by one, the fighters with whom Panther had been bought had earned their chances to compete in solo matches, much to their own and Maxus' delight. To everyone's surprise, Javelin had earned his chance first, and he was all too happy to graduate out of the "stable" so that he didn't have to live in the dingy, crowded slave quarters of Maxus' estate with the likes of Panther anymore. He'd done fairly well for himself in his matches, losing only a few times in his first year but always putting on a respectable mid-bill show and never earning more than a crooked gray scar in his occasional defeats. He'd made a name for himself fighting with staff, trident, spear and (naturally) javelin, and he'd volunteered for as many fights as he could reasonably take. Eventually, his efforts had attracted the attention of an independent arranger who'd bought his freedom from Maxus and allowed him to fight as a free man for his own money. The fact that he'd managed to win himself a patron before Panther had seemed to finally set aside any lingering enmity the wiry beanpole had for him. Regardless, he'd left Panther's life at last, and that was good enough.

The next to achieve particular notoriety and skill were Boar Spear and Snow Tiger, but they'd proved uninterested in one-on-one matches. In their circuit travels and various low-bill free-for-alls, they'd found that they complemented each other exceptionally well and worked fantastically as a team. Therefore, they'd opted to join the burgeoning and underpopulated tactical team-fighting division as their period of training indenture had drawn to a close. The next time Maxus bought fighting slaves, Boar Spear and Snow Tiger had culled three like-minded candidates from the pack of newcomers and forged them into a dynamic, cohesive team. Then, before that team's first tactical-division event, Snow Tiger and Boar Spear had borrowed a moderate sum of money from a local loan shark and bet it on their total victory against a group of more experienced (though less-cooperative) fighters. The gamble had paid off many times over when Snow Tiger's intuitively brilliant small-group tactics and Boar Spear's stubborn unwillingness to concede defeat had led to a victory that had shocked even the new division's most savvy arrangers. With the winnings, the team had paid off its loan and put a sizeable chunk of money into Maxus' hand toward the freedom of its junior members. In less than a year, when the founders' indenture expired, the entire team was free and independent.

And while the fighters with whom he'd been bought had advanced, Panther had exercised and trained and fought and learned, with no ambition beyond winning his next match. In time, he'd earned a chance for some one-on-ones, in which he'd learned to listen to the fans and play to their moods. When he could tell the spectators wanted to see the higher-billed combatants such as Peregrine or God-Blooded Thunder, he'd made his victories as spectacularly brutal as possible. When he could tell the oppressive heat rolling off the Yellow River had made everyone lethargic and restive, he'd toyed with his opponents, humiliating them to the mean-spirited crowd's delight. When he could tell that the low-billed melees hadn't warmed the crowd up at all, he'd drawn his fights out as long as he dared, pretending to be close to defeat, only to turn things around just when all seemed lost. He'd learned to play with the crowd's emotions by way of exaggerated taunts, grandly expressive gestures and flashy, graceful fighting moves that even the people on the cheap rooftop seats surrounding the arena could make out. Eventually, Maxus had forced him to try out for the dangerous and elitist free-fighting division, and he'd won himself a place in its lowest tier after a fight promoter saw only one match.

And he'd never lost, which had astounded and captivated the arrangers and crowds alike. No matter what odds were stacked against him or how outmatched he *should* have been, Panther won every match he entered, which had finally helped the trainer realize how much more valuable an asset he was than Wolf would ever have been. Wolf had been an excellent fighter and would have made as talented a trainer as Maxus himself, but he'd lacked Panther's charisma and intuitive talent for the game. No matter what Panther did, people had responded to it just as the dark-skinned fighter wanted them to. Any weapon he'd picked up had simply become a part of him, and he'd never shown the slightest fear of death or defeat. Panthers skills could make a man rich, Maxus knew, and in that light, all was easily forgiven.

Eventually, however, the glory he'd won and the reputation he'd built for himself had begun to outstrip his station as a slave in a fight-trainer's stable, and the time had come for him to try for his freedom. The bizarre and ever-changing legal scripture by which Nexus pretended to abide had carried a minor clause at the time that had provided him an opportunity to do just that. According to that obscure clause, once a "wholly-owned" pit fighter reached a certain age having won a certain number of victories in the arena, that fighter was entitled to compete against an opponent of his master's choosing, with his freedom at stake. Few pit-fighting slaves were qualified to take advantage of that opportunity, but Panther certainly was. What's more, he'd realized that all the money Maxus had made off him (and more) could be his if he were a free man. So, when the law had forced Maxus to make the offer, Panther had accepted it without hesitation.

It was to the events of the afternoon of that fateful match that Panther's unquiet thoughts were drawn now as he sat beneath his pillar of oak...

"I did it, Panther," Maxus was saying as Panther waited by the barred stall door leading out into the pit. Panther could almost feel the old man cringing, but he didn't bother to turn around. "I shouldn't have, maybe, but I did it anyway."

"And you sound heartbroken," he sneered over his shoulder. "Master."

"You think I want this, boy? You're the best fighter I got. This *pains* me."

"*Pains* you," Panther said.

"It does!" Maxus insisted, and his voice took on a weak, wheedling tone that made Panther scowl. He couldn't believe he'd once feared and revered this whining old man. He couldn't believe he'd once boasted that Maxus had taught him everything he knew.

"Of course. Master."

"Damn you, boy. It's going to be lambs to the slaughter out there, and you think you can just stand there mocking me. I'm trying to give you a last chance to change your mind."

"So, make me an offer," Panther said, shrugging. "But don't think you can scare me into taking it. If you thought I was still afraid of you, you'd have hit me for talking to you like this. *Master.*"

Maxus sputtered, but no blow fell. Panther watched Maxus' shadow on the wall ahead of him, smiling as the old man's hand rose, hesitated, wavered and finally sank again. He smiled at the little djala girl who stood waiting to unbar the door and let him out into the arena. She looked from Panther to Maxus and then straight down at her feet, quivering.

"All right, here it is," Maxus said through clenched teeth. "If you beg out of this match right now, I'll grant you your freedom."

"Keep talking."

"You'll come work for me as a trainer. You'll help me pick out my next crop of fighters, and you'll show them how to do what you do out there. How to fight; how to read the crowd. You'll be indentured like Boar Spear was, but you can move into my house and live with the overseers like a real trainer."

"Are you kidding?"

"And you can still fight," Maxus hastened to add. "We'll go halves on your winnings, and anything you ought to keep can come to me to buy off your indenture faster sooner. I'll still take care of you like one of mine, and you can be out on your own as soon as—"

"Get out," Panther said through an incredulous grin. "Go tell them I'm ready to fight. I'm not listening to any more of this."

"You should think harder, boy," Maxus said with a trace of his old venom. "You don't know what I've put you up against. You know who's meeting you out there? It's God-Blooded Thunder. He came all the way from Great Forks when he heard you were up to go free this year. He doesn't think you belong in the free-fighting division, so he's come to keep you out. He even thinks he's doing you a favor."

That admission gave Panther pause, but if the old man was looking for panic or even fear, Panther didn't give it to him. "Whatever," he said with another shrug. "I've seen him fight. He's tough, but he's got no style. I can take him." He paused a second then laughed quietly. "Even if I can't, you're still out a fighter because I'm not going to stop until he kills me."

"Hey, that's the spirit," a second and familiar voice said from the back of the stall. Maxus whipped around to see who was intruding, and Panther glanced back to find both Boar Spear and Snow Tiger standing by the stall's rear entrance. They both wore leather pants and matching leather vests that had been embossed with a bright red image of a shark.

"Thunder ain't so tough," Boar Spear added to what his partner had said.

Panther turned his attention to Maxus one last time. "Go on and tell them I'm ready. You and I have nothing more to say. Master."

"Then good riddance to you," Maxus barked, trying to hide the shame in his voice. "I *was* going to flag the match when you fell, but now, maybe I'll let God-Blooded Thunder do what he wants with you. Maybe teach you a lesson about what your place is in this world."

"Good news, then," Snow Tiger said, artificially chipper. "That's why we're here too."

"Then talk some sense into him," Maxus said, pushing between the two newcomers on his way out of the stall. "If you can." He limped away as best he could and shut the door, leaving Panther alone with his two former teammates.

"You aren't supposed to be here," Panther said, turning toward Boar Spear and Snow Tiger. He hefted the squared-off steel blade he'd chosen for this match and propped it on the leather harness he wore on his left shoulder as his only armor. "What do you want?"

"Don't tense up now," Boar Spear said. "You've got a big match ahead of you. Don't worry about us, we're not here for anything nefarious. We wouldn't have come ourselves if we were."

"That doesn't make any sense," Snow Tiger said.

"What *do* you want?" Panther asked again.

"Right," Boar Spear answered. "We came to make you an offer. But not threaten you with one like the old man was trying so hard to do. Ours actually comes with a wish of good luck."

"So what is it? Wait, let me guess. You want me to join your little team if I win."

"Absolutely," Snow Tiger said.

"The Leather Sharks would love to have you," Boar Spear added. "Snow Tiger and me already talked it over with—"

"The Leather Sharks?" Panther scoffed. "You're kidding, right? That's ridiculous."

"I *told* you the Iron League sounded better," Boar Spear said, punching his comrade in the shoulder.

"I told *you* it was already taken by a mercenary outfit in Cinnabar," Snow Tiger said, socking his partner in return. "But he's not even talking about the name. Are you, Panther?"

"I'm not. I mean me joining up with you guys is ridiculous. I don't do tactics—I'm solo. Besides, I'm not even in your league."

"I know it's not what you're set on, Panther, but hear me out," Snow Tiger said, crossing the stall toward him. "You want to free-fight, I know, but you haven't really thought about it. If you look across all the leagues, you'll see that the most maimings, career-ending injuries and deaths happen in the free-fighting league. The average free-fighter career expectancy is shorter than it is for any other league. Even the criminals who get trotted out for one-on-ones against those rabid chauns every vernal equinox have a better survival rate than you do."

"So what? You think I'm not better than average? What's the last fight you saw me lose?"

Snow Tiger rolled a long-suffering look to his partner, but Boar Spear was too busy making eyes at the diminutive djala girl by the arena door to notice.

"That isn't the point, Panther," he said instead. "There's always somebody better. And that's doubly true with you just being a mortal. You're never going to draw the crowds that the God-Blooded do over in Great Forks. No way in Creation you're going to draw crowds like the Dragon-Blooded gladiators do over in Arjuf. That might be what you want, but it's just not going to happen."

"Don't sell him short," Boar Spear piped up, tearing his eyes away from the djala girl. "Maybe he's got a dragon in the woodpile, and we just don't know it yet."

Panther glared at Boar Spear and tried not to let the offhand remark sting too deeply. After his mother had died and he'd been sold into slavery, he'd wished that very thing many times. He'd wished that his unknown father had actually been a Dragon-Blood who would return for him some day and Exalt him into the nobly divine society of the Realm. He suspected every orphan in Nexus wished the same thing.

"You don't know what's going to happen," Panther said, gripping the hilt of his sword painfully tight. "Neither of you. But what *I* know is I'm not joining your team."

"Just hear us out," Snow Tiger said.

"Yeah," Boar Spear put in. "Listen, man, you're more likely to get your head cracked in during your first year as a free-fighter than you are to ever make any real money in it. Or you'll lose a hand. Or bust up a leg like Maxus. Nothing's certain. You don't know what you're going to be up against or what they're going to throw at you or anything. But let me tell you, in the team-tactics division, you always know what you're up against—chumps."

"I believe that," Panther said.

"Yeah," Boar Spear said. "We picked up a trainer who's ex-military—from Lookshy by way of the Blessed Isle, if you can believe it. We're soaking the sand with all our competition. We're the stars of the league, and with you on the team, there'd be no stopping us."

"Still not interested," Panther said. "I don't care about team tactics. Nobody does except you two and any mid-bill rejects who can't stand on their own. I've got a future in free-fighting."

"You could be pretty good," Snow Tiger said. "We've seen you fight, and frankly, you've won us a lot of money. But what about *after* your fighting career's done? What about when you get too hurt or too old to go on?"

Panther didn't say anything, and the look on his face became unreadable.

"Haven't thought much about that, have you?" Boar Spear asked. "Well, we have. This whole tactical-fighting thing is just one small step for us. We're going to be winning for years in the arena, and we're going to be pretty rich and pretty famous before we're as old as Maxus is now. It's not as glamorous or high up on the daily fight bill, but it's good money and it's easy work for people as good as us. And it's just a start."

"Before what?" Panther asked in spite of himself.

"We're starting a mercenary company," Boar Spear said, grinning. "We're going to build our reputations in the ring then 'retire' at the height of our popularity. Then we turn all that fame into good word of mouth that gets us some paying customers on some small jobs. We'll recruit some new fighters and have the core of a solid, professional unit. And if it does well enough over the first few years, we'll see about expanding or absorbing a couple of smaller outfits. Or better yet, we'll see if we can't subcontract under one of the bigger companies like the Hooks or the Hooded Executioners."

"Well, good luck with that," Panther said as a dull roar arose outside. The crowd was getting ready for him. "But count me out."

"Hey, come on," Boar Spear said. "This is a good offer we're making here. We want you in as an equal partner. We can take this thing places. We can do good things."

"I'm not interested in just good things," Panther said, nodding to the djala girl who stood waiting with her hands on the bar across the stall door. "I'm interested in great things. A great life. And this is the path to it. *My* path. I won't settle for the edge of obscurity like you two."

Boar Spear opened his mouth to say more, but Snow Tiger raised a hand and stopped him. "Suit yourself, Panther," he said, holding back his disappointment. "This isn't a one-time-only offer. Think about it some more. We won't turn you away if you change your mind. Maxus might hold a grudge, but we won't."

"Sure," Panther said. "Whatever. Now go take your seats. Fight's on."

With that, the djala slave opened the door, and Panther strode out into the arena for what was to be his last match as a slave. If either Boar Spear or Snow Tiger wished him luck as he left them behind, he didn't hear it. All he heard was the roar of the crowd and the rhythm of people chanting his name. Sure, there were more people, and louder, cheering for God-Blooded Thunder than there were for him, but that didn't matter. By the end of the match, they'd all be chanting for him, he promised himself that.

And by the end of the match, it was true. The fighter from Great Forks glared and smacked one meaty fist into his palm, but he was soft on the inside and Panther could tell it. Granted, God-Blooded Thunder was big—half again as tall as Panther was—and as thick around as a tree, but he wasn't as agile and powerful as Panther. Being quicker, nimbler and unafraid, Panther had the advantage over his opponent, and he knew it from the start. The fight was as good as his from the moment he stepped out into the sand.

Of course, he still took his time, drawing the fight out and showing off for all the fans who filled the stadium. He knew that some small fraction of the spectators were arrangers and fight managers come to scout his freedom match, so the last thing he wanted to do was put on a lousy show. So he let God-Blooded Thunder take a few swings at him here and there, rolling out of the way just in time. He even let himself be disarmed by a wild near-miss kick just so he could dramatically dive for his fallen weapon and roll up onto the defensive as God-Blooded Thunder barreled down on him. Through it all, he stood his ground and fought, never showing the first sign of fear despite being constantly on the defensive.

Only when his opponent had grown frustrated and tired did Panther go on the offensive. He taunted and harassed his opponent, making the larger fighter take wilder swings and practically chase him around. He could hear the crowd laugh a little when his dodging and ducking made God-Blooded Thunder stumble and miss a punch by almost half a dozen feet. A moment later, he teased out an ill-aimed kick then dove between the larger fighter's legs and hacked at the back of his knee. God-Blooded Thunder actually fell on his face in the dirt, and even his most ardent fans had to laugh at that one. And when they did, Panther knew that they were his and that he was a free man.

Minutes later, when all was finally said and done, the crowd roared in ecstasy, forgetting their erstwhile hero and showering praise on their new one. Drinking in their adulation, Panther headed for the Freeman's Gate, which led out of the arena to the streets of Nexus. A procession of judges met him halfway, surrounding his (now former) master, who walked with his head down. Maxus was holding a velvet pillow in shaking hands, and on it lay a short ironwood sword, lacquered white with a jade-inlaid hilt. On the blade of the sword was inscribed an ancient symbol for the word "freedom," as well as the word "panther" in the common tongue known as Riverspeak. The old man stopped in Panther's path and held the object out to his erstwhile slave, and Panther took it and raised it over his head, to another outburst of generous applause. Long-stemmed flowers fell to the sand from the front several rows of seats, sticking upright like arrows, and silver dinars wrapped in silk ribbons rained down as well as a gesture of good luck. Panther smiled and acknowledged the crowd with a broad salute. Maxus opened his mouth to say something then, and he put a hand on Panther's shoulder. From the look in the old man's eyes, Panther could tell that Maxus had something soft-hearted to say, which he obviously thought was going to sound fatherly and forgiving, despite the ugly words they'd exchanged before the fight.

Panther shrugged and knocked Maxus' hand away, and he pushed past his former trainer and owner before the old man could say anything. The judges murmured in astonishment, but Panther ignored them and headed for the Freeman's Gate. As soon as he walked through it, he was a free man, no longer beholden to the pit or expected to fight just to keep himself fed. He could leave this place, leave Nexus if he wanted to, and start a new life doing anything he pleased. He could be a farmer or a merchant or even a mercenary. He could take up with the Guild and earn a living on the open roads of trade and exploration. He could even get married and raise a family somewhere out there. An entire world waited, with all those choices and countless others before him. But then…

Panther stopped just past the threshold of the Freeman's Gate, looking at the dusty street that lay before him. He didn't really *want* any of those things. He didn't know anything about living any of those kinds of lives, and none of them appealed to him in the slightest. All he wanted to do was to keep fighting in the pit until he was a rich and famous as he'd always dreamed he could be (and poor orphans had inexhaustible imaginations where fame and money were concerned). It was all he knew how to do, and he was good at it. He had a chance here to make a name for himself—one leagues better than the birth name that even he had forgotten. His skills had won him his freedom, and now, it was time for him to do something worthwhile with it. Something that *he* wanted to do. Something he deserved because he'd earned it, fought for it, won it.

With the crowd still cheering behind him and Maxus staring at him like he'd turned into a snake and bit the old man, Panther stepped back through the gate as a free man and turned his back on it. With the sun beating down on him, he walked away from the Freeman's Gate and headed for the fighter's exit at the opposite end of the arena. He'd entered this pit a slave, and now he was leaving it his own man. But just as he'd come in, he was leaving it a fighter. Now and forever, that was what he was going to be.

Chapter Four

Panther sighed, and the wind through the leaves above him echoed the sound. Meditation was proving to be impossible, and enlightenment was proving elusive at best. He'd always been proud of the fight that had won him his freedom and his choice to keep on fighting as a free man, but now, looking back on it, he couldn't banish a lingering discomfort. Had he done the right thing? Before his first fight in the pit, all he'd wanted was to be free, to live far from Nexus on a farm somewhere, doing a free man's work and raising a family. In only a few short years, he'd changed his mind completely. Before, he'd wanted a life all his own; in time, he'd come to want the same life he already had, only on his own terms. Was that progress? Was that maturity? Or had he simply compromised his dream of freedom and chosen to accept the life that had been thrust upon him?

Had he done the right thing? Looking back now, he didn't think so, though he hadn't given it so much as a second thought at the time. By that day's end, he'd won the services of an arranger and rented out a small place to live in the city of Nexus' eponymous central district. It hadn't been a large or lavishly appointed place, but it had been convenient to the arena as well as his arranger's home, and it had been Panther's own. After years of poverty and scavenging on the streets after his mother's death, followed by even longer as nothing but Maxus' property, the place had been a mansion to Panther, and he'd found more self-sovereignty than he'd known what to do with. As his fame and fortune grew, which it did quickly, he'd indulged his every taste and whim in women, drugs, liquor, fine foods, expensive clothes and ridiculous finery. The newfound pleasures of the flesh available to him had addled his senses and made him complacent in the life he'd won. All he'd had to do was practice daily at his arranger's training grounds and continue to win fights that stole his spectators' hearts, and it had seemed like that life would be his forever.

It had never occurred to him to wonder what his life would have been like if he'd chosen to give up competing in the pit when he'd won his freedom. In time, he'd grown unable to imagine himself as a farmer or a merchant or a father. Those people were peasants, and he was a rising star. He might never Exalt as one of the Dragon-Blooded, but that was okay. That dream had lost its luster as his fame and fortune had grown. No other life mattered anymore. The ability to conceive of it had died inside him. He'd gladly buried it and laid the grave goods of his better judgment and nobler aspirations overtop it so that its spirit would trouble him no more.

Or rather, he'd thought he had until a certain trip into Bastion to entertain a rich man had forced him to take drastic measures in hopes of excising it for good. The rich man's name was Kerrek Deset, an aspiring merchant prince for the Guild and an inventor of no little skill if rumors about him were to be believed. Those same rumors also attributed to him some bizarre predilections and experimental tastes at which Panther didn't even have the imagination to guess, but that sort of thing hadn't bothered Panther. Kerrek was rich and influential and rising in the Guild's ranks, and he'd contacted Panther's arranger specifically to set up a dinner introduction. The way the arranger had explained it, such meetings often turned into offers for patronage, and if Panther could be as charming and entertaining up close as he was in the pit, he might be able to make out handsomely with just a night's socializing.

That hadn't even mattered to Panther, though. The very idea of spending an evening in the chic and exclusive Bastion District—uphill and upwind of Nexus' industrial smelting forges, sweltering humidity and polluted bottomlands where the sewage and garbage from upstream collected—had been enough. He was being offered a chance to see and pretend to be a part of the life he'd thought he wanted, so no force of reasoning or violence would have prevented him from attending. It hadn't been until much later that night that he'd realized what he was truly in for.

The night began with a handsomely appointed carriage arriving at the street in front of Panther's apartment, surrounded by an escort of some fifteen armed men in brown-and-gold uniforms. The insignias they wore on their shoulders didn't match either the Guild symbol or the personal crests on the pennants flying at the carriage's corners, so Panther guessed they were professional soldiers hired out of Cinnabar. The gesture seemed a grandiose one, which Panther found both amusing and respectable. People on the streets gave the carriage a wide berth as they passed it, which snarled traffic for blocks, and people on their balconies or rooftop gardens all around gawked and whispered among themselves. Panther found it a little annoying that these same onlookers had gotten used to seeing him—an honest-to-gods arena celebrity—on these streets, but fifteen no-name sell-swords were some sort of a big deal.

Of course, they might have just been staring in wonder at the conveyance Kerrek had sent for him, Panther had to admit as he descended his building's steps and approached it. The thing was a black-and-burgundy lacquered carriage with brass accoutrements and detailing and thick, semi-reflective glass in the windows. It was large enough to accommodate six people, even with a mahogany tea table in the center and a circular velvet couch around the perimeter, yet it balanced on only two large wheels. What's more, it was not hitched to a team of horses or any other sort of beast of burden. Instead, only two men stood at the front of a long, wooden crossbar on the front of the carriage wearing thick boots, leather pants and not much else. Panther looked at them then at the carriage's underside, where some sort of mechanism of gears and chains and free-spinning disks connected the crossbar to the wheels. Before he could really get a good look, though, the footman at the back of the carriage opened the door for him, and the hired guards stepped aside so he could board and be on his way.

The ride to Bastion District was largely uphill, but the two men out front seemed to have no trouble pulling the carriage all by themselves, and the hired guards jogged alongside easily. The mechanism beneath the carriage hummed and clicked, and it occurred to Panther that it was probably doing all the work keeping the cart moving and balanced. He couldn't begin to ponder how that might be, and there was no one else riding with him to ask. Maybe it was a relic from the First Age that had been scavenged from the undercity or a modern construction whose design was based on one. It didn't really matter.

What did matter was the changing urban scenery rolling by outside as he was carried uphill to the better part of town. The yellow sulfurous haze that drifted downhill from the industrial forges and clung to the streets diminished and finally disappeared. The streets became less crowded and were kept in better repair. Streetlights burned on every corner—some lit by gas, others simply burning lamp oil. The quality of garb on the average person on the street steadily improved as well. The façades of the buildings and shops that lined the street became generally larger, cleaner and more wholesome looking. Then, finally, the carriage was moving among walled estates that were larger than Panther's entire apartment building, and he knew that he'd arrived in Bastion.

The carriage passed through a series of gated stone arches that served to segregate the district's various neighborhoods based on how old a family's money was and what occupation had earned it for them. These also acted as watchposts for the neighborhood watch soldiers, rather than the spindly watchtowers that marred the skyline of the less affluent districts. The guards around the carriage flashed hand signals to the watchers over the gates and were allowed safe passage. In no time at all, the entourage had wound its way through Bastion to the estate of Kerrek Deset on one of Nexus' moderately high hills. The carriage guard slowed in formation and opened ranks at the gate, turning the safety of the carriage over to the estate guard proper, and the carriage rolled on in up the smoothly paved drive. It stopped by the front door, where a squad of servants descended the broad marble steps, opened the carriage, offered hands to help him down and led him inside.

Within, Panther found so many servants on hand and guests in attendance that it was difficult to tell exactly how large or well decorated his host's house was. He could see that the floor and the columns holding up the roof and balcony were marble and that every wooden surface from the doors to the stair rails to the windowsills was a deep teak or mahogany that had been polished to a reflective sheen. Tapestries and expansive portraits hung on the walls, and marble statuary stood in lighted niches around the walls. And that was only the foyer and main hall.

The small entourage of servants led Panther through the milling throng of guests toward a somewhat smaller dining room. Panther nodded to the local elite as he moved through them, mostly receiving blank stares, sardonically raised eyebrows or self-righteous smirks in return. He didn't actually know any one of them from the Scarlet Empress, but acknowledging them as equals seemed the proper thing to do. He'd half expected to be met with disdain by some of them or outright ignorance of who he was—possibly to not be so much as acknowledged in return—but he wasn't truly prepared to experience it. Apparently, these people didn't get down to the arena all that often, and if any of them even knew who he was, they had no respect for what he did for a living. It was something of a relief, then, to be led among them quickly and taken to the dining room to meet his host.

Kerrek Deset sat at the center of a long, curved table with a chestnut-haired woman at his right and a black-and-white-haired woman at his left. The table was stacked high with food, wine, flowery display pieces and even abstract ice sculptures at either end, and the nozzles of a hookah had been worked into the underside of the table, sticking up at intervals for the guests to partake if they so desired. Around the outer edge of the table, between it and the walls, Kerrek's dinner guests jostled each other on a long, low bench as they talked, ate and occasionally puffed on whatever drug their host was providing. Servants bustled in and out of the room from another door in the rear, replacing plates and cups as the diners finished with them and discreetly cleaning up messes as the guests made them. Panther's own small group of servants separated as they shut the door behind him then made a quick report to their host. The gabble of conversation in the room dulled to a murmur as Kerrek stood and spread his arms wide in welcome. The host was a slight man with pale skin, short hair and the wide-open eyes of a prey animal. He wore a long red-and-green jacket over a white linen shirt and leather pants, and his neck and fingers twinkled with jewelry. His hair was oiled into a tight ponytail and held in place by gold wire that had been braided into it. Panther would have been willing to bet the outfit alone cost more than a week's stay in his apartment over in Nexus District. He felt more than a little shabby in his sleeveless silken tunic and loose white pants. With its few gold accoutrements, the outfit was the most expensive and best-looking one he had, but it was a potato sack next to what his host and the other guests were wearing, even the ones sitting farthest from Kerrek at the table or consigned to mingle out in the rest of the house and enjoy each other's company.

With warm words of welcome, Kerrek thanked Panther for showing up and urged him closer. Panther came forward and stopped in the center of the room beneath the enormous iron-and-glass chandelier that lit the place. He stood in the middle of the horseshoe-curved table so all the guests around the edge could see him and gave a quick, respectful bow. Polite and eloquent words weren't exactly his strong suit, so he thanked his host and gave sort of a general greeting to everyone else who was listening. Few of the guests seemed all that interested in his arrival—in fact, most went back to their own conversations immediately—but Kerrek went on and on about how glad he was that Panther could join them and how thrilled he was to have a local celebrity in his own home. The chestnut-haired woman to his right rolled her eyes in extreme boredom and talked to the person on her right in low tones. The black-and-white-haired woman on Kerrek's left—a pale, severe beauty in an odd outfit of black leather and lacquered iron—smiled at Kerrek indulgently, though, and appraised Panther with a quick, calculating stare.

Panther thanked his host uneasily, unsure of how to react to such effusive praise in such a setting, and then, Kerrek started in with a long list of questions. Most of what he wanted to know covered the same topics that avid spectators at the arena always seemed to want to know. How long had Panther been fighting? How did he get into it? What division did he like best to fight in? Who was the first gladiator he'd ever killed? Was he ever scared facing older, more experienced fighters? What was the worst he'd ever been hurt? Could they see the scar? His neighbors and apartment staff and the people who paid good dinars to stand in line and shake his hand after a fight all asked the same types of things.

Panther gave his host the same answers that always got the best reactions from others who asked—moderately long half-stories that had room to grow but were complete unto themselves—and Kerrek cooed and gasped in all the right places. He never offered Panther a place at his table, though, which Panther found odd and a little embarrassing. He stood awkwardly for a moment when Kerrek's questions dried up, then decided to ask one of his own before he had to lamely drift away and join the other guests in the other rooms.

"So how long have you been a fan of the fights, sir?"

"All my life," Kerrek answered with a peculiar light in his eyes. "When I was with a caravan, I made it a point to visit local arenas all along my trade route, and since I set myself up here, I've been to the main pit downtown every weekend. I've seen you fight many times. In fact, you're one of my favorites. Probably my second in the entire league."

Panther blinked, a little nonplussed. "Second. I see. Who's the first, sir? Anyone I know?"

"I'm sure you do," Kerrek said with a huge grin. "In fact, that's part of the reason you're here. I wonder if you wouldn't mind favoring myself and my guests with a little entertainment before we ask you to sit down to dinner with us."

The wheels turned in Panther's mind, and his eyes narrowed. "Entertainment? Does Rejis know about this? Or is that why you didn't invite him?"

"Your arranger set this up, you silly boy," Kerrek said.

"That's what he does. You aren't obligated, of course, and there isn't any prize money in it for you, but we would all be most grateful if you'd indulge us in a demonstration. In fact, let me show you how excited I've been…"

At that, Kerrek took a crystal bell out of his breast pocket and rang it. A moment later, a line of servants emerged from the rear room carrying items that made Kerrek's eyes dance. Two of them were carrying a pair of poles that were twice as long as Panther was tall. Another was carrying a folded-up black and white robe similar to an arena judge's outfit, and yet another bore a velvet pillow with a jade rod carved to look like a judge's wand. The last servant in through the door held a bundle of rolled-up silk flags. The flags, robe and wand were carried to Kerrek's seat, while the men with the wooden poles came around the enormous table to stand behind Panther. There was enough room within the curve of the table to lay both poles down end to end.

"Aren't they wonderful?" Kerrek asked, slipping the judge's robe on over his clothing. It was trimmed in arctic fox fur and decorated with black and white pearls. "I had them all made for me for events just like this. As I said, I've been a fan for a lifetime." He lifted the jade rod from its velvet pillow and made an imperious flourish that was supposed to look like a judge's start-of-fight signal. "It doesn't work, of course, but it went with the outfit."

"Right," Panther said, looking around. Kerrek's dinner guests had grown quiet all of a sudden, and the servants were opening the door out into the main hall so the crowd outside could see what was going on.

"Now, if you'll indulge me," Kerrek continued, looking at the two women who sat on either side of him, "I wonder if you would play arrangers for me." He unrolled the silk flags his servant had brought to him and laid them flat on the table. One was green with a gold-lamé panther on it, one was burgundy with Kerrek's family crest in silver lamé, and the last two were silken judge's flags. Kerrek handed the green one to the woman on his right, who accepted it reluctantly at best, and said, "You'll represent my guest, if that's all right." He handed the burgundy flag to the woman on his left. "You'll take my man." The pale woman looked Panther in the eye and smiled. "And both of you remember how I showed you to do the signals? Which signal means which thing?" Both women nodded. "Excellent, excellent. Now remember, when the fighter on your flag falls, it's up to you to decide his fate. That's the way these things work." Then, to Panther, he said, "Have you made up your mind?"

"You want to see a fight," Panther said, still uncertain what exactly was expected of him. "Me versus your first favorite fighter. That's what you've got in mind?"

"Only if you're willing. Though I would be very disappointed if you weren't."

"I see. Who's the other guy?"

"He says you know him, actually," Kerrek said, his excitement growing. He rang his crystal bell once again, and the crowd in the main hall parted to make way for someone. A moment later, Panther was stunned to see Javelin stroll into the room, flanked by a bustling entourage of Kerrek's servants. He was still tall and thin like Panther remembered, but his body had filled out with hard, wiry muscles, and his hair was cropped short like a raw mercenary recruit. He was dressed in leather shorts, sandals and shoulder harness like he was on his way to an actual pit fight, and he wore a leather patch over his left eye. He practically sneered when he saw Panther, and he walked right up beside him with a cocky swagger.

"I think one of us is overdressed," Panther murmured. "Or under."

Javelin ignored the remark and stopped next to Panther, facing Kerrek with a proud smile. "Noble host," he said in a performer's voice, "thank you for your gracious invitation and this opportunity to attend you in your lovely home. May the entertainment we provide find you well pleased."

"Would that it will," Kerrek said, "though our second guest has yet to accept my invitation. Have you had time enough to think about it, Panther? Will you do us the honor?"

"You'd better," Javelin whispered under his breath. It was the first time the man had spoken to him in years. "I've been asking him to set this up for almost a year now. I've wanted a piece of you ever since—"

"I'll do it," Panther said to Kerrek, which earned him a smile from the pale woman with the burgundy flag. "What are the terms? Whose rules?"

"Rules?" Kerrek said.

"I'll stipulate to the free-fighting rules," Javelin said to cover his host's confusion. "As long as he agrees to cesti only—and to the poles."

"Whatever," Panther said, though he frowned at that last part. The long poles the servants behind him were carrying were mainly used in training unschooled fighters or for corralling low-bill fighters in the pit who were too cautious or timid to engage each other. In the pit, a pair of judges would hold them parallel at about waist height on either side of the fighters so that neither would have anywhere to go but toward each other. To suggest that Panther would need such a thing in even an impromptu match like this was a slap in the face.

Kerrek, who obviously hadn't caught the insult, beamed with delight and rang his crystal bell one last time. A servant came in from the rear room bearing a silver tray laden with two pairs of studded leather cesti. He walked all the way around the table to where the two fighters stood, and Kerrek joined him to playact as judge. Javelin snatched up one set and began to buckle them on, and Panther shrugged out of his tunic. The other guests were all buzzing with delight and even exchanging bets, and several of them gasped when they saw the sunburst design that covered Panther's chest. It was an eight-pointed emblem with an empty ring at the center, tattooed with a bright golden ink that showed up wonderfully in contrast with his dark brown skin. He'd had it done a couple of weeks after winning his freedom, on the recommendation of his arranger who'd recently had the same procedure done on himself. Javelin's good eye widened fractionally when he saw the decoration, but he showed no other reaction.

When both fighters had strapped their studded fighting gauntlets over their fists, they stood a few paces from each other facing Kerrek, who leaned back against the table with his silk judge flags tucked into the front of his belt. His face was beaming, and he held up his jade baton in salute. Panther and Javelin saluted him back, and the two servants with the wooden poles got into position. They knelt and held their arms out at full extension to either side, the ends of the poles dangling from their outstretched wrists on leather loops. Panther and Javelin turned to face each other and saluted brusquely.

"You know, Javelin," Panther whispered with a calculating smile, "if not for Wolf, neither of us would be where we are today. Seems like one of us ought to thank him."

"You'll be the one," Javelin hissed. "Just wait 'til he finishes brutalizing your dead mother before you talk to him, though."

Panther smiled. "That was pretty clever. Take you all these years to come up with it?"

Rage lit Javelin's face, and as soon as Kerrek made his imperious start-of-fight gesture with his wand again, the wiry gladiator launched himself at Panther, swinging almost wildly. The long studs on his cesti whistled through the air, and it was all Panther could do to turn the blows aside or catch them on the leather pad covering his palm. He had to be intensely conscious of the fight space between the two poles, unaccustomed as he was to fighting in such close confines, and concentrating on that cost him an early advantage. The spectators gasped at Javelin's ferocity, and Kerrek laughed with delight.

Panther fell back three long steps—right up to the servant on his end of the poles—but on the third, he braced himself and stood his ground. He feinted a high jab to lure Javelin in then twisted out of the way when Javelin counterattacked with an uppercut. Panther had no leverage to capitalize on the mistake with a full punch, but he slammed an elbow into Javelin's forehead, rocking the taller man back. He then pressed his advantage, trying to get within only a couple of steps of his opponent and negate his reach advantage. He landed a couple of solid blows into Javelin's midsection, chipping flesh from the man's ribs with the studs of his cestus. A less experienced fighter might have doubled up or dropped his arms to protect himself, but Javelin knew better. He stomped down on Panther's ankle, scraping the edge of his sandal down the whole length of Panther's shin, and wheeled around with a left cross that caught

Panther squarely in the cheek. Sparks danced behind Panther's eyes, and he almost fell over the boundary pole on his left. Javelin followed up with a wild rabbit punch that fortunately landed between Panther's shoulder blades, rather than on the back of his skull. He curled and tried to roll with the blows as Javelin laid into him with punches, elbows and even a couple of sharp kicks. Panther had seen Javelin fight before, but he was never so ferocious, even when he'd snatched victory from the threshold of defeat.

A detached, analytical part of Panther's mind was starting to wonder if he could really compete with the strength to be found in such passion. He was certainly losing on the tactical front, what with Javelin's long reach keeping him at a distance and the inherent weakness of Javelin's missing eye negated by the fact that Panther couldn't move to either side because of the poles. He was starting to get weak from the punishing blows he couldn't block, and it was starting to look like the only option he had left was guile—not a quality he possessed in abundance. So instead of something original and clever, he did what he did when he could tell he was boring an arena crowd by winning too quickly. He let more of Javelin's blows through and pretended to be more hurt than he really was each time one fell. He gave up all efforts to counterattack and made it look like Javelin was murdering him where he stood. The crowd started to fall silent by degrees, the tension broken only the sound of Javelin's exertions and Panther's yelps and cries of faux distress.

Only Javelin could tell that he wasn't doing as much damage as Panther would have the crowd believe, but he didn't recognize it as a feint. From the rage burning in his hateful glare, the man must have thought Panther was mocking him, which cost him his temper and his advantage. He leaned back for a savage, fight-closer punch, but Panther saw it coming in low from the left, and he loosened up and rolled with it as much as he could. It still hurt like there was no tomorrow, but it didn't have the closing power it *looked like* it had. Panther spun almost all the way around, spitting out a little blood for effect (though more than he might have liked). He dropped thunderously to a knee, taking a moment to rest and regain his strength while he pretended to be delirious with fatigue. From the table, he heard the sound of a silk flag snapping into position, followed by a quizzical grunt from Javelin.

"Not now," he heard Kerrek say, a little annoyed. "First the fighter has to petition me, then I signal the question to you. *Then* you decide the downed man's fate. Sorry, Javelin. Are you ready?"

"Just a second," Javelin said, coming over to Panther and tilting Panther's bleeding head back so he could face the crowd. Panther could see in Javelin's face that the wiry bastard thought that last punch had sealed the deal. He might have smiled if he weren't worried the effort would dislocate his throbbing jaw.

"So," Javelin said then, loud enough for everyone to hear, "the rumor is that you're pretty tough. Undefeated in the pit, even. I'll bet this is probably the worst night of your life, then, isn't it? About to get beat down in front of all these people, and not even in a sanctioned match. And by me, of all people. Someone you were willing to just let die so you could go free. If you want, you can beg out. It won't hurt your record." Some people in the crowd laughed, and Kerrek was drinking the melodrama up like sweet fruit juice. Javelin then leaned down to Panther's level and whispered for him alone, "I recommend you beg out. Because I'm not about to petition our host for judgment, and that jade toy he's got isn't going to be able to stop me when I bust your skull open for what you tried to do to me."

"Gods bless you, Javelin," Panther whispered back through clenched teeth, glancing up at Kerrek's table and catching the gaze of the black-and-white-haired woman holding Javelin's flag. He winked at her, and she smiled thinly in understanding. "You just talk so much."

Javelin's good eye widened, and that was all the hesitation Panther needed. He launched himself up from the floor and caught Javelin with an uppercut right under the point of his chin. He spun lightly with his body's momentum as Javelin stretched up onto his tiptoes in shock and drove a reverse elbow into the wiry fighter's stomach. Exclamations and even a few appreciative outbursts of applause popped throughout the crowd, and Panther soaked it in. As Javelin doubled up, Panther drove a knee into his face, rocking him backward into the arms of the servant holding the boundary poles. The servant braced and kept himself from falling over, and Panther darted in to close the distance. He backhanded Javelin across the face then grabbed him by the hair and by the belt. With a mighty heave and a triumphant shout, he hauled Javelin off the ground, over his head and then down hard, all between the boundary poles. He then rolled Javelin over onto his face, pinning his wrists under his chest and sitting on his legs. The taller man thrashed and wriggled like a landed fish, but Panther was stronger and heavier, and he had all the leverage. Bracing himself with his left hand in the center of Javelin's back, Panther looked up at Kerrek's stunned face and petitioned him the way a victorious pit fighter was supposed to.

Kerrek recovered as astonished murmurs and disbelieving laughter filtered throughout the crowd. He lifted his judgment flags and signaled in the direction of the pale, leather-clad woman seated behind him and to his left. She looked Panther in the eye but did nothing. She cast him an inquisitive look and shrugged. Panther mouthed the words *Let the crowd decide* then looked around at the spectators from his vantage on the floor.

"Well?" he called out to them, shocking several. They looked as if a wild animal had just strolled in, mauled someone and started speaking with blood on its muzzle. "I'm here to entertain you folks, aren't I? What do you want to see? He lives or dies on your word."

"Panther..." Javelin said, turning his head away from Kerrek as much as he could.

"Our host calls this one his favorite, though I don't know why," Panther continued, ignoring his opponent and the taste of blood in his mouth. "Maybe he told some lies, or maybe he's a better actor than he is a fighter. He'd almost have to be, right?" A handful of people laughed, though Kerrek looked embarrassed and a little angry. "But I don't think that's it. I think this beanpole offended our host somehow and didn't have the good sense to realize it. I mean, you see how he's dressed for dinner." A few more people laughed, and a couple let out drunken catcalls for blood. "How likely is it he's got the social grace of a yeddim?"

"Panther," Javelin said again. "Let me just—"

"What I think happened," he went on, gouging Javelin's side with his knee, "is our host decided to teach this ruffian a lesson. He went out and found the youngest undefeated free-fighter in Nexus—me—and set this little punk up." A handful of dinner guests actually hooted at that and banged on the table enthusiastically. They knocked over all the wine goblets near them, but they were all tellingly empty. "So help us out. Show how much you respect our host here tonight. Tell us how much of a lesson you think this man deserves. What's the proper price to pay for a slight against Kerrek Deset? Does this one live on in shame…? Do I kill him…? What's he deserve?"

The crowd exploded into an uproar, shouting their various opinions of what Javelin deserved. The black-and-white-haired lady smiled at Panther, and even Kerrek himself seemed pleased with the show his guest had turned this event into. The guests would be talking about this party all their lives. Only Javelin seemed not to be enjoying himself, and a note of panic crept into his voice as he tried to get Panther to listen to him. Panther ignored him and instead looked again at the pale woman on Kerrek's left.

"What's your decision?" he asked her.

"Predictable," she said with an enigmatic smile. She held her silk signaling flag straight out, turned it once in a circle then rolled it up against her other hand. The crowd went crazy with excitement, and Kerrek smiled in surprise, obviously taking all the noise and energy as a sign of respect for him as master of this house.

"Panther," Javelin said, struggling in vain. "Wait."

"Javelin," Panther said, raising his hand and coiling it into a fist. "That's just too bad."

"Panther! Pan—"

Chapter Five

That night had been Panther's first private one-on-one but not his last. His performance had so impressed his host that he'd won Kerrek Deset's patronage. The Guildsman had set him up with a new arranger and introduced him to a stratum of wealth he'd never been able to conceive of before. He'd still had to fight, but he hadn't wanted for anything so long as he'd kept winning. Money, drugs, wine, women, clothes, jewelry… he'd had but to mention it to Kerrek, and it was his. He'd moved out of his first apartment and into a much larger one on the top floor of a building just a block away from the luxurious Guild harlotry in downtown Nexus. He'd rented time and private rooms at the most upscale gymnasiums and bath houses in Nexus. He'd even convinced Kerrek to take him to see a low-bill match at the Theater of the Bright Panoply in Arjuf on the southern coast of the Blessed Isle. All he'd had to do was spend most of his free time at Kerrek's manor in Bastion or in Kerrek's company as the Guildsman made the social rounds. As long as he'd kept Kerrek happy and played the part of the wild, untamable gladiator, the money and the privileges had kept coming Panther's way. It had been just a matter of putting on a show, no different than one down at the arena, and he played it exceptionally.

Of course, he'd known even back then that the arrangement couldn't last forever, but that hadn't worried him. He'd learned from caretakers in Maxus' employ how to take care of his money, so he'd always been careful to put away in a Guild bank just about as much as he frittered away in leisure. He'd also used the time he spent pretending to socialize with Kerrek's peers to look for the next willing patron once Kerrek's interest withered. When that time had inevitably come—about the same time Kerrek entered some sort of business arrangement with his white-haired lady friend—Panther had simply moved on without a hint of trouble. He was never so secure financially as he'd been with Kerrek, but neither had he fallen back to the level he'd been at immediately after winning his freedom.

Yet, as he'd gotten his feet under him and learned how to either find a patron or keep competing without one, he'd come to realize that the happiness he'd had as a child and in his first pit fights was no longer within him. The good things in his life had simply lost his interest. Certain pursuits were expected of Nexus gladiators of Panther's caliber, and he'd gone through the motions of engaging in them, but as he'd aged, he'd grown quiet and empty within. The ability to put on a good show for screaming, bloodthirsty fans had never abandoned him, but the savagery and energetic hunger he'd aped in the pit had ceased to touch his heart. As days had passed into weeks and then on into months and years, he'd found himself drifting almost in a trance from fight to fight, always winning but no longer trying so hard to do so. The contests became closer and closer, and the crowd howled in rapture at what it perceived as excellently wrought drama, but Panther had hardly even noticed. He'd fought without thinking, too numb to truly defend himself, but too tough and well trained to fall.

Panther had never been given to introspection, but it had eventually occurred to him that the way he'd dealt with Javelin had affected him more than he would have thought possible. Twice in his life he'd sacrificed Javelin's safety for his own benefit, and never before the first time had Javelin so much as offered him a dirty look. The second time had been even worse, because Panther had actively *taken* the man's life just to make a rich stranger happy. He hadn't even wanted to get out of the pit-fighting game. He'd just wanted to feel a little better about himself. Once he'd done it, though—once he'd made his life that little bit better at Javelin's expense—some part of him hadn't even been sure that this was the life he wanted. He'd wanted to be free once and raise a family somewhere, but he'd given up that opportunity time and again. He'd never so much as tried to run away from Maxus. He'd turned his back on the dusty streets of

Nexus once he'd won his freedom. He'd even stopped traveling once he was assured two high-bill one-on-ones a month in the Nexus arena. And once he'd killed Javelin, it had been like he'd signed a contract on his future. He'd destined himself to a life like Maxus', where he either died in the pit or lived long enough to retire and pass on his skills to the next generation of people who were just like he used to be.

Yet he'd known that he had no other big opportunities coming to him in his career, so he'd vowed to just keep on fighting until someone came along who could take him down. In a way, a part of him had considered it a fitting tribute to Javelin, who'd gotten him where he was thus far. Panther hadn't yet sunk so low that he felt he deserved to die for what he'd done, though, so he'd never let himself lose. The worst he'd allowed to happen was he hired a new arranger and told him to put him up against any foe short of a Dragon-Blood that would draw a crowd and keep the bookkeepers in the betting pools guessing. That had gotten him into fights against beasts and God-Bloods, Fair Folk and gangs of less experienced brawlers, but he'd remained undefeated. The fights had gotten tougher and the stakes had risen commensurately higher, but still, no one had been able to bring him down. Finally, he'd started to wonder if anyone *could* bring him down. Maybe it turned out that fate wasn't terribly imaginative, he'd thought once, and he was right where he was supposed to be doing just what he was supposed to be doing. The very idea had driven him into his cups for the next several days, but when he'd sobered up, he'd done so in a state of weary resignation.

And it had been in that frame of mind that he'd entered his last match as a professional pit fighter in Nexus…

The match was the highest one on the bill, so the sun was already low in the western sky when it started. It was lower than the cheapest of the cheap seats, in fact, casting the pit in shadow. Three rings of bright lamps with huge swivel-mounted mirrors had been lit around the top of the coliseum and at its two mezzanines, though, so the pit was lit up as bright as day. Panther emerged from his private waiting room onto the field of battle as the caller introduced him, and the rambunctious crowd did its best to bring the house down. He might as well have been the Scarlet Empress herself for all the noise these people were making. The ghost of a smile touched Panther's lips, and he thought that this must be what the Dragon-Blooded felt like whenever they went among mortals. These cheering fans had praised Panther's opponents with wild abandon, but he was their god, their undefeated champion. They worshiped him. They threw flowers and dinars and long, rolled-up prayer strips, and though few of their offerings actually made it down to the sand of the pit itself, Panther respected their devotion.

He also abstractly respected the team of five men who'd taken the field to oppose him. Normally, he couldn't fight more than three men at a time in the pit—one of the free-fighting division's few rules—but this was a special occasion. His arranger had spoken to the officials who ran the free-fighting and team-tactics divisions and had gotten from them special dispensation to schedule a day of cross-division fighting to help boost ticket sales. The year's end Calibration was coming, and people were normally leery about spending their money or making bets at that time of year. The promotion was helping to offset the loss the managers of the arena were going to take when it was forced by civil law to close for the five days of Calibration proper, though.

Panther didn't really care about all that, but he'd absorbed the information as his arranger had explained it to him. All he really cared about was who he was fighting, and it had come as a surprise when he'd found out. He, the reigning undefeated champion of the free-fighting division, was being pitted against the reigning undefeated champions of the tactics division, the Leather Sharks. The match had been hyped and touted as a clash of juggernauts from which only one side could emerge truly victorious and undefeated. It had pulled in the big-money crowds from both divisions, and the arena was packed from pitside to wall top and even into the aisles. The cheap rooftop seats on the buildings were more expensive than they'd ever been, but they were still packed to capacity. The streets around the arena for blocks were clogged with foot traffic and people holding impromptu cart parties as they waited to hear how the fight was going. Mostly, the folks out there listened to the caller's amplified narration, and they cheered reflexively as inside crowd roared. Panther envied them the excitement they could feel for something they couldn't even witness, while he, at the locus of all the fuss, barely felt a thing.

For their part, the Leather Sharks seemed to be taking things pretty seriously as Panther approached. They stood waiting for him now in a precise fang formation, all loose and relaxed but ready to take action at the wave of a flag. They wore matching outfits of leather armor that enwrapped them almost entirely from head to toe. Only their joints were not covered in thick, black leather, and that only inasmuch as they needed the extra mobility. Each one carried a long wooden spear with a black-iron head, a weighted throwing net on one side of their belts and a stout leather-wrapped cudgel on the other. They all wore thin, black helmets with grills over their faces, and the metal had been painted to resemble a shark's head with blood around the wide-open mouth. A bright red shark insignia practically glowed on each fighter's chest too, catching the reflected lamplight perfectly. They looked like the grizzled, professional mercenaries their two captains had always dreamed of becoming. Panther stopped two spear lengths from them, crossed his wrists in front of his chest in an old-fashioned bonded-slave salute and bowed with a veneer of respect. The fighter at the head of the fang formation stepped forward, took his helmet off and balanced it with one hand on his right shoulder. It was Boar Spear, and he looked exactly as young and energetic as he had the last time Panther had seen him.

"Good to see you again, Panther," he said. "Ready to make a lot of strangers rich and poor?"

"You mean by whipping your team for you?" Panther said automatically. It was pit-talk, and it just came naturally. "Suppose so. It's been a slow day."

"Sure you don't want to arm up?" Snow Tiger said over Boar Spear's shoulder. He kept his helmet on and stood with his arms crossed, balancing his spear in one massive fist. "Those things aren't going to do you much good." He nodded toward the dinged-up and tarnished fighting gauntlets Panther wore, which appeared to be Panther's only weapons.

"Won't do you much good either," Panther said, shrugging. He hadn't bothered to select any better weapon or even so much as don any armor. He wore nothing but the gauntlets, some loose pants and his oldest pair of sandals. The golden sun tattoo gleamed on his chest, either inviting his opponents' weapons or mocking them. "Less, probably."

"He's just like I remember," Boar Spear said with cheerfully sardonic sentimentality. "Isn't it good to see him again, Snow Tiger?"

"Just ask him and get it over with," Snow Tiger said. "Crowd won't keep hollering forever."

"Sure," Boar Spear said. Then, "You remember what we asked you about last time, Panther? Hadn't heard from you much these past few years, but we wanted you to know that offer's still out there."

Panther was so amazed he barked a laugh, the first real one that had come out of him in months. "What's that? Join up with you guys, was that the offer? You're kidding, right? I mean, you remember why you're here, don't you?"

"Told you he'd laugh in your face," Snow Tiger said.

"No, we're still serious, Panther," Boar Spear said. "I mean, we're *going* to whup you, but after that, we'd love to have you on the team. And I don't just mean pit fighting. We've got a lot of money riding on this thing—enough to get out for good and all. We're starting up our merc outfit, and we still want you with us. You don't even have to fight with us if you don't want. You can train recruits for us or just let us put your face up on posters. Whatever you want."

"Judges are coming," Snow Tiger said, tapping Boar Spear on the shoulder.

Boar Spear put his helmet back on and got back into formation as a pair of robed judges swept into position on either side of the line between the opponents. They raised their signal flags high, petitioning the fighters' arrangers before they could give the start-of-fight signal. The crowd cheered, anxious for the fighters to get on with it already.

"We go way back, Panther," Boar Spear said over the surging noise, "and we can help each other. Think hard about it."

"I'll tell you what," Panther said. "If all five of you put together can beat me in front of all these people, I'll retire from this life, sell off everything I own and set you up myself. And I'll be one of your raw grunts out there on the front line every time some rich bastard lines your pockets to fight his battles for him. How's that?"

If Boar Spear replied, the spectators' hollering washed it out as the judges gave the start-of-fight signal and backed out of the way. Panther held out his hands in a loose defensive stance and lazily let the Leather Sharks come toward him and close in around him. They each shifted their spears to a casual one-handed grip under their right arms, using them more to keep Panther at bay than to threaten him, and they drew their nets. As Panther postured and slowly circled, occasionally making eye contact with a random blank face in the first row of seats and snapping off a showy salute, the Sharks surrounded him in a five-pointed star formation. They circled him widdershins and kept enough distance between themselves so that if one missed a net-cast, it wouldn't entangle an ally. Every one of them held their nets by the center and twirled the barbed weights in lazy circles, just like Maxus had taught Panther, Snow Tiger and Boar Spear years ago.

Panther wasn't thrilled about that. He'd never liked fighting opponents who used nets, and he was fighting more people than he cared to face at a time; putting both unfavorable factors into the same fight was just no good. Even worse, the fighters kept their spears trained on him so he didn't have enough room to dodge and duck around between them. If he wanted to seize the advantage in this fight, he'd have to rush one, take his spear away and see what he could do with it. It might get him run through the guts for trying it, but maybe not. Either way, he figured he might as well give the crowd a good show for its money.

As was expected of him, he held up his arms, banged his

gauntlets together and taunted the fighters as they circled him. He called them cowards. He called them weaklings. He told them the fight was as good as over and that he'd already won. He belted out the tired old pit-talk and emphasized it with grandiose gestures that even the people in the roof seats could see. The crowd loved it, and the caller repeated some of it for benefit of those who couldn't hear. Panther saw Snow Tiger's eyes roll behind the grill of his helmet, and he caught Boar Spear smiling. Fortunately, a quick flick of Boar Spear's eyes to the right alerted Panther to the first actual attack of the match, and he twisted out of the way just in time to avoid a whistling, spinning black net. One of the weights scratched his back, but it didn't bother him. He turned to face the Shark who'd thrown the net, coming up much closer to her than he'd intended. She lashed out with the point of her spear to urge him back into position, and rather than snatch it out of her hands, Panther knocked it aside with the back of his gauntlet. The parry rang like a temple bell, and he danced back into the center of the circling formation as the crowd heaved a sigh of relief and disappointment.

The fighter who'd cast her net first shifted her spear to a high thrusting position like someone would use from behind a shield wall, and she jabbed at Panther apprehensively. Panther correctly judged this attack as a feint, and he heard a Shark behind him grunt with the effort of throwing his own net. To dodge it, he spun toward the first Shark, slipping inside her spear's effective range, and elbowed her hard in the chest. The leather absorbed most of the force, but he'd surprised her and, more importantly, missed the second net. The fighter kicked him hard in the shin, though, which surprised him enough for her to get another attack in. She reversed her spear in one hand and whipped the butt upward into his chin. The sound of it was deafening inside Panther's skull, and all he could see was a blue-white lightning bolt of pain. He staggered back into the cursing Shark who'd just missed him with his net and was foolishly reaching for the cudgel on his belt. The fighter's spear was up and out of position, but he recovered quickly and brought the weapon's shaft down across Panther's shoulder, cracking the long weapon in half. Panther lurched and fell forward as the crowd gasped in horror, but he turned the fall into an almost graceful shoulder roll that brought him up into a tight defensive crouch. It also let him drag his gauntlets along the ground and come up with two fistfuls of sand.

The Leather Sharks didn't realize this at first, but the next one of them to try to throw a net learned it soon enough. Snow Tiger was the lucky winner, and as he reached back to let fly, Panther sprang toward him throwing dirt. It was a rookie tactic and a desperate one, but seeing a professional and a champion do it was like a rare treat for the fans. They hooted and hollered like idiots. They loved it even more when the surprise blinded and flustered Snow Tiger so much that his throw was weak and far off the mark. The net flew so slowly, in fact, that Panther was actually able to stand up, reach back as it went by him, and snag it by the throwing ring in its center. He swung the net in a huge arc like a fighting chain to keep the change in momentum from tangling it up, and he ended up with it coiled around his arm like an obedient pet viper. Posing like a stage actor as Snow Tiger fell back, Panther gave the spectators a moment to react to that, and they let him know how much they'd enjoyed it. Then he turned to the two remaining Sharks who still had nets.

Boar Spear twitched and pump-faked like he was going to throw his net, but Panther could tell he was faking by the way his eyes kept drifting toward Snow Tiger. That left only one teammate with a net, so Panther rounded on him before the others could close on him with their spears. That Shark held his spear out in front of him to keep Panther back, and he spun and hurled his net fast. It was a good, hard throw, but the fighter had no skill with the weapon beyond the very basics, and Panther could tell where the throw was going before the Shark even released the net. He jumped aside as the net swung open, but not before swinging his own net lazily behind his back and catching the barbed weights on it in the mesh of the Shark's net as it went through the space where he'd been. Feeling them tangle, he then whipped both of them around his body in a huge arc and let them fly. The Shark tried to block them both on his spear, which only made the throwing rings on each end come around and hit him in the shoulder and the helmet. To his credit, the fighter didn't drop his spear or fall down. It would take him a second to extricate himself, though, so Panther capitalized on that. He jumped forward, grabbed the fighter's spear by the head and jerked it straight out of the fighter's hands. Without even looking, he then turned around and flipped the spear end-over-end directly at Boar Spear. The spear wobbled gracelessly, but it never touched Boar Spear. Midway between him and Panther, the spear hit the net Boar Spear had just flung at Panther's back, and the two weapons fell to the ground in a tangled heap. Boar Spear flinched, and the crowd gasped, and then the caller went crazy recounting everything that had just happened. And when he did, the fans went wild. Panther mildly realized that he hadn't yet broken a sweat. Was that because this wasn't hard, or did he just not care enough about the outcome?

While Panther knocked the sand out of his gauntlets and took a moment to ponder that, the Leather Sharks got themselves back into fighting order. They abandoned their nets, and those who still had them readied their spears. The other two drew their cudgels and stepped in a little closer than their teammates. Apparently the plan was to keep him trapped between the three spears while the other two fighters moved in and beat him into submission. If even one of the nets had managed to wrap him up, Panther figured, all five of them might have closed in with clubs. It seemed the Leather Sharks only wanted to beat him down and prove a point, not kill him or drive him out of the game with a career-ending injury. They circled him now, letting the crowd cool down from the show Panther had just put on.

"You guys are seriously the best in your division?" Panther goaded them out of habit, making his dismissive wave huge for the crowd's benefit. Then, in a quieter voice, he added, "You must not have been kidding when you told me every other team was made of chumps."

"Hey, careful with all that," Boar Spear whispered, a little hurt. "We go back too far for real jabs like that."

Panther just shrugged and went back to circling defensively, trying to decide how he was going to turn this match around.

He could wait for someone to get too close with a spear, snap it over his knee and go to work... Maybe he could grab a spear haft, use it as a lever to crush a couple of Sharks together and take out two for the price of one... What did the crowd like? Actually, they seemed to like it when he improvised...

On impulse, Panther looked to the fighters holding cudgels and extended a gauntlet toward each of them, beckoning with as much cavalier disrespect as he could convey. It worked too, because both fighters rushed him, swinging their weapons in broad, dangerous arcs. He moved with them as best he could, dodging high and wide strikes, parrying overhead blows and even jumping over a couple of low slashes aimed for his shins. It was so easy to evade the attacks that he started to wonder if maybe the Sharks were going easy on him to stretch out the match. Of course, before he could get too cocky, one of the spear-wielders behind him nicked him across the thigh, drawing blood from a burning thin line. Panther staggered a step, and one of the Sharks took that moment to rush in. Dividing his attention three ways with nigh-suicidal detachment, Panther stepped back, grabbed the hafts of the two spears closest to him and jerked them forward unexpectedly. He crossed the two weapons in front of him and blocked the cudgel's overhand smash, then he unleashed an ugly and powerful kick into the Shark's groin. The club dropped into the sand, and the fighter crumpled. A judge moved toward him to rule whether he would keep fighting, and Panther kicked the guy once more, hard, across the side of his helmet.

As the judge got in position, both Sharks whose weapons were trapped in Panther's gauntlets tried to free their spears. Panther let one of them go as both fighters jerked backward, but he jumped toward the other one—dodging a cudgel blow from the fighter who still had one—and knocked that fighter to the ground. She lost her grip on the spear, and Panther wrenched it out of her hand as he came down on top of her in the sand. He popped up into a crouch and planted the butt of the spear in the woman's chest to lever himself to his feet. He turned in time to meet the attack of the other fighter, and he just barely managed to block the wild cudgel blow. He bashed it aside with his newly acquired spear and brushed the fighter back with an ungainly thrust. He'd never been as good with a spear as a sword, cestus or khatar, but he'd been decent with a simple staff, so he spun the spear into a comfortable staff-fighting position and posed again to give the crowd a hint of what was coming. The move got both Boar Spear and Snow Tiger into the game at last, and the three Leather Sharks who were still standing rushed him at once.

Panther met their attacks with a whirlwind of parries, redirections and stop-thrusts that would have done a champion staff fighter in the signature-weapon division proud. His spear made for an unwieldy staff, but it was light enough, and he was strong enough, to compensate. And since all he was doing was defending himself—and all Boar Spear and Snow Tiger were doing was trying to flank him and distract him so their teammate could bash him with the cudgel—that was okay. Boar Spear managed to simply muscle a couple of good shots in through Panther's defenses, but they were either hard raps with the butt of his spear or flat slaps with the edge of his spear head that stung and stunned but inflicted little real harm. Panther found that he could stand his ground with reasonable stability and that he could even maneuver the triangle of attackers if he pretended to go on the attack toward one of them. The Sharks, it seemed were drawing the fight out, making it look good so the crowd wouldn't feel disappointed. They wanted the match to last. Panther had no problem with that from a strictly ethical standpoint, all pit fighters did that if they wanted the fans to remember them, but it put him at a tactical disadvantage that he did have a problem with. It wasn't happening yet, but pretty soon, he was going to start getting tired. He'd taken only one of the Sharks out of the action—as a quick glance at the pit judge told him—but they were still four strong, and he was only one man. If they kept toying with him, and he kept letting them, they were going to wear him out and beat him down. He had to start getting more aggressive. Mean, even. But not first.

"Come on, you cowards!" he shouted with a huge, explosive wave and a twirl of his spear. "Quit toying with me like a bunch of cats and *fight*! Or don't you know how?" As he taunted, he left a gap in his defenses big enough to drive a merchant's wagon through. Boar Spear and Snow Tiger were too smart to fall for the ploy, but the Shark whose name Panther didn't know went for it. He came in with a sideways cudgel swipe intended to crush ribs, and Panther made him pay for the mistake. He stepped into the arc of the swing and planted his own spear point-down like a battle standard, blocking the attack while it still had no power. Then, before the fighter could recover, Panther pounced on him and drove a sledgehammer of a punch right into the grill of his helmet. The Shark's head snapped back, and Panther kicked him in the stomach. When the fighter doubled over, Panther drove both gauntleted fists down on the back of the kid's head while simultaneously ducking under Boar Spear's and Snow Tiger's high counterattacks. The Shark crumpled, and the crowd thundered as a judge came to rule on him. That just left Boar Spear and Snow Tiger, and Panther didn't mind his two-on-one odds against them one single bit.

Except in the sudden rush, Panther had forgotten about the Leather Sharks' fifth member—the woman from whom he'd taken his spear before the other three had closed in on him. As he turned around to either retrieve his spear or pick up a different one, the woman appeared suddenly in his peripheral vision and whipped her cudgel in under his guard. He got a hand on her elbow, but it wasn't enough to turn the attack in time. Her weapon slipped past his gauntlet and pounded into his left side. It wasn't a mortal or debilitating wound, Panther didn't think, but it had an instant effect nonetheless. For just a moment, it burned away the haze of numbness that had been creeping up on him these last two years since Javelin's death, and it seriously pissed him off. He barked in pain, and the anger took over. He clamped his gauntlet down hard on the Shark's wrist before she could withdraw it, and he barely flinched when she punched him in the face with her free hand. A cut opened beneath his right eye, but he ignored it. Staring in the woman's eyes, he ground the bones of her wrist together with one hand while the other reached up and grabbed the underside of her helmet beneath her chin. Her eyes widened, and with a mighty heave, Panther lifted her off the ground, spun around and flipped her over his shoulder onto the sand, knocking her helmet off in the process. He then ripped the cudgel out of her hand, knelt on the woman's right shoulder and raised the weapon to smash her skull. A judge came gliding toward him to accept his petition, but before it got there, a spear haft came in from the left and cracked a couple of Panther's ribs just above where the woman had bashed him. He fell over and rolled to his feet in subsumed agony to see Snow Tiger standing over the fallen Shark and Boar Spear running up to stand next to him. *Now* they were the only two Sharks left.

"Damn it," Boar Spear said, looking over his shoulder at his fallen teammate. "I warned her about losing her temper."

"Told you she wasn't ready for the show," Snow Tiger said, his eyes fixed only on Panther, who was crouching and trying to catch his breath.

"Shut up," Boar Spear snapped. He came a couple of steps toward Panther then, holding his spear out in front almost defensively. "Look, Panther, try to calm down," he whispered. "I'm really sorry about that. We told all our guys we were only out here to knock you down, not to kill you. You're no good to us dead or so mangled you can't fight anymore. You know? Real sorry. Let's just try to keep this a straight fight, yeah?"

"Piss off," Panther said, rising slowly to his feet. "I don't need your charity." With that, he hurled the cudgel in his hand right at Boar Spear's chest. Boar Spear dodged it with a wide-eyed glare, and Snow Tiger had to bend out of the way too. When the weapon had spun past him, he hefted his spear and started coming toward Panther cautiously behind his partner.

"Damn you, we're trying to do you a favor!" Boar Spear shouted, leveling his spear now like an angry god in judgment and bearing down on Panther with increasing speed. "Even after the way you treated us before!" He slashed the air savagely with the flat of his spear, and Panther had to duck and jump back to keep from taking a nasty hit. "Even after the disrespect you showed Maxus after all he did for you!" Another attack, this one much wilder. The point actually cut Panther shallowly across the chest, doing nothing to abate his mounting rage. Boar Spear's frustration grew as well, the harder Panther made it to hit him. "Even after what you did to Javelin and what you let happen to Wolf, we're still trying—" *slash* "—to—" *chop* "—help—" *hack* "—you!"

With the last word, Boar Spear lunged straight in with a ferocity that surprised his teammate. Yet Panther had been waiting for that very attack, and he did what Boar Spear least expected—he caught the head of the spear in the palm of one metal gauntlet. The impact jarred all the way up Panther's arm, but it made Boar Spear miss a step and almost fall over. He did actually fall over a second later when Panther jerked the spear toward himself and snapped its head off with a solid chop from his other gauntlet. Boar Spear went down in the sand, and Panther had only a second to do what seemed like the best thing for the situation. He flipped the broken-off spear head around in his hand and hurled it as hard as he could at Snow Tiger, who was just starting to charge him now that Boar Spear had fallen. The projectile flipped over only once in midair before sinking deeply into the unprotected segment of his armor where the leg met the hip. Bright blood welled all around the blade, garish and lurid in the reflected lamplight, and Snow Tiger collapsed with an undignified scream.

Boar Spear was on his feet an instant later, and his face was livid as he looked from Snow Tiger to Panther. A judge was already gliding toward Snow Tiger, and the crowd was apparently locked in endless paroxysms of joy, but Panther was hardly aware of these things. Boar Spear didn't seem to care either.

"That's a mortal wound!" he shouted in plaintive rage, pointing at his fallen teammate with the broken off haft of his spear.

"He won't die," Panther said, plastering on a smug, malicious grin as he took on a defensive stance once more. "Damned if he'll walk again, though. You think he still wants to start that mercenary company now?"

"What in Creation is wrong with you, Panther?" Boar Spear hollered, throwing fuel on the fires of the spectators' passion, though they couldn't make out what he was saying. "Damn you, all we wanted was a better life than this! And even though you don't deserve it, we wanted to offer you that chance too. But you just keep spitting in our faces. What in hell is wrong with you?"

He didn't wait for an answer. As the crowd roared and egged him on, Boar Spear brought up the spear haft and swung it like a club, trying his best to bash Panther's brains out. Panther didn't flinch or try to duck, he just stepped up and grabbed the end of the stick before it could connect. The move surprised Boar Spear—again—and Panther punched him in the face with that same hand. Then he snatched the stick away and swept Boar Spear's feet out from under him with it. When the last Leather Shark fell to his knees, Panther ran up and grabbed him in a chokehold that used the stick for leverage against the ground. He leaned forward against the leather-clad fighter, whom he'd known his entire professional career, cutting off air to his lungs and blood to his brain.

"Listen up," Panther whispered as the noise from the crowd threatened to drown him out. "Here's how it is. There *is* no better life than this, you got it? Not for me; not as long as I keep winning. I made my choices, done what I've done, and it's all been to get me exactly where I am today. And nobody, *nobody*, is going to tell me I'd be better off somewhere else. So you think about that from now on any time you start wondering who's got the better life."

He could have just let it go at that moment, but the burning pain in his side and the anger in his breast wouldn't let him. So, before he let Boar Spear drop into unconsciousness, he stood up straight with the Leather Shark in his arms and gave his opponent's head a hard, sharp twist. Something cracked in the center of Boar Spear's neck, and all the life went out of his limbs all at once. Yet Boar Spear wasn't dead, and as Panther dropped him to the bloody sand, the fighter's eyes went wide and fixed Panther with a complicated glare. It burned with hatred and promised eternal damnation, but at the same time, it welled up with tears and a panicked desperation.

Panther looked at him for a long moment, waiting for Boar Spear to say something, but when nothing seemed to be forthcoming, he turned his back and walked away. The fans cheered and threw tokens of their praise, but Panther didn't notice. The fire in him was going out once again, leaving only the comfortably familiar numbness. He wrapped himself in it and left the arena victorious.

Chapter Six

The remembered sound of applause faded away into the rustle of wind through the canopy of leaves, and Panther hung his head. Snow Tiger and Boar Spear had arranged the match with a clear agenda, and Panther had turned it around with the power of his conviction. Yet once his victory had been won and his enduring fame had been assured, he hadn't found the sense of fulfillment or purpose he'd expected to find. After the lifetime of sacrifices and compromises that had culminated in that match, he was no more assured of his place in this world than he'd been as a frightened child kneeling by his dying mother's side in their half-forgotten Nexus tenement. In fact, that match and the career-ending injuries he'd inflicted on his former teammates had only served to bring into sharp relief the fact that his life had no purpose. He had no purpose. He was but one wave in a sea of faces. People recognized him and respected him and even loved him, but none of that mattered because, when he was gone, Nexus would carry on as if he'd never existed. Another champion would come along, the people would forget him, and daily life in Nexus would keep on being the same until the end of this age. He contributed nothing, and he would leave no legacy.

These were the thoughts that had overwhelmed him as he'd left the arena that night after his last match, and they had pounded on him relentlessly as the waves and winds of a storm would pound the shore. These were the thoughts that had driven him back to his plush but empty apartment once the night's celebrations were through, contemplating them through a numb haze. He had simply lain there on his bed the next day, sprawled like a mindless animal in the summer heat. And in his sour, fruitless contemplation, his Exaltation had come upon him, revealing the face of the Unconquered Sun and giving him his mission to take light into the darkness as a priest of righteousness.

But why? Panther silently demanded, glaring up at the sun through the tree canopy. He knew he wasn't a righteous man. If he hadn't been willing to admit it before, the memories that this painful meditation had dredged up would have convinced him. Twice he'd been willing to sacrifice a former teammate's life—once passively to cheat his way to freedom, once actively to cement his worthless position in life as a killer. The first time, that cavalier attitude had cost Wolf his life though Javelin's had been spared. Wolf, who'd done nothing but defended his teammate. Panther had caused Wolf's death, and he'd reaped the audience's praise for avenging that death. It hadn't been cowardice but cold-blooded, calculating self-service.

His murder of Javelin at Kerrek Deset's manor had actually been more of the same, now that he thought about it. In all his career as a pit fighter, he had grievously wronged his former teammate. Yet, when it came time to pay for his crime, he'd scoffed in the face of justice. He'd not only killed Javelin to protect himself, he'd callously taken from Javelin what the wiry young man had worked so hard to earn. He'd stolen Javelin's place at Kerrek's side and usurped whatever advantage Javelin might have gained there. And worst of all, he'd known all along that he didn't even *need* the benefits that Kerrek Deset's patronage had offered him. It had merely been expedient. Panther had been lazy, choosing to pay in blood for the position and advantages he could have earned honestly if he'd been patient enough to work harder for them.

Laziness had also informed his decision to remain a pit fighter after he'd won his freedom from Maxus. He could have done anything with the money he won in the pit, but all he'd ever done was blow it on trifles that vanished all too quickly. He could have saved it, planned with it, but instead, he'd thrown it around like there was no tomorrow. In fact, there had never been a tomorrow for him. He'd never looked beyond the next fight, the next party, the next fix. He'd simply assumed that he'd fight in the pit until someone killed him. And until then, he'd be famous and rich and respected—and maybe even feared. Never had he given the first thought to what he would do if he survived to retirement age with most of his fortune still intact. Never had he thought of what he'd do with his life once he could no longer fight. He'd never wanted to. Fighting was all he knew how to do, and he'd never taken the time to learn anything else. Maybe if he had, he could have put his energy and talents toward something that actually made a difference in this world. Maybe if he had, he could have actually had a positive effect... helped people somehow... done righteous works that made him worthy of what the Unconquered Sun had given him. But he hadn't. He'd never bothered to try to make the world any better, because it had always been good enough for him.

In the end, Boar Spear and Snow Tiger had apparently realized that about him, and they'd tried to help him. Though he'd spit in their faces, they'd offered him partnership in their dreams because they knew he had none. They'd seen what his life was worth, but better than that, they'd apparently seen what his life *could have been worth,* if only he'd had the dedication to pursue a cause. And since they knew him and respected him, they'd tried to share their cause with him. Yet he'd ruined them despite every effort they'd made on his behalf. He'd more than likely destroyed their reputation as a fighting team by defeating them five-on-one, but worse, he'd crippled Snow Tiger and Boar Spear both. Snow Tiger might be able to walk again someday (provided Panther hadn't punctured the main artery in the man's leg), but he'd never fight. If the surgeons hadn't had to amputate his leg, the man would have a worse limp than Maxus ever did. And Boar Spear would never move again of his own volition. Panther had made sure of that.

And the only reason Panther had done it was because Boar Spear had called him out. He'd said that the life Panther had made for himself wasn't worth the effort and would profit him nothing when he was an old man. Panther had not disagreed, but that had made the message no more palatable, so he had lashed out. He had broken men and killed men in the pit for years, but never with such malicious, venomous intent. Never had one of them struck him and wounded him so profoundly as Boar Spear's insight had. What Panther had done to them had been in no way righteous, so why had the Unconquered Sun chosen him? Frankly, Panther had looked righteousness in the face and had chosen not to be a party to it. He'd turned his face away from it in pursuit of his own selfish desires.

Turned his face away...

Panther set aside his self-recriminations for a second and thought about that. The Unconquered Sun had said something like that before Panther had left Nexus. *I turned my face from the world of men,* the god had told him, *but I shall do so no longer.* When exactly had that happened? At the end of the First Age when the Dragon-Blooded had slaughtered their Solar Exalted masters? The Solar Exalted had ruled this world once, and they'd made of it a paradise that suited them well. They'd derived their power from the Unconquered Sun, the mightiest of gods. Yet, somehow, they'd been torn down and hunted to extinction by their lieutenants and servants, the Dragon-Blooded. That revolt had brought the First Age to an end, but how could it even have come about unless the Unconquered Sun had already turned his face away from his chosen ones? But if the world was a paradise under the rule of the Exalted, why would he ever turn away? Could it be that the paradise that had suited its Exalted rulers so well had not suited the god who gave them their power?

Panther contemplated this, and though he was loath to accept it, an ancient part of his soul—now reborn for the first time since the revolt of the Dragon-Blooded—acknowledged that it was true. That ancient memory would reveal no more of what it had seen or even done, but the certainty of its shame filled Panther now. What was worse, it mirrored Panther's own feelings, and the two reinforced each other. Panther knew that the sins he'd committed against his fellow man were nothing compared to those his ancient, reborn self had committed, but that made him feel no better. He knew that both people—himself in the present and the Prince of the Earth he'd been long ago— had done wrongs to the limits of their respective abilities, and though they'd known what righteousness was, they'd turned away from it. And when it had happened at the end of the First

Age, the Unconquered Sun had turned his face away from the world of men to punish his chosen ones and let the world suffer for their sins.

Yet, now, the god had made it a point to say, at least to Panther, that he would turn away no longer. His punishment had left the world to wallow in decline, and he could apparently stand it no longer. The passage of time and... something even Panther's most ancient memories couldn't remember... had whittled the souls of the first Exalted down until all that was left was the memory of power and glory and the shame of letting it all go to waste over vain pursuits. And in its rebirth, one such soul had found a comfortable home in Panther. Like it, Panther had become lazy and cruel and self-absorbed as his power and glory had grown. Like it, Panther had denied wise counsel and lashed out at those who would give it. Like it, Panther had turned in upon himself, forsaking all others. And now, like it, Panther had been given a second chance to make something of his life by the grace of the Unconquered Sun.

That realization hit him like a thunderbolt, and as he opened his eyes to this new enlightenment, the golden disk on his forehead that marked him as one of the sun's chosen began to glow. He who had no father and no purpose, had now been given both. Not because he'd lived the life of a monk and remained steadfast in his worship of the principles of righteousness, but because he'd been selfish and vain and done great harm to those who were essentially innocent. He'd done wickedness and succumbed to its temptations, and he'd seen the effects that wickedness had had on the people around him. Never once had he stopped to consider those effects when he'd been committing the acts, but looking back on them now, he remembered every one, and he was ashamed. That shame had always been with him in one form or another, mostly in the numbness that had enwrapped him, but never had he faced it or sought to overcome the source of it. He'd never found the power within himself to rise above the constraints of that life he'd made for himself.

Now, he had that power, and now, he knew why he'd been chosen. He knew righteousness by its opposite, just as he'd learned all his life, but his Exaltation had put an end to that life and begun a new one. In it, he had a chance to see that he never let righteousness fall by the wayside out of greed, vanity or indolence. He could teach people how to walk the path of righteousness because he could so intimately recognize the signs of falling from that path. He could inspire people to do as he was now learning to do because his fame had traveled far throughout the Scavenger Lands, of which Nexus was the commercial heart. People would listen to him because of who he'd been, and they would follow him because of what he'd become. They would see how much he'd changed. He would show them. They would come to understand that, by the Unconquered Sun's power, even the worst of them could be redeemed if they but chose to follow the path of righteousness. And if they chose not to follow it even after he showed them the way... If they still chose to do evil despite what he had to teach them...

Panther stopped to ponder that a moment. It was a squalid and dangerous age, and evil men had grown fat and wealthy in it. The Dragon-Bloods had risen to their position through bloody revolt, and they'd grown decadent with no one to challenge them. And in the last five years, they'd begun to turn their gazes ever more attentively toward their internal affairs on the Blessed Isle. (The fact that Panther had come this far since his Exaltation without so much as seeing a single rider of the Wyld Hunt testified to that.) As the Dragon-Blooded had withdrawn, criminals, barbarians, ghosts, little gods, monsters and murderers had seemingly multiplied overnight, swelling up in every outpost of civilization like infections on the still-healing wounds that rent Creation. They were thriving and having their way with the world, and they would not be redeemed by words alone. Panther knew that just as surely as he knew that no words from any man or woman in his life would have changed the destructive path he'd been on. Only the grace of the Unconquered Sun had had any effect. And now, Panther was the instrument of that grace in Creation. Where words would not suffice to stop the spread of evil and defend the way of righteousness, Panther had been given the power to back up his words. His entire life had taught him how to fight and win and how to get people to take notice. Only now did he have a message worth getting noticed and an ideal worth fighting for. He would make this world a righteous place, and he would make himself a righteous man.

Panther stood and quelled the fire within him that made the golden disk on his forehead burn. His meditation was over. He didn't have every answer he could have hoped for, but he no longer needed all the answers. He had a mission now and a goal for what to do with the rest of his life. More importantly, he knew that he had the blessing of the most powerful god in all Creation so long as he stayed on his path and defended those who chose to walk with him from those who never would. His life stood to be much simpler now, even than it had been before. He would be righteous from now on, and he would let no unrighteous act stand. Granted, that was a much more difficult philosophy to practice than it was to adopt, but he was no longer willing to settle for a life of aimless ease. There was important work to be done now, in the Scavenger Lands and all over the world, and only those who were chosen like himself could do it.

So, he left the peace and solitude of the ancient sanctuary he'd found and walked back the way he'd come, ready now to accept what he'd been given and to make the world a righteous place as he knew best.

Chapter Seven

Having arrived at his new understanding concerning his Exaltation and what was expected of him, Panther found the concerns of the mortal world weighing down on him once more. He discovered that he was tired after his long pilgrimage, not to mention somewhat lost. When he'd left Nexus, he'd known only that he was heading east and that he had to avoid population centers. He had no idea now how far he'd walked or exactly where he'd ended up. He knew only that he was still somewhere far north of the Yellow River, and he was fairly certain that he hadn't crossed into the Great Eastern Forest that spread out from the Elemental Pole of Wood at the edge of Creation. The only other thing he knew for sure was that he was hungry and in need of a good night's rest. So, as he made his way out of the forest into which his wandering had brought him, he randomly picked fruits and edible plants and filled himself. He'd never been taught how to forage in the wilderness during the life he remembered, but the knowledge came to his mind unbidden in half-remembered dream fragments. And as he trusted this knowledge and acted on it, the forest provided without complaint. It accommodated him as befit a Prince of the Earth, which the most ancient part of Panther's Exalted soul recognized and respected.

Carrying on thus, his hunger sated and his mind at ease, Panther made his way out of the forest and stopped at its edge when night fell. He found that he was fairly high up on a hill and that a village lay some miles away in the valley below. A dusty, narrow, rutted road stretched into the distance, and crooked needles of smoke rose from cooking fires. Panther could just make out fertile farm fields and hear the low sounds of farm animals. He could also hear the hour chimes of a modest temple of the Immaculate Order, around which the small farming hamlet had likely been built. That gave Panther pause, and he sat among the bushes at the top of the hill to rest and think. It was the dogma of the Immaculate Order that labeled people such as him Anathema, and most people across Creation had no experience to refute it. Most people saw only the spiritual and ethical bastion of civilization that the Realm represented when they looked at the monks and temples of the Immaculates. What Panther saw was an entanglement that could result in a Wyld Hunt being called down on him, which would distract him from his mission, to say the least.

Therefore, he decided to wait here, still fairly far from the hamlet, and skirt it on his way back toward civilization. Once he did that, he could look for a larger town into which to disappear—though perhaps not one so large that he might be recognized. Then he could find out where he was and decide where to go. But first, he would rest and get some sleep. As helpful as his meditation in the arboreal sanctuary had been, it hadn't been particularly restful. In fact, he couldn't even remember the last good night's sleep he'd had. So, he lay back now, atop a hill overlooking the world whose care he had inherited, and slept.

Awaking at dawn the next morning, Panther ate to curb the light hunger rumbling in his belly, then washed his face in a stream and relieved himself like a normal, mortal human being. His dreams had been filled with indistinct but wondrous images of glory and power that no waking mind in this age could conceive, but this simple biological act reminded him of who he was and where he'd come from. When it was done, he went back to the spot where he'd slept and lay back down in a boneless sprawl, looking at the world below. As the haze of sleep and dreams cleared, he saw that something wasn't right in the hamlet he'd noticed the night before.

The first thing he noticed was a pillar of smoke rising where the cooking fires had been coming from last night. The pillar was black and thicker than any cooking or brush-clearing fire should be—as if buildings in the village were burning. He wondered if an accident of some kind had started a fire in the village. Yet, looking to the edge of the valley and beyond, where the village's farming fields lay, he could see that many of the crops had been trampled by a large number of men, horses and wheeled vehicles. Some were burning too, adding more smoke to the morning sky. And as Panther sat up and focused his attention, he could hear faint whispers of animal panic and piteous human distress, along with hard laughter and guttural shouts that were supposed to be intimidating. What he'd awoken to was no accidental tragedy, but a raid, likely by one of the barbarian tribes that roamed the Scavenger Lands looking for prey. He couldn't guess which tribe it might be because he didn't know exactly where he was, but that didn't really matter.

Though perhaps there was a reason for what was happening, the most ancient part of his reincarnated soul mused. After all, everyone needed to live. The barbarians raided for food, for metal—for things they needed to survive. After his mother's death, even Panther himself had stolen to eat and committed crimes to survive. He understood the need. But no... that didn't matter. A barbarian horde that grew strong on the rape and pillage of civilization would just keep on burning and destroying and despoiling until someone stopped it. And the sooner someone stopped it, of course, the better. Panther stood, strapping on the sword he had worn all the way from his erstwhile home in Nexus.

Maybe once the imperial army would have come, and the legions would have marched forth in precise military fashion with their well-armed and armored foot soldiers led by Dragon-Blooded officers who wielded jade weapons and ancient magic. Even though being saved from chaos by the Dragon-Blooded more or less amounted to being conquered by a more civilized occupying power, at least the people would be safe. And in their gratitude, they would pay tribute, and the Realm would stay strong enough to keep protecting them. Yet now, the Dragon-Blooded were too concerned with their own affairs, so the only ones left to stand up for the Scavenger Lands were those who took it upon themselves to do so. Fortunately, it also left people like Panther, who'd been given a power that the Dragon-Blooded could only envy. The time had come for him to make a difference.

"The world can be made pure and whole once again," he said to himself as he started moving down the hill. "And it starts here."

Panther lost sight of the village behind a hill as he descended to the road, but the black smoke and the growing sounds of slaughter made sure he never lost his way. His long strides ate the distance, and he covered the few intervening miles in little time. As he approached the last bend in the road before the village proper, he could hear the specific words of the villagers' cries for help and every sound a barbarian's weapon made as it cut one of them down. Before he was quite there, he met a handful of harried-looking refugees fleeing up the road toward him. He paused briefly to ask how large the force was that had attacked and how many people were still alive in the village. The refugees took one look at him, made crude warding gestures and ran off as fast as they could. Panther scowled at that before it occurred to him that running into a tall, scarred man sporting a metallic-ink tattoo of the sun across his chest might not set one's mind at ease when one's home was being ransacked by armed barbarians.

When he arrived on the scene at last, taking in the entire horrid tableau in an instant, it was worse than he'd imagined. Even a lifetime of shedding blood for money and public adoration couldn't have prepared him for the carnage that lay before him. All of the homes that made up the village were constructed of wood and roofed with thick logs, and most of them were burning. Some blazes still roared and ate voraciously, while others were guttering in the blackened skeletons of the structures they'd destroyed. The dirt road through the center of the village was churned to a bloody mire, and chips of broken glass lay everywhere like a spring dew, reflecting the sun and the fires in a thousand directions. Wagons lay hobbled, smashed and burning, some with dying horses still attached to them, trying desperately to break free. Trash and detritus had been strewn everywhere, and the smell of smoke and blood turned the air into a noxious miasma. The roar of the flames welcomed him like a chorus of demons.

And then, there were the bodies. They lay in the street, across the thresholds of the ruined homes and in the alleys between the homes. They lay in graceless sprawls—some with dozens of slashes splitting their skin, others with blue-black concavities of blunt-force wounds twisting them out of shape. Many more were choking and dying in the bloody muck of the road, while still others burned and thrashed in the throes of a hideous death. The blood of these lost souls washed the ground, and the odor of it hung thick in the air, coating everything in the stench of death.

Among them, laughing and shouting and destroying everything in sight, were the barbarians who'd brought ruin down upon the village. Each one had somewhat short and bandy legs, and thick mats of curly black hair covered their hard, muscular bodies. Their eyes gleamed a dull, cherry red, and tufts of hair stuck up from their pointed ears. They wore little actual clothing beyond scavenged, ill-fitting armor, and their bodies were painted in odd tribal glyphs. Most of them gripped swords, hatchets, spears or maces in three-fingered hands. Those who went unarmed used bony black claws or their sharp, crooked teeth to tear their victims' flesh. There was not one of them who was not splashed with blood.

Panther angled toward a knot of the Wyld-twisted barbarians who clustered near the center of the village. Three were standing and looking down at something that lay between them, and a fourth was rising from his knees and raising a stone axe. He didn't see Panther coming up behind him, and his preoccupation gave Panther a moment to see what had captured the barbarians' attention. On the ground between them lay a girl of about sixteen, wearing nothing but a torn homespun dress. She curled up on her side, clutching her hands between her legs, and her face was a mass of bruises. There was blood on her dress, and all four barbarians around her reeked of it. Panther didn't have to guess what had happened, and a blaze of righteous rage exploded from him. Only the distance between them kept Panther from killing the barbarian where he stood. The power of the Unconquered Sun shone from his body in a brilliant flare as he charged, and he shouted, "Stop!" with a roar like thunder.

The barbarians flinched and froze, and the one with the axe turned around to see what light had thrown his shadow over the girl he'd just violated. Panther didn't even let the realization sink into the barbarian's mind before he lashed out with a punch that rang like iron and broke the raider's skull. The brute twisted and collapsed like a bag of stones, and Panther snatched the stone axe out of his nerveless fingers. The other three scrambled backward hissing in fear and surprise, and Panther looked them each in the eyes, golden energy still roiling off his body. The barbarians hesitated, then rushed him, howling primitive war cries. Trailing a blinding fan of energy, Panther swung his axe through the first two to reach him, severing their heads almost effortlessly. The third checked his assault as his comrades' blood blinded him, and Panther buried the back-swing of the attack in the center of his hairy chest. The axe's stone head shattered, but the barbarian flew backward a dozen feet through the air and landed in a lifeless heap.

Panther dropped the useless haft of the broken weapon and started to lean down to check on the girl who lay before him, when the barbarians' foreshortened war cry was answered from several directions at once. He looked up to see more than a dozen raiders rushing him, whooping with bloodlust at the prospect of a real fight. A handful led the charge with long, iron-tipped spears, and Panther rushed forward to meet them. They tried to stab him, and he smashed through the hafts of the weapons like they were chopsticks. That broke their stride, giving Panther a second to draw his sword. He cut down the three who'd attacked him then shouldered his way between their falling bodies into the thick of the rest of them. His opponents outnumbered him by more than double the number he'd ever faced single-handedly in the pit, but with the divine power flowing through him, he was unafraid. If anything, his attackers seemed afraid of him as their inhumanly intelligent red eyes took in the bright light rolling off his body, the burning disk glowing on his forehead and the golden sun gleaming on his chest. Panther didn't know if these raiders recognized or understood the source of his power, but they certainly seemed in the right frame of mind to witness it. He brushed all the attackers around him back with three wide, scything swings of his blade, cutting down two barbarians who weren't quick enough. The others gathered around him in a tight circle, feinting with their weapons to frighten and distract him. Panther turned around slowly between them, daring them all to come to him and pay the price for their rapine and destruction. Some of them could hardly stand to look at him, much less attack, but not all. One leaped at Panther's back, only to catch an elbow right between the eyes, blinding him and flipping him over in midair. Another tried to tackle Panther around the knees, but Panther jumped straight up and crashed down on the barbarian's back with both feet. Two more tried to attack at once, and Panther stopped them with his sword. He drove the blade between the bones of one's forearm and into the other's stomach, then uppercut the first one under the chin with a blazing fist.

They all fought desperately and without strategy, and Panther punished them for their carelessness. He almost hoped that the ease with which he did it would frighten the other attackers away, but it had just the opposite effect. The rest of the barbarians in the diminishing circle rushed him all at once, trying to grab his limbs and just bear him to the ground like a pack of wolves. They got in past his outermost guard, sacrificing the leverage and room necessary to use their weapons, and he could feel their teeth and claws trying to tear away his blazing flesh. With a roar, he thrashed and twisted and lashed out in a frenzied blur, chopping the raiders down or sending them flying. They landed in great heaps all around him, either choking out their last breaths or howling in agony. None of them rose again to face him.

There were still more of them scattered throughout the town, and in the moment of tranquility he'd carved out for himself, Panther could hear them coming. He heard the sounds of running feet and feral snarls of bloodthirsty rage. It sounded like a force many times the size of the number of raiders he'd already put down was coming, but that didn't especially bother him. He was strong and unharmed, possibly indestructible. He was a demigod with a righteous cause and a horde of weak enemies arrayed against him. The righteous feeling of triumph was heady and intoxicating—more powerful than anything he'd felt in the pit. *Let them come*, he thought. *Let them learn to respect the power of righteousness.* The satisfaction that bubbled up at that thought was ancient and sweet, and it disturbed him a little.

The sudden sound of running feet in the mud behind him startled him, and he whirled around with his sword held high like a javelin. He almost hurled the blade into the running figure, but he saw that that person wasn't coming toward him. In fact, the person was running toward the fallen woman whose life Panther had saved, and the person wasn't one of the raiders at all. He was a young, red-haired man, dressed like a farmer but with blood and soot staining his clothes and sticking to his skin. The man froze when Panther turned on him, and even when Panther lowered his weapon, the man only stared dumbfounded. He took a hesitant step in the woman's direction but froze again when Panther looked down at her.

"I think she's still alive," the man said, twitching with uncertainty as his gaze darted from Panther to the woman to the direction from which more barbarians were likely coming next. "Can… Can I… go to her? Help her?"

"Where did you come from?" Panther asked him. "Where were you hiding?"

The man bit his lip and held it in his quivering jaw.

"Where?" Panther demanded, coming toward the man.

The man fell back a couple of steps but then stepped up on shaking legs to put himself between Panther and the woman on the ground. "Stay back," he said in a choked whisper.

The man's fear—fear of *him*—took some of the battle fire out of Panther, and he forced himself to calm down even though the other barbarians would be here any second. Why had he wasted time toying with the others and being proud of himself when he should have been looking for survivors?

"Don't be afraid," he told the man, holding his sword down next to his leg. "I'm here to help. How many survivors are left?"

"N-not many," the young man said. "Th-the rest are—"

"Where? Quickly."

"The temple," the man said, nodding back the way he'd come. "There. The Arczeckhi can't burn it or get in, so they're destroying everything else they can. Everybody who survived the first onslaught ran in there."

Panther looked toward the temple to see a handful of barbarians alternately throwing rocks and spears at the high, thin windows and pounding on the heavy wooden door with cheap stone axes while one rode around in frustrated circles on a horse-drawn black chariot. Broken and mutilated bodies of villagers lay in the dirt all around the door, arrayed as if they'd been cut down on their way to the temple. Among them lay a handful of corpses of white-robed monks, who appeared to have fallen either defending the temple or helping the surviving villagers get inside. The barbarians at the temple door ignored all the bodies that lay around them, just as they appeared to be ignoring their comrades' call to battle. By the sound of it, though, most of the others had heard that call and were converging on the center of town in response.

"All right," Panther said, looking around to see how far away the closest attackers were. "Pick her up, and follow me. I'll get you there."

The man struggled to lift the wounded, unconscious woman, who seemed to be swearing venomously through a delirium of pain and shock. He settled her weight as best he could then said, "B-but there're still Arczeckhi over there."

"I'll deal with them."

Panther started walking, and the red-haired man followed him. The man was young and thin, and the girl he was carrying was almost as tall as he was, so he staggered with her limp weight and had to struggle to keep up in the clinging muck of the road. He looked around for other barbarians, but the closest and most dangerous ones to them were the ones between themselves and the temple doors. He tried to explain to Panther

why he didn't think it was a good idea to go *toward* danger, but
Panther ignored him. In fact, Panther sped up and put the red-
haired farmer behind him, though he waved for the farmer to
hurry. As the young man increased his pace, Panther broke
into a run and started shouting for the barbarians' attention.
He called them weak, called them cowards and rebuked them
for attacking the village in the first place. The raiders stopped
harassing the temple doors and turned around. Panther could
see the surprise on their faces as his glowing power reflected in
their eyes, but he saw no fear. Instead, the non-mounted raiders
began to run at him, brandishing their weapons, and the one in
the chariot wheeled around toward him and snapped his reins.

That one closed the distance the fastest, and he bore down
on Panther with a malicious zeal. Panther skidded to a halt in
his tracks and waved off-handedly for the redhead to take a
wide path around what was about to happen. He glanced up to
make sure the raiders on foot were still converging on him, then
he stood his ground and let the chariot come. The vehicle was
drawn by only one horse—a stout and shaggy beast—and the
entire carriage could have fit inside a well-appointed coach back
in Nexus. It was trimmed piecemeal in ugly bits of iron, though,
and its wheels were sturdy and thick. Someone had designed it
to break up formations of foot soldiers, and it would surely be
the death of any single soldier who stood in its way. The driver
held a short spear over his head in his left hand, holding the
reins with only his right. The barbarian flashed his awful teeth
in a huge smile when he saw Panther just standing there.

Panther didn't smile, but neither did he quail in fear as
the chariot came at him. He switched his notched and bloody
sword to his left hand then raised his right fist and stood
waiting. The corona of energy around him pulsed and ran
down his body until all of it was concentrated around that one
fist in a throbbing ball of light. Still he waited, until he could
feel the thudding of the horse's hooves through the ground and
practically taste the horse's breath on the air. Then, the instant
before it was too late, he sidestepped out of the horse's path,
raised his blade to deflect the surprised barbarian's hasty spear
thrust and drove his blazing fist like a sledgehammer into the

side of the chariot right in front of its left wheel. The force of the blow boomed like a thunderbolt, and the vehicle practically exploded around Panther. The left wheel shot off in a random direction, and the entire left side of the chariot splintered into a thousand pieces. The carriage flipped over and twisted apart the bar that harnessed it to the horse, and the animal stumbled and crashed to its knees in the mud. The barbarian chariot-driver flew through the air over Panther's head and crashed to the earth, impaling himself on his own spear.

Standing serene in the middle of the explosion, Panther raised his sword in his left hand, then raised his right and opened his fist. The hard, bright glow that pulsed around his fist shot back up his arm and surrounded his entire body once again. He then shifted the sword back into his right hand and looked up at the barbarians who remained between him and the temple where the surviving villagers took refuge. His glare stemmed the barbarians' rush, making them backpedal furiously in the ruined road. Before they had time to recover from what they'd just seen or flee for their lives, Panther rushed them, hurling his sword ahead of him. It buried itself in the closest barbarian's shoulder, and Panther laid into the others, smashing their skulls with fists, elbows and the heels of his hands. They died where they fell, and Panther stopped again. He looked back to see where the farmer and wounded woman had made it to.

The man stood up out of a shallow depression that was hidden by tall grass off to the side of the road. He tried to lift the woman again but only managed to get her sitting up with her arms sticking out uselessly in two directions. "Come here and help me with her," he said. "You're stronger."

Knowing that the barbarians would be charging down on them any second, Panther hurried over and snatched the woman off the ground. The light pouring off him cradled the injured woman in its embrace, though the redhead seemed afraid to let it touch him. Panther nodded toward the temple doors, glanced back at the barbarians in the center of town, then followed the farmer to where the survivors had holed up. The farmer reached the thick wooden door first and started banging on it and pleading for entrance.

"It's Kellen!" the man shouted. "Laless is hurt! Let us in!"

Panther ran up beside the redhead, Kellen, and eased the now-semiconscious woman, Laless, to her feet between them. The sound of a heavy wooden beam being slid aside whispered through the door, and a seam appeared between the thick wooden panels.

"Hurry!" Kellen said, pushing the door open wider against resistance. A man with a white bandage wrapped around his head peeked out, glaring. He scowled at Kellen, looked more sympathetically at Laless and then blanched in horror at Panther. His eyes bulged, and he tried to slam the door. Kellen tried to hold the door open with one hand while helping balance Laless with the other.

"Stay out!" the man inside hollered. Then to the people behind him in the temple he shouted, "They've summoned a demon! Help me!"

The force against the door increased, nearly knocking Kellen over, but Panther had had enough. He shoved the door back one-handed. The people pushing it fell onto each other and lay on their backs in shock. Panther held the door open and waved for Kellen to get moving. The redhead dragged Laless inside and snorted in contempt.

"Idiots!" he snapped. "Get up, and help me. And don't worry about the Southerner. He's no demon, he's just… God-Blooded, I think. Anyway, he's here to save us."

Panther glanced back over his shoulder and saw that the barbarians were coming toward the temple in force now. He turned back toward the temple and shoved both doors open wide so the people inside could see what he saw. Those closest to the door gasped and froze.

"No," he said. "I'm not here to save you, I'm here to help you. You can't let what they've done to your families and your homes stand. This is your fight. I'm just here to show you that your enemies aren't invincible." He turned his back on the temple then and began to walk toward the advancing raiders. "If you love your homes and you want justice for what's been done to you, come see it for yourselves."

He began to jog toward the barbarians now, but no one

followed him. Neither did he hear the sound of the temple doors slamming, though, which he took as a good sign. Yet that meant that the people were waiting and watching to see if he lived or died, not unlike an arena crowd. Whether through fear or indecision, they'd made themselves spectators in a show where far more than money was at stake. *Well,* Panther thought, *if it's a show they want, I can give it to them. But better they learn something from it.*

He decided what he needed to do as the first rank of barbarians rushed into range. They snarled and hissed and shouted at him, but he slipped between them with unnatural speed and grace, disarming them with crippling blows and knocking them into one another so that no one could get past him. He halted their advance all by himself in the road, feeling not an inkling of fear over their fury or the weapons they raised against him. But though he felt he could hold them off right here until they broke around him and tried to flank the temple from either side, that wasn't what he wanted the villagers to see. Instead, he let one of the barbarian's maces get in under his guard and come down on the edge of his shoulder. He rolled with the blow and deflected it, but the *way* he rolled with it made it look from behind like he'd nearly lost his whole arm to the attack. He fell back a step and "just barely" managed to drive the attacker back with a "wild" kick. The attacker was dead before he hit the ground, but the illusion of grievous injury made the villagers gasp. The barbarians pressed in all around him, and Panther fell back three more steps as more blows fell and appeared to hurt him.

This sort of playacting was one of the tricks of showmanship he'd learned from Maxus after his first few successful pit fights, and he'd been so good at it that his fans had always fallen for his antics. His professional opponents had usually recognized the theatrics for what they were, but the crowds had bought it every time. These barbarian raiders, likewise, could tell they were doing no damage and making no progress, and they redoubled their efforts to bring down their radiant nemesis. The villagers who were watching him, however, had no reason to suspect him of pretending during what was supposed to be a life-or-death battle, and they fell for it like fresh country rubes. They believed that, although this stranger was brave and powerful and clearly doing well, he wouldn't last forever fighting alone. Panther knew that his message had gotten through when a roar of outrage finally built up behind him and the villagers came rushing out of the temple. They held pitchforks, hoes, barrel staves and skinning knives, and those who had no weapons picked up what few weapons their enemies had dropped. They charged into the mass of the raiders, swinging wildly but catching the barbarians completely by surprise. They had no style, skill or strategy, but their righteous fury and pent-up frustration gave them a strength that was undeniable.

"That's it!" Panther shouted to the villagers, smashing the skull of the nearest barbarian. "Drive them back! Punish them for what they've done to your families, your homes!"

His words gave the villagers strength and stole it from the barbarians. Dozens of raiders fell under the onslaught, and those who could do so finally broke and ran. They scattered back across the fields from which they'd come and fled into the countryside, howling in pain and crying in shame. The farmers chased them to the edges of the village and then stood at the borders waving their improvised weapons and shouting defiantly at their would-be murderers. Panther stood alone in the middle of the street for a moment, letting the beleaguered townsfolk revel in their unexpected victory, then he called out to them before anyone could get any funny ideas about chasing their assailants farther into the wilderness.

"Everyone get back here and gather round!" he called in the same kind of loud, clear voice that Maxus had always used to get people to do things in an emergency. "The battle's won, but there's still work to do. You've got wounded to tend to and survivors to find, and if you want to save any of what's left of your homes, I suggest we get started fighting these fires."

Without question, the villagers rushed back to do as he said.

Chapter Eight

The fires were the most immediate problem, and the villagers didn't need Panther's leadership to realize it. Once their battle pride began to wear off, it took only one hard look around the village to show them what needed to be done. The most able-bodied of the surviving men set to work immediately with buckets and shovels and even thick blankets, doing what they could to beat back the fires the raiders had set. Their first priority was to stop the spread of fires that reached crooked orange fingers toward their crops, and it was with a grim-faced determination that they let their houses burn while they did so. The forest nearby would give them the materials they needed to rebuild their homes—it would not replant burned crops.

Panther set those who didn't have the energy to fight the fires to the task of locating other survivors. He turned to the young girls and older women of the village to do this work, as he'd never met a man who could easily stomach seeing his loved ones dying or in pain. Killing was one thing, especially in the heat of a real battle, but dealing with gruesome trauma was not work Panther had ever seen a family man do well. Maxus, for instance, had once broken down into panicked tears in front of gods and everyone when his son had been thrown from a horse and dislocated his hip. One of the house slaves had had to run out and reset the joint before Maxus regained the presence of mind to call for a carriage so he could take the boy to a surgeon in town. In this village's women, Panther saw the same dispassionate self-control that the house slave had shown, so he knew he could rely on them. He even saw a couple of midwife-aged women rush into a still-burning house and come out carrying a moaning, badly burned child between them.

As the fire-containment progressed and the search for survivors got underway, the issue of what to do with the wounded among the raiders came up in short order. It arose as Panther came around the corner of a burning home to find a gang of five men in torn and bloodstained buff jackets carrying a struggling and hissing raider between them. The barbarian was bleeding from half a dozen small wounds, and his right arm had too much play in the elbow. The men holding him were not villagers, but he'd seen a couple of them fighting alongside the villagers to drive the raiders away. Their faces were lit with malice now, and with an unspoken single-mindedness, they swung the raider between them and tossed him through a broken window of the burning structure. The raider screamed and disappeared, as if he'd been swallowed by a demon from beyond the Southern pole.

"What are you doing?" Panther shouted, startling the men. They flinched, backed off and regrouped like a pack of dogs. "What's wrong with you?"

He pushed past them and knocked down the home's front door as the barbarian screamed inside. He went into the building, careless of the fire and smoke, and emerged a moment later with the raider in his arms, writhing and coughing and reeking of burnt flesh and hair. Panther dropped him unceremoniously in the filthy street, but the barbarian looked grateful nonetheless.

"What are you doing?" one of the men said. "We're just giving this bastard what he deserves."

"Go help the other men fighting the fires," Panther said, "and stay out of my sight until it's done. All of you. You don't want to know what *you* deserve for what *you've* just done."

"What did we do?" another of the toughs asked.

"You ganged up on a wounded man four-to-one," someone else said, jogging up from the opposite direction. This man was dressed in a jacket that was cut in the same style as the toughs, but it was older and looked to be made out of better material. He was balding with a severe widow's peak, and an arrowhead of black hair grew under his bottom lip. The toughs stood up straight when this man showed up, but none of them raised eyes toward him. "Better than that," the man continued, "you threw a wounded man into a burning building and stood around to make sure he couldn't come out. Maybe you'd best do what the Southerner says and make yourselves scarce for a while."

The toughs looked back and forth at each other, then bolted. The balding man glared at them and then turned toward Panther. He nodded, then knelt beside the wounded barbarian and drew a stained khatar from his belt. "I'll take care of this one," he said as the barbarian's eyes widened. "Quick and painless."

"No," Panther said, touching the man's wrist. "He's hurt, maybe for life, but he'll live. Bring him. We'll put him with the others."

"Others? Haven't you been dispatching them?"

"No," Panther said again. "Once a man's down and can't fight, that's it. You don't take his life without a judgment. And if you don't live here, you don't get to pass judgment."

"You're joking, right?" The man looked in Panther's eyes, then shook his head. "You aren't. So what are we supposed to do with the ones we find still alive?"

"Bring him," Panther said. "I'll show you where I've been putting the other ones. And if he tries anything funny, twist his right arm under the elbow. It looks broken."

The balding man did as Panther said, but lifted the barbarian by the right wrist. The raider yelped and promptly passed out, which made dealing with him a little easier. The balding man hoisted him onto one shoulder and followed Panther back toward the center of town.

"Who are you?" Panther asked. "And what are you doing out here in the middle of nowhere?"

"My name's Rolan. My men and I are caravan guards for the Guild. Just plain bad luck we were here when the raiders came. If they'd waited another two hours, we'd have been gone already. We already had the horses hitched to the wagons and ready to move out. They took off without us the first sign the raiders meant business. That is, the horses did. Wagons, drivers and merchants were pretty much incidental when that happened."

"But you stayed? Why?"

"What do you mean?" Rolan said. "You saw what the raiders were doing."

"Of course," Panther said. "Sorry. I wasn't thinking." He waited a moment, then said, "Listen, it's going to be a while before we can get the survivors sorted out from the dead, and fate can decide the borderline cases. These people need all the extra hands they can get right now. Can you and your people stay and help out?"

"That was the plan."

"Good. Then while we're settling things down and figuring out what to do next, do what you can to keep your men in line and help these farmers keep their heads. Now that their rage is spent, the last thing they need to do is start taking their grief out on the wounded."

"But what you said before about passing judgment..." Rolan said. "It sounded like you were implying that it'd be fine for the people who live here to kill any wounded Arczeckhi they find. Because of... all this."

"Not so soon after everything's happened it wouldn't," Panther said. "I'm going to put it to them all when the time's right. Once the fires are out and everybody's accounted for. Right now, let's just try to restore some order and take care of these people."

"Sure," Rolan said, a little uncertain. "Makes sense."

"Oh, one last thing. I didn't introduce myself. My name's—"

"I know who you are," Rolan said. "Your name's Panther, and you're the undefeated free-fighting division champion in the Nexus arena. But that isn't *all* anymore, is it?"

Panther's face went blank. "No, it isn't. But listen—"

"Don't worry," Rolan said, making an awkwardly dismissive wave beneath the burden across his shoulders. "I'll do what I can to help people keep their heads about *that* too. Until the time's right to put it to everyone as well."

"Good," Panther said. "Now, bring him right over here..."

It took the rest of the afternoon for things to calm down in the village and for the farmers to take stock of their situation. Most of their homes and the entirety of their communal storehouse had been destroyed, and more than half of the villagers were gone. Some had fled the attackers and lost themselves in the surrounding countryside, but most of those "gone" were dead. The village wasn't large or densely populated by the standards with which Panther was familiar, but the death toll was a staggering, grievous blow to the community. As the survivors counted the dead and brought them to the center of town, their faces were ashen, and their hearts were heavy. Panther tried to set aside his own feelings for the victims of this tragedy so he could concentrate on what needed to be done, but he couldn't do it. Every few minutes, his spirits sagged, and his will to remain involved diminished. He'd saved the village and shown the farmers they could fight to protect themselves. Maybe that was all that was required of him. There were bigger and harder battles to fight out there in the Scavenger Lands... Maybe he was needed more elsewhere.

Every time Panther found these thoughts creeping in, he thought of the day he'd won his freedom but turned his back on life outside the pit. He'd made the wrong decision then, and he knew now that he couldn't repeat it by turning his back on these people. So, he redoubled his efforts each time, taking strength from the sun on his back and finding small moments of joy in the eyes of wounded survivors reunited after assuming each other dead.

As he worked, Panther found people shying away from him or falling silent whenever he drew near. By paying attention when individuals weren't aware of it, though, he managed to glean his general whereabouts relative to the only landmarks he knew of in the region. In his long, semi-lucid pilgrimage, he'd somehow made it all the way into the Hundred Kingdoms—a chaotic patchwork of shifting alliances, tidally fluctuating borders and regrettably frequent warfare. Most of the Hundred Kingdoms were insular and provincial to the point of xenophobia in terms of custom and social convention, but if nothing else, many of them shared tense economic understandings that kept the region fairly developed and in decent health. Yet that health and development tended to attract barbarian raiders from the edges of Creation, and none of the tense economic alignments between kingdoms amounted to pacts of mutual defense when raiders were at the gates. And like most regions in the Scavenger Lands, few of the Hundred Kingdoms had any allegiance to the Realm. Many kingdoms paid regular tribute to the titular ruling dynasty of Creation, but only out of inertial habit or fear. After all, the idea of armed forces from the Blessed Isle sailing up the Yellow River past Lookshy, Nexus and Great Forks to punish any of the Hundred Kingdoms was an improbable fantasy at best. There was still a garrison of imperial troops at the city of Greyfalls just to the northeast up the Rock River, though, and it was commanded by Dragon-Blooded officers. That garrison was largely cut off from the Blessed Isle, but the fact that a small number of its Dragon-Blooded officers had remained on duty there after so many others had withdrawn to the Isle in recent years was worrisome enough to keep some of the Hundred Kingdoms in line. Some of this information Panther knew from idle gossip circles he'd been part of as a hanger-on of Kerrek Deset's. The details he was able to piece together from context as farmers talked about what was happening.

As for this particular village, Panther learned that it was called Saikai and that it was but one of the hamlets in a sovereign nation that called itself Nishion. The kingdom was only a handful of days' ride from Greyfalls in one direction— at least from Saikai—but the royal family back in Nishion City staunchly refused to seek any sort of alliance with the Dragon-Blooded soldiers and magistrates there. As a result, Nishion's border cities had resigned themselves to the fact that Greyfalls' military wouldn't come to their aid should trouble arise.

Panther wasn't able to find out much about the recent barbarian-related tribulations that Nishion had been going through, even when he asked outright and found someone willing to answer. The Hundred Kingdoms had always suffered the predations of various tribes of Wyld-touched barbarians, but that was no different anywhere in the Scavenger Lands. The people of Saikai had thought themselves safe because their hamlet was relatively small and wasn't even one of the top-producing villages in Nishion, yet the Arczeckhi had come nonetheless. The walled fastness of Nishion City hadn't been attacked yet as far as anyone knew, but the capital of the kingdom seemed incomprehensibly far away now that the raiders had come to Saikai. And if their own leaders seemed distant and unwilling to come to their aid, how much farther and more disinterested must the Dragon-Blooded defenders of civilization seem to these people? It just wasn't right, and from what he was overhearing, Panther suspected that he wasn't the only one who thought so.

Eventually, afternoon wore on into evening, and the skies began to dim. All the wounded who'd survived the barbarians' onslaught had been found and gathered in the largest intact houses, and everyone who'd died had been collected and cremated as local tradition demanded. The Arczeckhi had been brought out as Panther had asked as well. Their dead were laid out in unruly heaps, and their wounded sat or lay in a group orbited by six men dressed in buff jackets and wielding swords. They were Rolan's men, and they all eyed the wounded Arczeckhi with eager malice. They waved their weapons in the barbarians' faces and told them to be ready to join the corpses of their friends, but their efforts did little to intimidate the captives. Those wounded Arczeckhi who were lucid enough to need guarding in the first place barely even acknowledged the presence of their wounded comrades, much less the bodies of the fallen.

Panther found it gratifying when the work was done that the barbarian corpses outnumbered those of the villagers dead and wounded, but as the villagers began to drift toward the center of their village and regroup, there was little good news to be had. Though their lives had been spared, many of their homes had not. Nor, it turned out, had many of their crops. Their meager storehouses had all been burned, and what little of the crops in the fields hadn't been burned or trampled wasn't nearly enough to support the village. If the villagers pulled everything that was even close to ready out of the ground that very night, they would have enough to last them only a couple of weeks. (And that wasn't taking into account the extra that the wounded would need to regain their strength and fight off infection.)

Worse, all of their livestock had been slaughtered or set free, or the animals had simply broken free in panic. As the tired, dirty and bloody villagers of Saikai congregated, they pieced together their state of affairs and were forced to acknowledge that their future looked grim. Panther had to agree.

A concern arose over their more immediate future, however, and after a long, heated discussion between several of the oldest surviving men, one of them approached Panther and brought it up to him. The man tasked to do so was the redhead named Kellen. He broke off from the knot of locals with a frown on his face, and he approached Panther at a jerky, hesitant pace. When Panther saw the young man coming, he met him halfway.

"Hello," he said, making the villager flinch. He realized he was scowling and had been all day, so he tried to soften his expression and look less intimidating. If nothing else, at least the blazing disk on his forehead and the glow that had surrounded his body had dimmed and gone out shortly after the battle had ended. "It's Kellen, right?"

"And he knows my name," the redhead breathed in a quavering voice. "That's fantastic."

"All right, just try to take a deep breath," Panther said. "I came here to help you, remember? You've got nothing to fear from me." Kellen tried to relax, but he seemed to find it difficult not to look at the golden sunburst tattooed across Panther's chest. And when he did look up, his gaze went right to the center of Panther's forehead. "So, what's on your mind?"

"Oh, nothing," Kellen said inanely. Then, "Well, no. It's just..." He looked over his shoulder at the group of men he'd been talking to a moment ago. They watched and spoke with their heads together, but when Panther looked over at them, they dispersed to go join other villagers in separate directions. "It's just that we're starting to get a little worried about these barbarians. I mean even the dead ones there. I mean, the sun's going down, and even though they're like wild animals, they might have enough soul in them to come back for us as hungry ghosts. Then there's what to do with the ones we didn't kill. We sure don't have enough to feed them even if we didn't want to just drown them or cut their throats or stone them to death for what they've done to us. We just wanted to know, I mean, if you're ready to tell us… that is…"

"Calm down," Panther said. "I was just about to get to that now that everybody's here. Are you sure these are all the dead Arkzecks?"

"Ar-*check*-i," Kellen corrected absently, looking over his shoulder at the barbarians' ugly corpses. "And yes. Unless more of those the mercenaries are guarding pass on."

"Good. Then go back and tell everyone I'm going to deal with the corpses myself, then we'll all deal with the survivors. After that, we've got to decide what to do with you all."

"What does that mean?" Kellen asked with a mixture of disgust and horror. "How are you going to deal with them?"

"Relax," Panther sighed. "I'm not going to eat them or anything. I'm just going to make sure their souls go where they're supposed to."

"And how's *that*?"

"Watch if you want to know," Panther said, brushing past Kellen now to approach the heaps of Arczeckhi bodies. "But first, tell your people to start thinking about what they want to do about the survivors."

Kellen murmured some vague reply, but he followed Panther from a few yards back. Other villagers came up to him to watch what Panther was doing, but none ventured any closer than Kellen did. Panther could hear them whispering, but he ignored them. As a priest of the Unconquered Sun, he had a duty to perform over these dead that went beyond what the villagers had done for their own. Since the end of the cataclysmic battles that had given birth to the First Age, many dead souls found themselves shackled to the living world as hungry ghosts or trapped in the bleak, stillborn Underworld, rather than moving on to the cycle of reincarnation as was natural. Seeing this, the Unconquered Sun had given to his priests the ability to dissolve the bonds that often trapped a departing soul. Panther respected the funereal rites that the villagers of Saikai had practiced over their own fallen, but he knew that the barbarians had no one to pay their memories the proper respect. So, speaking words that rose to the surface of his mind from the depths of his last

Exalted incarnation, he knelt in the muck and prayed over the Arczeckhi raiders' bodies. Every few words he said, he laid a hand on another corpse's skin and willed the cleansing power of the Unconquered Sun to come forth.

Crowding around the scene now, the villagers gasped and retreated like a flock of raitons as the fallen barbarians' bodies began to glow and disintegrate one by one. Golden fire seemed to consume the corpses from within, and as each body disappeared, a shimmering mote of blue-white energy arose from it. These motes spun in place for a moment, then shot into the darkening sky and disappeared as the barbarians' souls reentered the cycle. All that was left was a handful of fine black ash and whatever accoutrements the raiders had been wearing. The villagers gaped at this display, barely finding the breath to whisper among themselves. When the work was done, Panther stood and turned to address everyone.

"May we find our way so easily when our times come," he said solemnly. "May the Unconquered Sun light the path so brightly for us all." These lines were the last from the prayer he'd been reciting all this time. He hadn't realized he'd spoken them aloud, or in Riverspeak, until he saw the awed and confused looks on the Saikai villagers' faces. The words had come unbidden to his lips across the vastness of time, and that flustered him.

"What did you do to them?" Kellen asked, surrounded now by his friends and neighbors.

"I sent their souls forward," Panther said. "They won't trouble you again in this life. Hopefully, they'll have better luck in the next one."

"Can you do that to these ones, then?" Kellen asked, pointing toward the circle of wounded Arczeckhi, none of whom seemed to be paying the slightest attention to the proceedings.

"That's better than they deserve," Rolan said from over there. He'd rejoined his men now that the bulk of the emergency work seemed to be done.

"I won't," Panther said, "because what I just did doesn't work on the living. Their fate is up to you."

"Us?" Kellen said as a wave of murmurs went around the

crowd. Several people, Kellen included, looked at the wounded barbarians with ugly hatred, but most averted their eyes fearfully or physically shied away. "You said you were going to deal with them."

"I said I would deal with the dead," Panther answered, "and that *we* would deal with the survivors. I have an idea about what needs to be done, but this is your home. You're the ones they've wronged. It's you whose justice they have to answer to."

"Then kill them," Kellen said, not meeting Panther's eyes. "I think we're all okay with that. Right?" A few of the men in the gathering proclaimed their agreement, but most of the noise the crowd made was indistinguishably noncommittal.

"That's what you want?" Panther asked. "You want me to kill them?"

Kellen looked around for encouragement, but none came. "Yes. Yes, kill them."

"No."

Kellen blinked, and nothing came out of his open mouth for a second. Then he said, "Um… please?"

"I'm not going to do it," Panther said, crossing his arms. Kellen looked over at Rolan and the mercenaries, but Panther cut him off before he could speak. "They're not either. That isn't why we're here." He looked significantly at Rolan as he said that, and the balding mercenary shrugged in resignation.

"But they killed our families," Kellen sputtered, leaving the safety of the crowd to walk toward Panther. "Our friends. They've left us with scars that will never heal." His voice rose with every accusation. "They burned our homes. Destroyed our crops! Killed our livestock! They've ruined our village!" Kellen was shouting now, and his eyes had started to water and turn red. He stood within arm's reach of Panther and gestured savagely, forgetting the fear that had ruled him thus far. "They killed my father. They, they *violated* my Laless! They deserve to die!"

"Fine," Panther said, stepping forward and grabbing Kellen by the wrist. "Then let's go."

"Hey!"

Panther pulled Kellen away from the crowd over toward

the Arczeckhi captives. Confused, angry and with a hint of returning fear, Kellen dug in his heels and tried to shake loose, but he couldn't get away. Panther dragged him over in front of Rolan and held out his hand for a blade. Looking just as surprised as Kellen, the mercenary supplied a short khatar. Panther reversed the blade and thrust its hilt into Kellen's hand. Then he held Kellen by the back of the neck and pushed him toward the barbarians. The Arczeckhi who could still move looked up with interest at last. Fear painted many of their faces.

"All right," Panther said. "Do it. Find the one that murdered your father. Find the one that burned your home and ruined your crops. Find the one that wronged you the most, and kill him if you say that's what they all deserve."

Kellen turned back, the sword shaking in his hand. "I don't... How can I tell...?"

"Which one most deserves to die?" Panther asked, glaring down at him now. "Which one do you most deserve vengeance against? Do you even know?"

Kellen looked at the Arczeckhi one more time and then looked back with shame and frustration screwing up his face. "No, I don't know! But who cares? I don't! They all deserve it!"

"So do it," Panther said.

Kellen just stood there, a tear running down his dirty cheek.

"Do it!" Panther said, shoving Kellen forward again. The redhead stumbled over his feet and landed next to a barbarian with a bloody gash on the side of his head that had peeled back most of his ear. Kellen dropped his weapon, but the Arczeckh flinched away rather than reaching for it. Kellen snatched it up and scrambled back to where Panther was standing.

"I can't, all right!" Kellen howled, nearly throwing his weapon at Panther in his haste to be rid of it. "Not while... not while they're..."

"Weak? Wounded?" Panther asked. Kellen shook his head, and tears started running freely. Panther turned back to the assembled villagers. "Can any of you? Can you bring yourselves to strike down defenseless men who are completely at your mercy?" Nobody stepped forward or so much as made a noise. "Good. I'd hoped not. You're decent people. You're civilized.

You're not like these mongrels." A couple of Rolan's mercenaries glowered until they realized Panther was talking about the barbarians. "You're better."

"So what *do* we do with them?" someone in the crowd said.

"We turn them loose," Panther said. "We send them crawling home."

"Free them?" Rolan piped up. "Are you sure about that?"

"Are you kidding?" Kellen snapped. "They'll just come back and kill us later."

"I'm serious," Panther said. "We're going to let them go home, where they'll either die of their wounds or live to make better decisions next time."

He turned to the barbarians then and made eye contact with the only one he recognized. It was the one with the broken arm and the burned skin, whom he'd saved from Rolan's men earlier that day. "And you understand me when I say that, don't you?" he asked. "Both my words and my meaning?"

"Do," the Arczeckh growled, looking at him with blank red eyes. "Both."

"But…" Kellen began.

"What?" Panther asked over his shoulder.

"You're just going to let them go?"

"No, you are. All of you. You're going to do what each and every one of you would want them to do to you if your positions were reversed. You know you can't hold them here indefinitely or even support them while you've got them now. So, you're going to show them mercy instead."

No one spoke for a long time until Kellen finally said, "But what if they come back?"

"Then you'll fight again, and maybe you'll kill them next time." He looked back at the one Arczeckh and said, "You understand that? If you come back here, it'll be the last thing you do."

"Last thing," the barbarian answered. "Won't come back."

"We'll see," Panther said. Then he looked over at Rolan and said, "Let them up. Let them go."

Rolan looked skeptical, but he shrugged and relayed the order to his men. When they only grumbled and stood still, he said, "You heard the man. Anyone who doesn't agree with him can square off with him and work it out one on one." They kept grumbling, but they complied after that. They started lifting the barbarians who could walk onto their feet and gesturing with their swords for the raiders to go back the way they'd come. Cringing like whipped dogs, the Arczeckhi started to move along.

"Hold it," Panther said before the burned one he'd saved got moving. "I want *all* of you gone. Even these here."

The barbarian looked down at some of his more severely wounded cohorts who couldn't stand on their own. He shook his head and shrugged as best he could. "No good. Worthless dreams. Not even last the morning."

"You heard me," Panther growled. "Take them."

The squat, hairy killer scratched his head, shrugged like Rolan had done and grunted something to his least wounded comrades. None of them liked hearing what he had to say, but they did as Panther wanted. They grabbed their compatriots by the arms or legs and began to drag them away. The burned one looked back a couple of times on his way out of the village, but Panther couldn't fathom what he might be thinking. Nor did he especially care. Eventually, the Arczeckhi disappeared into the darkness of falling night.

"That wasn't a terribly nice thing you just did," Rolan murmured to Panther, glancing at Kellen as the redhead went back to stand with his fellow villagers.

"I've done worse," Panther said. "And he could have. Eventually, he'll be glad for what I did."

"How glad will he be when those barbarians come back here looking for revenge?"

"They won't be back. Without treatment, the worst of their wounded won't survive the night, and from the looks on the toughest ones' faces, nobody's getting any treatment. Besides that, the ones in the best health aren't strong enough to take the village right now. If they meet up with a larger band and get absorbed into it and *that* band comes here, we've got bigger problems anyway."

"Maybe," Rolan admitted. "But I think I ought to send a

handful of my men to track them. Make sure they're behaving themselves."

"If you want," Panther said. "But not just yet. There's still something these people have to decide, and it could be important to know before you divide your forces."

"And what's that?"

"What to do now."

Rolan nodded, and Panther posed the issue to the villagers. No one said anything for a few moments, and again it was Kellen who broke the tense silence.

"Why don't you just tell us what to do and save us the trouble of guessing," he muttered.

"I won't tell you what to do here," Panther said. "It's completely up to you. There's no right or wrong in this like there was before. As far as your options go, though, it looks to me like you can either stay and scrounge or you can leave and take your chances making it to somewhere safer."

"We can't stay," one of the women in the crowd said. "We don't have enough food to take care of us until the next harvest. If there even is a next harvest. We don't have hardly anything left."

"We can't leave," a man on the far side of the crowd answered her. "We've got too many wounded to take care of. We can't cart them all over Creation."

"We don't all have to go," someone said from the comfortable obscurity of anonymity. "We could leave all our remaining supplies with the least wounded and—"

"No!" Kellen snapped, looking around for who was speaking.

"Nobody's leaving the wounded here and running for his own life," Panther said.

"This is useless anyway," someone else said. "Where would we go?"

A number of possible answers were raised to that question, in the form of several nearby villages, but none of them were suitable. Most of the names that came up were either too poor to support refugees or too unfriendly to accept them. Others were the names of towns that had already been sacked at least once in the last season by barbarians. Some had even been razed to the ground, though not everyone in the crowd had heard about it. Finally, Rolan suggested a possibility that silenced the crowd and even made Panther frown a little.

"What about Greyfalls? It's only a few days by horseback, and it shouldn't take us more than a week if we can salvage some of the carts or wagons to haul the wounded."

"Or we could just send a couple of riders," one of Rolan's men added. "Get them to send some help or float a barge downriver with some supplies to help out in the short term."

"I don't know," Panther said, swallowing uneasiness seasoned with uncomfortable fear. "There's no guarantee the Terrestrials there would actually send help."

"The what?" Kellen asked.

"The Dragon-Bloods. Anyway, there's no guarantee they'd even listen to a couple of riders who show up unannounced."

"So, we'll all go," Rolan said. "Just show up and dare them to turn us away, wounded and all."

That got the crowd murmuring and casting furtive glances at Panther, and Panther had a firm suspicion of what they were talking about. He clenched his jaw in agitation and squirmed a bit, then finally said, "I don't know."

"Why not?" one of Rolan's men, one of the ones who'd tried to burn the wounded barbarian alive, asked with a hard, knowing glare.

"I doubt I'd be very welcome there," Panther said.

"But you're a celebrity, right?" the mercenary said, sneering. "Surely, they'd just love—"

"Shut it, Maruf," Rolan said.

"—just love to have a celebrity show up with his entourage," the mercenary continued. "I bet they'd welcome you with a full honor guard, wouldn't they?"

"What's he talking about?" one of the Saikai villagers asked, although many of the others were murmuring even more intently now.

"Nothing," Kellen replied awkwardly. "Nothing but a possible complication arising from a foreseeable misunderstanding."

"There's no misunderstanding," Maruf said to Panther. "Is there, Anathema?"

"Don't be silly," Kellen said with a mixture of fear and anger under a sloppy veneer of diplomatic charm. "This man's a hero. He saved us. He's no Anathema. He's... he's just God-Blood. That's all. Isn't that right?"

All eyes turned Panther's way, and the horror in many of them was unmistakable. He stood up straight under the scrutiny, squared his shoulders and shook his head.

"No," he answered. "It isn't true. I'm not God-Blooded, but I'm not Anathema either. I'm not infected by the infernal taint of Malfeas or in league with heretical gods. Those are the lies the Immaculate Order spreads to keep you ignorant and dependant on the Blessed Isle. My power comes from the Unconquered Sun, a god more powerful than the Immaculate Dragons or even the Elemental Dragons. An age ago, people like me ruled Creation, and the Dragon-Blooded were our lieutenants. We've been gone a long time because the Unconquered Sun has been disgusted with the mess this world's become, but we're back now. I've been granted a measure of his power and a mandate to make this world a righteous place again with it. The stars and the prophets have long foretold a day when the forces of righteousness would come to vanquish that which is wicked. I've come in from the wilderness to tell you—that time is now at hand."

Everyone in the crowd was still looking at him, but the fear was gone from most of their faces. They had seen the way he'd dealt with the barbarians both during and after the attack and the way he'd helped fight fires and rescue wounded people from damaged, collapsing homes. And never had he made any demands of them except to do what they knew in their hearts was right. Hearing his words now and feeling the power of conviction that filled them, they couldn't help but believe. None of them had the presence of mind to reconcile this man's words with the lies they'd been told their whole lives, but under these circumstances, those lies simply lost their relevance. Even if it someday turned out that Panther was stretching the truth for his own benefit, all that mattered was that he'd helped them and that he was guiding them to make their own decisions. As a result, they chose to trust him rather than fear or hate him. Panther gathered this from their grateful faces and was relieved. He'd known that this subject would have to come up eventually, and he was glad it had gone as well as it had. That only left the actual immediate problem of what the survivors of Saikai were going to do now.

"So, we can't go to Greyfalls," Kellen said, speaking for his family, friends and neighbors. "They haven't seen what we've seen. They'd only act first and ask questions later."

"What does that leave?" Rolan replied.

"Well," Panther said, scratching the back of his head, "What about Nishion City?"

An uproar arose over that, which turned from a conversation to an argument to a debate that lasted long into the night. It heated and cooled as tempers rose and fell, but the best thing it did for the community at that moment was that it took everyone's mind off of just how bleak Saikai's future looked. The villagers appreciated the argument as it rolled on because it kept them all together and wouldn't let anyone focus on how much had been lost. When it was over and everything was decided, everyone would find some place to let exhaustion overtake them at last, and they would be able to put off until tomorrow the harsh realities that the Arczeckhi raid had brought forward.

Chapter Nine

In the forgotten ruins of a place once called Kementeer, Bear Fist sat on a throne of broken marble. The marble had once belonged to the columns of Kementeer's palace, but the palace had long since fallen into ruin, and the columns that had supported its vast domed ceiling had collapsed and been strewn about this courtyard. The gutted, hollow ruins of the palace stood behind Bear Fist now, falling far short of the canopy of the forest that had since encroached on it. Trees and wild growth had usurped this bygone domain more thoroughly than any invading army ever had, such that all that remained today was the ghost of the palace and the occasional cluster of mausoleums that Bear Fist's people found nearer the river.

Now, though, Bear Fist was overseeing the renovation of this place by the hundreds of slaves who'd been captured by his ruthless Arczeckhi warriors in the months since he'd impressed Mokuu into Ma-Ha-Suchi's service. The slaves were mostly humans taken from sacked and ruined villages in the weakest of the Hundred Kingdoms, but among them were weak and sickly Arczeckhi from tribes who'd forgotten Mokuu and worshiped other gods. The barbarians of those tribes had not yet obeyed Bear Fist's command to join his growing army, so his beastmen had had to beat down their chieftains, and he'd had to scourge their lowly tribal gods. Fortunately, he'd had to do so only a few times before the other scattered tribes began to fall in line.

Bear Fist had converted the warriors of the first few tribes by reminding them of who Mokuu was and what he represented and by telling them that Luna had chosen Mokuu for a glorious fate. Bear Fist was to be the agent of that glory, he told them, and the Arczeckhi were to give him the power he needed. That power would restore the Arczeckhi to the position of fame and awe that the entire tribe had once held, and their god Mokuu would lead them again as he had when he was alive. As he'd told the various tribal chiefs this, Bear Fist had called upon Mokuu to appear and endorse him, and the god had complied. The Arczeckh spirit had reminded his people of what the Arczeckhi had once accomplished when they'd been unified under him, and he'd assured them that he was still real in spite of his death. He'd then demanded obeisance and sacrifices in his name, as well as in Bear Fist's—whom he implied was *his* agent, as well as Luna's. The subtlety had not been lost on Bear Fist, but the barbarians had responded favorably, so he hadn't punished the war god for it. Nor had the war god pushed his luck any further.

The barbarians had done as Mokuu told them, then select shamans among them had gone out to the tribal refuges of their brothers and sisters to spread the word. They'd found great success among the most poor, hungry and downtrodden of the tribes, but they'd had to fight to convince the largest and strongest groups of Arczeckhi holdouts. They'd clashed with their brothers and cousins, but their faith and their unity of purpose had given them unflagging strength. They'd fought down and captured as many of their own people as they could, and where the holdouts' shamans had invoked the power of their vicious gods, Bear Fist himself had stepped in. In just two months, Bear Fist had united or subdued every Arczeckhi family, clan and tribe under his command, and he and Mokuu reaped the benefit of their combined worship daily.

Shortly thereafter, Bear Fist had led the building army here to the lost city once called Kementeer. It was a toppled and vine-shrouded place north of the Yellow River not far from where Mokuu's last totem pole had been hidden. Once it had been the capital of one of the Hundred Kingdoms, but it had been so long lost and overgrown that only Ma-Ha-Suchi had remembered where it lay. Now, Bear Fist used it as a staging ground for his growing Arczeckh army to cut a swath through the weaker, unprotected petty nations of the Hundred Kingdoms. The men who weren't cut down immediately were enslaved and brought back here to tend to the ruins so that the place might be made fit for habitation once again. The recalcitrant enslaved Arczeckhi were put to this same work, but every week they were given the chance to forswear their worship of their old gods and praise the names of Mokuu and Bear Fist. Many still refused, but more were changing their minds every week as the free barbarians won victory after victory under Bear Fist's leadership.

"Things are going well," Mokuu's voice said from behind Bear Fist's improvised chair of broken stones. "Better than I thought."

Bear Fist turned, but the god had chosen to remain immaterial and invisible. Still, Mokuu's voice was fuller and more confident than it had been months ago when Bear Fist had first heard it. His people's worship was making Mokuu more powerful every day, though not yet powerful enough to make him a threat to one of the Chosen of Luna. Bear Fist turned back to look out over the slaves' progress.

"You should have more faith, little god," he said over his shoulder. "You had more confidence in your people once. And you weren't even a god then."

"My people were stronger then," Mokuu said. "And proud. We didn't need one of your kind to bring us together. We had no fear of civilization. We took everything we wanted, and nothing could stop us."

"Except the people who did," Bear Fist said, smirking. "But those people have grown complacent and weak now. The Hundred Kingdoms, for instance, are more scared of one another than they should be of the world beyond their borders. They're going to be the first to feel the thunder of your people's footsteps. And when enough have fallen, Greyfalls will be next."

"Yes," Mokuu hissed in delight. "Where the Exalted are. My people will bathe in wyrm blood, and the whole world will know how real I am."

And that'll be your last glory, little god, Bear Fist thought, smiling to himself. *Because while your people are harrying and weakening Greyfalls like wolves, the full strength of Ma-Ha-Suchi's army will be coming to raze the city in my master's name. And if you don't bend knee to him then, I'll destroy you.*

"But first things first," Bear Fist said aloud. "The Hundred

Kingdoms. Some of them are ripe, and it's finally time for the harvest."

"Which first?"

"Verdangate," Bear Fist said, looking up in thought. "They've actually got a decent military as far as that goes so far east. After that, Nishion, Freeden and Tulpa. That should make a nice buffer in case the Dragon-Bloods at Greyfalls decide to get involved before we're ready."

"And what exactly is supposed to stop them?" Mokuu asked, coming around to stand in front of Bear Fist now. Bear Fist couldn't see the god, but he could hear the voice moving. "Bastard Dragon-Bloods *like* to get involved. They can't leave well enough alone."

"It's taken care of, little god. We stay away from the kingdoms that border the river for now, just in case. We attack fast and hard, and when we do, we let no one escape to spread the word. Your people are especially good at that, aren't they?"

"They are."

"So, don't worry about the Dragon-Bloods at Greyfalls. By the time they realize how strong we are and just how much we're out to accomplish, we'll be on them, and there won't be anything they can do about it."

"It sounds like you've thought of everything so far," Mokuu said, moving away now.

"Not I," Bear Fist answered. "One greater than I. Ma-Ha-Suchi. We only share in his glory."

"Then pray, let him be generous," Mokuu said.

Bear Fist leaned back against the stones and smirked again. *Just including you and your people in this was generous enough*, he thought. *If he didn't need shock troops and a distraction, he would've been content to let your entire race decline unto extinction.*

"Yes," he said. "Generous."

Mokuu said nothing more, and after a moment, Bear Fist had to sniff the air to confirm that the war god had departed. He stood up then and began to look around for signs of where the god had gone. The idea that Mokuu was moving around and acting without his supervision didn't sit well with him, so he figured he'd better go make sure that the god wasn't getting up to any mischief. He knew that Mokuu would never stray far from the staging area, so he suspected the god had gone to loiter around the spirit lodges where his most faithful shamans were carving and dedicating a set of new ironwood totem poles. The god seemed to like observing the shamans' progress, and he even manifested before the devout Arczeckhi worshipers sometimes to praise their faith and exhort them to greater displays of piety. He'd even imposed bans on them in earlier manifestations and commanded them to pass those bans on to their faithful chieftains and soldiers. Now, none of the Arczeckhi slept without a weapon in hand, they spit and cursed whenever anyone said anything about the Dragon-Blooded, and they smeared any white object with a bloody thumbprint. These small signs, as well as the sacrifices of forest animals and elderly or wounded slaves, venerated Mokuu and made him stronger. Bear Fist had found that he sometimes had to forcibly remind Mokuu and the shamans to include himself and Ma-Ha-Suchi in these praises lest Mokuu forget his station in this enterprise. The Arczeckh god had complied thus far, but Bear Fist knew that he had to be wary of how far and how fast he let worship of the god spread.

He was halfway to the lodges when a commotion arose at the perimeter his beastmen lieutenants had established. He heard one of them, Last Runner, bleat out a wordless signal from the opposite side of the palace courtyard, then Scar Horn and Bark Back echoed it. The slaves all around stopped what they were doing, and the barbarian warriors exchanged glances before moving in that direction. They chuffed and snarled hungrily, clearly ready for a fight, and Bear Fist could see that the subtlety of the sentries' call had been lost on them. He bent low and flowed into a faster shape, then darted between the milling warriors as a sleek jungle cat to go see what Last Runner and the other beastmen had noticed. He made it to the edge of the tumbled-down palace's courtyard and out into the forest before any of the Arczeckhi did, and he found Scar Horn and Bark Back standing with spears at the ready over someone who lay face down. Neither warrior saw him as he crept up on them, and Bark Back even whistled out the all-clear signal before he realized that Bear Fist had arrived. When Bear Fist stood back up into his human seeming not three yards from them, Bark Back jumped.

"Bear Fist," he said, shifting his weight in embarrassment. "If you were a snake, you'd have bit me."

"I'll remember that next time," Bear Fist said. "What's going on? Who is this?"

"Can't tell," Scar Horn said. "Arczeckh definitely, but past that, who knows? They all look alike."

"Pretty beaten up, though," Bark Back said, crouching over the prone figure now as Bear Fist approached. "He collapsed when Last Runner called out."

"Maybe he's one of ours," Bear Fist said. He waved his men out of the way and rolled the fallen barbarian over. The Arczeckh was bloody, sweaty and dirty, but Bear Fist could still make out the remnants of reddish war-paint on the barbarian's face, stomach and legs. It was the same ancient pattern and color that Mokuu's shamans had shown their chiefs, which meant that this warrior was one of the locals. That didn't bode well, considering the state the barbarian was in. His right arm was swollen and twisted improperly at the elbow, and much of his back and arms had been grievously burned. His feet were blistered and raw from hard, unflagging travel, and his eyes were deeply sunken in from dehydration. He carried no weapon, and what was left of his clothing hung on him in tatters. Somebody had whipped him good, and it looked like he'd only barely managed to escape with his life.

"Still alive?" Bark Back asked, standing beside Scar Horn a few feet away.

Bear Fist leaned over the wounded warrior's mouth and nose for a second then said, "Barely."

Scar Horn knocked heads with Bark Back and said, "Told you."

"Damnation," Bark Back grumbled, scuffing the ground with one hoof and rubbing his forehead between his horns.

Scar Horn shrugged. "Should've taken my word for it, then."

"Both of you shut it," Bear Fist said, kneeling beside the barbarian. "Go clear the area, and keep the rest of the Arczeckhi out of here. They probably think we're being invaded." The three of them could hear a large group of barbarians coming from the courtyard into the forest in response to Last Runner's signal, doubtless looking for trouble.

"Sure," Scar Horn said, nudging Bark Back in the direction whence Bear Fist had come. The two beastmen went on their way, leaving Bear Fist with the fallen Arczeckh.

"Are you unconscious or just exhausted?" Bear Fist asked when he and the barbarian were alone. "Can you talk?"

The barbarian's eyes opened a crack and focused on Bear Fist, but the man made no effort to sit up.

"Not bad," Bear Fist said. "What's your name? What happened to you?"

"No name," the barbarian said in a thready whisper. "Not real enough anymore."

Bear Fist ground his teeth but tried not to let his frustration show. One thing that was both very convenient and terribly irritating about these barbarians was how quickly they were willing to give up once they'd been beaten. Either they rolled over in service to the ones who'd done it, or they just lay down and got ready to die.

"You're plenty real enough. Now, concentrate. Who are you?"

"Sar... Sarkur," the barbarian finally managed, coughing up a mouthful of blood.

"What happened?"

"We were beaten," Sarkur wheezed. "By ones more real than us. All of us."

Bear Fist frowned. "Who were you supposed to be fighting? Where?"

"A human kingdom," the barbarian said. "A village. Farms. Animals. Muddy streets."

"Where was it?" Bear Fist snapped.

"In a valley near a forest. It was too small to have one so real."

"What does that mean? What happened?"

"We attacked with the sunrise like we were supposed to," the barbarian said. "We burned and killed and chased everyone.

Some died at a temple doorway, but others passed through it. A few tried to get in."

"A temple? An Immaculate temple?" Sarkur nodded. "So what happened? Was there a Dragon-Blooded priest inside?"

The barbarian tried to spit but only succeeded in slopping a little blood down his chin. Then he shook his head. "No."

"So, what happened? Who did this to you? The villagers?"

"Not them. One more real than them and us. He shined. He wore the sun, all in gold."

"The sun." Bear Fist sat up, frowning. He certainly didn't like the sound of that. Ma-Ha-Suchi had told him about warriors of unimaginable power who'd once strode Creation like gods and venerated the sun just as he venerated Luna. But according to Ma-Ha-Suchi, those beings had been absent from the world for centuries. They hadn't been seen in numbers or in power since the end of the First Age, when Ma-Ha-Suchi was young. And those who were born into this age were hunted down and destroyed like rabid dogs by the Dragon-Blooded.

"Are you sure about that?" he asked the wounded man, lifting him off the ground to look in his eyes. "Absolutely sure?"

"The villagers fought too. But he led them. He beat us back, then spared our lives and turned us away. He made us leave and carry our wounded with us. We tried to come here, but only I was real enough to make it this far."

"And where were you fighting?" Bear Fist demanded. "Where did this happen? And how long ago?"

"Days and nights," the Arczeckh said, lolling in Bear Fist's hands. "In a valley by the edge of a forest. A village too small for one so real."

"Damn it," Bear Fist hissed, dropping the barbarian. Sarkur was going to be no more help until he got well again, if he even survived. Bear Fist whistled out for Scar Horn and Bark Back, who he could hear not far away talking to the Arczeckhi who had come to investigate. He needed a litter, and he needed to get this barbarian to a spirit lodge so the shamans could nurse him back to health. He didn't especially care if one warrior more or less died, but he needed to know what this man had seen and where he'd seen it. If Sarkur wasn't just feverish and remembering a dream or hallucination about how his raiders had been driven off, things might have just gotten damnably more complicated.

He left Sarkur where he lay and rushed to give orders to his men.

Sarkur, the most real of his band, lay on his back on the forest floor. In the distance, he could hear the moon's chosen, Bear Fist, speaking to his servants, and he could hear soldiers of his own kind responding in excitement. They spoke his name in questions, wondering if he was still real or if they should forget about him. They'd already forgotten the rest of Sarkur's band, just as he had, and they were preparing themselves to do the same for him. Sarkur wondered as well, though he could hear Bear Fist's anger when the others questioned him. Bear Fist believed that Sarkur was still real, and that made Sarkur proud. It honored him.

Yet honor and pride were not assurance, for which the dimming recesses of Sarkur's mind sought. He could still see, but that fleeting sensation could mislead a weak mind. He could still feel the pain that ones more real had inflicted on him. That gave him hope because, if one more real could touch him and affect him, that one imparted a mote of his own reality. The sounds of birds in the trees gave Sarkur hope as well. The way his brother-equal had explained it once in a dream, animals were the least real creatures of all, and they didn't exist except for the needs of ones more real. To hear the birds sing, even when he couldn't see them, assured him he was at least more real than them. That and the pain and his own lingering sense of "I am" were reality enough for him. He only wondered how long it would last.

"Sarkur," a voice whispered as the Arczeckh lay dying. "Sarkur, are you still real?"

The warrior recognized the voice, and it gave him strength. "I am, Mokuu. Real enough to hear the birds and to be seen by a god."

"And you will be more yet," Mokuu whispered. "As real as I, in time, if you will but worship me. If you devote your reality to my own and obey my bans. Have you done so?"

"I have, Mokuu," Sarkur said. He tried to turn to look his god in the eye, but he could barely move.

"Will you do so for as long as your reality endures?"

"I will, Mokuu."

"Then share in my reality."

With those words, Mokuu's body wove itself into existence, crouching by Sarkur's head. He was much larger than the shamans had described him, standing taller now than Bear Fist, though still proportioned like an Arczeckh. He sniffed the air and tasted it on his tongue, then lay broad, three-fingered hands over Sarkur's chest. Sarkur closed his eyes and felt a portion of Mokuu's reality flow into him. His arm wrenched itself back into its proper alignment, and the deepest of the wounds he'd been given pressed themselves back together with a feeling like they were drinking cool water. He gasped and tried to sit up, but Mokuu held him down.

"Tell no one but the shamans of what I've done," the god said when he was finished. "And when you do, tell them that they may all share in my reality thus if they will but worship me."

"What about Bear Fist?" Sarkur asked. He was still weak and in pain, but the songs of the birds were clearer now, and he knew that he would wake again if he slept.

"You are equals in my esteem, but he is still more real," Mokuu said, his form unraveling once more until only his red eyes lingered in the air. "That will soon change, though, and when it does, you will take his place. Tell the shamans this also, but no one else."

"I will, Mokuu," Sarkur said, relaxing at last. "Thank you."

"Your gratitude isn't real," Mokuu said, moving away. "Only your worship. And it must grow. Only thus will our people become as we once were."

"I understand," Sarkur said, finding a sharp stone to hold as a weapon before slipping away into dreams.

"Understand what?" he vaguely heard someone say as he

closed his eyes. "Who's he talking to?" Someone else answered, then the first voice spoke again, approaching from some distance. "Must be delirious. Get him on that litter, and move him quickly. He doesn't look quite as bad as I thought, but he still needs attention. We need him alive. We need to know what he saw."

Chapter Ten

It took the rest of the night and a little bit of the next morning, but eventually, the people of Saikai chose not to accept Panther's suggestion. Nishion City was just too far, they decided, and they preferred a more immediate assurance of security. No one could agree on what exactly might constitute such a thing, though, so they eventually compromised on traveling to the next nearest village to see how their neighbors had fared in light of recent events. None of the villagers were especially thrilled with this idea—and both Panther and Rolan called it a waste of time—but no one could come up with a better one that pleased everyone.

They spent the day after the attack, once that tentative agreement had been reached, salvaging what they could of gear, weapons and supplies and burning the remaining implements of war the barbarians had abandoned. They managed to find and repair two wagons, and even rounded up a couple of the oxen that had run off during the raid, and they devoted those vehicles to transporting those who were too wounded to walk or ride. Those less wounded took turns riding what mules and oxen could be rounded up for the task, and everyone else had no choice but to walk. It was a grim procession the villagers made as they left their ruined home behind them, but their spirits were higher than expected under the circumstances. Panther was leading them, and his strength gave them strength.

What good spirits sustained them at the beginning of their journey quickly faded, however, as they reached the village of their nearest neighbors. Every structure that made it up lay in blackened, tumbled-down ruins that had long since stopped smoking. Fly-shrouded bodies lay in the streets and in the wreckage, some burned, others hacked apart. The village's storehouses appeared to have been picked clean before being burned down, and all the fields had either been trampled to ruin or burned to their roots. Most of the damage appeared to be at least a week old. The only fresh sign that anything had happened here was a set of wagon and yeddim tracks that arrowed straight through the village's center—an indication that Rolan's Guild employers had fled this way in a hurry.

The Saikai villagers were horrified by what they found, but not so much that they refused to do right by their victimized neighbors. At Kellen's urging, the least wounded among them spent the day cremating the dead and performing the necessary funereal rites over them. The young redhead then asked Panther to recite for them the same prayer he'd said when he'd sent the Arczeckhi's souls back to the cycle of reincarnation. This request came as something of a guilty afterthought, and only after much cloistered arguing with the surviving Saikai elders, but Panther complied.

That night, they discussed their options again, and Rolan took a more active hand over the proceedings. He stood before the villagers and explained to them that they didn't have enough supplies to keep traipsing from village to village hoping that things would get better for them. If they couldn't go home again, he'd explained, they'd have to seek refuge at a town large enough to accommodate them. They'd find doctors for their wounded, safety of numbers against future barbarian raids and, potentially, jobs to sustain them if they couldn't get back home soon enough.

Rolan and Panther had been putting forward that very option since the villagers had left Saikai, but only when confronted by the reality of this neighboring village did they choose to accept it. The fact that Rolan had pointed it out to them rather than Panther—whom the villagers didn't quite know what to make of just yet—also helped. That then raised the question of *which* town to approach, an issue that sparked a whole new round of debate. It needed to be one large enough to support all of them, one with enough surgeons and doctors to treat their wounded, one built up enough to offer them some measure of protection and one that would actually be safe once they were inside. Plus, it needed to be within range of how far they could get with their limited supplies. Several possibilities were raised, mostly the names of nearby towns with which the villagers had done business in the past, but ultimately, none of them offered enough of the qualities they were looking for. Nishion wasn't exactly a nation of walled and fortified city-states.

Eventually, Panther settled the issue himself. He stood up and told everyone that they were wasting time and that their indecision wasn't making them any safer or their wounded any healthier. What they needed to do, he told them, was go to the one place in their kingdom that they *knew* would take them in and protect them. That place was Nishion City. Kellen tried to argue against this idea, saying their supplies wouldn't take them that far, but Panther didn't back down. He finally told them flat out that he was taking the wounded to Nishion City and that the decision was final. The others could stay and debate if they wanted, but it wouldn't change what he intended to do. That decision settled the issue for most of the villagers—those who wanted leadership more than an equal say—and those who still disagreed could do nothing but go along grudgingly. Rolan, Kellen and some of the older villagers then set to work plotting out the quickest route that night and working out a harsh ration for their supplies. They set out again the next morning.

Either good luck or the grace of the Unconquered Sun kept them from running into any more bands of Arczeckhi, but their luck wasn't universal across this region of Nishion. As they made their way toward their nation's capital, they eventually ran into another train of refugees who seemed to be in equally sorry shape. These refugees had escaped Arczeckhi raids, though they'd had no one to save them or fight for them. They were weary, bedraggled and deeply in shock. They had come from villages and towns to the southwest of Saikai, and the story they told of their hardships chilled the Saikai villagers' bones. The Arczeckhi had been busier than anyone had realized, it seemed, and not just in Nishion. These survivors told of vicious, coordinated attacks that left villages smoldering in ruins and saw every citizen either murdered or bound into slavery. The barbarians descended on their victims at dawn or in the dead of night, howling like madmen and painted up like demons set free. To hear some of the survivors tell it, some of the barbarians even *had* demons working for them—towering, goat-headed beings that walked and used weapons like men. They'd been merciless, and they'd given no indication of what had provoked them to such callous and widespread violence. The Arczeckhi seemed to have banded together and declared war on the Hundred Kingdoms. Even some of the larger towns to which the villagers had originally fled had been sacked and looted.

Hearing the misery of their countrymen made the Saikai villagers realize just how lucky they'd been, and it stoked their compassion. They joined up with the less fortunate band, pooling their meager supplies and offering a measure of safety in larger numbers. It didn't occurred to them to do so at first, but they also realized that they could offer a measure of hope as well. It happened the second night after they'd joined up, when some of the worse-off refugees asked about Panther and Rolan, who looked significantly out of place among the simple farmers of Saikai. Kellen fielded these questions, explaining that the two of them were outsiders from different parts of the Scavenger Lands, and quite without warning, he found himself talking about the morning Saikai had been raided. He started the story with hardly the import of a fireside chat, but by the time he got into the middle of it, he found that every one of the refugees in the band was hanging on his every word. They stared at him and at Panther alternately, barely believing what Kellen said the man had done. Only when Rolan and some of his men confirmed it did they appear to accept it. Panther neither elaborated on nor corrected anything Kellen said about him, but neither did he deny it. The crowd was buzzing in awe when the tale ended, and that's when the inevitable questions came out.

"How did you do all that?" someone asked, drawing everyone's attention to Panther. "What are you?"

Kellen opened his mouth to explain that Panther was God-Blooded, but a look from Panther stopped him. He then tried to explain the truth as Panther had, but it came out all jumbled and didn't make much sense. Panther stood up then, released some of the divine power inside him through the celestial brand on his forehead and told the refugees exactly what he'd told the Saikai villagers. Everyone gaped at him in awe, and just as before in Saikai, none of them could gainsay him when he claimed to be put on this earth to help them. His power calmed and reassured them like the rays of the sun breaking through dreary storm clouds. As one, they relaxed a little, and even the Saikai villagers found themselves more at ease. They went to sleep that night with a kernel of hope growing inside them, and they set out the next morning unified in their faith that an agent of a higher power would see them to safety and make sure everything was all right.

And the more stragglers and refugees the Saikai caravan took in, the more times Panther's story was repeated. It remained fairly true to its roots whenever Kellen told it around the nightly fires, but as others began to learn it and repeat it, it accreted embellishments and increasingly outlandish additions. The story became such that one might have thought Panther had descended unto Saikai on a golden cloud and destroyed the entire Arczeckhi army with one glowing punch.

When Panther discovered that this was going on, perhaps a week distant from Nishion City, he stopped the refugee caravan in its tracks and tried to set the record straight. He recounted the events of the raid on Saikai as they'd actually happened, but his account of the things the Unconquered Sun had enabled him to do only glorified him further in the refugees' eyes. He then turned the story into a sermon on the Unconquered Sun and how all the most powerful divine blessings came from him and were to be used only to make the world a righteous place. That settled some of the refugees down, Kellen among them, but the others heard only what they wanted to hear and continued to exalt Panther as their savior. Their praise touched something in Panther that harked back not only to his days showing off for bloodthirsty Nexus crowds, but to something older and deeper as well, which not only enjoyed it but *craved* more of the same. The pleasure those memories evoked in him made him feel guilty and uncomfortable, though, and he knew he had to shut them down before they could overwhelm him. That couldn't be what the Unconquered Sun wanted for him.

So, in order to break their burgeoning worship of him without tarnishing their faith in what he represented, Panther began to tell the refugees about who he'd been before the Unconquered Sun had spoken to him. He told them about the sort of person he'd been and about the choices he'd made to get where his life had taken him. He pulled no punches describing the less-than-righteous things he'd done, especially as a hanger-on in Kerrek Deset's circle of Nexus' high society. He showed the refugees that, although he'd been famous and wealthy, he'd come up out of abject poverty and slavery, never learning how to be a good man. He'd wasted every chance he'd been given to lead a righteous life, until he'd felt trapped by his own choices. Yet, though he'd despaired of ever finding a better way to live his life, the Unconquered Sun had spoken to him and wiped away his sins. As such, he explained to them, it was not the man who deserved their praise and adulation, but the power of the Unconquered Sun. It was that power that made him strong and gave him purpose. It was that power that would help them and see them to safety. It was that power that could take a lowly and debauched man and make him an instrument of righteousness. The man was only the vessel for that power.

Panther didn't know how well the sermon had gone over, but it silenced the crowd and turned everyone in it thoughtful. It also ended the embellishments and put a stop to the fawning looks that some of the refugees tried to hide from him. No one spoke to him the rest of the day or night—even Rolan or Kellen, who'd grown the least uncomfortable around him—and no one seemed eager to talk about him either. Only as the weary caravan set out once more the following morning did anyone seem willing to talk much about anything. Everyone was still keeping a respectful distance from Panther, but at least they were talking to each other and trying to put one another at ease about the tragedies they'd suffered in common. Panther walked along in comfortable silence at the head of the band, with only Rolan and his men farther forward, scouting ahead for trouble.

About midway through the day, Rolan dropped back from

scouting and fell into step beside Panther. Panther had just completed a walking circuit of the refugee band, making sure that everyone was still accounted for and no one was having any problems, and he nodded to the mercenary captain. Rolan returned the gesture with an air of uncomfortable solemnity, and the two of them just walked in silence for another few minutes before either spoke. Rolan opened and closed his mouth a few times, searching for words, and Panther let the mercenary find his way without prompting him.

"Let me ask you something," he said at last, tapping the thin strip of beard beneath his lip with a gloved finger. "If you don't mind."

"Go ahead," Panther said.

"Is everything you've told these people true? About the kind of man you used to be? Do you really think you were such a wastrel?"

Panther nodded, looking sideways at the mercenary. "Those were the most strident examples. There's more I could have told, but I didn't think I could take any more… honest self-reflection."

"And the rest is true too?" Rolan went on. "You're a good man now? A righteous man?"

"I'm not a righteous man," Panther said. "My old life hasn't just gone away. I'm still Panther… mostly, I think. Well, that part's pretty complicated. I don't understand it all."

"So, you're *not* a righteous man?"

"I'm a man who's got a lot of things to answer for," Panther said. "In this life I've made and in one that came before. I didn't just turn righteous all of a sudden when the Unconquered Sun spoke to me."

"So, you're doing penance for all the bad things you've done."

"Nothing so self-serving," Panther said, though he wasn't entirely sure of that. "I'm just doing what the Unconquered Sun wants. I'm trying to help people make righteous choices and make them myself. And since I've made so many *unrighteous* choices in my life, I have plenty of experiences to judge against."

"So, you know what's wrong and what makes people make bad decisions? And since you know that, you can help them make the right decisions instead. Is that what you're saying?"

"More or less."

"And that doesn't make you a righteous man?"

"Not really," Panther admitted. "I think a righteous man would always just choose the right thing to do without having to back-check it against a list of mistakes and awful decisions."

Rolan frowned and scratched the back of his neck. "Maybe you're right. Honestly, I was actually hoping that you'd just say yes with confidence and let it go at that."

"If any of them had asked," Panther said, nodding back over his shoulder, "I might have. You didn't sound like you wanted just a pat reassurance, though. You sounded like you wanted an answer with some meat on it." Rolan nodded but kept frowning as if he were still thinking hard about something. "Was there something else?"

"No, there... Well... There is one thing, actually. I don't even want to ask it anymore, but after what you told the refugees about yourself, I have to know."

"Go ahead, then."

"It's just... Do you remember me? When you first talked to me back at Saikai, did I seem familiar?"

Panther took a long sideways look at Rolan as they walked, then said, "No, I'm afraid not. I can't place your name or your face. Did we meet before? When you said you knew who I was, I thought you'd just recognized me as a pit fighter."

"Well, I did, but that wasn't it entirely. We've met, actually. Before all this. In fact, I saved your life once."

Panther nearly tripped. "Pardon? When was this?"

"A couple of years ago," Rolan said, embarrassed color rising in his cheeks over the upturned collar of his jacket. "You'd just become champion of the free-fighting division, and your arranger sent you out on a tour of all the venues you'd fought in to make it there."

"I remember *that*," Panther said. "It was a fame tour."

"It was you, your arranger and all your... *escorts*, to put it politely. You might not even remember this part, but on the way back to Nexus from the last stop in Great Forks, the carriages you were all traveling in were attacked by bandits."

Panther thought hard about it, trying to part the obscuring veils woven by drugs and sex and self-importance.

"They came down out of the trees and up out of dugouts by the side of the road, raining arrows on your carriages and horses. They killed over half the mercenary guards the Guild had rented to you before anyone knew what was happening."

"I remember the carriage stopping for a minute," Panther said, digging the memory up at last. "And I remember hearing shouting. I was... preoccupied at the time. I didn't know what was going on." He'd been preoccupied by opium and the trio of "escorts" the Guild's Nexus harlotry had provided for the trip, to be exact, but he didn't think Rolan wanted to hear that right now.

"What was going on," Rolan said, "was that good men were dying because they'd been paid to keep you and your people from getting hurt. And they did. They fought the bandits off so the carriages could tear off to the next town. All but one, that is. Yours."

"What happened?"

"An arrow dispatched your driver, and the bandits jumped up in his place. They decided to cut their losses and run, and your carriage was their prize."

Realization dawned on Panther. "And you know this..."

"Because I was one of the mercenaries guarding you, and I was the one who got your carriage back to safety. I chased the bandits down, jumped on the carriage myself and fought them off it. And I nearly drove the thing to pieces in the dark, but I got it to the next town with the others."

"I see. You did save my life, then, Rolan. I had no idea."

"I know," Rolan said, looking at his shoes as he walked. "When we got to town, your arranger pulled you out of the carriage and stuffed you in an inn before I'd hardly reined in the animals. And we left in too much of a hurry the next day for anybody to take stock of what had happened. You stayed in your carriage the entire way back to Nexus, though, and I never saw you for more than a few seconds at a time. By the time you were finally settled again at home, I had a new assignment and couldn't stay around."

"I think I know what you—"

"Let me finish," Rolan snapped. "I just want to say that I kept up with your career after that, and the next time I was in Nexus with more than a few days to spare, I made it a point to see you fight. I even paid an entire jade obol to get into a line to shake your hand. I waited for two hours in the blistering Nexus sun with Yellow River haze making everything stink to high heaven, but I thought it would all be worth it once I got to actually see you face to face."

Panther exhaled heavily and frowned. Now he was the one looking down at his feet.

"And when I did, I don't suppose you know what happened, do you?" Panther shook his head. "Well, that's because nothing actually happened. You just nodded, shook my hand and gently ushered me aside so you could get to the next person. I looked you and your arranger both dead in the eyes, and neither one of you showed me the first glimmer of recognition. And that was the last I saw either of you, until Saikai."

"And I bet you've been wanting to tell me off about that ever since, haven't you?"

"Among other things."

"So, what can I do? Say I'm sorry? Because I am. You saved my life, and I didn't even know it. There's no excuse for that."

"Of course, of course," Rolan said, waving the words away like gnats. "But that blade won't cut after all this time."

"So, what can I say? What can I do?"

"Just this," Rolan said. "Just answer this question. This is actually what I came over here to ask you about anyway. Gods, I've been trying to ask you this since we left."

"What is it?"

"Are... Are you still that same man? Are you still who you were then, or are you better now?"

Panther thought about it and tried to form just the right turn of phrase that would ease all the angry frustration Rolan must have been feeling all this time. Something profound and powerful that would make Rolan see him in a new light of respect and reverence. All that came out, however, was the truth.

"I'm afraid not, Rolan. I'm still Panther. Being Exalted hasn't made me any better than who I was. But I do know *how* to be better now, and that's what I want to do. That's all I can say." Rolan gritted his teeth, crossed his arms and sighed heavily, and Panther chanced a glance up at him. "Sounds like you were hoping I'd say something else."

"I was, I think," Rolan said, holding back the edge of a wry smile. "Something effusively apologetic, maybe, so I could feel like I'd scored a moral victory. Or something sanctimonious, perhaps, so I could label you a pedagogue and stop taking what you say seriously. But what you said sounds like something I would have said if our roles were reversed, and that's terribly annoying. Where does a man go from there?"

"That does sound like a quandary all right."

"You shouldn't make light of this," Rolan said, smiling a little in spite of himself. "I'm still indignant. And justified in that."

"Of course."

"I'm serious," Rolan said, sounding less so the more he spoke. "The next time I save your life, I expect to be lavished with gratitude. Preferably out loud and in person. With witnesses as well, if you please."

"Maybe I'll even return the favor," Panther offered.

"Oh, that already goes without saying. But the rest... that shouldn't."

"Then it won't."

"Good," Rolan said, relaxing at last and picking up his pace a little. "Then I'm glad we had this talk. See that it doesn't." And with that, he left Panther behind, returning to scouting with his fellow mercenaries. His step seemed lighter now, and he carried himself straighter and with more casual grace than Panther had seen in the man thus far.

"Don't worry," Panther said quietly as Rolan outpaced him. "I'll see that it doesn't."

Chapter Eleven

Three days passed at Kementeer, and the Arczeckh named Sarkur hadn't said anything about what had happened to him or where. He'd been taken to the spirit lodge that his people's shamans had erected among Kementeer's ruined stones, and though his condition hadn't deteriorated, it hadn't improved either. He'd lain unconscious on a pallet of straw and animal hides with poultices wrapped over his most serious wounds, rousing only to drink the water that was brought to him and choke down thin broth before lapsing back into deep dreams. None of the shamans had taken great pains to revive him or even care for him as he lay still, believing that if Sarkur were truly real he wouldn't need their ministrations anyway. If he wasn't, spending days trying to put him back together would only be a waste of time that could be better spent venerating Mokuu.

Their attitude frustrated and infuriated Bear Fist, and the first few times he'd failed to convince them to *heal* their wounded tribesman, he'd nearly lost his temper and torn the whole lodge down around them. After that, he'd decided it was best not to spend more time around the shamans than absolutely necessary. He'd ordered Soft Claw and Red Leg—those of his beastmen with the most knowledge of how to care for a wounded man— to check in on Sarkur regularly and take care of him. They were responsible for the bandages and poultices, and to them was supposed to fall the responsibility of questioning the Arczeckh when he became lucid again.

Bear Fist was tired of waiting, though, and he came now to the Arczeckh spirit lodge to tell his men what he'd decided to do about that. He strode up to the deer-hide-flap door as Red Leg was coming out, and he pulled his man aside to talk.

"What is it?" the beastman asked, shying a little at the scowl on his leader's face.

"How's the Arczeckh?"

"No fever, no infection. His elbow doesn't look broken—just sprained or dislocated. It looks better today than three days ago."

"Just tell me what I want to know, Red Leg," Bear Fist growled, glowering down at him. "I don't care about any of that."

Red Leg hunched submissively. "He's… he's still out."

"Damn it! Has he said anything?"

"Nothing yet. Their language is a mess, but as far as I can tell, he's only talked about the fire or about fighting."

"But not where or what happened?"

Red Leg shook his head. "That's right."

"This is taking too long. Are you sure you're doing everything you can?"

"We are, Bear Fist, but we're not surgeons. We can stitch people up and keep them alive, but making them better faster isn't—"

"Fine, whatever!" Bear Fist said, slashing a hand through the air. "No excuses."

"Sorry."

"So, he's not coming around any time soon. Well, I'm tired of waiting. This is holding up raids and slowing everything down."

"Slate Knife and the others are still out there, but I could take Scar Horn and Last Runner and—"

"No, I need you here. Your work organizing these apes is more important than one setback."

"So, what's the plan?"

"I'm going to trace back his steps," Bear Fist said. "I'll figure out for myself where his band fell and what happened there."

"You're just going to leave?" Red Leg asked without thinking.

"Is there a problem with that?" Bear Fist snapped, clamping a broad, tattooed hand around the beastman's throat. He lifted, and Red Leg's cloven hooves left the ground. "The plan hasn't changed, the raiders are still softening up the kingdoms nearest us, and cleanup on this place is still going fine. Are you saying everything isn't under control?"

"N-no, Bear Fist," Red Leg choked out.

"Are you saying you and the others can't maintain order until I get back?"

Red Leg tried to speak again but could only squeak. He shook his head instead, trying not to claw desperately at Bear Fist's hand.

"Good," Bear Fist said, throwing the beastman down in the dirt. "Then just keep doing what I already told you to do. If the plans need to change, I'll change them when I get back."

"Yes, Bear Fist," Red Leg wheezed, rubbing his throat. "Should we still look after the Arczeckh while you're gone?"

Bear Fist looked at the door of the spirit lodge in contempt and shook his head. "The hell with him. Let him die or live if he's going to. Go back to what you were doing before, and tell Soft Claw to do the same. And tell him to remind you to remember your place when I make decisions."

"I will," the beastman said, rising only to a crouch. "I apologize."

"Don't apologize," Bear Fist growled, "just get it right from now on." He turned on his heel then and headed for the spot where Sarkur had returned to Kementeer.

Red Leg crouched where Bear Fist had dropped him, getting his breath back, and he soon felt Soft Claw's hands under his armpits, helping him up. He rose, dusted himself off and turned to face his cohort.

"You heard that?" he said.

"I did," Soft Claw replied. "Only took him three days to blow his top and go off on his own. That's sooner than last time."

"A little. So who had it?"

"Scar Horn, I think," Soft Claw said. "I'll ask Last Runner when his watch is over. He's keeping up with that. All I know is I had five days and you had a whole week."

"I guess my deep and abiding faith in our leader never pays off."

"Doesn't look like it. Not when the stakes are so small, anyway."

"Let's hope my luck's better when they're bigger, then."

As he left, Bear Fist melted down into the shape of a jungle cat to better follow the wounded Arczeckh's trail. He tasted the heart's blood of the panther he'd killed to win this shape, and as the transformation overcame him, his vision, hearing and sense of smell all sharpened considerably. The spot where Sarkur had fallen emanated a smell of blood and burnt flesh, and signs of the Arczeckh's passing stood out against the forest backdrop like stars in the sky. Bear Fist had noticed only about half of them in his human shape, but the sensory acuity that this form gave him revealed all the rest. Keeping low to the ground and out of the sun, he followed the trail the barbarian had left, tracking it out away from Kementeer.

He followed the erratic, delirious trail for miles and miles through the forest, bounding over boulders and splashing through shallow streams without slowing down. The mortal Arczeckh scouts and even his beastmen would have lost the faint, thready trail by now, but his divine senses did not fail him. Eventually, he made it to the edge of the forest and reached more expansive, open terrain, where he found the first Arczeckh corpse. This barbarian had been dead for several days, and raitons had already begun to pick at his flesh. Sarkur had obviously forgotten all about this fallen compatriot and just left him here to rot when he had died. *Being beaten down and scattered for so long serves them right*, Bear Fist thought as he chased the black carrion birds away and sniffed at the corpse. *No respect for their fallen.*

The corpse showed signs of having been beaten and stabbed and then forced to walk for gods knew how long without adequate supplies, but it revealed nothing out of the ordinary beyond that. There was nothing to indicate that anything had happened to Sarkur's band except that their victims had turned against them with surprising results. It marked the head of a more distinct stretch of Sarkur's back-trail, though, which was all the easier to follow for having been made by two people. The new stretch of trail was so distinct to Bear Fist's animal senses that he knew he'd be able to follow it from farther away and at greater speed—specifically from the air, now that he was out of the thick of the forest. He bounded up the side of a broken tree that was leaning against a stronger neighbor and leaped out into space. His body melted and re-formed in mid leap, filling his mouth with the tang of a different animal's heart's blood. This was the blood of an eagle, and as the memory of its taste came to him, Bear Fist dwindled and changed into one of those majestic raptors. He climbed on a current of warmer air and followed the trail once more. Every dragging footprint or spot of blood on a broken brush stood out with perfect clarity to Bear Fist's sharpened eyesight, and he made much better time in the air than any scout would have on foot. As he flew, he whispered a prayer of thanks to ever-changing Luna for the gift of physical fluidity that made this possible.

His search took most of the rest of the day and part of the night too, but it got easier the closer to his destination he came. As he approached, he more frequently found places where wounded Arczeckhi had fallen and been left to die. Predators and scavengers had already found most of the bodies, but each corpse was a landmark promising an even more distinct trail. His eagle eyes had no trouble finding the way even for a while after the sun set, though he did have to land and resume the panther shape once full dark was upon him. The half moon was hidden behind thick veils of cloud, so it offered little help, and he suspected that he was close to the village that had repelled Sarkur's raiders. He didn't want to miss it or any clues it offered just because he liked flying in the night sky too much to want to come down.

His feline sense of smell was of little use, he found, since the raiders' back-trail was several days old at this point, but his eyes were better accustomed to hunting in the dark. In no time at all, he found himself in the center of a mostly ruined village that smelled of mud and burnt flesh and an undertone of dried blood. No human nose would have been able to pick these subtleties out of the air, but Bear Fist was exalted far above any human. Yet, while his Exaltation provided him the means to sharpen his senses, it wouldn't give him answers he wasn't willing to work for. So, he started trying to figure out what had happened here.

The first thing he did was work out where he was. Judging from the direction he'd been traveling and how long it had taken him to get here, he was somewhere in Nishion along the eastern edge of the Hundred Kingdoms. That was especially troublesome, considering the fact that Greyfalls was so close by. If the villagers had fought off the raiders and escaped, they might have run there, which would be problematic. It would put Greyfalls on alert well before Bear Fist or Ma-Ha-Suchi were in any position to lay siege to it. That might not jeopardize Ma-Ha-Suchi's ultimate goals for the region, but it would certainly make achieving them harder and cost the lives of more warriors than was necessary. And while an increased loss of life among the Arczeckhi shock troops Bear Fist was grooming would not be significant, costing Ma-Ha-Suchi more beastmen than he expected to lose would be... unpleasant.

With that in mind, Bear Fist tried to reconstruct in reverse order the sequence of events that had occurred in this village. The first thing he made sure to do in that regard was to determine if and how many of the villagers had escaped. He did a rough count of the number of houses the village comprised and checked that against the number of fresh grave-urn markers he discovered in the village's graveyard. That indicated that about half of the villagers had been killed and the rest had run off or been taken before the raid had fallen apart. Second, he sought out signs of which way the villagers might have gone. Circling the center of the village revealed that answer, and he was relieved to see that the signs didn't point toward Greyfalls. Actually, they pointed deeper into Nishion, which was promising. What was odd, though, was how solemn and sedate the tracks leading out of town seemed. They didn't indicate a headlong mass rush like the barbarians' tracks leading into the village did. They even consisted of ox and cart tracks as if everyone left alive had simply packed up what they had and gone on. It belied the evidence all over the center of town and around its Immaculate temple.

That, he determined, was where the actual fighting had been done. Even in the dark of night, the signs of struggle and bloodshed stood out plainly for one with the eyes to see them. The ground was churned chaotically, there was blood mixed with the dirt, and scraps of clothing and bits of tooth lay trampled and forgotten. This was where his barbarians had fallen, but there was no sign that anything truly unusual had happened here. Certainly, there was no indication that one of the Children of the Sun had been here, as Sarkur's rambling had implied (or *seemed* to imply). The village was still ruined and worthless. The Immaculate temple was still standing. Surely, one of the reborn Solars would have left things the other way around…

Yet, for all his certainty that nothing was amiss beyond the fact that farmers had routed ruthless warriors, something about the area disturbed Bear Fist. He couldn't quite put a name to it, even when he resumed his human shape and stood in the center of the village to survey the entire scene. He crossed his hands behind his back, ringing his orichalcum-alloy smashfists against one another, and paced in deep thought. Something wasn't right here, and he couldn't see it. What was it?

"It's the bodies," a voice said out of thin air, startling him.

Bear Fist turned around to see Mokuu materializing in the middle of the muddy street. First, the little god's gleaming red eyes blazed into existence, then the rest of his body wove itself together from shadow and ephemera. He stood with his long arms crossed over his chest, flashing long, vicious teeth when he spoke. He'd grown considerably since Bear Fist had last cared to look at him—more than Bear Fist was ready to appreciate. Mokuu was roughly the size of one of the bull god Ahlat's war aurochs, and he looked as strong and tough as one of them too. He still carried no weapon, as that was not part of the reality that had made him a god, but his fingers terminated in long claws, and he appeared to be dressed in fine black-lamellar armor. Bear Fist glared at the Arczeckh war god. Someone, it seemed, had been skimming more than his share of the Arczeckhi barbarians' praise and worship while Bear Fist was attending to battle plans and damage control. He and Mokuu were going to have to have words about that. But first...

"What about the bodies?" he asked. "What bodies?"

"Exactly. Where are they?"

"They're burned and buried," Bear Fist said, flexing his fists in irritation. The leather straps that fastened his weapons to the backs of his fists creaked. "I saw the markers."

"Not those," Mokuu said. "The Arczeckh bodies. My people. If the farmers drove some off, they must have killed the others."

Bear Fist ground his teeth. He should have realized. "You're right. This place hasn't punched through into the Underworld and their hungry ghosts aren't lingering, so it's not like they just left the bodies to rot. So where *are* they?"

"They're gone. Destroyed. In the fires, maybe, though those don't look as extensive as I might like."

"As you might like," Bear Fist snarled. He stepped up in Mokuu's face and thumped him in the chest with the ram's-head motif on the back of his smashfist. "What are you even doing here, little god?"

"I followed you, of course," Mokuu said, refusing to back down. Even with his odd stocky proportions and bandy legs, he stood taller than Bear Fist now. "One of my people was severely injured doing your work. I had to know what happened."

"Don't insult me," Bear Fist growled. "What are you really after?"

Mokuu smiled. "Fine. I was simply curious. My shamans told me what Sarkur told you about what happened. If it was true that one more real than all those raiders stood his ground here, I had to see for myself. I had to know how real one like that could be. Was he more real than me? Than you? You understand how attractive a notion that can seem."

"What I understand," Bear Fist said, shoving Mokuu backward a few steps, "is that you're having trouble remembering your station. This is no concern of yours. You should be with your people, preparing them to do what I tell them."

Mokuu's eyes widened in surprise, but he recovered quickly.

He came forward, planted a broad hand in the center of Bear Fist's chest and shoved him down. Bear Fist landed on his back and slid half a dozen feet in the dirt.

"I'm getting tired of doing what you tell me, Moon-Chosen," he said. His red eyes glowed with malice, and he stalked toward Bear Fist with a toothy smile of supreme confidence. "And my people have—"

Before Mokuu could finish the sentence, Bear Fist was up and charging into him. The man tucked low and put a shoulder in Mokuu's stomach at a dead run then popped up straight, hurling the shocked Arczeckh god into the air. Mokuu huffed and turned a somersault in the air with his arms and legs waving madly, but Bear Fist wasn't content to let him just drop. The silvery tattoos on his hairy chest and right arm glowed a bluish white, and a blazing leash of pure energy snaked out from his palm with a will of its own. He twisted at the waist, reached backward and whipped the end of the leash around Mokuu's neck before the god had even hit the ground. He then jerked it forward so that Mokuu landed awkwardly and skidded toward him along the ground. One of Mokuu's waving arms almost got a hold of him, but he jumped over it and came down on Mokuu's chest. He punched the god twice in the head, smashfists ringing on Mokuu's skull, then he closed both of his hands around the god's short, thick neck. The move wouldn't choke the life out of a spirit, but it communicated his superiority clearly enough.

"Damn you, you *will* do as I say!" Bear Fist shouted, banging Mokuu's head and shoulders on the ground. "Do you understand me?"

Mokuu only hissed and tried to pry loose either the hands or the glowing leash around his neck. Neither budged.

"Answer me!" Bear Fist shouted. He let go with the hand from which the leash extended and backhanded Mokuu. The blow and the force on the leash would have snapped any mortal's neck. It didn't cripple Mokuu, but it hurt. The next two hurt just as much. "Answer, damn you!"

Mokuu was dazed, but still he had some defiance left in him. "They're my people…"

Bear Fist roared like his namesake totem animal, and divine power welled up inside him. His tattoos glowed with it, and a milky full moon blazed on his forehead. Even the moonsilver iris of his left eye shimmered. His form rippled and stretched until it was no longer human in shape, and the taste of heart's blood filled his mouth. Now, an enormous brown bear hunched over the fallen god, and it began to drive its massive paws down on Mokuu, who couldn't even raise his arms to defend himself. The blows boomed like a hammer on an anvil, and the earth shook with their power. The force of Bear Fist's fury buckled the ground and drove the two of them into an impact crater that deepened with every blow. At last Mokuu lay still and dazed, and Bear Fist resumed his human shape, his fury spent. He stood up off the beaten Arczeckh god and dragged him out of the crater by the energy leash.

"I'm sorry," Mokuu wheezed, cringing and shielding his face with his hands. He bowed and scraped as much as he was able. "You're right. I'd forgotten my station, Exalted One. Please forgive me. I won't... It won't happen again."

"You're right about that," Bear Fist said, kicking the god in the ribs. "I made you what you think you are." Another kick. "And I can destroy you." Kick. "In fact, give me a reason I shouldn't do that right now." He wrapped the excess length of his leash around Mokuu's neck and forced the god to his knees. He raised his right hand, and the half moon broke through the clouds to bathe the serrated blade of his orichalcum smashfist in eerie luminescence. "I could do it and tell your people your lack of reality forced me to destroy you. I could break them and make them wholly mine."

"Yours..." Mokuu croaked. "Yours and Ma-Ha-Suchi's..."

"I... of course. So, tell me why I shouldn't."

"Because I... I know what really happened here."

Some of the red rage cleared from Bear Fist's mind, and he slacked the leash a little bit. "How?"

"I talked to the spirit of the forest back there," Mokuu said, pointing back toward the tree line in the distance. "Before I spoke to you, I went to him and asked what happened."

"Then that should have been the *first* thing you said!" Bear

Fist growled, slamming Mokuu down face first. *Though I do appreciate you revealing your delusions of superiority*, he thought.

"I'm sorry!" Mokuu replied, spitting mud and trying to sit up. "I lost my head. I forgot myself. I won't do it again."

"I know," Bear Fist hissed. "Because if you do again, I won't hesitate to destroy you."

"I understand, Exalted One! Please don't! I abase myself before your mercy!"

"No. I abase you in order to show you mercy. Don't forget it."

"I won't. I promise."

"Good. Now tell me what the forest's spirit told you."

"I will. I will. But please forgive me..."

After which, the crafty god thought as the Chosen of Luna gloated over him, *I'll forgive myself for choosing to endure this illusionary humiliation. Because if you think it's so easy to put me down, you're a fool. But you'll learn, "Exalted One." You'll find out when my people do, and when that happens, the Arczeckhi will be reborn in my image. Then we'll talk about whose station is greater.*

Chapter Twelve

"What are you doing?" Panther asked, startling Kellen half out of his wits. Kellen was just climbing down from a wagon, and Panther was just walking around it on one of his regular circuits when he saw Kellen. Startled, the farmer jumped and dropped a rolled-up wad of cloth he'd been carrying.

The two of them were near the end of the long train of Nishion refugees, at the rear of one of the wagons carrying the most seriously wounded. The wagons were still reserved for those too wounded to walk, but the refugees had accrued enough animals now that they could take turns riding or just letting the animals carry their belongings for a while if they wanted. Those who were healthy enough to walk or ride weren't supposed to be on the wagons, though.

"You scared the life out of me," the redhead said, scooping up what he'd dropped. "What are *you* doing?"

"What I always do," Panther said. "But you didn't answer. You know the wagons are for sick and wounded only. There's hardly room for them as it is."

"I know," Kellen said, scratching the back of his neck. Panther just stood staring at him with his arms crossed. "I *know.*"

"People notice this sort of thing. Especially people from Saikai. They pay attention to you."

"Tell me about it," Kellen said, shaking his head. "My father's the mayor of Saikai, and the village wives have been doing it since I turned old enough to marry." He paused then, and a shiver ran through him. His face twisted up for a moment like he'd bitten an onion thinking it was an apple. "That is," he added quietly, "he *was* the mayor."

Panther tried to keep glaring at the young man the way he would if some pickpocket in Nexus had tried to justify his crime after being caught, but he couldn't do it. He quit glaring and put a hand on Kellen's shoulder.

"It's all right," he said. "I know things are pretty terrible right now. I just don't want you setting a bad example for the others. You've been strong, and people are starting to look up to you. Especially the kids. If you're getting tired, ask for a spell on one of the horses or—"

"I know, I know," Kellen said. "It isn't that. It's..." He hesitated, looking back at the wagon he'd been climbing down from. "C'mon, we're getting left."

He jogged off up the road after the train of refugees, and Panther strolled up next to him. They walked side by side for a moment, and Kellen seemed content to walk in silence. He looked at neither the wagon nor Panther.

"So what were you doing?" Panther asked at last.

"I... I was seeing Laless. Some of the women tending the wounded said she's been crying. A lot. More than some who are worse off. She doesn't do it at night when I get to see her, but she wouldn't do that. You know? I thought I'd sneak back here and catch her at it."

"I see," Panther said.

"She wouldn't tell me if I just asked her about it, you know?"

"I understand. It's hardly a crime wanting to comfort sick people. So how is she?"

Kellen looked at the wad of fabric in his hands as he answered. "Hurt, sick, scared and sad. But on the whole, she's better. Kind of. Well, better and worse. It's kind of a mess, really."

Panther nodded.

Kellen didn't say anything more for another few minutes, and he slowed to let the wagon get a little farther away. It was the last wagon in the line, and being behind it made Panther and Kellen the last in the line of refugees. Only one of Rolan's mercenaries was farther back, riding one of the newly acquired horses and making sure barbarians weren't riding down on the refugees from behind.

"Her mind's clearer now than it's been for a few days,"

Kellen eventually continued. "She's not in quite as much pain, and her fever's subsided. And thankfully, those animals didn't give her any diseases." Rage rose in Kellen's eyes at the memory that statement brought up, and it took him a moment to get control of himself.

"What makes that worse?" Panther asked.

"Well, the shock's finally wearing off. She's starting to realize what all happened. She lost her whole family—parents, brothers, sister... She watched them die. She fought the ones that did it, but she couldn't stop them. And when she tried, they... they..."

"I know," Panther said. He did partly so that Kellen wouldn't have to say it, but also because he didn't want to hear it. If he'd come down from his contemplation earlier, if he hadn't been meditating so long in the first place, he might have been able to help the girl sooner.

"She can hardly stop thinking about it," Kellen said. "She'd been trying to hide it from me, acting like she doesn't remember, but how could she not? Her hips were both separated. She can't walk. She can hardly even make water without pain. And now, she's stuck in that wagon all day with those other people who are all worse off than she is. It's been getting to her. And she wouldn't even have told me about it if I hadn't come back here at a different time than usual and found her crying. I've been just sitting with her all afternoon trying to comfort her—for all the good it's done. Makes a man feel pretty worthless, you know?"

"I know," Panther said, thinking back to the day his mother had died. She'd died scared and in pain from an ugly wasting sickness, and nothing he'd said or done had made the end any easier for her. She had almost seemed relieved at the very end when she'd finally slipped away. It had definitely been a relief for him. It had also been the last time before his Exaltation that he'd watched with anything other than satisfaction or disgust as another human being died.

"I mean, what am I supposed to say to her to make her feel the least bit better?" Kellen went on. "She's got nothing left. No family, no home, no land, no safety..."

"She's got you," Panther said. Kellen shook his head and

frowned. "No, that's something whether you want it to be or not. I haven't seen anyone else visiting her or trying to make her feel better. It's obvious you want to take care of her. That is what you want, isn't it?" Kellen nodded. "That goes a long way with someone who's been through what she has. Just remember, there's only so much you can do."

"I know," Kellen sighed. "I'm only human. Knowing that doesn't make—"

He stopped then and looked at Panther with a dawning expression of wide-eyed hope. Even still, he had trouble saying what Panther could clearly see was on his mind.

"Wait a minute," he finally managed. "I... Isn't there something *you* can do for her? Something with your..." He shrugged uncomfortably and pointed furtively at Panther's forehead. "You know? Can't you lay your hands on her and, I don't know—"

"Magically make everything all better?" Panther cut in, frustrated. "Fix her? Turn her troubles into money? Something like that? Don't you think I would have by now if I could? Or do you think I'm just holding out on everybody?"

"No," Kellen mumbled, stung and disappointed. "Sorry. Sorry, okay?"

Panther forced himself to stop scowling. "No, no. It's no problem, Kellen. Didn't mean to snap at you. It's just you're not the first person to ask me that." The new refugees they took on always asked him the same thing whenever they heard the story about what he'd done at Saikai. "Look, I wish there was something more I could do for that girl—for everyone who's hurt—but the Unconquered Sun didn't give me a healer's touch. I wish he had. But I've only ever been good at one thing, and that's what I've been given the power to do. For everything else, I'm on my own."

"Just like the rest of us," Kellen said.

"Right."

Another few moments of silence passed as Kellen thought about that, and the two of them walked along behind the wagon. The road had started to angle upward some time ago, and the head of the refugee train had already crested the rise and started down the other side. Kellen looked up at the apex of the rise, then back down to the fabric wadded up in his hand, then back over at Panther.

"So, that turning trouble into money thing," he said, forcing a smile that didn't quite reach his eyes. "Are there actually Anathema who can do that?"

Panther smiled thinly, rolling his eyes. "Never met any. And I know it's a centuries-old cultural bias, but could you not call me Anathema to my face?"

"Oh, did I?" Kellen said, with color rising in his cheeks. He was genuinely embarrassed, but a smile tugged up the corner of his mouth. "I didn't even realize. You said 'savior' was out too, didn't you?"

"I did."

"How about help-ior?"

Panther rolled his eyes again.

"How about 'enemy of chariots'?"

"How about not asking?" Panther said. "I don't honestly know what we're supposed to be called. I don't even have any proof there are others out there the Wyld Hunts have missed. It stands to reason, I suppose, but I don't know it for a fact. I don't even really know the Wyld Hunts have actually missed me. One could be looking for me as we speak, thinking I'm a villainous Anathema."

"There's a comforting thought," Kellen said, turning slightly pale at the notion. All trace of a smile vanished from his face.

"Sorry," Panther said. "It's just one of the unpleasant realities of living in this age. As our problems go, though, it's really pretty low on the list, wouldn't you say?"

"I suppose. It's just... We need you right now, and we don't care if you're Ana... if you're *considered* Anathema or not. I don't know if we could take losing you to a Wyld Hunt after everything you've done for us."

"I wouldn't much care for that either," Panther admitted. "But that isn't your problem to worry about. You think about how to take care of yourself and your people, and I'll worry about the rest. Deal?"

"Sure. But I'd almost rather trade."

"I know," Panther said. *Frankly, I agree,* he added in thought. *And probably for the same reason. Other people's problems hardly seem real when we put them up against our own.*

"So, what's that you've got there?" he asked instead of voicing that sentiment. "Is that a scarf?"

Kellen looked absently down at his hands and held up the roll of fabric he'd been toying with since Panther had walked up to him. "This? Yeah. It's more like a token of how comforting I'm not, though." He tried to smile, but it had a hard, bitter, self-deprecating edge.

"How do you mean?"

"Laless gave it to me," the redhead explained. "It was years ago on my naming day. Her mother made it, and I've pretty much always carried it around with me. When I was in talking to her—Laless—just now, I tried to use it to wipe her tears. But look here…" He unrolled it then and held it out so Panther could see it. It was tattered, dirty and stained with blood. It looked awful. "I had it with me the morning the Arczeckhi showed up. I'm glad it didn't get burned or torn up, but when Laless saw it…"

"It didn't help," Panther said.

"No." All signs of humor were gone from Kellen's face, but he didn't look as upset or frustrated as he had a little while ago. He just looked old beyond his years. "Quite the opposite. Felt like kind of an idiot there, truth be known. Once I got her calmed back down, I figured I'd better just get out of there before I did any more damage."

Panther put on a smile and squeezed Kellen's shoulder in what he hoped was a reassuring way. "Don't be too hard on yourself about it. She knows you care about her and you're trying to help. I'm sure she appreciates it as much as she can anything. Just keep being there for her, and you'll both get through this all right." Kellen didn't seem convinced, but he didn't seem inclined to argue the point. "Besides, I think most women find the stupid things we do around them faintly endearing in retrospect."

"Yeah, maybe," Kellen said. He looked at the scarf for a long moment then started to roll it back up. "Let's hope."

They were just cresting the rise at that point, and as they did so, they saw what the refugees before them must have already noticed. The land stretched down and away, giving them a nice long view over the fertile fields at Nishion's heart. The road ran straight, joining up with a couple of others to form a much larger highway that led right to the gates of Nishion City itself. And from where the two of them stood, they could just make out the walled city in the distance.

It was surrounded on three sides by flat, empty grassland, which was itself bordered by thick forests and the foothills of the faraway mountain ranges to the northwest. It backed up to an enormous freshwater lake that was fed by a river on the opposite end of the plain. Irrigation canals from that lake fed the rich farmland around the city and also filled the wide, deep moat that surrounded the city's high stone walls. The earth that had been removed to make that moat had apparently been piled up in the center of the fortification to form a high, manmade hill. At the top of that hill stood the castle of the ruler of Nishion, which was separated from the city below by another moat and a moderately high curtain wall. It was a decent city for a kingdom of this size, but the entire thing would have fit neatly within *one* of the economic districts of Nexus. Panther tried not to let his disappointment show, especially when he heard Kellen gasp and saw the young man stop walking.

"There it is," the redhead said as his people made their way down the road ahead of him. "Nishion City. We made it. Isn't it something? I haven't seen it since I was a kid."

"Sure is," Panther said, trying his hardest not to condescend. He had to remind himself how awestruck he'd been at the size of the Nexus pit-fighting arena and how ridiculous he'd felt about that when he'd finally gotten to see the Theater of the Bright Panoply in Arjuf on the Blessed Isle. He just hoped Nishion City was larger up close than it appeared from this distance. "And I bet you're not the only one who feels that way. It's been a long, hard road coming here."

"Yeah, but we finally made it. Well, by nightfall, anyway, if we don't stop anymore 'til we get there." He started walking again.

"You're probably right," Panther said. "I'm going to move back up the line now and make sure everyone's all right with that. You're welcome to join me."

"I will in a minute," Kellen said. "But first, I want to tell Laless the good news. It might cheer her up a little."

"Probably right about that too," Panther said. "Go on ahead. I'll meet you."

"I'll catch up in a little while," Kellen said over his shoulder, as he headed back toward the wagon. "And, Panther, I can't let it go without saying. We wouldn't have made it without you. Thanks."

"You're welcome," Panther said, putting on a smile that appeared totally genuine. "Now, go on."

And I'm glad you appreciate my helping you get here, he added silently. *Because I'm not entirely sure what I'm supposed to do now.*

Chapter Thirteen

Just shy of a week after he'd left, Bear Fist returned to his lost city of Kementeer. The last of the rubble had been cleared away in his absence, and many of the barbarians who had been away raiding had since returned. The ranks of their human captives had swelled to the limits of their ironwood cages, and most of the Arczeckhi holdouts had converted at last. The place buzzed with activity, and his return went unnoticed for several long moments. Dozens of chariots were either being built or repaired. Short, shaggy horses were being cared for in their enormous corral in the center of the encampment. And in a leaning, deteriorated stone building that had once served as a barracks for the city guard of Kementeer, equipment had been set up for the mass production of weapons and leather armor. This activity bolstered Bear Fist's spirits, but it did not cut through the unease that had settled over him since his confrontation with Mokuu.

According to what Mokuu had eventually related, the barbarians had all but laid waste to the village of Saikai, when suddenly, a man with dark skin like a Southerner and a golden sun tattoo on his chest had challenged them. The man had glowed with unbound power and stood up to the barbarians' weapons without fear, and he'd inspired the villagers to defend themselves. They'd done so and won the battle, then they'd laid their dead to rest and left with the dark-skinned man, though not before the man had destroyed the bodies of the dead Arczeckhi and sent their souls back to the cycle of reincarnation. This information had soured Bear Fist's disposition, but Mokuu had explained that the nearby forest spirit had been thrilled by what it had witnessed. In its excitement, the spirit had confirmed what the barbarian Sarkur had implied when he'd returned to Kementeer beaten, bloody and near death a week ago. The savior of Saikai had been one of the Chosen of the Sun.

In light of this revelation, Bear Fist and Mokuu had lit out after the traveling refugees to see where the Sun-Child might be taking them. They'd followed the trail to the next village and discussed it, eventually coming to the conclusion that they were going toward the capital of the kingdom, Nishion City. Bear Fist had taken to the sky in the form of an eagle to make up some time, and what he had seen had born that conclusion out. He'd then turned right around and headed back toward Kementeer.

He had to adapt his plans for war now, and he knew that he'd have to do so quickly. According to what Ma-Ha-Suchi had told him about the First Age, the Chosen of the Sun were strong and proud and able to sway mortals to their causes with hardly any effort at all. If he let this Southerner get to Nishion City and entrench himself there, the man could turn the soldiers and citizens into a formidable private army. The citizens of Nishion might even feel they owed it to him since the man had protected them from the Arczeckhi. Rather, they might believe it if the man told them that. And if he was able to put on an impressive enough show of strength in Nishion, he might even be able to sway the less stable neighboring kingdoms. Given enough time, this single Child of the Sun could establish a significant power base here in this backwater of the Hundred Kingdoms. That power might not rival Ma-Ha-Suchi's, but it could certainly prove problematic to it as Ma-Ha-Suchi emerged from his nameless lair and began his war against civilization in earnest. Granted, that possibility was extremely remote, but Bear Fist knew that he had to get to Nishion City and keep it from becoming a reality. Ma-Ha-Suchi had invested in him a great deal of trust in the early stages of this enterprise—he would expect no less.

Circling Kementeer now in the shape of an eagle, Bear Fist surveyed his forces. They would be enough to overwhelm whatever power the Sun-Child had amassed thus far, but time was of the essence. The Exalt spiraled in toward the center of the staging area and resumed his human shape in a flash of energy and a puff of feathers. The barbarians around him started and backed away, but a handful of his beastman lieutenants showed more eagerness. Slate Knife knocked heads with several of them, then they all jogged over to him.

"You're back," Red Leg said. "Faster than we thought."

"Some of us," Slate Knife said, smiling. "Did you find what you were looking for?"

"More," Bear Fist said. He walked toward the empty ruins at Kementeer's center, drawing the beastmen along. "We have to get everybody moving. By morning, I want everyone ready to march to war."

"Going to Verdangate early, are we?" Scar Horn asked.

"Not Verdangate. We're going to Nishion City."

"We're not finished clearing the way," Last Runner said. "Verdangate's almost—"

"Verdangate can be damned!" Bear Fist hollered, grabbing Last Runner by the long hair under his chin. "We're going to Nishion City first!"

"Of course," the beastman replied through gritted teeth. Bear Fist shoved him away, sending him stumbling into Soft Claw. The other beastmen gave Bear Fist some room after that, but they all kept following.

"What's in Nishion City?" Bark Back said in low tones. "What changed the plan?"

"They've got a champion," Bear Fist said. "He beat back an entire raiding party on his own."

The beastmen grumbled among themselves.

"What is he?" Scar Horn asked. "A mercenary? God-blooded?"

"Is he… like you?" Bark Back added. "One of Ma-Ha-Suchi's rivals, maybe?"

"I doubt it," Bear Fist replied. "All he's got with him are scared farmers and backwater town guards at best, anyway. Nothing like what we have."

"No," Last Runner said. "At least, not yet, right?"

"Right. So we're going to Nishion City before this champion starts putting stupid ideas in the people's heads."

"Are you expecting that to be a problem?" Scar Horn asked. "How big a threat is he?"

"Not too big to handle," Bear Fist said, glaring. "But I want to handle it quickly, and I want word of it getting out. I want to make an object lesson out of Nishion City. It's time to put fear in the hearts of all the Hundred Kingdoms. It's time to show them what this army can do."

"And we need to be moving by when?" Last Runner asked.

"Tomorrow, and we're taking everyone. We'll send word to the bands that are still out and have them join up with us on the move. We're going to roll over any villages or towns in our way and knock down the gates of Nishion City like a sandcastle. And when this champion of theirs shows himself, I'll destroy him myself for all of them to see."

"It'll be good to be making war by your side again," Slate Knife said. "Nothing against raiding and looting, but it's not the same." Some of the others echoed the sentiment.

"Nothing's the same," Bear Fist said, looking up at the ruined façade of the forgotten castle before him. "But we're going to fix all that. Starting tomorrow."

Mokuu watched silently as the hirsute, tattooed warrior led his goatmen into the ruins of Kementeer to formulate plans. He waited several long moments to see whether the warlord would call for his advice or input, but he doubted Bear Fist respected him enough to do so. When his prophetic doubts were fulfilled, he cut across the overgrown courtyard to the spirit lodge where his most faithful shamans were gathered. The wounded, diminishing Sarkur was there as well, in the semi-real state he'd been in when Mokuu had last spoken to him. The god moved to the farthest, darkest end of the lodge and waited. Not long after that, an Arczeckh boy rushed inside with the news about Bear Fist's return and related the message that the warlord intended to march everyone to Nishion City and sack the place. That news riled up the shamans, who immediately set to work burning pungent roots and drowning white river stones in a mixture of blood and horse urine. As they did this, they spoke the name of their god and begged for his aid and counsel. Mokuu smiled at all this attention and materialized before them in the shadows. When the god had fully manifested, crouching to fit under the low roof, Sarkur's eyes opened, and the warrior sat up on his meager pallet.

"I am real," Mokuu said as his shamans bowed and praised his name. "I am here."

"The Child of Luna has returned," the eldest shaman said. "He leads us to war when our dreams diminish."

"He does so in my name," Mokuu said, "and at my urging. He serves me well. You will follow him and praise his name."

"We will praise his name," the shamans all intoned.

"But only through me," Mokuu added. "He will be praised in words, but the deeds you do and the sacrifices you make will all honor me. Without me, the Child of Luna would not be real at all."

These words confused some of the shamans, but they dared not gainsay their real and present god.

"His plans and designs have given us victory," Mokuu continued, "but his strength depends on mine. Remember this, and tell the others. He has no strength but what I give him."

"We will," the eldest shaman said.

"Do not tell the Child of Luna or his half-goats what I've said. That isn't your place. I've already shown them their station. Do you understand?" The shamans all indicated that they did, and Mokuu smiled. The gesture was sinister and horrible in the shadows of the lodge. "Good. Now, go and make ready. We move as one when the sun comes up, as our people have not done in centuries."

The shamans abased themselves and vacated the spirit lodge to spread their message to their respective bands, and Mokuu gave them his blessing. Only Sarkur remained, and as he tried to stand and go, Mokuu waved for him to remain. The warrior crouched and froze, and Mokuu came toward him. On his way, he stopped at the crude copper brazier where the herbs and roots were burning, and he breathed in the noxious smoke that wafted from it. The stench pleased him greatly, and he popped one of the filthy stones from the bowl next to the brazier into his mouth with great delight.

"Sarkur," he said at last when the two of them were alone. "You are much diminished. I expected you to be more real by now."

"I am as you've allowed, Mokuu," the warrior said. "I only share in your reality."

"Just so," Mokuu said. "Have you spoken to anyone about how you were injured or what happened to the rest of your band?"

"I have not," Sarkur said. "As you commanded."

"Very good. Your faithfulness honors me. But now, you'll speak of it to me."

"Mokuu?"

"You'll tell me about the farmers' champion, Sarkur. You'll tell me everything, yet you'll breathe no word of it to any other—especially the Child of Luna. Tell me how he fights. Tell me how he leads. Tell me what he tried hardest to protect. Tell me what made him angriest."

Sarkur's eyes widened fractionally at the memory of the glowing, golden warrior who had not only led the farmers to fend off the raid but had also spared his life and forced him to trudge home in shame, burdened by dreams that weren't worth remembering.

"He was… Doesn't Bear Fist need to hear this as well if he's leading us in battle against that one?"

"The Child of Luna knows everything he needs to already," Mokuu snarled, his red eyes flashing. "He'll face the farmers' champion, and if he has faith and trust enough in me, he'll defeat that champion."

"If?" Sarkur asked quietly. "That one is fearsome. What if Bear Fist loses faith and proves not real enough?"

"Then I will destroy the champion myself," Mokuu said. "But to do so, I would need your faith and worship. Yours and the others' as well. If the Child of Luna should fall, there is an act of worship and sacrifice that you must perform to show everyone how real I am. Are you real enough to do as I will ask?"

"I am not a shaman," Sarkur whispered in shame. "I'm a warrior, and one barely real."

"You are a warrior, just as I was," Mokuu said. "I don't need a shaman for what I want done. As for the rest, I can make you more real. I will commit in you a divine work to make you a worthy vessel for what I need. But you must be willing."

"I am, Mokuu," Sarkur said, his red eyes shimmering with reverence and pride. "Do as you will, and I will do as I must."

"Good," Mokuu said, grinning. "And if Bear Fist should fall, I will tell you what to do."

Chapter Fourteen

The layout of Nishion City was simplicity itself, and after several days of taking refuge there, Panther knew it like he knew his old neighborhood in Nexus. From the drawbridge at the outer wall, one road ran straight from the gate to the foot of the hill on which the castle stood. Branching off from that road were concentric streets that ringed the entire city and were connected by smaller cross streets. The streets closest to the gate were taken up primarily by inns, restaurants and other businesses, and residential neighborhoods clustered together farther back. The city's army garrison and its associated businesses took up the entire ring street closest to the base of the castle hill. The more affluent residential community lay opposite the castle hill from the front gate, and the least affluent community found space where it could along the base of the outer wall itself. Somewhere among all that, the city still found room for a public park, a long open-air market and an impressive stable and exercise yard for the locals' horses. And towering over the entire city stood the castle of Nishion's royal family. It nestled atop a large, man-made hill that was exquisitely landscaped and decorated by a spiraling path that had been cut deep into it. The sides of the path were so sheer that they offered no straight path of approach, but defenders atop the castle walls could still fire projectiles down at them. At the top of that hill stood another high wall with its own gate so that the city's defenders could fall back to the high ground in the event that the outer walls were ever breached.

To prevent that eventuality, however, wooden towers stood at the cardinal points around the perimeter of the outer wall, and catapults and oyumi mounted on huge wooden turntables stood ready between each one. The top of the wall was crenellated and ringed with a broad parapet so that a large number of troops could stand ready there. The walls were several feet thick and made of heavy stone, and they offered only one good means of entry: the front gate. That gate consisted of a drawbridge, an iron portcullis and a second set of heavy double doors. The city was tough and well fortified for a place of its size, and it would acquit itself well if the Arczeckhi barbarians came. The refugees would be safe here for as long as their leaders would keep them. Panther had spent the last several days making sure of this, among other things, and now, he was only marking time before the inevitable.

He contemplated that as he walked. Now that he'd seen the refugees safely here, the time would be coming soon for him to leave Nishion City. It wasn't exactly the sort of place he wanted to spend the rest of his life, especially with Greyfalls so close. There were bigger wrongs to put right out there in the Scavenger Lands, greater evils going unchecked. His home city of Nexus, for instance, was a cesspit of turpitude and vice, and it was one of the most prosperous and influential cities east of the Blessed Isle. He'd experienced every stratum of life and society there, and he knew how the place worked. Maybe that was why the Unconquered Sun had chosen him. Maybe he was supposed to take a hand in cleaning Nexus up and making it a decent place once again—assuming it had ever been one. He was an agent of the most powerful god in Creation, so surely, he was supposed to be taking on the largest, most important tasks. Not that saving people who needed help wasn't important, of course, but there was only so much he could do now that he'd gotten the refugees here. They had to be able to take care of themselves. He couldn't just stay beside them every day watching out for them.

Then again, it would be so easy to let himself do just that. The refugees loved him for what he'd done, and they didn't care that he was Exalted above them. The lies spread for centuries by the Realm had little cachet here when compared to what they'd seen him do and heard him say. The people respected and accepted him like his fans had after he'd won his freedom.

More than that, they loved him. Even those refugees who weren't from Saikai had developed similar feelings just by walking with him and hearing what the Saikai villagers had to say. What's more, the people of Nishion City respected and admired him just as much, though for different reasons. They had no idea what he truly was—as he'd asked the refugees to keep that quiet for the first few days, lest the city guards refuse them admittance—but they knew what he'd done. They knew he'd fought to save Saikai and protected the refugees all the way to the city gates. Some of the most worldly and cosmopolitan of them even recognized him by description and reputation as the champion of the free-fighting division back in Nexus. They had no idea what he was doing so far from home, but the fact that someone so famous would stick up for their citizens was a joyful wonder to them. They were honored to have him as their guest in Nishion City, and he'd been spending evenings with some of the local merchants and minor nobility who insisted on honoring what he had done by throwing parties in his honor. (The ruling class and the royal family hadn't yet deigned to have him as a guest, but at least they'd acknowledged the refugees' plight and taken steps to alleviate it.)

If he wanted to, Panther could take advantage of his celebrity to live a decent life out here. It wouldn't be quite so free and debauched as the life he'd had with Kerrek Deset and that crowd back in Nexus, but that wasn't necessarily a bad thing. He could earn these people's respect as he'd earned the villagers', and he could teach them about righteousness as he understood it. He could tell them about how the Unconquered Sun expected them to live their lives. He could tell them about how life had probably been during the First Age and how it could be that way again if they were willing to cast off the Realm's lies and stand up to the corrupt power of the Dragon-Blooded. In time, he could make this kingdom his and spread the word even more effectively with the Saikai villagers as the core of his new ministry. And as his fame and power grew, the nonbelievers wouldn't be able to ignore what he had to tell them. It could all begin very soon if he was just willing to wait here and make it happen one day at a time.

It was an alluring fantasy that Panther had let charm him since he'd arrived, but a fantasy was all it was. It might be easy to stay here subverting and tending to a petty kingdom, but it would be even easier to lose sight of why he'd started. It would take nothing at all to let such a thing exist for his own glorification and worship rather than that of the Unconquered Sun. He couldn't do that. He'd devoted his life to the pursuit of fame and glory once. He wasn't about to do that again.

Such thoughts had been in orbit within him since his arrival here, and today, he'd finally made his decision. The wider world needed what he had to offer now that the refugees were safe. It was time for him to leave. He had only to break the news to the refugees themselves, and he'd be lighting out for points west that very day. He didn't look forward to having to say farewell to the people who'd grown so attached to him, but there was work to be done, and he had to see to it.

Panther made his way out of the affluent residential district tucked away behind the castle hill, moving toward the city park where the refugees had been temporarily settled. The park was a moderately wooded, mostly flat stretch of land that straddled one of the middle ring streets on the east side of town. A handful of cobblestone paths wound lazily through it, one of which was dotted with elaborately carved marble fountains. The park had been named Fountain Walk after that particular path, and it was apparently one of the most tranquil and beautiful places to go in Nishion City, excepting the private gardens of the castle itself.

Since the arrival of the refugees, though, Fountain Walk was anything but tranquil or beautiful. Tents and bivouacs and converted wagons covered almost every available inch of terrain, and the refugees who lived in them milled around with little to do. Some had found work in the city, not knowing how long they would have to stay, but those who hadn't or couldn't basically spent their time here in the park waiting to see what would become of them. Some chatted with neighbors and new friends, some lamented the sorry state to which they'd fallen, and some just stolidly kept themselves busy with whatever small chores they could find or invent. Others waited listlessly for the daily wagonloads of charitable donations sent from the denizens of Nishion City to make their stay here more comfortable. (These donations came as a result of Panther's words on the refugees' behalf whenever he spent time as a guest in one of the local's homes.) The rest, such as Kellen and some men from other villages, did what they could to keep their friends' and neighbors' spirits up. They organized the dispensation of the donations, checked in daily on the wounded—who'd been taken to the city's Immaculate temple for care—entertained the orphaned, homesick children and made plans for how to get their lives back in order once it was safe to leave the city again. Their efforts and Panther's acting as liaison between them and the more influential locals had kept the refugee situation from becoming more of a nuisance than was absolutely necessary.

As the afternoon sun was reaching its zenith, Panther strolled into the encampment smiling to the people he passed and exchanging a few words with them here and there. He scooped up an errant ball that had gotten away from some children who were playing with it and made them laugh by tossing it up and head-butting it back to them. He shook hands with some of the off-duty city guardsmen who'd taken it upon themselves to check in on the refugees and make sure no one was giving them any trouble. Finally, near the opposite end of the tent city, he found who he was looking for sitting on the edge of one of the fountains and looking at the Immaculate temple that was barely visible over a low hill.

"Kellen," he said, approaching the redhead. "Busy?"

"Hi, Panther," the young man said, looking back over his shoulder. "No, I'm just holding this fountain down. Need something?"

"Yeah, I wanted to talk to you. Rolan too, but I haven't been able to find him."

"He's probably still at the Guild outpost on the west side," Kellen said. "He and his men are looking for work again now that they're back in civilization."

"Ah, right. Any idea whatever became of the caravan that ditched him back at your village?"

Kellen shrugged. "Don't know. If he's found out, he hasn't

mentioned it. They could be here for all I know. Or across the border in Verdangate."

"I see. How about Laless? Been to see her today?"

"I have," Kellen replied. "She's as good as can be expected. The monks are taking really good care of her. She's in better spirits now, and they think she's going to heal up just fine with no lasting problems."

"Good, good," Panther said, sitting on the rim of the fountain's basin in front of Kellen and trailing his fingers in the water by his side.

"And I spoke with most of the other wounded folks too. None of them have told the monks anything about... you know. You."

"That's fine. I don't like keeping it a secret, but there's more than my comfort at stake if word gets out."

"Yeah. City folk tend to spook easy."

Panther paused for a long moment, and the only sound between the two of them was that of the water splashing in the fountain.

"So, have the royals sent anybody down here yet to talk to you folks?" he eventually said.

"Is that what you wanted to talk to me about?" Kellen asked. "Because it kind of sounds like you're avoiding something."

"I am a little," Panther admitted. "But I'm getting to it. So have they?"

"The royal family? Not yet. The city-guard folks say they're still discussing the situation with the nobles. Trying to decide what to do about us."

"Seems like it's taking a long time."

Kellen shrugged. "My father used to say it's better to let people in charge talk all they want and take all the time they want. That way, if they make a bad decision, you've at least got time to brace yourself."

"Fair enough."

Panther took a long look around then—at Kellen, at the tent city and out over Nishion City.

"So, what *is* on your mind, Panther? Is it bad? Is something bad happening?"

"No, nothing. Nothing I know of. It's just... I've made a decision I don't much like, but it's the only right thing to do. I wanted you and Rolan to be the first to know. You've both helped keep these refugees together, and you were both the first to accept me after you found out what I am. I thought you deserved to know first."

Understanding dawned in Kellen's eyes, and he sagged in disappointment. "Oh. You're leaving, aren't you?"

Panther nodded.

"When?"

"Today. Maybe tomorrow. I wanted a chance to talk to you and Rolan first, then I wanted to say so long to everybody all at once."

"That's good at least," Kellen said. "Where are you going to go? Back to Nexus?"

"Probably."

"Back to being a pit fighter?"

"No. There's work to do out there. Work only somebody like me can do."

"There's that kind of work here," Kellen said softly, not looking Panther in the eye. "We've got to get back to our homes soon, those who aren't staying here. We've got to start over and try to rebuild what we've lost. But those Arczeckhi are probably still out there, and it's going to take more than pitchforks and surprise to turn them away next time."

"I know, Kellen, but—"

"But what? Your work out there's different somehow? More important, maybe? Well, while you're out doing that important work, what are we supposed to do?"

"You're supposed to look after yourselves," Panther said, although it pained him to do so. "Just like you did back in your village. You're strong, decent people. You can take care of yourselves."

"The only reason we didn't get slaughtered back in Saikai was because you were there," the redhead replied, standing up and pacing back and forth a few steps. "If you hadn't showed up—"

"No. You survived because you stood up for yourselves and

decided not to be victims. All I did was show you it could be done. And you can't have honestly thought I was going to stay here with you forever holding your hands and tucking you into bed at night."

"Well... no. But I didn't think you were going to ditch out the first chance you got either."

"I'm not ditching out," Panther growled. "Look around you, Kellen. You've been welcomed and taken in at the safest place your kingdom has to offer. You've got soldiers here to protect you and concerned citizens doing their best to take care of you. You don't need me."

"But we could. What if we do and you're not even here?"

"Well, what if somebody else does?" Panther asked instead of answering. "What if somebody out beyond these walls needs the kind of help only I can give, but I can't give it because I'm here? I'll tell you, Kellen, it's not even a what-if situation. This world's a wreck, and there *are* people out there who *do* need my help, more than just a little bit. You think it's right to co-opt me just to ensure your peace of mind?"

"Well, no, not really," Kellen snapped. "Not when you say it all glowering and scowling at me like that." He paused and sat back down on the edge of the fountain. "It's just... this isn't easy, you know. None of us knows what's going to happen or what we're supposed to do."

"I know," Panther sighed. "But you're strong, decent people, like I said. You're going to be fine as long as you look out for each other and stand up for each other. I know it's hard, but that's life in this age, and you can't be afraid to face it. If you are, it's only going to make you weak and invite the unrighteous to take advantage of you."

"Well, I've had just about enough of that," Kellen murmured.

"I know you have. And I know you're not weak. Gods, the first time I saw you, you were sneaking around your village looking for wounded while the Arczeckhi were sacking the place. The last thing you are is weak."

"Actually, I was mostly just looking for Laless..."

"Still, you weren't hiding," Panther said. "Don't try to make yourself feel worse than you deserve. Being out there and trying to help was a brave thing."

"Thanks. That means a lot coming from someone like you. Someone who could fight without being told to."

"I know it's true, Kellen. And I know you're going to be fine even after I'm gone. Just remember what I'm telling you, and don't be afraid to do what you know is the right thing. Hear me?"

"I hear you." He looked down at his wavering reflection in the water, then stood up again and extended his hand. "And thanks again, Panther. Not just for this, but for everything. You've done more than… more than we know how to say thank you for."

"You're welcome," Panther said, standing and shaking Kellen's hand. "Just try to remember that I wouldn't be leaving if I didn't think you folks could take care of yourself."

"I know. I guess."

"And if fate wants it…" he shrugged. "Who knows? Maybe I'll wander back this way sometime."

"Who knows?" Kellen said. He smiled, but it had a grim cast to it. "Maybe."

The two of them stood for another moment, neither saying anything, until Kellen finally broke the silence.

"Well, if there's nothing else you wanted, I'm going to go back and see Laless again. Try and explain things to her. I think she'd like a chance to say farewell in person before you go too, if you can manage the time."

"I can. I'll stop by later, after I've told Rolan and all the others. Probably tomorrow in the afternoon or so."

"Sure," Kellen said. "I'll see you then." He nodded and turned away, heading back toward the Immaculate temple where the wounded were being cared for.

All right, Panther thought as the redhead walked away. *That wasn't so hard. I wonder if Rolan will take the news that well.* He turned around and headed back toward the ring street that would lead him to the city's local Guild headquarters, where Kellen said Rolan probably was. *I guess there's only one way to find out.*

"Finally?" the mercenary said. "I thought you might drag your feet a whole season as slow as you were going."

"You see, the way of it is, Rolan... Wait. What?"

The two of them were talking on the spacious walkway at the top of the rear wall of Nishion City. At this time of afternoon, there were few guards on this part of the wall, so the two of them had the parapet to themselves for the moment. Panther had found the mercenary here after an hour of asking around at the Guild headquarters and talking to a couple of city guards who just happened to have seen Rolan come this way. The man stood now in a civilian outfit of a simple woolen tunic and leather pants, leaning against a weather-worn crenellation and smoking a long, thin wooden pipe. He smiled, exhaling a puff of smoke that smelled of cherry wood and... something else Panther remembered well.

"I'm sorry," he said, tapping the arrowhead of hair under his lip with his pipe's stem. "Did you think I'd be surprised you're leaving? I'm more surprised you waited around so long. Surprised you even came in with us, actually."

"Is that so?" Panther frowned. "You know, I can't tell if you're being sarcastic or just having some fun with me."

"I've only the lightest of intentions," the mercenary said. "Nothing to worry about. Everything's placid."

"Right," Panther said. He glanced at Rolan's pipe then smirked to himself. "I'll bet."

"You want some?" Rolan asked, holding the pipe toward Panther.

"No thanks."

The mercenary shrugged, then stuck the stem back in his mouth.

"So, you're moving on then?" he asked a moment later. Panther nodded. "Good. Good decision. I was worried you might think you had to stay."

"Worried? Why is that?"

"Well, it's a nice place, isn't it? Fairly civilized, but not decadent. Adequate fortifications, but not militaristic. Hell and gone from the Blessed Isle, but not a week's ride from Greyfalls. Well, maybe that part isn't so good for you…"

"Sure, Nishion's a nice city," Panther said. "But you're rambling."

Rolan made a little salute with the pipe then laughed at himself for doing it. "Sorry. Anyway, all I'm saying is it might seem like a good place for someone like you."

"But…"

"You've already come to that yourself, it looks as though. It's nice, but you can't stay here. These people don't need you anymore, so you have to go."

"I looked at it more like *other* people still need me *out there*," Panther said, "but that's basically it."

"Whatever suits you. Point is, I was worried you might not realize that… well, ever. Because of what we talked about on the way here, you see. Because of how you are—or were—you see?"

"I do see," Panther said, unsure whether he truly appreciated this candor. "I thought we'd set that straight."

Rolan shrugged. "You know what they say. Leopards, tigers, spots, stripes…" He waved a hand vaguely. "It's a whole thing."

"Right."

"Right. But I'm not worried anymore. You'll be leaving soon, and I didn't even have to sit you down and explain it to you. You know the right place for you to be is out there in the world, and that makes me happy."

"I can see that," Panther said. *And I can smell it.* "So what about you, Rolan? What are your plans now that the refugees are all safely here?"

"I've been thinking about that," the mercenary said. He leaned back against the low parapet and looked out at Nishion City stretching beneath him. "I think I'm going to stay."

"Makes sense," Panther said. "There's a Guild headquarters here. You could probably get plenty of work…"

"No, I mean *stay*," Rolan said. "Live here. Join the city guard. I talked to the watch commander yesterday, and he said I could qualify as a lieutenant with a proper recommendation from the Guild."

"I see. What about your men—the other mercenaries, I mean?"

"If they want to keep doing the thing, they're set up to continue without me. Maruf would take over in a heartbeat. It wouldn't bother me one bit."

"So, just like that?" Panther mused. "You like it here that much?"

"I do, but it's not just that. These people could use my help, I think. There's turmoil all over the Scavenger Lands, and I can't remember the last time I heard of any Dragon-Bloods riding out to fix any of it. Years at least. And all I've been doing in all that time is filling my pockets and shedding blood to protect other men's investments. It sounds less noble now than it used to sound glamorous."

"Tell me about it."

Rolan nodded and took a long, thoughtful drag from his pipe. "So, now I suppose I'll try helping for a bit. Actually contributing something. Who knows? Maybe the gods will reward me some day with a little bit of what you got."

Panther smiled a little sadly. "Don't hold your breath," he said. "The most important thing I got was a second chance and a little perspective. It doesn't sound like you need either one."

Rolan shrugged. "Maybe, and thanks for saying so. Still, it would be nice to be able to stand up unarmed against armed men dozens to one and not be scared about it."

Panther's smile was more genuine this time. "That is pretty nice."

"So, here I'll stay and do my part. Settle down. Maybe look into starting a family. I've heard it spoken of well."

"I wouldn't know. But I wish you luck, Rolan. It sounds like a good thing you're doing. The people of Nishion are lucky to have you. And of course, I share in that luck."

"You do, at that, don't you?"

"That's right."

"Because I saved your life that time."

"Yes, because you saved my life that time."

Rolan smiled, deeply pleased with himself and took another puff from his pipe. Panther grinned and turned toward the lake that the walls of Nishion City overlooked. While they stood together in amiable silence, a two-man team passed by on a routine patrol circuit. They exchanged a few words with Rolan and nodded in nervous awe at Panther before hurrying on their way. When they were gone, Rolan smile was even wider than before. Panther cocked an eyebrow and stared hard at the mercenary.

"Don't worry," Rolan said. "I've just been talking you up a little around town is all. Not the new truth, mind you, just the old one. About you being the free-fighting champion of Nexus. They're all very impressed. You're quite the celebrity at the Guild building."

"I wondered why they were all looking at me like that. But you haven't mentioned—"

"I haven't," Rolan assured him. "They might not look too kindly on you if they knew *that*, would they? You or any of us who came here with you."

"They wouldn't."

"So, nothing to worry about. I've just been saying nice things. After all, you did save a number of people's lives."

"I suppose I did." Panther thought for a moment, and an idea brightened up his expression. "You know, to say thank you, maybe I can return the favor."

"Really, how's that? Or rather, 'Think nothing of it. That isn't necessary.'"

Panther smirked. "You said a good word might help get you a good position here with the city guard, right? You think they'd give weight to a recommendation from me?"

Rolan's face brightened, though he tried not to look too eager. "I think they might, at that. It would make a difference with the Guild at least. If you're willing."

"It seems the least I could do," Panther said. "And I'd be glad to. After all, you did save my life once."

"I vaguely recall something about that."

"Of course. So, who would you recommend I talk to at the Guild?"

"Actually, there will be several people you can mention it to at the thing, if it isn't too much trouble."

"What thing?"

Rolan sat up and tapped the ashes from his pipe over the side of the wall. "I guess word hasn't circulated to everyone down in Fountain Walk yet." Panther shook his head. "Prince Bolon is coming down at the end of the week to throw us a royal feast. Presumably, he's going to tell everyone about what his family's decided to do about the refugees' plight. It'll either be a welcoming feast and a show of the royals' generosity, or it'll be the royals' way of letting everyone down easy and turning them out with their stomachs full. Frankly, though, I think Prince Bolon only wants to ingratiate himself with the local nobles to strengthen his bid for Prince Regent once his parents snuff it. You see, when Nishion's royal family—"

"Time to rein it in, I think, Rolan," Panther said. "Rambling again."

"Sorry. The important part is that there's going to be a feast on Fountain Walk for all the refugees at the end of the week, and for you and I and my men as well. That'll be the time and place to be seen if you're interested. If you can stay that long, that is."

Could be the last time for a long time I get to do something like this, Panther thought. *I don't expect to be making a lot of friends in high places once I leave.*

"Also," Rolan went on, "it'll give you a chance to say your farewells to everyone all at once while they're all in a good mood."

"True. I was going to leave in the morning, but I suppose I can wait a little longer. I'll be there. See you then."

He waved and started to walk away, but Rolan coughed and asked him to wait up a second.

"What is it?"

"Well," Rolan said, stuffing the stem of his pipe through his belt, "it might sound a little silly, actually. And you're free to say no, of course. But I was wondering if you wouldn't mind showing me and my men and some of the off-duty city guards a thing or two."

"What do you mean?"

"You know," Rolan said, "some moves. Like from when you

were still a pit fighter."

"You mean fighting moves."

"Right," Rolan said, shrugging and looking down at his feet like a teenager. "If that isn't a problem. Also, if you aren't busy. And you wouldn't mind. Nothing flashy, mind you, just useful. Something that works in a fight. Well, a little flashy wouldn't be so bad."

Panther couldn't help but laugh at that, and Rolan's cheeks turned bright red. "I think I can find some time for that," he said, clapping the mercenary on the shoulder. "Gather some people up, and meet me back at Fountain Walk. I'll show you some of the moves I used on God-Blooded Thunder when I knocked him off the top spot. How would that be?"

"That..." Rolan said, grinning in delight, "that would be just fine. Thank you."

"I don't understand it," Bark Back mumbled to Slate Knife as the two of them walked side by side. Behind them marched the bands of Arczeckhi that Bear Fist had given them to lead, and behind that marched those given to their beastman cousins. Bear Fist was far away at the head of the formation, leading his army.

"Bear Fist already explained it," Slate Knife said, barely looking at Bark Back. "When the battle starts, you and I break left with our fighters and take out their archers and artillery on top of the walls."

"I understand *that*," Bark Back said. "We're the spear's point. But—"

"More like the ram's horns."

"Whatever. Anyway, I understand what our job is. We clear the way so the others can get in mostly whole."

"So, what don't you understand?" Slate Knife asked. "Do you not know what to do once we've taken care of the wall-top guards?"

"No," Bark Back said. "Cart, horse—that isn't the point.

What I don't know is *how* to do what we're supposed to do. We've got no towers, no ladders, not even so much as a battering ram among us. I thought we'd be stopping to get ready at one of those villages we rolled over in our rush here, but we've hardly slowed down since we left Kementeer."

"You want towers?" Slate Knife gestured over his shoulder with his long spear. "You really think these pox-riddled Wyld-mutants are sophisticated enough to build and use siege towers? I'm surprised they've mastered the chariot. Anyway, this isn't a protracted siege. It's a shock-and-panic raid. That's what the Holy Patriarch wants the Arczeckhi for, and that's how Bear Fist is using them."

"What Ma-Ha-Suchi wants is fine and good, but these people aren't ants. Nishion City has a wall and a moat—defenses designed to keep exactly this sort of army out. I mean, even if we had ladders, just getting to the wall tops would be—"

"You're missing something, Bark Back," Slate Knife said, "and it's a good thing this came up before we got nearer the city. You and I—and Scar Horn and Red Leg's fighters on the other side—aren't scaling the walls and attacking from the outside. We're scouring them from the inside."

Thunderstruck, Bark Back could only blink for a moment. He stopped in his tracks, and Slate Knife had to stop with him. "How in all the circles of hell are we getting inside in the first place?"

"We're following Bear Fist," Slate Knife said. "He's going to open the way, and we're going to run right through the front gate."

"That's... That's bold. I guess we don't need towers or ladders for that. But how—"

"Look," Slate Knife said, pulling Bark Back along, "Bear Fist is going to go over all the specifics again once we're in position. But it's very simple. We run in, we kill the defenders on the front wall so the others can come in behind us, then we let our fighters loose on the city. While they're enjoying themselves, Bear Fist finds who he's looking for and puts him down. When that's done, we try to force a surrender. If that doesn't work, Bear Fist gets angry, and we get to see what happens. Doesn't that make sense to you?"

"I suppose," Bark Back admitted. "Sounds kind of like a raid on a village or a trader town, just on a larger scale."

"Only this will be better because, once we're inside, there won't be anywhere for anyone to run. Their own walls will trap them inside with us in the dark, in their homes, where they thought they were safe and protected. And when they see what these maniacs want to do to them and what Bear Fist has done to their champion, they'll surrender. I'm not even betting here. That's just the way it'll happen."

"If you're that convinced, I'll follow your lead."

"Trust in Bear Fist," Slate Knife said. "He's got this all worked out. He won't let us down. The Holy Patriarch wouldn't have given him this job if he couldn't do it."

"Of course not. But you know how I am. I don't like not knowing the whole plan before something big like this."

"Do you at least feel better about it now?"

"It sounds fine enough for me now."

"Oh, good. We don't have to cancel it."

"Shut up."

Slate Knife smiled and punched his cousin in the shoulder. "Come on, we're lagging behind. Just keep the faith, and trust in Bear Fist. This is all going to work out great."

Chapter Fifteen

The end of the week came quickly, and though Panther was anxious to leave, he didn't regret spending the extra time with the Nishion refugees. Invitations to dinner with the local nobles had fallen off in anticipation of Prince Bolon's royal feast, and he'd passed the time in relative peace with the people he'd shepherded safely here. They left him alone in the hours surrounding midday so he could pray and meditate, but the rest of the time, they clustered around him amiably as if he were an old friend with whom they'd all grown up. They talked to him about themselves or their home villages or about local history, and he told them about Nexus and what it was like growing up there as a slave and a pit fighter. Those stories tended to turn into homilies or cautionary tales, but never by design. Panther simply found as he spoke about his old life that his experiences all too often stood as examples of what not to do, as they'd never brought him the peace or sense of rightness he'd found that day meditating in the clearing before he came to Saikai village. Fortunately, none of the refugees seemed to mind when his stories waxed spiritual, and Panther took it as a promising sign that they kept asking to hear more.

The days before the feast were not uniformly idyllic, though. More of the wounded who'd made it this far died in the care of the monks treating them, and their survivors' hearts broke to hear the news. What was worse, they then had to harass and argue with the keepers of the city's graveyards to be allowed to bury their kin's ashes within the city walls. Eventually, the matter had come down to Rolan spending a considerable sum of money to bribe the undertakers and see that the dead were treated properly.

Yet, solving that problem thus gave local opportunists ideas. They came to the refugees secretly and in small groups, offering their services as facilitators and mediators between the outsiders and the townsfolk or offering to help the refugees find jobs while they were in the city. Others tried to present themselves as entrepreneurs who needed manpower or start-up funds with which to build a new business unlike the kingdom had ever seen. Still others were simply crooks who came in among the refugees to either steal from them directly or recruit them into the criminal underworld at the lowest levels of Nishion society.

Kellen was the first refugee to realize what was happening when several Saikai villagers told him about an "opportunity" they'd gotten themselves involved in, and he told Panther about it immediately. Panther had then spent the rest of that day and those that followed ferreting out those crooks who would prey on their less fortunate neighbors. Most of the scams the scoundrels were running were old ones he recognized from his life on the street in Nexus, and the Nishion crooks were rank amateurs by comparison. It took only a couple of lessons on what to look for before the refugees were able to defend themselves and their meager possessions against the urban predators. Panther did have to step up once when a leg breaker for a local "protection" broker started threatening some of the farmers, but the brute had backed down without even a fight.

The ratio of problems to peacefulness had turned out in Panther's favor, though, so he was well rested and in good spirits by week's end when the prince's royal feast was to be held. He stood now on the highest hill in Fountain Walk beside a fountain that looked like a tall wine glass growing out of a marble lotus blossom, watching the prince and his retinue process down from the castle at Nishion's center. A long caravan of expensive covered wagons led the way down the spiraling path around the castle motte, each with pennants flying. Horsemen bearing tall lamps led the way, and a line of musicians and other entertainers followed the wagons. Even at this distance, Panther could hear strains of the music and see colorful handheld fireworks going off as the entertainers danced and played with them. The sight caused a stir among the refugees, who all came out to watch, and even the city folks seemed impressed. They lined the streets, kept back by a cordon of city guards, and cheered as Bolon's parade descended among them.

"Is that entirely appropriate?" Kellen asked, standing next to Panther. The redhead was standing on the rim of the fountain, leaning with one hand against the top of the stone wineglass. Water was running down his skinny arm and soaking the cuff of his rolled-up sleeve. "I mean, we're here because we need help."

Panther shrugged. "Your prince just wants to make an impression, it looks like. Or he thinks a parade's the perfect way to raise your spirits."

"Don't need it," Kellen said. "You've been doing that fine all by yourself without all this noise and spectacle."

"Remember, he didn't have to come at all," Panther said.

"Sure, but he's only doing it because he wants something. Make himself look like our friend or just do all this so we don't get mad when he gives us bad news. I mean, you never know with royals. They never spend their money or make a fuss unless they want something out of it."

"You're in a mood," Panther said. "You don't like parades or something?"

"They're fine. I just wonder where all this fuss and generosity was when the Arczeckhi were killing our friends and neighbors. Where was it when we needed it? I mean, they can tax us and tell us how to behave, but they can't protect us?"

"Try not to take it so hard," Panther said. "The raids caught everyone by surprise. I doubt the army could have gotten to you in time even if they'd known you were in danger. It was only good luck that I made it there when I did."

"Or fate."

"Sure."

"But still, that's what the army's supposed to be for, isn't it? That's part of what our taxes are supposed to be for, I thought. Instead, I bet some of that money's funding this parade so Prince Bolon can get whatever it is he's after out of all of us. I mean, if you think of it that way, we're paying for all this."

"You're probably right," Panther said. "But that's just life. In Nexus, the city doesn't even have a standing army. If you live out in one of the villages and you start having problems with raiders or whatever, you just have to hire mercenaries and hope for the best. It's even worse in Realm territories. The taxes are higher, and you're still not guaranteed any protection. And that was before the imperial troops started focusing on their business on the Blessed Isle. These days, forget it."

"You know, just saying it's worse other places doesn't really make it better."

"Just try to keep it in perspective, Kellen," Panther said. "And remember, the royals are just people. Your government is just people. If you and yours don't like the way those people are treating you, stand up for yourself, and do something about it. Just because they're not trying to kill you doesn't mean you have to take whatever else they do to you."

Kellen scratched his head and looked at Panther with the start of a smile on his face. "Are you trying to start a peasant uprising?"

"Oh, absolutely," Panther said wryly. "That's exactly what I was driving at."

"You want a bloody coup and ouster of the ruling class," Kellen said, shaking his head in mock disappointment.

"Sure, I figure that's the best way to make a good name for my kind. Advocating rebellion in times of crisis."

"Anything to lift our spirits, right?"

"Whatever works. Now, why don't you be quiet and try to enjoy the parade."

"Yes, sir."

It took a couple more hours for the procession to make it all the way to the center of Fountain Walk, but the refugees heard it well before it arrived. The music grew steadily louder, and everyone could hear the cheering and laughter of the crowd as the entertainers passed. Before the parade's actual arrival, several advance wagons arrived at the tent city to set up tables and benches for the feast and to start unloading the food. A detachment of city guards cordoned off an area in the center of the park for the festivities to take place, and servants in palace livery scurried frantically setting everything up. They didn't let anyone sit or approach the tables for almost an hour, and even when they did, they only filled the tables that were smallest and farthest from where the prince would be seated.

When those seats were filled and the royal retinue was only about twenty minutes away, the servants began to serve wine and bread, which at least kept the refugees from complaining about the wait. Then, slowly, they began to fill in tables closer to the head table where the finest food and dinner accoutrements were on display. While that was going on, Panther, Rolan, Kellen and the nominal civic leaders among the refugees were singled out and asked to come forward. The servants and royal retainers then arranged them into a receiving line in front of the head table and took down their names. No sooner than they had done so than the noise swelled, and Prince Bolon's carriage finally arrived. Everyone seated stood and clapped as the man himself emerged and made his way to the table that had been prepared for him.

Prince Bolon was relatively tall for the region, and he appeared to have been a muscular man once. His muscle had turned to flab, though—and quite some time ago if the gray in his mustache and the wrinkles around his eyes were any indication. Also, the bald pate that prefaced his old-fashioned topknot seemed to be natural, rather than an artifact of cosmetic design. He wore what passed for stylish finery in the Hundred Kingdoms, wrapping himself in long silk robes the same shade of blue and red as the colors of Nishion's flag. He strolled up the aisle of applauding refugees with the languid grace of someone born to power and luxury, pausing occasionally to shake a farmer's hand or offer a courtly bow to a wide-eyed milkmaid. Behind him, musicians and entertainers circulated among the far tables, and servants began sitting everyone down and serving them food.

As the prince's wife, concubines and children all emerged from their carriages and come toward the head table, Bolon stopped at the receiving line to introduce himself to those who'd been assembled by his staff. As he met and exchanged bows with each one, a scribe whispered each person's name and personal information in the prince's ear, and the prince recited this information as if he had known the person all his life. Panther and Rolan exchanged bemused glances once the prince had moved on past them, but the locals seemed to accept this custom with honored grace. It was over in a few minutes, and everyone was shown to a seat.

Panther wasn't expecting dinner conversation—in fact, he wasn't expecting the prince to stay around for more than a few moments—but Bolon surprised him. The prince actually went out of his way to engage his refugee guests in small talk. He asked them about where they were from and how badly their homes had been abused by the barbarians. He asked them if they'd been having trouble with the Arczeckhi before and if they knew what it was that had inspired the barbarians to come together in such force and number now. While the prince conversed on that subject, his oldest children drew the farmers out by asking about mundane subjects such as crop yields, soil quality and average rainfall. Their knowledge of those subjects went no farther than what one might read in an almanac, but they were at least polite and deferential to their elders. Meanwhile, the prince's wife deftly distracted the refugees from their losses by asking questions about how they'd escaped and how they'd made it so far from their homes without incident.

Panther and Rolan's names came up regularly when these questions were asked, and eventually, all attention at the head table turned to them. Rolan gave short, embarrassed answers to questions that came his way and seemed to spend more time apologizing to the nobles for his rough speech than actually responding. Panther was equally uncomfortable with so much attention, but not for the same reasons. His anxiety was never realized, though, and once he was able to relax, he charmed the prince's family and took some of the pressure off Rolan. He employed what high-society social graces he'd learned as a hanger-on of Kerrek Deset's back in Nexus and simply tried to enjoy himself. He told stories about his days as a pit fighter and about the places he'd been in the course of his career. His descriptions of life in Nexus and Great Forks fascinated those who could hear him, and even Prince Bolon himself sat rapt as

Panther talked about the one trip he'd taken to the Blessed Isle to see a low-bill fight in the Theater of the Bright Panoply.

The only awkward moment came when the prince's wife asked Panther what had brought a Nexus pit-fighting champion so far from home to the eastern outskirts of Nishion. The question hit during a conversational lull, and everyone in earshot at the main table turned to hear Panther's answer. Kellen's eyes widened as his face paled, and Rolan swallowed a mouthful of wine the wrong way and coughed half of it back into his cup.

"I just couldn't live that life anymore," Panther said. "I had a revelation one afternoon about the paths I'd taken and the many different lives I could have had, and there wasn't one that didn't seem preferable to the one I'd been living. I realized that day that I didn't have anything left to accomplish and that I wasn't trying to make anything of myself. I was just marking time until someone in the pit managed to put me down, but I was too well trained to let that happen. I had money and fame and a life to envy, but it was all meaningless when I looked back on everything I'd done to get it. So, I walked away."

"Just like that?" Prince Bolon asked. "You left everything behind, never to be seen again until you reemerged here in Nishion. In Saikai, where you saved the villagers and brought them here."

"He helped us," Kellen corrected, staring down at his plate but glancing in the prince's direction. "He showed us we could fight for ourselves."

"Yes, of course," Prince Bolon said, waving toward Kellen but still looking at Panther. "And tell me, has this heroism made you feel better about yourself? Has it redeemed you for that life you no longer relish?"

"I don't know," Panther said, unsure if the prince was legitimately asking or trying to antagonize him. "Is one good act all that's required to make a man righteous? Is one good act sufficient to cleanse a man's conscience after spending a lifetime serving himself? You tell me."

A couple of the prince's sons and concubines sat up straight and murmured in indignation, shooting Panther hard looks, but Bolon only raised his chin and frowned in thought.

"Interesting," he said. "I suppose it isn't. How could it be?"

"How indeed?" Panther replied, nodding.

The prince nodded in return, and his acceptance cooled the tempers of his family. It also put Kellen and Rolan at ease, and both of them let out quiet sighs of relief. The conversation returned to more mundane subjects after that—life in the city, events at the castle and the like—but Panther said little, and a pinched, contemplative look settled on the prince's face. Panther kept glancing at Bolon throughout the rest of the meal, and whenever he did so, the prince was looking out at the tables upon tables of displaced refugees with that same expression. One of his concubines tried to say something to Bolon, but the prince only waved her away without looking at her. When one of his sons by that concubine tried to get his attention, the prince snapped his fingers for quiet. He even brushed off a drink steward who stood opposite him across the table blocking his view. Panther had a good idea what the prince was thinking about, and he could tell that the man was annoyed by the distractions. He didn't want to speak up too soon and add to those distractions before the prince reached whatever decision he was driving at.

Before Prince Bolon could speak, though, a pair of high-ranking city guards approached the table from behind and bent low to speak with their prince. Bolon tried to shoo them away, but the older of the two insisted, going so far as to touch Bolon's silk sleeve and demand the prince's attention. Several of his sons jumped up from their chairs brandishing knives, but a gesture from Bolon stilled them. He listened to what the soldiers had to say, then stood up with a look of equal parts anger and fear on his face. He looked at Panther and then out at the crowd and banged his metal cup on the table several times. When everyone was looking his way and relative quiet had descended, he spoke.

"Everyone listen," he called out. "This dinner is over as of this moment! I want you all out of here! Now! Begone immediately!"

The refugees broke out into confused murmuring, and Panther froze, dumbfounded, as the prince and the two soldiers who'd delivered their message turned as one to stare at him.

"All right," Bear Fist said as Slate Knife finished buckling on the Lunar's orichalcum smashfists, "does everyone understand what they have to do? Bark Back, I'm looking in your direction."

"I understand now, Bear Fist," the beastman said as his cousins chuckled at his expense. "It all makes sense."

"Good. Because it's a little late to call this off if you still don't get it."

Bear Fist climbed onto a large boulder overlooking Nishion City and looked back over his lieutenants' heads. Behind them, the masses of the Arczeckhi army thronged like great black locusts. They were restless and bloodthirsty, and that suited Bear Fist just fine. The garrison outposts, watch stations and farming settlements they'd ground under their feet and chariot wheels in their mad rush here from Kementeer hadn't sated their appetite for violence at all. They wanted to get into Nishion City. They wanted to raze it to the ground if Bear Fist would let them. They wanted to prove how real they were over each other and over the simpering weaklings who hid behind the city's walls. If not for their respect for Bear Fist and his near-divine lieutenants, they would be swarming over this rise already and descending on the unsuspecting city even now.

"I understand it," Bark Back said, scuffing his cloven hooves in the dirt. "It's a good plan. Let's start already."

"Not just yet," Bear Fist said, turning back toward the city below. "But almost. Another couple of minutes, and it'll be time."

He looked up at the sky then, and the beastmen did likewise. They all waited in respectful silence as the fat, white full moon climbed across the sky toward its highest point. Its light reflected faintly on Bear Fist's looping, graceful tattoos and shone in the moonsilver iris of his left eye. He breathed in deeply to center himself, then stood up on the topmost crag of the granite boulder. His lieutenants readied their weapons, and seven of them went back to give orders to their barbarian soldiers. Only Bark Back, Scar Horn, Slate Knife, Red Leg and

Last Runner remained.

"Remember," Bear Fist said to them, "give me a count of fifty after you see me cross the face of the moon, then the first of you follow. When they leave, give me another count of one hundred, and bring all hell and damnation with you."

"We will, Bear Fist," Slate Knife said.

"Count on it," Scar Horn said.

"We won't let you down," Bark Back chimed in.

"Or I you," Bear Fist said. "Now, watch carefully. I'll be moving fast."

The beastmen nodded, and with that, Bear Fist launched himself upward. His leap carried him high into the air, higher than any mortal could jump, and at the apex, his body flashed, shrank suddenly and all but disappeared against the black night sky. He'd taken the form of an eagle and started climbing at a high angle toward Nishion City. He would be at the walls in no time at all.

"All right," Last Runner said, keeping a steady eye on the face of the full moon. "Won't be long now. Go get the first groups ready, and get them up here. When I give the word, charge."

"Charge, and hope Bear Fist has that gate open," Red Leg said.

"Or pray," Bark Back said.

"It'll happen," Slate Knife snapped. "I told you, it's not even worth betting over. He'll do it."

"Fine," Bark Back said. "It's just… I kind of wish Mokuu were here for this."

"You what?" Slate Knife breathed, scandalized.

"What?" Bark Back said. "No, not like *that*. I don't think we need him for this. I just don't like the idea of leaving him back at Kementeer unattended for so long."

"Don't worry," Slate Knife said. "Bear Fist showed him who's boss. He knows his place."

"Maybe," Bark Back said. "I just hope these barbarians know it too. I don't trust their god not to pull something while Bear Fist isn't standing over him holding a leash."

"You give their god too much credit," Scar Horn said. "He's just a ghost who got promoted, and if push comes to shove, Bear

Fist can take him. We've all seen it."

"Plus," Slate Knife added, "when these fighters see what Bear Fist does to Nishion's champion, there won't be a doubt in their minds about who their leader is."

"As long as—"

"Okay, there he goes," Last Runner cut in. "Get ready."

The savory taste of raptor blood filled his mouth, and Bear Fist streaked upward wearing his eagle shape. The features of the night jumped into sharp relief, and a rush of air hissed in his ears as he climbed straight up into the cloudless sky. He pulled up higher than the top of the tallest watchtower on Nishion City's wall, then arced over toward the city with his wings at full extension. The soft light of the full moon caressed his back as he tilted forward and down, appearing to cross the silvery orb's face from Last Runner's vantage. Yet, despite the teams of men in the city's watch towers, the patrols of city guards making regular circuits of the parapets and the lamps and torches burning within the city itself, no one saw Bear Fist coming toward them. Though the city guard knew better than to carry lamps or torches with them up onto the parapet itself, they restricted their watchful care to the ground surrounding the castle to the horizon. They could think of no reason to check the sky, so Bear Fist's approach went unnoticed. Even better, his army needed no lamps or torches because his Arczeckh soldiers could see in the dark almost as well as the day. And since the bulk of it was hidden behind a rise beyond the guards' line of sight and they'd allowed no report of their approach to reach the city, the guard had no idea what Nishion was in for this night.

When he'd crossed the moon's face, Bear Fist tucked in his wings and shot downward in a perilously steep dive, knowing that time was short and that he had to act fast. He plunged toward the guard station at the top of the wall nearest the gate like an arrow seeking a target, throwing out his wings and stopping short just shy of the guardhouse door. The city's night sounds below covered the flap and rustle of his hurried landing, then he changed forms again, flattening and elongating into the shape of a glossy black moccasin. He slid under the uneven wooden door of the guard station into a brightly lit room that reeked of dust, oil, pitch and human sweat. The ability to hear was lost to him in this form, but he could still see well enough even with the sudden change in brightness. One man in a blue-and-red city-guard uniform was leaning against the wall by the door talking to another who was seated on a one-legged stool and idly drumming his fingers on a broad wooden wheel. The wheel was connected by cog and axle to a set of pulleys and counterweights that Bear Fist knew worked either the drawbridge or the portcullis. A similar mechanism stood in an identical guard station on the other side of the city wall's main aperture. He'd have to operate both to open the city to his army, and that meant first dealing with these two guards.

As neither one of them had noticed him slithering in beneath the door, the first guard's death was free. Bear Fist rose up to half his ophidian height, to where the guard's leather boot ended, and sunk his curved fangs in deep. Bitter venom coursed through him into the guard's body, and the soldier lurched off the wall in horror and pain. He grabbed his leg and sat down hard, and that was when he and his partner both noticed Bear Fist on the ground. Before either of them could react, Bear Fist rose up into the form of a stout, shaggy ram—the first animal he'd ever sacrificed to Ma-Ha-Suchi—and charged into the guard who was still standing. The guard barely had room to move, and he was too surprised to even draw his weapon before Bear Fist's curling horns doubled him over and knocked the wind out of him. The guard fell over into a three-point stance, barely able to even wheeze, and Bear Fist finally resumed his human shape again. He kicked the gasping guard's hand out from under him and shoved the man's head down hard onto the stone floor. He then grabbed the snakebit guard's face in one callused and tattooed hand and smashed the back of his head against the wall. Both guards collapsed before either could make a sound.

Checking through the guard station's one window, Bear Fist

saw that the guard (or guards) across the way hadn't noticed his entrance. They'd know he was here soon enough, but he didn't want the alarm raised just yet. To make sure he wasn't disturbed, he took the dead men's short swords and wedged one between the door and the frame and the other through the handle so that the weapon's hilt caught on a heavy iron bolt. Then he turned his attention to the wheel and pulley apparatus that the two dead men were ostensibly responsible for. Seeing that it worked the drawbridge, he gave it a mighty heave that set the counterweights moving and dropped the bridge like a hammer of judgment. Naturally, *that* attracted attention, which was just as well since he knew that the fifty count he'd told Last Runner to give him was up. His men would be here soon, and he was only half finished.

Bear Fist smashed out the glass in the guard-station window as the sound of running feet grew loud outside, followed by frantic pounding on the door and demands that the door be opened or an explanation be given. He ignored all this and, instead, turned his attention one last time to the wheel and pulley apparatus he'd just sent spinning. The moonlight through the window reflected on his ram-headed smashfist as he raised the weapon and brought it down with one thunderous punch on the drawbridge mechanism. The wood and iron machinery blew apart and rained down the stone shaft that the counterweights moved in. Bear Fist then jumped out the guard-station window, becoming an eagle as he did so, and flew across to the opposite station.

The other station's window was not open, but he could see that the door opposite it was and that a handful of guards were running this way. The guard on duty at this station was looking out the window to see what was happening at the drawbridge station, and the last thing he saw was an eagle with one black eye and one silver eye streaking right toward him. Moving at his full speed, Bear Fist transformed back into his human shape less than a foot away from the window and crashed through it like he was tearing through rice paper. The window exploded in the guard's face, and Bear Fist hurled him all the way out of the station. The guard flew back into the three who'd almost made it to his side, and the four of them went down in a heap. One even fell off the parapet some thirty feet to the ground.

Bear Fist jumped up and tore off the ruins of his shirt, then turned to the portcullis mechanism. He sent the wheel spinning and the counterweights whirring so that the portcullis retracted out of the way, then he smashed this mechanism like he'd done the other. That left the way open for his men, and not a moment too soon. No sooner had he heard the portcullis mechanism falling through the wall shaft to its demise when he heard the roars and battle cries of his first groups of beastmen and Arczeckhi raiders tearing across the field down from the rise and heading straight for the city's open front gate. At about the same time, alarms started ringing out all along the walls, while the guards in the watchtowers rang the enormous bronze bells that hung beneath their lookout posts. The sound carried from one corner of the city to the other, and men began to rush along the walls to man the catapults and heavy oyumi that alternated positions between the watchtowers.

"Too little, too late," Bear Fist said with a hard grin as he saw the men rushing around just outside the guard station. Many of his first-wave raiders were already inside effective catapult and oyumi range, rushing up the steps to engage the wall-top guards hand to hand. "Go ahead and do what you think you can, though," he said. "I'd be disappointed if you didn't put up a fight."

He emerged from the ruined guard station then, just as the guards he'd knocked down and scattered were rising to their feet. They looked at him with almost the proper amount of fear and reverence, and Bear Fist smiled like it was his naming day.

"Is something the matter?" Panther asked Prince Bolon, wondering if he'd been exposed. Nishion wasn't a Realm satrapy, and it didn't have Dragon-Blooded rulers, but that didn't necessarily mean that it was so enlightened a society that it would accept the presence of one of the "Anathema." Especially one who hadn't been up-front about his Exaltation.

"These people need to leave," Bolon snapped, urging his family to get up from the table. "The sooner the better. And as for you—"

Before the prince could finish, a faint ringing could be heard coming from all directions, followed by the deep, sonorous booming of the city's watchtower bells. The city guards all snapped upright, and a thrill of fear and excitement ran through the refugees. Many of them jumped up from their seats and started gabbling in wild confusion. Prince Bolon picked up his pace, heading around the table with his family right behind him.

"Hold it," Panther said, though the prince was ignoring him. "What is that? What's happening?"

"It's the alarm!" Rolan said over the mounting noise. "It means the city's under attack."

Bolon had made it around the table and was heading for the central aisle, at the opposite end of which his carriages waited. Panther stood up, vaulted over the top of the table and blocked the prince's way. The royal stopped, his eyes wide, and demanded Panther clear the way.

"Where do you think you're going?" Panther demanded.

"Back to the castle, where it's safe," Bolon said. "Out of my way."

"If you're going, you're taking these people with you."

"There's no time for that. The city's under attack, and there's something wrong with the gates. They came open by themselves before the attack started. These people need to get out of here before it's too late!"

"Get out of here and go where?" Panther shouted. "They've got nowhere safe to run to."

"I do!" Bolon said desperately.

"Maybe," Panther said. "But I'll be damned if I'm going to let them watch their leader abandon them to their fate." He looked past the prince at the man's wife, concubines and children and jerked a thumb backward toward the carriages. "You get back to the castle to safety. Tell the others what's happening and that Bolon chose to stay with his people to do what he could to protect them."

"Wait a minute!" Bolon croaked. "You can't—"

"Quiet," Panther snapped. "Go," he said to the others.

The women and youngest children all happily complied with Panther's orders, rushing past the seething, protesting Bolon like he wasn't there. The prince's three oldest sons stayed behind, though, drawing their knives and encircling their father back to back to back. They signaled to a handful of city guards and ordered them to stay formed up on the prince at all costs until whatever was happening was all over.

The commotion of everyone talking and city guards rushing around trying to secure the area without really knowing what was happening was significant, but Panther could still hear some of what was happening beyond the lamp-lit borders of the park. He could hear many people running and shouting in the far distance, as well as the occasional faint scream. He could also hear guards rushing from different parts of the city in the direction of the front gate, but he couldn't see where they were coming from or what numbers they were moving in. Even that noise was drowned out, though, as refugees began to come toward the head table asking what was wrong and why the alarm bells were ringing. Panther had nothing to tell them except that the prince believed the city was under attack and that everyone might have to be ready to defend themselves if the worst happened. The people he told this to moved back into the crowd relaying the message, and the noise increased tremendously. And over it all, the bronze watchtower bells continued to ring.

"Hey, Panther," Rolan said, pushing through a knot of refugees to Panther's side. "Panther!"

"Rolan. Any specific idea what's happening?"

"Nobody knows more than what the prince said yet. Something's wrong with the gate and the city's under attack. The guards who brought the message have already gone back to their posts, and the ones still here don't know more than we do."

"Who's attacking?"

"They didn't say, but... one guess."

"Probably," Panther said. "Damn. Where'd the prince go?"

"His sons and guards took him to the temple," Kellen said, coming up behind Rolan. "They said they're going to 'watch over the wounded,' if you can believe that."

"Right," Panther replied. "Did his family get out of here yet?"

"They're off safely," Rolan said. "That was fancy quick thinking on your part, I have to say. Send word back to the royal family that Bolon is staying down here being a hero to his people while they're just hiding in the castle. Very nice."

Panther shrugged. "It only works if they don't tell the others I made Bolon stay."

"He'd lose face," Rolan said. "I doubt his family would be willing to do that to him. Or to his sons who chose to stay with him."

"Fair enough."

"Hey, quiet a second," Kellen said, looking around suddenly. "Did you hear that?"

Rolan frowned and looked up. Panther nodded.

"What?" Rolan asked.

"A crash," Kellen said. "Pretty far away, but loud enough to reach us here. Sounded like the walls coming down."

"Not the wall," Panther said, "but probably one of the towers. I heard one of the warning bells go down."

"What could do something like that?" Kellen asked.

Rolan glanced nervously at Panther in response but didn't say what was on his mind. Instead, he said, "I think we need to find weapons. Immediately."

"You're right," Panther said. "I can hear chariot wheels."

Chapter Sixteen

The Arczeckh attack on Nishion City began as wonderfully as Bear Fist could have hoped. Since so many battle plans rarely make it through first contact with the enemy intact, Bear Fist was thrilled to see his plan carried off with such vicious competence and resounding initial success.

As he was opening the way, four large bands of Arczeckhi led by four of his beastman lieutenants were moving across the open the open plain to Nishion City's gate. They needed no torches or lamps, and they brought no chariots and made no battle cries. They crawled low to the ground, covering their backs with camouflage they'd scrounged along the way. Their efforts to date had allowed them to approach the city unawares, and they didn't want to give up their critical element of surprise here now. So, they crept toward the moat with none of the parapet guards the wiser until the drawbridge finally crashed open. As soon as that happened—when they were more than halfway to their goal—the barbarians jumped up and charged the city in earnest, seeming to appear out of the very ground. Even the guards in the gatehouse across the moat from the city wall hadn't been able to pick them out, and Bark Back sprinted forward and made it to them before the rest of the barbarians did. He got into the gatehouse with them and killed them before they could react effectively. Then he stepped out again just as the charging barbarians reached the end of the drawbridge. As they stepped onto the long wooden beams, howling and shouting and gnashing their teeth, the portcullis yawned open before them, welcoming them to the city.

When the first wave had just reached the city gates, Last Runner arrived at his one hundred count and gave the signal to those of his beastman cousins whose forces still remained out of the city defenders' sight. This second wave was much larger than the first, and it comprised more than just foot soldiers. It counted among its number archers with short horn bows, spearmen who'd been specially trained by Bear Fist's lieutenants and charioteers, the pride of the raiding army. Most of the fighters wore piecemeal bronze and leather armor, and they carried weapons of all varieties and states of repair. They'd also painted their faces and chests with the bright green and yellow tribal slashes of Mokuu's ancient raiding band to make themselves look fearsome and demonic. Even the smallest effort in that regard went a long way where the Arczeckhi were concerned.

At Last Runner's signal, Bear Fist's beastmen bellowed great, echoing war cries, and the second wave of attackers descended on Nishion City. Their charging footsteps and their horses' hoofbeats rolled like thunder, and the bone rattles and wooden whistles they'd affixed to the wheels of their chariots lent their advance an otherworldly air. They rushed headlong toward the city in a relatively loose formation, so as not to cram into a deadly bottleneck at the gate, and the tactic also served to make the wall-top city guards' artillery less effective.

This is not to say that the second wave incurred no losses, though, because, even caught completely unawares, the city guards were well trained and tough to panic. They rushed to the crenellations with their bows strung and launched volley after volley of arrows at the oncoming masses. Their desperate efforts were not terribly effective, but they did manage to thin the barbarian ranks somewhat. The teams manning the clunky, unwieldy oyumi had a little better luck. Each team managed to get one shot off from the bulky, ballista-like apparatuses, which rained dozens of hunting and frog-crotch arrows down on the horde with every shot. The enfilade withered the foremost rank of second-wave chargers, even taking out a handful of charioteers and horses, but their effectiveness was limited. Manually reloading and cocking each oyumi took a long time, and the speed-loading devices that had been designed for the weapons still had to be broken out of their crates and made ready because no one had been expecting an attack.

The catapult teams fared somewhat better, loading, cranking and firing off two volleys of heavy stones, but the stones' paths of destruction were limited. Each impact obliterated a handful of charging barbarians, and the stones' bounce and roll took down another half as many, but when the stones came to a stop, they ceased to be a threat. The projectiles were intended to actively defend against siege machinery or tighter formations of men and cavalry, not relatively undisciplined bands of raiders. (The walls, moat and gate were supposed to be defense enough against such a threat.) The arsenal did stock clusters of fist-sized stones that separated when fired and were more effective against looser formations, but the arsenal seemed very far away now that the surprise attack had already begun.

Questions of ammunition and artillery soon became moot points, however, which was part of Bear Fist's plan. While the wall guards tried to train their weapons on the oncoming second wave of Arczeckhi and beastmen, the first wave was already rushing into the city and swarming up the stone steps to the front wall's parapet. Red Leg led the charge up the right side, and Bark Back took his men up the left, and they engaged the defenders with a savage will. On the right side, Red Leg rammed the nearest guard right in the stomach with his head and cleared a space at the top of the steps. He swept the man's feet out from under him with his spear then swung it in a wild arc, giving the Arczeckhi behind him a foothold on the parapet. The mass of them flowed up and around him, tearing into the stunned city guards. On the other side, Bark Back actually leaped over the first knot of guards to engage him and planted his hooves right in the back of the closest one's helmet. The man fell flat, and Bark Back tackled the next three all at once. The Arczeckhi behind him leaped and scrambled up the steps like animals, capitalizing on the room he'd made for them.

The city guards fought desperately, scared and confused by this unimaginable assault. They acquitted themselves well at first, as they controlled the high ground, had more room to move and controlled their enemy's only access route, but their advantage did not last. Primarily, they were outnumbered, and though they killed many of the first Arczeckhi to make it up the steps, they couldn't check the momentum of the barbarians' charge. The sheer mass of the attacking force pushed them back so more barbarians could make it onto the parapet. The defenders also lost ground because many of them were still trying to fire stones and arrows down on the oncoming raiders. Bark Back and Red Leg both focused their efforts on those teams of defenders and urged their raiders along behind them. They overwhelmed the first oyumi teams and hurled the catapult operators to the ground, taking most of the pressure off their oncoming comrades outside. But while Red Leg had no trouble clearing the entirety of the right side of the front wall of artillery teams, Bark Back almost paid for his gains with his life. As he and his men incapacitated and bounded over the second catapult, the next alternate team of oyumi operators stood ready for them. They had broken the stops on the swivel mount that restricted the bulky weapon's field of fire and were pointing the device right down the empty parapet at them. Bark Back froze with wide eyes as he took in the vicious grin on the operator's face. The guard pulled back on the lever to cock the firing apparatus, then reached toward the trigger with extreme satisfaction.

Yet, before the man could loose the dozens of arrows into Bark Back and his raiders, a screeching eagle with one silver eye swooped right down in front of him. The eagle transformed in a bright blue-white flash into Bear Fist, who glared and started walking toward the oyumi without the slightest fear. The swirling tattoos and scar patterns of raised dots on his chest and arms glowed, and the golden weapons he wore reflected the light. The oyumi operator's satisfaction turned to abject terror, and he fired right at Bear Fist's chest, praying aloud for deliverance. His prayers turned to screams when Bear Fist only crouched *into* the mass of projectiles with his arms crossed and his tattoos glowing brighter than the moon above. The arrows hit his forearms and smashfists and bounced off in all directions as if Bear Fist's arms were made of solid steel. A handful of deadly missiles made it past him and wounded a few of the Arczeckhi, but Bark Back went untouched and none of the raiders was killed. A couple even lodged in Bear Fist's shoulders, but he paid them no mind. The oyumi operator backed up with his hands out in front of his face, and Bear Fist continued his measured advance. He wrenched the oyumi off its swiveling platform and hurled it to the street below, then pounced on the operator like a jungle cat. Bark Back and the raiders cheered their leader's divine prowess and charged past him into the city guards who'd been waiting for the oyumi to fire.

Shocked and demoralized, the guards stood very little chance. The raiders pushed them back and forced them to regroup with their reinforcements on the adjacent wall. As more guards rushed to join them, the front-wall guards gained some confidence and backbone, but Bear Fist didn't allow them to capitalize on it. With not only his tattoos, but his left eye and the full-moon mark on his forehead glowing with terrible brilliance, he forced the defenders around the corners of their adjacent walls to the opposite side of their corner watchtower, beneath which the bronze warning bell still pounded and rang. His raiders howled and screamed loud enough to drown the noise out, and Bear Fist drew power from their worship and encouragement. With two mighty backward sweeps of his fists, he drove the long orichalcum blades of his smashfists through the leading support posts holding up the watchtower, splintering the wood like rotted branches. The tower lurched and groaned, and Bear Fist jumped back behind it to give it a powerful heave from the opposite side. The city guards screamed and tried to bolt as the tower fell toward them onto the parapet and crashed with a thunderous splintering of timber and horrid clanging of the warning bell. Most of the guards were able to get out of the way—though many by leaping from the parapet altogether—but killing them wasn't entirely Bear Fist's intention. Instead, he'd cut off the surviving city guards on the front wall from reinforcements and forced the other guards to either go all the way around the wall or climb down and look for another stairway if they wanted to help. Trailing ribbons of blue-white energy, Bear Fist turned to Bark Back.

"Finish up here, then get down with the second wave," he said loud enough to be heard over the ringing in Bark Back's ears.

The beastman nodded his understanding, and Bear Fist left him. The glowing, tattooed warrior looked once out over the city, then leaped from the parapet edge to the roof of the nearest building, some four dozen feet away. He ran to the opposite side then leaped a similar distance down to a lower roof, doing so again and again until he was back at street level. He landed on the main road that led from the gate to the castle motte in a four-point crouch that cracked the pavement in a circle all around him. He stood to find city guards running his way from the castle end of the road and the central ring streets that fed it as his second wave of raiders flooded in from the open gate with wicked, red-eyed charioteers in the lead. Bear Fist smiled in the instant of calm before the storm of chaos broke out.

"Forward!" he shouted to his men, urging them on. They charged around him to engage the city guards, and he stood among the throng a moment giving orders. "Find the garrison! Destroy every soldier! Swarm the streets! Make them send their champion down from on high! Make him come to me and face the glory of Luna!"

The raiders cheered as they surged forth to do as their leader commanded. Some praised the name of Mokuu as well, but Bear Fist let it slide for now. Their god might give them strength, but their leader gave them victory and glory. As long as they remembered that, everything would be fine. If the rest of this battle went as well as the beginning, in fact, everything would be better than fine. Bear Fist wouldn't need Mokuu at all if he made a good enough impression here tonight. These people would be his... Rather, they would be Ma-Ha-Suchi's. And with these savages at the head of an army of beastmen, civilization would tremble before Ma-Ha-Suchi's wrath.

The refugees at Fountain Walk park didn't have to wait long for the battle for their capital city to reach them, but Panther put the time they had to good use. He jumped up on the nearest table as refugees milled around, and he clapped his hands twice to get everyone's attention.

"Listen up," he called out over the noise of fearful babbling and the ever-closing tide of chaos out beyond the ring of lamp and torchlight. "Quit your gabbling, and get it together. Your city's under attack, and your lives are in danger. You're going to have to stand up to your enemies now and drive them back if you ever want to be safe in your homes again."

A handful of people out in the crowd cried out that they weren't soldiers or that they didn't know how to fight or that they wanted the city guard to protect them, but their protests only served to make Kellen angry.

"You can fight!" the redhead said, jumping up on a wobbly bench beside Panther's table. "Those of us from Saikai have already done it once. We wouldn't be here now if we hadn't. And if you think about what's at stake, you'll see you don't have a choice."

The sound of screams and bloodshed drew closer and grew louder on the end of Kellen's words, and no more protests came from the crowd.

"Good," Panther said. "Now grab weapons where you can find them—knives, bench legs, broken bottles, serving platters, whatever. And get as many of these tables turned over in a circle around this area. Do whatever you have to in order to keep them out."

"And if you start getting in trouble," Rolan added, "come back toward the temple. That's where the wounded are, and that's where your prince is. Don't let those barbarian bastards touch it."

"Go now," Panther said, and the refugees set to doing what he'd said. He jumped down from the table and joined the nearest group to help carry out the orders he'd given. Rolan and Kellen joined him, kicking over tables and helping folks pry the legs off overturned benches to make rude clubs. Many of them grabbed knives or serving skewers from the tables, and Panther was pleased to see city guards staying around to help. Some of them even offered some of the refugees their holdout khatars or bits of their armor. The sudden burst of activity and cooperation held back everyone's fear for the moment and distracted them from the sound of running feet and chariot wheels that was coming ever closer.

When the attack finally did come, the refugees were as well defended as they could make themselves, inside a double ring of overturned tables and benches with the Immaculate temple behind them. Some crouched behind the tables they'd knocked over, while others stood well back and huddled together for security. The city guards who'd stayed behind tried to spread out and help coordinate the defensive efforts, but their tactical advice fell mostly on scared deaf ears. Rolan had a little better luck getting refugees to think like a team, but that was only because they knew him or were too scared to question him. Kellen hurried over to the temple to help over there, but he found himself doing just as much work preparing the defense as keeping cowards from running inside to hide with their prince. Only Panther, standing calm and still in the center of the park was truly ready for what was coming. He murmured an ancient prayer to the Unconquered Sun, then steeled himself for battle.

It wasn't the main force of raiders who descended upon Fountain Walk, but it was sizeable nonetheless. More than a dozen charioteers came charging up the street, followed by many times that number of hunched, black-furred barbarians in hellish war paint. And between the charioteers and the raiders ran three tall man-shaped beasts with goat heads and hirsute bodies. Each goatman carried a long ash spear with a long, broad iron head and a tuft of red-tipped crow feathers attached at the top of the haft. These three appeared to be in charge, and their war cries inspired the Arczeckhi. As soon as they came in sight, Panther heard gasps and moans of dread run rampant among his refugees. Before he could shore their courage up with any more words, the raiders were on them.

The charioteers arrived first, and they did thankfully have to dodge around the tables the refugees had turned over. That didn't make them any less dangerous, though, as they simply rode alongside the makeshift barricade and lashed out at anyone standing too close on the other side. Many citizens fell wearing masks of shock as Arczeckh whips cut into them or javelins flew out of the darkness and impaled them. The charioteers made an entire pass, laughing all the way, then circled back to look for weak open spots between the tables.

While they did that, rattling the refugees' courage, the raiders advancing on foot made it to the table barricade and climbed over to fight. The goatmen made it over first, leaping the obstacles like they were skipping rope and attacking with their spears. Their ferocity knocked many defenders down and panicked those who were out of reach, and when their neighbors' blood ran, several of the defenders lost their courage altogether. They fled, dropping their improvised weapons, and the squat, bandy-legged raiders cut them down gleefully. Panther started to move toward the three leaders when he saw that not all of the raiders were attacking from the same direction. A great many of them broke to the right, where their charioteers had done the most damage along the barricade, and were pressing the attack from that side. Those who made it over first pushed back the refugees while those behind pulled the tables out of the way so the circling charioteers could come through. As that danger was more immediate and closer, Panther broke off and went to help out.

When the first knot of Arczeckhi made it past the refugees into the clear, they found Panther waiting for them. He laid the first one out with a straight right to the face and smashed another with an elbow. As the two went down, he dodged a third's club and snatched up an iron mace the first had been carrying. He brained four more in quick succession, striding through them toward the barricade. When he was up among the refugees, he stepped up on a city guard's blind side and intercepted a barbarian who was leaping toward the man with a knife in each hand. The mace whistled through the air and caught the barbarian in the midsection, not only stopping him in midair, but hurling him backward into more of his comrades. The act gave the refugees courage and put some strength back in their arms. With Panther's help, they held the barricade together and forced the charioteers to circle back the other way. That didn't stop the barbarian drivers from loosing another volley of spears or lashing out with whips their again, forcing the defenders back.

With a quick word of encouragement, Panther backed off and headed toward the center of the conflict where the goatmen were still fighting. He could hear their inhuman laughter mixed in among the Arczeckhi's vicious snarls and the wounded refugees' piteous cries, and it made him angry. The half animals were enjoying themselves.

Before he could teach them a lesson, however, the barricade on the opposite side gave way completely and a pair of chariots thundered into the torch-lit perimeter. Refugees fled them or fell beneath them, unable to withstand the vicious onslaught. Arczeckhi poured in behind the drivers, scattering defenders or clashing with the ones who refused to run. The gain of ground shriveled the defenders' morale and stoked the fires burning in the barbarians' red eyes.

"Fall back!" Panther heard Rolan shouting. "Come back toward the temple! Don't let them touch it!"

Panther looked back to make sure the temple wasn't currently being overrun and was glad to see that at least that much was going right at the moment. He then had to jump out of the way as a whip cracked right beside his ear and a chariot almost ran him down. He rolled on his shoulder and came up in a wide crouch as refugees fell back past him and barbarians pulled down the barricades to give chase. The chariot driver turned as he was able, casually running down refugees who happened to be in his way, and gave himself room to charge at Panther once more. At the far end of the park, the goatmen adopted a more casual air themselves, killing at their leisure and letting the Arczeckhi lead the way. Panther took all this in during a long, clear moment of detached peace like many he'd experienced in the Nexus arena. He hadn't realized it, but he'd been holding back thus far, fighting like nothing more than a strong, well-trained warrior so as to conserve his energy for what was sure to be a long night. Yet, the longer he held back, the more lives he was throwing away instead of saving.

His lingering moment of peaceful detachment shattered, and Panther snapped around to face the charioteer who'd tried to run him down. The golden mark of the sun at its zenith glowed on his forehead, and he leaped not away from but toward the barbarian driver. The Arczeckh's malicious smile vanished, and the hand holding his whip suddenly froze as Panther sprung all the way over the horse and crashed into him like a stone from a catapult. Panther hit the barbarian with both knees and fists, and when the two of them hit the ground, the terrified horse ran wild, lost control of its chariot and crashed into the upturned tables, wiping out several Arczeckhi who were late to the melee. The driver's broken body made no sound, and Panther stood to face the others.

After what had just happened, a dozen barbarian foot soldiers came at him. He put his hands up in a ready stance, and a glimmer of the golden light emanating from his forehead shone around his hands and forearms as well. When the raiders rushed him, he knocked aside their clubs and short blades like he was blocking punches, without taking so much as a scratch. He realized almost absently that he was still holding the iron mace he'd taken from a fallen barbarian, and when he had a chance to attack, he swung it in a wide arc that met little effective resistance. Dead and wounded barbarians flew backward from him, and he stood there alone and untouched. Another charioteer tried to charge down on him, but Panther turned and hurled his mace through the air. It struck the horse right in the head, which wrecked the chariot and threw the driver into a tall fountain.

This sudden development shocked the barbarians and filled the refugees with awe. As many of the Arczeckhi gaped at him or cringed, desperate refugees cut their foes down and fell back to the safety of their compatriots. Others recoiled in terror just as the barbarians were doing, while still others found a new strength in the presence of this divine entity who fought for their lives. Many of these last were villagers from Saikai, and they even let out a cheer when Panther began to reveal his power.

For their part, the goatmen weren't afraid, but they were suitably impressed. They looked at each other, then at Panther, then at their raiders, before bellowing a war cry and converging on him. Most of the barbarians were either too occupied with the reinvigorated refugees or too afraid to approach Panther in the first place, but a significant number of them did so as well. Panther came forward to meet them, and emboldened refugees swelled up around him on either side. The defenders' help and the powerful blows of his glowing fists cut through the Arczeckhi, and in mere moments, he found himself surrounded by the three goatmen. They were strong and fast and fearsome to behold, and the weapons they carried were wicked and deadly, but they fought like savages or intelligent animals rather than trained warriors. Panther had dealt with the same odds and the same circumstances many times in the pit, but with the power welling up inside him now, he almost felt sorry for these three.

Golden light trailed from his body as he snatched the spear from the fastest one, blocked the second one's blow on the haft and skewered the slowest before that one could even attack. He then levered the dying goatman back toward the second one, knocking them both over. The one he'd disarmed recovered quickly and tried to tackle him, driving his caprine horns up under Panther's chin. Panther sidestepped and grabbed him in a headlock, then lurched over onto his back, driving the goatman's face into the cobblestone path. He felt the beast's neck crack on impact, and he shoved the body aside. An Arczeckh tried to jump on him before he stood up, but Panther rocked back onto his shoulders and planted both feet in the barbarian's chest. He hurled the painted warrior straight up in the air with a double kick, then popped back up to his feet and stepped back. The only remaining goatman was just struggling to his feet and wrenching the spear free from his partner's chest, and he had no chance to attack Panther after he did so. Panther stepped toward him, grabbed the leg of the falling Arczeckh he'd just kicked into the air and brought the barbarian's body down on the goatman like a hammer. Both raider and beastman collapsed in a heap, but Panther kicked the goatman in the side anyway just to be on the safe side. The warrior flew a dozen feet and crashed.

When it became obvious another moment later that none of the three goatmen would be getting up, a cheer went up from the refugees and the city guards who were still standing. At the same time, a wail went up from the barbarians who'd witnessed the event, and they fell back. The intensity of Panther's gaze repelled them, and the light coming from him burned their hateful red eyes. Even the refugees, who showed no fear of their protector, became terrifying in the barbarians' minds, and they lost their will to fight. They hesitated on the brink of outright panic, and all it took was Panther walking toward them for their courage to fail entirely. Without even a cheap parting shot or a backward glance, they broke ranks and fled, leaving their dead and wounded like someone else's trash. Another cheer rose from the refugees, especially those from Saikai who'd seen Panther in action like this before. Some pointed at him and stared, while others shied away, but all of them looked relieved that the barbarians were gone. Of all the survivors, the city guards looked the most uneasy and fearful.

"This isn't over," Panther said in the quiet following the barbarians' retreat. "They're still out there. I can hear them, and there's a lot more. We need to get out there and help your city guard. Them and the civilians they're trying to protect."

The survivors' blood was up, and they cried out in vehement agreement.

"All right," Panther went on. "I want everybody who's not hurt to find a weapon—a good one—and come with me. Everybody who's only scratched up and bruised a little, you stay here and start taking care of the wounded. Half of you help get everybody who can't get into that temple on their own inside. The other half start rounding up the barbarian wounded and keep an eye on them. Don't let them out of here, and don't let anybody who's not one of your own so much as touch that temple."

As the brave and unhurt started picking up weapons the Arczeckhi had dropped, Panther searched the survivors' faces for signs of either Kellen or Rolan. He found the two of them next to a fountain just a stone's throw from the doors of the temple. Rolan was sitting on the rim of the fountain with his hands in the water, and Kellen was kneeling in front of him with a wet strip of cloth. Rolan's forehead was gashed badly and his left eye was a black and red mess. Kellen was dirty and sweaty but appeared to be unhurt.

"If that's not Panther behind me," Kellen said as Panther's radiance cast his shadow over Rolan's wounds, "we're in an awful lot of trouble."

"What happened?" Panther asked.

"Damned whip," Rolan said, wincing. "I had one of those furry little monsters on my shoulder screaming in my ear, and didn't even hear the chariot until it was right on top of me. The driver did this. I think he ran over my foot too."

"He was very inconsiderate," Kellen said, holding Rolan's chin still so he could look at the mercenary's ruined eye. "Rolan taught him a lesson." Rolan held up a bloodied leather whip and tried to smile with artificial good cheer. "If you give me a second, I'll get him inside and be all right to join you."

"Actually, you're staying here," Panther said. "I need both of you here to make sure nobody gets any funny ideas about how to treat the wounded barbarians."

"I'm thinking of a joke or two I'd like to tell them, actually," Rolan said.

"You know better," Panther said. "Just make sure nobody causes any trouble on either side. I'm counting on you two."

"Sure thing," Kellen said.

"We'll see to it," Rolan said, swaying slightly where he sat. "Oh, and Panther?"

Panther looked back.

"I know you weren't planning to, but I'm glad you stayed. If something… happens, I want you to know how much we all appreciate your help."

Panther nodded, though his eyes were on a group of city guards who were doing their level best not to look at him. "I know. I'm glad I stayed too. Now, you all keep it together here, and we'll be back soon with some good news."

"We will."

With that, Panther walked away, the glow around his body intensifying. He paused only briefly to pick up the three black spears the goatmen had been carrying, then he went on to collect those who were coming with him for what still needed to be done.

Bear Fist walked among his men, letting them throng ahead of him and engage the defenders of Nishion City without stealing too much glory from them. He helped them when they needed it, knocking aside arrows or bowling over cavalrymen who tried to take on the barbarian charioteers, and he kept an eye on his beastman lieutenants. When one of them needed help, he came to them in an animal form to pull them back from the brink of disaster. Whenever it happened, they thanked him for his help, complemented him on his prowess and apologized for needing it.

Mostly, though, he kept his eyes open for the supposedly Exalted champion. Several men fought their way to him *thinking* themselves champions, but he proved each of them wrong. Many carved a path through the Arczeckhi only to quail at the sight of the divine power radiating from him. Those, he ignored. A few steeled themselves enough to attack him. Those, he dispatched without even breaking stride. One actually managed to get in past his guard and dig a shallow scratch beneath his right eye, though, and Bear Fist chose to honor him. He swatted the notched and bloody sword out of that one's hand and scooped him up in both powerful arms. His tattoos glowed fiercely, as did the moonsilver in his left eye, and the would-be hero's spine cracked like a handful of sticks. Before he dropped the man's broken but still-living body to the ground, he smeared his thumb with blood from the cut under his eye and pressed it against the man's forehead. He then kissed the man on the cheek and cast him aside.

The entirety of his barbarian army was within the city walls now, and he was very pleased with both waves' efforts. Hardly any fighters had been killed on their way from their hiding place to the gate, and a mass of nearly five thousand of the apelike Arczeckhi were surging forward now. The bulk of them pressed up the main street toward the castle motte, fighting upstream against the city guards who tried to erect hasty fortifications and hold them back. Those who didn't have room to get into the main fight expanded their forces down into the ring streets that fed off the central street, looking for cross streets that would lead to the next ring street up. The ones who made it to the successively smaller ring streets came back toward the central street to attack the city guards from the flanks. The rest either encountered military resistance as city guards attempted the same flanking tactics, or they happened upon confused and frightened civilian resistance. The barbarians, and sometimes their beastman spearheads, attacked both groups with equal zeal, thinking nothing of slaughtering those less real than themselves. Many of them even delighted in breaking the doors and windows of the homes and shops they passed, looking for anyone who might be hiding within.

As the massive raid went on, more guards appeared on the street, and the barbarians' progress stalled out just two streets shy of the city's interior moat. The main street was a scene of unimaginable slaughter, and the artery was so clogged that the Arczeckh charioteers had no room to maneuver their vehicles. Seeing this and realizing he was only wasting blood for little gain, Bear Fist whistled out to some of his lieutenants and signaled a change in tactics. He told a handful of them to keep pressing the forward attack but to move the entire back half of the raiding mass around the outer ring streets all at once. The raiders were to sweep up the ring streets around the sides and converge not on the castle or even the motte, but on the military garrison from which all these guards were emerging. Once the defenders of the city were crushed, Bear Fist reasoned, surrounding the holdouts in the castle proper and forcing a surrender would just be a matter of attrition.

The beastmen signaled their understanding, and as they moved to comply, Bear Fist pushed his way through the masses of fighting men to the front rank of Nishion's city guards that was doing such a good job holding his men back. He wasn't quite powerful enough to simply wreck the concentrated might of Nishion's standing army, but he was about to hurt it considerably and give his farthest-back soldiers an opportunity to do what he'd told them to. The glow from him flared as he stepped before the dug-in Nishion defenders, and he let out an ursine roar that shook them to their souls. To their credit, they didn't run, but that didn't make the first rank any match for him. He smashed apart the weakest of their makeshift fortifications and waded in among the pikemen on the front line. Their weapons rang like hammers on iron when they hit the smashfists strapped to the backs of his hands, and he turned them aside. He sheared through a line of men like leaves of grass and actually gained his force several yards before the archers farther back received the order to fire. Bear Fist crossed his arms and deflected most of the projectiles that came his way, but not all of them. His shoulders bristled with a couple more unfelt shafts, and the barbarians closest to him fell, having no protection over their heads. More rushed forward to take their place just as more city guards advanced to replace their fallen comrades, and the archers aimed farther back into the mass of Arczeckhi. The Arczeckhi had archers of their own, though, and they returned fire, many with flaming arrowheads lit from torches or buildings they'd already set alight.

Even with Bear Fist's occasional shows of strength and divine prowess, the going was slow and torturous. Bear Fist supposed he could really give everything he had and break through the defenders, but that would defeat the purpose of what he was trying to accomplish. The longer he held back, the more time he gave his soldiers to move in on the city guards' garrison and break the back of Nishion City's defense. It also gave Nishion's champion more time to show himself and kept a reasonable amount of Bear Fist's energy in reserve. Bear Fist just prayed the champion would hurry up and show himself already—if he was even going to—so he could prove his divine might to the Arczeckhi and wrap this first long stage of the attack up at last.

And by Luna's fickle grace, Bear Fist's prayer was answered.

Chapter Seventeen

The first time most of Nishion's city guards and the barbarian warriors saw Panther, they couldn't doubt that he was some divine entity come to either deliver them from evil or scourge them to oblivion. He came up the ring street near the back of the barbarian army, emerging whence a sizeable wing of barbarians and a handful of beastmen had disappeared quite some time ago. He came at the head of a column of armed civilians and rag-tag city guards, riding in a captured Arczeckh chariot that still howled and rattled from the gimmicks its original rider had fastened to the wheels. He wore loose purple pants but no shirt, and a metallic sunburst had been tattooed across his dark, muscular chest in bright golden ink. As if that weren't indication enough of who and what he was, a disk of incandescent gold blazed on his forehead, and the rest of his body had begun to shine faintly as well.

As he came forward, Panther held the stocky, sweating horse's reins in one hand and raised a wicked black spear in the other like a battle standard. He'd obviously taken the weapon from one of the fearsome goatmen, and the presence of the other two spears that balanced in the chariot in front of him told a similar story. He shouted a cry to the men following him and charged into the barbarians' flank, impaling three of them when he threw the first of his captured spears. The barbarians were so stunned by this blazing being's sudden arrival that they could only gape at him, making them easy prey. He and those following him cut deep into the heart of the massed troops before the Arczeckhi recovered.

Panther crashed ahead without fear, knocking demonically painted warriors aside or chopping them down with the second of his captured spears. He inflicted such damage that a path opened up for him, and he outdistanced his support fighters before he realized it was happening. The knowledge didn't come to him until his second spear broke over the skull of a beastman who almost managed to get onto the chariot with him and he glanced back to see how his comrades were doing. He knew he couldn't go back and help them, though, so he plunged ahead to where the city guards needed him more. He hefted the third black spear he'd taken at Fountain Walk and continued to thin the barbarian ranks.

At the same time, Bear Fist became aware of the sounds of battle being joined at the rear of his remaining force, and he turned to see a dark-skinned man riding toward him, glowing like the sun was in him. This, he knew, was the true champion of Nishion, and it seemed that Mokuu's information had been right. This man was one of the Children of the Sun, just as he himself was a Child of Luna. Ma-Ha-Suchi had told him next to nothing about the Children of the Sun except that they were oathbreakers and betrayers whose disappearance had let the world degrade into chaos these many centuries. They were once the caretakers of Creation, yet they had allowed it to fall to ruin, and those reborn in this age were too weak to escape even the Dragon-Blooded. They had to be punished for their failure, and Bear Fist looked forward to doling out some of that punishment. He scraped the blades of his smashfists together and began to make his way backward through his own men.

The way the Arczeckhi were behaving, the confrontation between Panther and Bear Fist seemed ordained by fate. They moved out of Bear Fist's way in respect, and they held back the city defenders who tried to push back now that the glowing, tattooed warrior was no longer laying into them. The barbarians also stayed well out of Panther's way because the spear he'd taken had tasted too much of their blood already. Even the beastmen who remained with this part of the army gave Panther plenty of room. The throng simply parted around him and around his opponent until the pocket of space in which his chariot traveled met up with that given Bear Fist out of respect and deference. They came together with no one standing in their way.

Panther had never seen anyone who'd been Exalted by Luna before, but the eldest reborn portion of his soul, that from which his divine power emanated, recognized the essence of the being coming toward him, and he felt a deeply buried sense of forsaken kinship. That part of him cried out to reestablish the ancient link and restore the way things had been done in the First Age, but the soul of the man Panther had become in this life overrode that instinct. Age-old kinship notwithstanding, this barbarian warrior was leading an attack on innocent people who'd done him no wrong. He'd slaughtered innocents and ruined countless lives. The only righteous thing to do was punish him for his transgression. And the only person in all of Nishion—perhaps all of the Hundred Kingdoms—equipped to dole out that punishment was Panther.

Panther rode on, more than ready to do what he had to. The Lunar warrior stopped in an island of calm and raised his hands, showing off the broad, bladed smashfists he wore. Panther bore down on him, answering the barbarian's challenge by hurling the black spear at the barbarian's chest with all his might. The barbarian reached out underhanded with his left hand and casually caught the spear with the point several inches from his throat. He then just as casually flipped it up into his right hand and hurled it back the way it had come just as hard as Panther had thrown it. The weapon was aimed at the horse rather than the rider, though, and Panther jumped clear before the inevitable happened. The spear sank into the horse's chest as Panther's feet left the floor of the chariot, and the entire vehicle lurched and turned over with a great crash. Its momentum carried it toward the barbarian who easily jumped over it without once taking his eyes off Panther's face. Panther jumped backward off the chariot just before it crashed and even managed to land on his feet with impeccable grace. His sandals skidded over slick paving stones, and he came to a stop just a spear's length from the tattooed, glowing barbarian with one blue eye and one silver eye. A disk of pale moonlight shone on his forehead just as the incandescent mark of sunfire shone on Panther's brow. The two of them stood staring a moment, sizing each other up.

"I know what you are," Panther said at last, flexing his fists and watching the barbarian closely. "I don't know *who* you are, what you're doing with these murderous savages or what you're hoping to accomplish, but I do know one thing. It's all over. Enough is enough."

"I disagree, Sun-Child," the barbarian said. "It won't be over—it won't be enough—until civilization lies in ruins and my master, Ma-Ha-Suchi, builds up the next age in his own image. I am Bear Fist, a general in his army by the grace of Luna, and these savages are my warriors by right of caste. Their lives are mine to spend, their strength is mine to wield, and this city is mine by their efforts."

"You're just plain wrong about that, barbarian," Panther said. "Because see, this isn't a city at all. Look around. There's four walls keeping us in. We're surrounded by screaming, bloodthirsty fools with too much at stake. And here we are alone together with other people's blood soaking in the dirt all around us."

"What are you talking about?"

"This is no city, 'Bear Fist,'" Panther said. "This is the world's biggest arena. And you and me... We're the show."

"You're insane," Bear Fist said, a hint of a growl coming out in his voice. "I've heard enough."

Panther raised his hands and gave a tiny, disrespectful shrug. "Do something about it."

Bear Fist could stall no longer, and with that, the battle was joined. The two of them rushed at each other with a single will and threw what should have been devastating right crosses simultaneously. Neither combatant tried to so much as dodge or block, and the impact of both blows landing at the same time was tremendous. Brilliant energy flashed around them both, and a deep, resounding boom split the air like lightning had just struck, flinging the two of them back in opposite directions. A shockwave flattened everyone standing at the periphery of their island of calm and blew out every intact window on the ground floor around them. The larger battle around them skipped a beat as every soldier in earshot paused in fascination.

Bear Fist landed among the wreckage of the chariot Panther had ridden in on, and Panther bowled over some Arczeckhi who didn't dodge quickly enough. They both glowed brighter than ever now, and they shot to their feet like nothing had happened. A nasty bruise was forming in the center of Bear Fist's chest, and the barbarian's smashfist had opened a deep cut on Panther's right cheek. Ignoring these minor hurts, the two of them rushed at each other again. Bear Fist attacked first, lashing out viciously with his golden weapons, and Panther found himself on the defensive. He blocked and dodged and ducked the first flurry of blows but got in too close and paid for it when Bear Fist kicked him hard in the stomach. He doubled up reflexively and forced himself to hit the ground and roll to the side. As he did, Bear Fist brought both fists down where Panther's head would have been. The blow missed Panther but cracked the pavement like a catapult stone had fallen on it. Panther rolled up to his feet.

As soon as Panther was up, Bear Fist attacked again, leading with another heavy, powerful right cross. Panther blocked it on his left wrist and followed up immediately with what looked like a terribly ferocious jab to the midsection. He pulled it, though, so it did little more than sting the barbarian's rock-hard stomach muscles.

"Ha!" Bear Fist barked. "Is that all you've got le—"

Panther rammed his forehead as hard as he could across Bear Fist's nose, driving the barbarian back clutching his face.

"Chump."

Panther stepped up to show the barbarian what a real punch could do, but Bear Fist came at him faster than he expected. The barbarian snarled and lunged at him, dropping a shoulder into his waist and wrapping both arms around him. Panther managed to keep his own arms from getting pinned, but he couldn't get the leverage to break loose. He could only get his arms up over his face as Bear Fist heaved upright, pulled Panther off the ground and lunged over backward, slamming him headfirst onto the pavement. Panther heard a crack that he hoped was just the ground, and he flopped onto the street on his back. He rose at the same time Bear Fist did, but it took his vision a second to clear, and that second cost him. The first thing he could make out was the face of a golden ram as Bear Fist backhanded him. The blow spun him halfway around and staggered him, driving him back to the ground once again. He landed on his face this time, and only his pit-fighting reflexes saved him. He rolled over on his back just as Bear Fist landed on him, pinning his legs.

"That wasn't funny," the barbarian growled, clamping a meaty hand over Panther's face. He slammed the back of Panther's head down again and again and again, his body glowing brighter with every smash. Panther couldn't see and could hardly breathe. He wrenched an arm out from under the barbarian's body and reached back for what he knew had to be somewhere nearby. When his fingers latched onto what he was looking for—namely, a broken wheel from his erstwhile chariot—he thanked the Unconquered Sun and swung it around desperately. The cracked and crooked wheel disintegrated on impact with Bear Fist's head, but it dislodged the barbarian so Panther could find some leverage. He hurled Bear Fist off him and stood up as quickly as his ringing head would allow.

Bear Fist clambered back to his feet, shaking broken bits of wood and iron off his body, and rage burned in his eyes, brighter than the moonlight that signified his divinity. He yowled and charged Panther with intent to tackle him to the ground again. Panther instinctively reached out and met the charge, catching Bear Fist's wrists in his hands and trying to hold him back with sheer brute strength. The impact was tremendous, actually driving Panther's heels backward and down so hard that they plowed short furrows in the street. A mortal's body would have broken, but Panther merely grunted and strained and pushed back as hard as he could. The paving stones behind him gave up another couple of inches, but eventually, Bear Fist could neither push him any further or make him submit. The two of them struggled and strained against one another a little longer, their energy swirling and crackling all around them, then finally jumped back and let go of each other. They paused and circled to catch their breath and regain control of themselves, at which point they realized that no one in the immediate vicinity was fighting any longer. Everyone was watching them, rapt.

"Place your bets," Panther murmured under his breath. "You don't get any more high-bill than this."

Bear Fist attacked first yet again, but this time, he changed tactics to one Panther couldn't have anticipated. He came in throwing punches like normal, but the first time Panther blocked high, Bear Fist dropped down into the form of a stout, shaggy ram and drove his curved horns right into Panther's guts. Caught completely off guard, Panther doubled up and staggered back several steps before tripping over the pavement that Bear Fist had broken earlier. He kicked his legs up and rolled over backward with the last of his momentum, narrowly avoiding Bear Fist crashing down in human form knee- and smashfist-first right where Panther's chest would've been. Panther jumped up and threw a couple of wild punches in an attempt to force Bear Fist back on the defensive, but the barbarian was no longer fighting wild.

In another flash, Bear Fist became an eagle, dodging Panther's attack by simple virtue of being a smaller target. He flew at Panther's face and clawed at his eyes, and Panther lurched gracelessly out of the way just like any person does when a bird flies right at his face. When Bear Fist passed, he turned back into his glowing human form and twisted in midair, landing right behind Panther's exposed back. He punched Panther in the small of the back, sending him staggering forward and almost falling on his face again. Only the power with which his Exaltation had infused his body kept Panther's back from breaking. The blows were taking a lot out of him, though, and slowing him down. He tried to turn around as soon as he got his feet under him and meet the barbarian shapechanger's next attack, but he was only half successful. He'd only turned halfway around when the curling, oak-hard ram's horns buried themselves in his side and he reeled in a huge half circle, scattering spectators who found themselves suddenly in his way. He staggered and went down on one knee, and Bear Fist stood back up as a man and kicked him gleefully in the ribs. Panther left the ground altogether and smacked into the wood and plaster façade of a nearby building. Cracks radiated out from the point of impact, and the crater only reluctantly released him onto the sidewalk. Dropping onto his hands and knees, he breathed heavily and spat out a mouthful of blood. He ignored it and listened for whether Bear Fist was coming at him again.

"Get up," the barbarian said instead, still standing as a man. "Are you coughing up blood already? I thought the Children of the Sun were supposed to be strong. Or is this the way your 'show' goes in 'the world's biggest arena'?"

"More than you think, maybe," Panther murmured under his breath. He rose very slowly, hauling himself upright with great difficulty. His body was covered with cuts and scratches too numerous to count, and there was blood on his lips, but the light shining from him was even brighter than before.

"There you are," Bear Fist growled with great satisfaction. He started to bound forward, and as he did so, his body flashed and melted down into the shape of a sleek black jungle cat with one normal eye and one of blazing moonsilver. It leaped for Panther's throat, fangs bared and claws out.

"You've got to be kidding," Panther said, deeply and profoundly unamused. He reached and grabbed Bear Fist around his black feline throat in his left hand. "But I'm not laughing."

The jungle cat looked at him in wide-eyed shock and let out a strangled hiss as Panther let go with his left hand and hammered the transformed barbarian with a glowing right cross that would've stunned an ox. Bear Fist flew back and smashed into a tall wooden lamppost. The base of the post splintered and the lamp came crashing down in the window of a second-story room of the same building Panther's body had cracked moments ago. Bear Fist's body flopped around the pole as he hit it, and he spun into a stack of empty crates by the building's side entrance. He was on his feet a second later as a man, and he emerged from the wreckage shaking and hissing through clenched teeth. His eyes were wide and blazing, and the moonlight emanating from him was many times brighter than that shining down from overhead.

"All right," he spat, knocking chips of dust and broken crate off his body with sharp, jerky motions. "You showed me your real power..."

"You sure about that?" Panther said, warily keeping his distance.

"...now I'll show you *my* real power, little Sun-Child. I'll show you the glory of what Luna's given me."

"All I see is you standing there talking," Panther said, falling effortlessly into his old rhythms of pit-talk. "Come show me something."

Bear Fist's reply to Panther's invitation was unlike anything Panther had ever seen in all his years in the pit, and it was enough to make him wish he'd kept his mouth shut. The light coming from within Bear Fist flared, and his body changed one more time. But instead of becoming some other animal, Bear Fist boiled up into a horrid combination shape that was far more deadly and fearsome than any simple beastman or Wyld mutant. This new shape was a vicious hybrid of man and brown bear that stood over nine feet tall and was almost half again as wide across the shoulders as Bear Fist had been originally. Its body was coated with thick brown bear fur, and Panther could still see the glowing outlines of Bear Fist's tattoos shining underneath it all. The full moon disk on the barbarian's head and the moonsilver in his left eye both glowed with terrible intensity, and the enormous totemic form of an enraged bear sketched itself in the air above him. He threw back his head and split the air with a monstrous growl that froze the blood and rattled nearby windows in their frames. Panther looked up and up and up into the monster's eyes.

Bear Fist smiled an ugly, awful smile at the look on Panther's face and growled, "This is the glory of Luna! This is the power Luna has given me!" His voice was an awful parody of roar and scream, and the sound of it drove even the staunchest spectators from both sides of the conflict fleeing in terror.

Panther had nothing to say to that, so Bear Fist took the offensive once more. He snatched up the crooked lamppost that his body had broken and spun it in two enormous paw-hands like an oversized spear. Panther jumped backward, unprepared for just how fast Bear Fist could swing that thing, and just missed getting his ribs crushed. He stepped to the side as the post smashed straight down where he'd been, then shoulder rolled over it to avoid a shin-breaking leg sweep. He counted himself lucky when his roll brought him inside the arc of Bear Fist's improvised weapon and allowed him an opportunity to close into striking range, but that turned out to be exactly what the barbarian wanted him to do. He tried to run in, stiff-arm the post aside and lay Bear Fist out with a punch, but Bear Fist simply couched the post under one armpit and backhanded Panther extraordinarily across the chest with his smashfist. The blow drew a deep red line across Panther's chest and tossed him off the ground like he weighed nothing. He might have flown another two dozen feet before hitting the ground, but before he'd gone more than ten feet, Bear Fist whipped the lamppost around and caught him with it in midair. The post swung Panther around in a wide arc and crushed him against the face of the building on the second floor, cracking the wall and shattering windows on either side of him. Bear Fist held him there a moment before using the post to slam him to the ground equally hard. Only when the barbarian raised the post to smash it down onto him again did Panther have an opportunity to move. He pulled himself out of the way and lurched to his feet, which was when Bear Fist swung the post around again and caught him across the back of the head.

Panther staggered and fell to his knees again, though he managed to land facing his opponent. His ears were ringing, his chest burned, his right eye was starting to swell shut, and he could feel blood pooling under his tongue, but at least Panther knew where the attacks were coming from now. When he saw Bear Fist bring his makeshift weapon down on him, he threw up a hand and absorbed the shock on his forearm. The ground cracked, and he sank an inch, but not taking that blow in the face helped him gather his wits. Another blow fell, and he blocked that one too, cracking the last couple of feet off the end of the post. He heard Bear Fist growl in frustration and take a couple of long steps in his direction.

The post came down again, and Panther blocked it once more, actually managing to rise as he did so. His body no longer simply shined like the golden disk on his forehead, but blazed with languid golden flames. The power coming off him was almost palpable, and seeing this display drove all sense and caution from Bear Fist's eyes. He rained blow after blow down on Panther from all sides, trying to knock him from his feet or drive him back or *something*. Panther stood still in the center of the storm, though, knocking the frantic attacks aside and relying on the Unconquered Sun to give him all the strength he needed. The more he asked for, the more he received, and he realized that the plain and simple fact of the matter was that he was in the right and the Unconquered Sun knew it. Bear Fist needed to be punished for the carnage he'd wrought, and Panther was determined to do just that. That was how he knew best to make the world a righteous place, and when he did so, there seemed no limit to the amount of power the Unconquered Sun would give him as he needed it. As more of it flowed through him now, a golden totemic image formed in the air above him, outlined in the excess energy that poured off him. He didn't even have to look up to know what it was.

"But you're weak!" Bear Fist hollered. "You're corrupt! You're lazy! You're decadent! Degenerate! My master told me the Children of the Sun are weak!"

Panther let the blows and invectives fall until he could take no more, then he reached out and caught the splintering, cracking lamppost in both hands. He stripped it out of Bear Fist's huge, clawed hands and hurled it over his shoulder.

"I don't care what you've been told," he said as Bear Fist goggled at him in shock. "But even the brightest full moon is only a pale reflection of the sun. It's unconquered for a reason. And so am I."

Then he strode toward Bear Fist with a look of utmost calm as golden radiance boiled off him. Bear Fist rushed at him and tried to tear him apart with his enormous claws, but his weight, strength and reach advantage all availed him nothing. Panther turned aside any attack Bear Fist tried to use against him, and he doubled the barbarian up with a resounding left jab to the stomach. He followed up with a right and a left, then an uppercut and another jab to the body, until Bear Fist crashed to his knees. In the air above them, their glowing totemic icons seemed to wage their own battle, and the results were much the same. The barbarian tried to put his hands up and defend himself, but Panther barely noticed. He simply rocked the beast's head back and forth with one earth-shaking punch after another until Bear Fist finally collapsed and seemed to melt back down into the scarred and tattooed human form in which Panther had first seen him. The glow from within his limp, battered body faded to a dull sheen, and the totemic bear image disintegrated in a shower of harmless sparks. Panther waited a moment to make sure the barbarian wasn't pulling some painfully clever trick, then rolled the man over on his back with one foot. Bear Fist's head lolled heavily, and he had no strength to lift his smashfists, but his eyes were still open.

"Go on and do it then, Sun-Child," the barbarian said, slurring around some broken teeth and a grotesquely swollen jaw. "Just make it look good for your audience."

"Shut up," Panther said. "Don't act like you know me."

He did take a glance around, though, and as far as he could see, Arczeckhi, goatmen and Nishion city guards were all staring at him in motionless wonder. That was better than killing each other, he supposed.

"Do it," Bear Fist said. "I'd kill you."

"I know," he murmured so softly that only Bear Fist could hear. "Be quiet, and let me take care of this first."

He then looked up at the rows of petrified Arczeckhi who stood staring at him, the man who'd just beaten down their divinely empowered leader. He made eye contact with several of them one after another, then stood up even straighter with the essence of his divine power roiling off him, and he addressed his next comments to all of the barbarians in the crowd.

"Listen up!" he shouted, startling many of them. "Every

single one of you murdering savages is next if you don't *leave…
right… now!*"

One step toward them over the body of their fallen leader
was all it took. Whatever courage the Arczeckhi had left
vanished, and they fled as one. They knocked each other down
and trampled one another, but nothing stopped them in their
headlong flight for safety. They even swept along the goatmen
trapped among them, and those who were strong enough to
resist the current still wisely chose to run for it rather than try
their luck. Panther was immensely gratified to see a goatman
with a patch of shaggy brown fur on his back rush out from
a side street, stumble forward onto his hands and knees, then
run off clutching his palms to his chest like he'd skinned them.
It was a mean-spirited sort of gratification, but Panther forgave
himself the indiscretion. Any guilt he might have felt over it
vanished like smoke the next moment anyway, as he turned
back toward his fallen opponent to find Bear Fist gone without
a trace.

"Son of a bitch," he spat, ever the epitome of divine grace.
"How did he do that? I was standing right here."

Chapter Eighteen

L ate the next morning, the attack on Nishion City was over, and no Arczeckhi left could pose a significant threat. Those who'd composed the main force on the main street had all fled after Panther defeated Bear Fist, which had left only those attacking the military garrison. Seeing the primary threat quelled, the main-street city guards had fallen back to their garrison to relieve their beleaguered forces, and they'd caught the barbarians from behind. The fighting might still have gone on for several more hours, but Panther had come along too, still glowing like a solar flare. His mere presence had terrified the barbarians, and his power had put theirs to shame. What should have been a desperate pitched battle had turned instead into a rout, and the Arczeckhi and lingering goatmen had retreated.

The hours since then had been devoted to scouring the city of any holdouts and making certain that no barbarians were lying in ambush. Panther had helped out with that effort somewhat, but he'd spent most of that time searching in vain for Bear Fist. The barbarian's escape irked him on a vain, personal level, but it troubled him on a more immediate and practical one. If the barbarian was gone and given time to recover himself, there was nothing stopping him from attacking Nishion again— or Verdangate or any of the other Hundred Kingdoms that looked like easy prey. These thoughts had added an urgency to Panther's search for his fallen opponent, but all he'd been able to find was a sinuous trail of blood at the spot where Bear Fist had fallen and a black scale smaller than his index fingernail. When he'd finally noticed it, he'd remembered the seemingly clumsy goatman with the brown back he saw scrambling away when the Arczeckhi first fled. It had looked at the time like the goatman had fallen down in his haste, but it was possible that he'd actually been scooping something up and running away with it.

That had soured Panther's mood, but no more so than the looks the people of Nishion City had given him as he'd walked among them. It had taken several hours for the radiance blazing from him to die down, and even as it had dimmed, civilians and city guards alike had shielded their eyes and turned away. None of them had been able to bring themselves to approach him, and some of those he'd tried to approach had actually retreated from him. None of them had seemed to care about what he'd done for them or what he'd helped them do for themselves. He'd even caught some of them whispering that maybe he was as bad as the barbarians' leader.

Disgusted and disheartened, Panther had eventually drifted back to Fountain Walk, which was where he found himself as the sun climbed toward its zenith. The place was still a shambles of overturned tables, discarded weapons, ruined tents, broken fountains and bloody cobblestones, but the mood was lighter here than elsewhere in the city. Refugees looked up at him with delight as he came among them, and some of them even ran over to him. He shook their hands and returned their embraces and praised their valor in defending themselves, but he didn't spend too much time with any of them in particular. He meandered across the park toward the Immaculate temple on the other side, where he eventually found Rolan talking to a handful of city guards and mercenaries, giving orders that all the men hurried off to follow in concert. The balding mercenary was sitting on the rim of the basin of the same fountain where Panther had left him the previous night. A large, stout stick was propped up next to him, and a broad white bandage covered his forehead and left eye. When Panther crossed out of Rolan's blind side, the man gingerly pulled himself to his feet, leaning on the stick.

"Rolan," Panther said. "Everything go all right? All the wounded are taken care of?"

"They are," Rolan said, nodding. His face was a grim mask, and he didn't meet Panther's gaze.

"And the raiders?"

"They just got through carting off the last of the dead."

"How about the live ones?" Panther asked. "The wounded and all."

"Well, they took them away first thing this morning. I'm not sure where, but they were all in irons."

"And you didn't—"

"No," Rolan said. "The first batch of clean-up guards wanted to put them all down, but... but we wouldn't..." He cleared his throat and scratched his arrowhead beard with the back of his hand. "We didn't let them, so they just took them away somewhere. Didn't think to ask."

"That's fine," Panther said. "That's what they've been doing with the rest too. Rolan, is something wrong?"

Rolan raised his head and met Panther's gaze at last. "It's Kellen. He's inside. I think you'd better come see."

The lifeblood ran cold in Panther's body, and he whispered, "Show me."

Rolan led Panther into the Immaculate temple. The two of them ignored the dirty looks the bald, white-robed monks gave them, and Rolan actually shoved one of them out of the way when he tried to say something about Panther coming inside. The two of them threaded their way around monks, the wounded, surgeons, empty pallets and bowls of water and blood-soaked rags until they arrived in the main sanctuary. The room was packed wall to wall with wounded refugees and city guards receiving what treatment the monks and volunteers could give them. It reeked of blood, sweat, urine, infection and worse smells Panther couldn't even identify. His stomach turned thinking of what hell these poor souls must be going through.

"Over here," Rolan said, leading the way. "We don't... We don't know how much time he has."

They stopped in the far back corner of the room where Kellen lay on a mean straw pallet barely breathing. Sweat soaked him, plastering his red hair to his skull, and his closed eyes rolled in their sockets. His shirt had been torn open, and stained and dirty bandages covered him from belt to breastbone.

"Kellen," Panther breathed, kneeling beside the man. "What happened to him?"

Hearing the voice, Kellen opened his eyes and looked at Panther. He smiled weakly, and Panther could see red flecks along his gums where he'd been coughing up blood.

"Is that Panther?" the redhead wheezed. "Thank goodness. I've been waiting forever."

"Kellen, what happened?" Panther asked, mopping some of the sweat off the young man's forehead with a cloth Rolan handed him. "You were fine when I left."

"It's stupid," Kellen said, then had to stop as his body was wracked with coughs. "Careless. That damn goat…"

"What?"

"It was one of those half-goats," Rolan explained, levering himself carefully to the floor on the other side of Kellen's pallet. "The one you stabbed in the chest. Turned out he wasn't quite dead. He was just lying there until you were gone, then when we were sorting the barbarian wounded from the dead…"

"Damn," Panther said. "Kellen, I—"

"I'm sorry, Panther" Kellen cut in. "We killed one of the wounded."

Panther barked out a tiny laugh to hold back a tear that wanted to come instead. He cradled the top of Kellen's head in one hand and said, "That's all right, Kellen. He made his choice. You did right. You did just fine."

Kellen sighed and actually seemed relieved. Then he glanced over at the city guard on the pallet next to him and said, "Laless isn't here, is she?"

"What? No." Panther looked at Rolan, who shrugged. "Is she all right? I don't see her."

"She's better," Kellen said, smiling as much as he seemed able. "Walking a little. She's okay. I talked to her when she was here before, but I asked her to leave when you came."

"Why? Is everything—"

"I'm dying, Panther," Kellen said, some of the haze behind his eyes clearing. "But I've been holding on. Waiting for you."

"You're just delirious," Panther said. He looked at Rolan and said, "Right? I know you've seen worse."

Rolan only clenched his jaw and shook his head.

"I know I am," Kellen said. "The monks said it, and I can feel it. But I knew if I just held on long enough, you'd..." He broke down coughing again, and this time blood leaked out of the corner of his mouth and ran down his cheek.

"Kellen," Panther said, "there's nothing... I... I can't—"

"I know you can't fix it," Kellen coughed, tears squeezing out of his eyes with the effort. "We talked about it already. You would if you could."

"You know I would."

"But that's okay," Kellen said. "That isn't why I waited. I want you to do something for me instead."

"What?"

"When I die, I want you to do what you did before. For those barbarians at home. I want you to make sure I go on like I'm supposed to."

"But you've got your own customs," Panther said. "Your family's going to want to—"

"Please," Kellen gasped. "This is what I want. Don't tell me it's good enough for the Arczeckhi and not for... and not..."

Kellen started coughing again, harder than before, and he couldn't even speak to finish his thought. It twisted Panther up inside to see the young man in such pain, especially with the undercurrent of frustration visible on his wracked and tortured face. Though he wanted to deny it, he could see that the redhead truly didn't have much time left, and he didn't want the man to die resenting Panther's unwillingness to heed his last request.

"All right, Kellen," he whispered. "I'll take care of you. I'll see your soul goes on like it's supposed to."

"Thank you, Panther. Thank you for everything."

Kellen closed his eyes then and tried his best to relax and let the inevitable happen. Panther and Rolan knelt in quiet reverence and settled in to wait with him.

Two hours later with the sun at its peak, Panther emerged from the Immaculate temple. He found Laless sitting outside where Rolan had been earlier, and as soon as they made eye contact, she stood up and burst into tears. He came over to her to comfort her, but she pushed past him and walked into the temple without a word. Panther made to go after her, but Rolan barred his way and shook his head.

"Comfort from you isn't what she needs, I don't think," the mercenary said. "Come on, let's take a seat and get you some rest. I wager you've been on your feet all night long."

Panther wasn't tired in the slightest, but he allowed himself to be led to the splashing wineglass fountain where he and Rolan both sat down. Neither of them had anything to say for a long while until Panther eventually broke the silence.

"He didn't ask me how the battle turned out. He didn't ask if we won."

"No," Rolan said. "I wasn't going to either. You don't have surprisingly bad news for us all, do you?"

Panther tried to smile. "No, we won. Nishion's safe again for a while."

"But for how long?" a new voice as someone walked up to where Panther and Rolan were sitting. The two men looked up to see a bedraggled and harried-looking Prince Bolon standing before them with two of his sons flanking him. "I understand you faced the barbarian's leader but didn't kill him."

"I didn't kill him," Panther confirmed, "but I did beat him."

"You let him get away," Bolon said. "Him and a significant portion of his barbarian horde."

"He drove them off," Rolan said, fighting back exasperation. "He probably saved your city single-handedly."

"As a matter of fact," Bolon said, "he endangered this city far more than he actually helped it."

"Beg your pardon?" Panther asked quietly.

"You, sir, led the barbarians here. You brought them right to us. Our reports indicate that they were concentrating their efforts in Verdangate with only minor incursions into Nishion. Yet they abandoned Verdangate altogether and followed you right here."

"I don't believe this!" Rolan spat, trying to stand up quickly, but only knocking his stick over and nearly falling down with it. Panther put a hand on the mercenary's arm both to steady him and to keep him in check.

"And now that you've revealed what... what you are, you'll be bringing Wyld Hunts from Greyfalls and only gods know what other sorts of trouble."

Rolan was livid, but Panther simply sighed in resignation and said, "Just go ahead and say what you're getting at."

"By order of the royal family of the Eternal Sovereign Kingdom of Nishion, you are commanded to leave our nation at once. You pose too great a risk to our property, our prosperity and our persons to allow you to remain. This royal order is to take effect immediately."

"Or what?" Rolan snapped. "What are you going to—"

"It's all right," Panther said, standing up. He towered over Prince Bolon, and the man began to tremble as Panther took a step toward him. "They want me to leave, so I'm leaving. My mind was already made up to go anyway. There's one thing I'm going to do first, though."

Bolon gulped audibly and backed up against his sons. "What's that?" Rolan asked.

"I'm going after the barbarians," he said. "And not alone either. I'm taking a detachment of soldiers who can track and who can move fast. We're going to go find Bear Fist where he's hiding, and I'm going to make sure he never bothers Nishion again."

"You can't do that!" Bolon said. "You can't just demand—"

"What's more, Your Highness, the barbarians have taken captives," Panther said. "Not from here last night, but from the other villages they've sacked while you sat in your castle reading your reports. That's what barbarians do with survivors. If those people are still alive, I'm going to find them and bring them home. You're welcome to publicly consign them to their fate if you want, but I'm not willing to do that, and I doubt the soldiers here who've got family out there in the farmlands are either. Now, I'm taking soldiers and I'm taking supplies, and we're setting out at first light tomorrow. And whether you like that or not, I expect you to make that happen. Because if you don't, you'll see what kind of risk I can *really* pose to this city."

Prince Bolon could only gape at Panther in abject terror, but his sons seemed to have a little more of their faculties under control. "It'll be done," one of them said, tugging his father's sleeve and pulling the man back. "You'll get what you need."

"Good. Rolan, you go with them and help coordinate. And if you can ride, I want you with us."

"Count on me," the mercenary said.

"I am," Panther said. "Make sure everything's ready by dawn."

Chapter Nineteen

Several days and nights after the disastrous raid on Nishion City, the surviving beast children of Ma-Ha-Suchi finally limped back to the forgotten city of Kementeer. They were whipped, dirty and tired, as they'd been traveling almost nonstop. They barely spoke to each other either, for between them they carried the weak and battered body of Bear Fist. Their Exalted leader would survive his wounds, they knew, but he was still recuperating, and he needed time to regain his full strength. The rapid overland trip had not been restful enough to help in that, though, and the worship his Arczeckh soldiers had dedicated to him had become faded and threadbare at best after their defeat.

"Finally made it," Scar Horn said, hobbling to a large piece of broken column and sitting down. "What do we do now?"

"We get him somewhere he can rest," Bark Back said. He and Soft Claw were supporting Bear Fist between them, and the effort Bear Fist was exerting to keep his legs straight was a token one at best.

"I meant after," Scar Horn said as Bark Back led the way toward the empty castle's ruins. "Are we supposed to go back to raiding now?"

"Maybe we should take him to Ma-Ha-Suchi," Last Runner said.

"Ma-Ha-Suchi will kill him for what he's let happen," Scar Horn said.

"Maybe," Red Leg said. "But Bear Fist would want a chance to fix things first. If we take him back now, we'll all lose face."

"We're not doing that," Bark Back said, pulling Bear Fist along in spite of Soft Claw's hesitation. "He's going to be fine.

He just needs to rest and heal. He can do that now that we're not hustling him all across Creation."

"There's something else we could do," Last Runner said. He pointed across the compound to the Arczeckh spirit lodge. Many of the barbarian survivors who'd managed to straggle back in were clustered around it listlessly, and the shamans they'd left behind for the raid were talking to them and painting indecipherable symbols on their bodies. "We could take him to them. See if they can do anything for him."

"We're not doing that either," Bark Back snapped. "How's that going to look?"

"There's how it could look, then there's what good it could do," Soft Claw said, looking over at the lodge. "Maybe if—"

"He'll be fine," Bark Back said, jerking Bear Fist away from the other beastman. "He doesn't need them or their primitive magic. He just needs time."

"Fine, fine," Scar Horn said as Bark Back half carried, half dragged Bear Fist along with him. "But what exactly are we supposed to do about the Arczeckhi now while Bear Fist is down? Did Ma-Ha-Suchi say anything to any of you about that before we left?"

"No," Last Runner said. "We'll figure that out once we've taken care of Bear Fist."

"Yeah," Red Leg said. "They're just as down and beaten as he is right now. If they're going to cause us any problems, we've still got a little time to get ready

At roughly that same moment, the Arczeckh warrior named Sarkur was sitting up on his straw pallet in the spirit lodge conversing with his god. Also in the lodge were a handful of shamans and the most real of the survivors from the Nishion City raid. Sarkur had been forced to stay behind as the rest of the army went on the attack, but from the sounds of things, that wasn't a bad thing. This survivor's words matched those of the survivors who'd been straggling in for days now, and they told a story that sounded very familiar to Sarkur. Their vicious nighttime attack on the unreal human city had gone well and started as planned until a black-skinned man with the sun on his chest and a glowing eye of power in the center of his forehead had come forth to oppose them. The man had attacked, proving himself more real than their entire host combined. And when Bear Fist, their divine leader, had challenged the man, Bear Fist had fallen.

Now, it seemed, Bear Fist and his semidivine beastmen had finally made it back here to lick their wounds and hide from the one who'd beaten them. The idea made Sarkur sick to his stomach, and it had broken the will of the survivors who'd returned. Even those Arczeckhi who'd remained behind to defend the compound and guard the captives had been sullen and quiet since word of the defeat had begun to circulate. Only one being showed any mirth at the situation in spite of the bad news. That being was the god Mokuu himself, though, and his attitude bolstered Sarkur's. Obviously, the god saw some advantage that the simple warrior didn't.

"You're certain he's returned?" the god asked, only his glowing red eyes visible in the cramped, smoky lodge. "Bear Fist is here now?"

"He is, Lord," the surviving warrior said, abasing himself with his head almost touching the floor. "We saw his beastmen carrying him up the trail behind us as we arrived. He must be here by now."

"And he's weak?" Mokuu asked. "He has fallen?"

"To one more real than I've ever faced," the warrior said, trembling. "How he wasn't destroyed I do not know."

"Then I'll find out," Mokuu said, his eyes glittering with malice. He looked around at his shamans and at Sarkur. "Come outside. Follow me. I want to see it with my own eyes."

The shamans did as Mokuu commanded, and Sarkur followed them. His wounds had all healed, and he was fully real again, but he was still weak from having been cooped up with his god and the shamans for so long.

The sun burned his eyes as he emerged from the lodge, but he could see clearly enough that the warrior had been right. Across the compound appeared five of the tall half-goats, two of whom were practically carrying the scarred and tattooed barbarian who'd forged them into an army. He looked far less real now than Sarkur would have ever thought possible. The supposedly divine being appeared to be on the brink of disappearing from existence altogether. The goatmen dragged him like a corpse toward the broken, empty castle they'd claimed as their home here, then they paused to argue about something. When they finally started moving again, a few of them looked toward the spirit lodge with either fear or contempt. Sarkur bristled at the disrespect.

"And where do you think you're going with him?" Mokuu said to those goatmen, displaying his reality for everyone in the compound to see. Sarkur's eyes widened in awe. The god looked much bigger outside than he'd seemed inside the lodge. His people gasped and began whispering among themselves, many of them coming to see what was happening. "Bring him over here."

The goatmen stopped but didn't comply. The one carrying Bear Fist, the one with the brown fur on his back, only stood still as the others gathered around him.

"He looks pathetic," Mokuu said, walking toward the castle ruins where the goatmen were standing. "Hardly real at all. What happened to him?"

"Not now, Mokuu," one of the goatmen dared to say. "Go back to your smoke hut. We'll tell you everything when it's time."

The Arczeckhi murmured at this insolence, and Mokuu's eyes glowed bright with anger.

"Silence!" he hissed, baring long, wickedly sharp fangs. "Bring him to me! Let me see him! Let me see this one who thinks himself my master!"

The goatmen chuffed and murmured, looking at each other for some sign of what they should do. The one in the middle who supported their master shook his head and scuffed one of his cloven hooves in the dirt in agitation.

"We're not doing *that* either," that one said.

"I did not ask you," Mokuu growled, looming over them. Then to his people he said, "My warriors, by defying me, that one cost you the greatest glory of your lives. Bring him to me now, that I may punish him. Tear apart his goat servants if you have to."

No one moved for a second, though the goatmen's eyes widened in shock, fear and outrage. The Arczeckhi themselves hesitated until finally Sarkur yelled out one of Mokuu's ancient war cries and broke their paralysis. Numbering almost one hundred—either survivors of Nishion City or those who'd been left behind—they rushed Bear Fist and his goatmen with feral growls and war cries of their own. Individually and even several-to-one, the goatmen were more real than they, but the Arczeckhi were not afraid. Most of them had been humiliated and defeated, and their rage was now boiling over and adding to their ferocity. Also, the goatmen were few in number and weak from days of hard travel. They set their leader on the ground and tried to defend him back to back, but they simply had no chance. Despite heavy initial losses, the Arczeckhi overwhelmed them and dragged them down, killing two and wounding the others. It was over in minutes.

Sarkur tried to get involved in the attack, but as the others raced ahead, Mokuu held him back with one large, three-fingered hand on his shoulder.

"Wait," the god said as Sarkur's comrades rushed ahead, proving their reality on the goatmen as they hadn't been able in Nishion City. "Stay here with me, Sarkur. You have a duty to perform in my name. You owe it to me for sharing my reality with you."

"I remember," Sarkur said, reining in his disappointment. "What can I do, Lord?"

"Soon," Mokuu said, squeezing Sarkur's shoulder. "Just be ready to do as I tell you."

Sarkur nodded, and Mokuu strode forward to join the eager throng of his people. The mass of them was just knocking down the last of the goatmen—the one with the brown back—and they swarmed over Bear Fist's body like greedy black ants. They hoisted him onto their shoulders, cheering in victory, and passed him over the tops of their heads to Mokuu. The god took Bear Fist in one hand and raised him high enough for everyone in the compound to see. Even the dejected human slaves in their wooden pens had a clear view. Bear Fist lay splayed across Mokuu's broad palm, arms and legs dangling.

"Yes!" Mokuu cheered, making sure everyone got a good view. "Look at him! Look at this one! Look and see what's become of one who thought he was my equal!" He shook Bear Fist like a doll, and the Arczeckhi cooed in wonder like delighted children. "Does this *look* like my equal? This looks to me like a loud-mouthed failure! This looks like one who took the blessings I gave him and tried to usurp my rightful place over you!"

The Arczeckhi were uncertain what to make of this, but their god's excitement infected them. They yelled out wordless encouragement as he spoke, growing in volume the more he said. Some of the caged slaves moaned, uncertain of their fate in light of this regime change.

"He tricked me and misled you," Mokuu went on, "and his treachery almost brought you to ruin. That might even be what he wanted all along." It took no more to convince many of the survivors of the Nishion City raid, and their vehement agreement startled many of the others. "And now, here he lies, beaten half-real for his transgression. He's failed you and betrayed my trust in him when I commanded him to unify you! He must be punished!"

The yelling turned into cheers, and Mokuu smiled in unmitigated joy. He turned around to face Sarkur, who stood staring up into his god's eyes. With great ceremony and deliberation, Mokuu placed Bear Fist's body on the ground at Sarkur's feet and then walked behind his warrior as everyone looked on in awe.

"This is Sarkur, my servant," the god said, putting both hands on Sarkur's shoulders now. "One of the most real among you. He earned these scars and disfigurations facing down the very one who has brought Bear Fist low. He survived the confrontation by believing in me and fighting in my name. In him, I am well pleased."

Sarkur's eyes shone with pride, and the Arczeckhi all around him regarded him with reverent awe.

"My reality is in him," Mokuu continued, "and he will be

the first of my *true* servants in this new age. He will bring you together as this Moon-Child never could, and he will lead you to victory and glory in my name. He will do what this Moon-Child could never do. And to him, I give this Moon-Child's life and reality. Let it serve you all as an example of the benefits of your worship. Through me are such things possible, and greater still. You must only worship me with your whole heart and rely on me with everything that makes you real, and I will give unto each of you as I have given unto Sarkur."

Wild excitement broke out at the god's words, and through the cheers and prayerful chants, all attention turned to Sarkur to see what he would do. Overwhelmed, Sarkur could only stare down at the barely real form that lay before him. Bear Fist's eyes were open as much as they seemed able to go, and the fallen Moon-Child looked at Sarkur with sad, frustrated resignation. The tattooed man couldn't even lift his head, though he seemed to be trying to.

"Now, Sarkur," Mokuu said, leaning over his warrior's shoulder to speak in his ear. "Show them what becomes of those who fail me and rob my people of their rightful glory."

"Mokuu?" Sarkur mumbled, unable to take his eyes off Bear Fist's.

"Kill him, Sarkur," Mokuu said, with much encouragement from the onlookers. "Make him a sacrifice worthy of me. Break his neck with your hands. Gouge out his eyes with his own weapons. Tear out his heart and devour it. Do whatever you must to make his reality your own." Sarkur only stood staring, and finally Mokuu gave his shoulders a painful squeeze and spoke again. "*Now*, Sarkur. Your people are waiting."

"But... But I can't," Sarkur said.

"*What?*"

"He's down, Mokuu," Sarkur gasped, barely able to speak at all. "He's beaten. I can't do it. Not like this."

The entire Arczeckhi gathering fell silent.

"What did you say?" Mokuu bellowed, throwing Sarkur to the ground on top of Bear Fist. "How dare you defy me when I exalted you above all these others? I'll destroy you *and* him for this."

"You'd better think twice about that," a loud, deep voice called out from the opposite side of the compound, cutting through the terrified silence at the end of Mokuu's raving. "And I mean right now."

Mokuu looked up, and the gathered Arczeckhi host turned as one to see a tall, brown-skinned man glaring at them from the back of a tall, black horse. He wore loose sandals and baggy purple pants, but his chest was bare, revealing the golden tattoo of the noonday sun he wore there. Many others were behind him on horses of their own, but they seemed of no consequence. The dark one in the lead stepped down from his horse and began to walk toward the Arczeckhi congregation without so much as a knife in his hands. And though he was unarmed, there was no fear in his eyes whatsoever.

Panther dismounted his tired, near-dead horse and stared at what looked like hundreds of black-furred barbarians. He and his detachment of Nishion soldiers had chased Bear Fist's men halfway across the country and almost into Verdangate, gaining serious ground on them each day. The beastmen didn't appear to have stopped for food or sleep like Panther and his men had, but doing so had gotten them only so far ahead. Now, all of them who were left lay dead or dying on the front steps of some long-lost ancient ruins, and their leader was in a pretty terrible spot.

"I know what you are," the Arczeckh god sneered as Panther came toward the milling barbarians. Many of the ones who'd survived the Nishion City attack fled outright. "You're the Sun-Child. You fought in Saikai village. You did this to Bear Fist."

"I did," Panther said, sizing up the god—Mokuu, the scarred barbarian had called him. Mokuu was proportioned like one of the squat, bandy-legged Arczeckhi, but he stood some twenty feet tall and was dressed in leather armor that was both far superior to anything the actual Arczeckhi were wearing and several hundred years out of date. "And if you don't back away from him, you're going to get a taste of the same."

Mokuu scooped Bear Fist up in one hand and laughed, taking a step toward Panther. "I'm not afraid of you, Sun-Child. You beat this one, but he was weak. He's nowhere near as real as I am. Especially here among my people."

"All right," Panther said with a cavalier shrug. "You better hope they still love you when I'm done with you." He started walking again, his eyes focused only on Mokuu.

"Destroy him," Mokuu said casually to his gathered people. "Tear him apart."

Those nearest Mokuu, namely the ones who hadn't been at Nishion City, tried to push back toward Panther, but the rest panicked and fled from him.

"Doesn't work that way," Panther said. "They already know what I'll do to them. You're the one who needs a lesson."

As he spoke and kept walking, the golden disk on his forehead began to shine, and his entire body began to glow with pure white light. The barbarians surged away from him. Those who didn't go to Nishion City still tried to get to him, but they were far outnumbered by their terrified brethren. The Arczeckhi horde parted around Panther and either fled the compound altogether or hurried to put their god between them and the glowing warrior.

"You cowards!" Mokuu shouted as his people fled. "Have you no faith in the power I can give you? Come back here and show him the strength you have through me!"

"Show me yourself, false god," Panther said. His power flashed around him, and he ran at Mokuu, drawing back a hard right hand.

Mokuu was impressed by the speed of the attack, but he was fast enough to counter it just the same. When Panther got in close, the god swung Bear Fist's body at him like a club, grinning with manic zeal. Shocked, Panther checked his rush and jumped out of the way, just barely avoiding a hard knock from Bear Fist's skull. Mokuu laughed at the surprise on Panther's face, and he swung Bear Fist back the other way to catch Panther across the spine. Panther was ready for the tactic this time, though, so instead of jumping aside, he leaped forward. He cleared Bear Fist's body by inches then vaulted off the back of Mokuu's wrist.

The impact forced the god to drop Bear Fist—who rolled to a stop half a dozen yards away—and it also propelled Panther up toward Mokuu's face. Panther punched him right between the crimson eyes, sending the god staggering back among his people. The Arczeckhi gasped to see their god struck, and they got out of the way to keep from tripping him.

Panther was less compliant. He landed between Mokuu's feet as the god staggered and swept both arms backward into the backs of Mokuu's knees. The impact knocked Mokuu's feet out from under him, and he crashed onto his back, crushing the roof and front wall of his spirit lodge. Panther's temporary advantage ended there, though, as the god kicked him square in the chest, sending him skidding across the grassy courtyard into a marble column that time hadn't yet brought low. Panther smashed into it, toppling it in a great cloud of dust, and Mokuu hauled himself up out of his ruined spirit lodge. Several paces away from where Panther had landed, Bear Fist lifted his head with tremendous effort to see what was happening.

Standing and shaking marble dust out of his hair, Panther was just in time to see Mokuu pounding toward him. He jumped out of the way as Mokuu took a swing at him, and broken stones flew from the impact. Panther escaped unharmed, though, and he stood to face the Arczeckh god once more. He dove out of the way as Mokuu tried to crush him with a giant piece of marble, but the maneuver brought him into kicking range again. The god's foot caught him right under the chin and flipped him backward onto the stone steps that led up to the empty castle of Kementeer. A corona of light trailed around his body as it flew, and the steps cracked where his chest and arms hit them. Nonetheless, he stood up again and even beckoned the god to come to him.

Mokuu did just that, picking up another chunk of broken marble for his other hand. He hurled the first one at Panther then charged toward him, switching the second stone to his other hand. Panther jumped straight up to avoid the first stone, which exploded beneath his feet, but that put him right in the path of the stone in Mokuu's other hand as the god rushed forward and tried to swat him down with it. Calmly, gracefully, Panther simply twisted in midair and swung his glowing right fist like a sledgehammer. The punch shattered the stone and nearly broke Mokuu's hand, spinning the god around awkwardly as Panther dropped back to earth. Capitalizing on Mokuu's lack of balance, Panther then grabbed the god's hairy wrist and hauled forward and down on it with every bit of strength he could muster. The god stumbled, lurched and flipped over Panther's shoulder, landing with a tremendous crash. As soon as Panther let him go, though, Mokuu thumped him hard in the chest with his middle finger, knocking Panther flat on his back.

The Arczeckh god recovered first, and he got to his feet while Panther was shaking stars out of his eyes. With an inarticulate growl, he stomped down on Panther's chest, driving the man down into the ground. Panther tried to roll out of the way when Mokuu lifted his leg, but the god drove it back down again three more times in quick succession. Panther got his arms up to block the last two, but he still couldn't get up. After the last hard kick, Mokuu twisted back and forth with all his weight on that one leg like he was trying to smear apart an insect. All of a sudden, though, the weight was gone, and Mokuu lurched backward gagging.

Panther sat up in the crater he'd been driven into to find Bear Fist on his knees on the opposite side of Mokuu. The barbarian's tattoos were glowing again, though only faintly, and a thin blue-white leash of braided energy had whipped out from the end of his wrist to wrap around Mokuu's neck. Surprise and feral outrage twisted Mokuu's face into a hideous demon mask, and he dug both hands under the leash's collar and jerked himself forward. Unable to pull back with any strength, Bear Fist slid forward and lost his balance. Mokuu screeched once in contempt and gave a mighty heave, tearing the leash into a thousand glowing shards like it was made of nothing more than tissue paper. He laughed in triumph and looked down at Bear Fist, and that distraction was all Panther needed.

When the god took his eyes off him, Panther kicked up to his feet and launched himself at Mokuu, energy trailing behind him like the tail of a comet. He flew forward and pounded both fists into Mokuu's stomach like twin battering rams. The god folded up in the middle, and with the last of his strength, Bear Fist grabbed Mokuu's right heel. The Arczeckh god lost his balance and wound up flat on his back one more time. Panther didn't give him a chance to get up this time, though. Instead, he leaped on Mokuu's chest and hit him again just as hard as he had last time. Mokuu tried to recover and punch Panther off his chest, but Panther caught the blow in his palm and slammed a punch of his own right into Mokuu's face. The ground beneath him cracked, and the god's eyes crossed as he lay temporarily stunned.

"Too bad you weren't afraid of me, false god," Panther said, dropping a knee into the fallen god's chest. "Might have saved yourself the trouble and the embarrassment."

Mokuu tried to get up or knock Panther off him, but his efforts only earned him another couple of heavy punches to the chin. He even tried to bite the man, but that only inspired Panther to knock four of his front teeth out. Finally, in desperation, he turned to the Arczeckhi who stood staring in awe at what was happening.

"My people," he cried piteously. "Aid me. Together, we can destroy him. Help me now, and I'll give you—"

"I don't think so," Panther said, punching Mokuu once more for good measure. "I already told you, they know better. This is about you and me, Mokuu, and they can see which one of us is more 'real.'" He turned then to look at the Arczeckhi and bellowed, "Can't you?"

The horrified fascination that had held the Arczeckhi still all this time finally broke, and the barbarians did just what they'd done back in Nishion City. They threw up their hands, threw down their weapons and fled. Mokuu alternately pleaded with them, hurled invectives at them and made them all manner of outrageous promises, but they didn't listen. They abandoned him to his fate and scattered in all directions. And as they did, forswearing the trust and recanting the faith they'd placed in him all these months, Mokuu's power began to fade rapidly. His armor frayed and rotted, and he began to shrink like ice melting in the noonday sun. In mere moments, Panther was straddling nothing more than a minor spirit in threadbare clothing, who was no larger than the people who'd once venerated him. Mokuu struggled at first but eventually just broke down sobbing at how radically he'd diminished.

"All right, little god," Panther said, standing up and lifting Mokuu up to his eye level. The radiance emanating from him seemed to hurt the god's eyes. "It isn't my place to destroy you, but I want you to remember what I did to you even when you thought you were really something here. You rose far too high above your station and at too many innocent people's expense. That sort of behavior might have run rampant all throughout this age, but it ends here. All of it. You hear me?"

Mokuu nodded, distilling his sobs down into pitiful sniveling.

"Good," Panther said. "Because things aren't going to be pretty if you don't shape up. No matter how fast you run, no matter where you try to hide, there's nowhere the light of the sun won't be able to find you. And when it does, somebody just like me is going to give you ten times worse than this little spanking. And, Mokuu," Panther added, holding the god very close to him and speaking softly, "Heaven help you if I'm the one who catches you getting out of line again. Because if I ever do, I might just forget what is or isn't my place. You understand?"

The god's eyes bulged in terror, and Panther finally let him go. The god fell in the dirt and scrambled backward, unable to take his eyes off the one who'd beaten him.

"Go on," Panther said, waving a hand in dismissal. "Get out of my sight, and go back to whatever hole you call your sanctum."

The god's restraint broke at last, and he bolted. As soon as he could tear his gaze away, he turned and ran, dematerializing before he was even five waddling steps away. Panther waited a moment to make sure the god wasn't pulling some sort of trick, then nodded in satisfaction. The celestial fire within him dimmed, and his body slowly ceased glowing. When he looked like nothing more than a mortal man again, he turned away. He intended to speak to Rolan and the Nishion soldiers who'd come along all this way, but instead, he saw Bear Fist lying not three yards away. He walked over to the barbarian first and stood over him with the sun directly above him.

"And as for you..." he said as the battered barbarian squinted up at him.

"Just get it over with this time," Bear Fist croaked at him. "I've got nothing left."

"If I were going to kill you, I wouldn't give you the chance to tell me to," Panther said, shaking his head. "Well, I *was* going to at first in Nishion City. I admit it. You've done a lot of evil, and for most people, there wouldn't be any coming back from that. But you and me, we're not most people, are we?"

"What?"

"We're Exalted," Panther said, kneeling beside Bear Fist so only the two of them could hear what he was saying. "We've got responsibilities. We're the pillars of Creation, and it's up to us to keep it from collapsing into chaos. And if we do our jobs, I figure, we're going to live a lot longer than any sins we've committed up to now. It's just a matter of choosing a life that's better than the one you've been living."

"Are you lecturing me?" Bear Fist managed to whisper. "Are you *preaching* to me? Now?"

Panther shrugged. "I wasn't going to, but something you said back in Nishion City got me thinking. You've done plenty wrong, and it's blown up in your face pretty spectacularly, but your problem might not be that you're an evil, unrighteous son of a bitch. I mean, you helped me with Mokuu there, and nobody said you had to. No, your problem *might* just be that an evil, unrighteous son of a bitch has led you astray. Maybe you're not so different from one of these furry savages in the bigger picture—doing bad things for no better reason than somebody a lot stronger told you to. I don't know why you'd listen to somebody like that—or why the Arczeckhi would—but then again, I don't know *you* either. It doesn't really matter. Point is, I'm giving you a chance here. I'm going to let you get up, and I'm going to let you walk out of here. If you live—and you probably will—you can go back to wherever you came from and think long and hard about what you're actually supposed to be doing with all this power you've been given. And maybe, when you've come to a decision, you can bring it up with this Mazuchi character who thinks he knows so much about the Children of the Sun. You got all that, Bear Fist?"

A strange, inscrutable look had come over Bear Fist's face, and he nodded in response to Panther's question.

"Good. Now, it's time to get up if you can and start walking. Though there is one last thing: Strip off those golden rams, and leave them there."

Bear Fist's strange expression turned into one of anger, and he tried to sit up, but Panther shoved him back down with one hand.

"This isn't just a free pass for you, barbarian," Panther said, shaking his head. "I wasn't kidding when I said you've done wrong. You've got rivers of innocent blood on your hands, and you even roped a delinquent god into this madness. If you don't do what I said, there's going to come an early reckoning."

The anger in Bear Fist's eyes smoldered there another tense moment more, but it slowly faded to be replaced by the strange, unreadable expression he'd worn before. Without another word, he unbuckled the orichalcum smashfists he'd been wearing since the attack on Nishion City and lay them on the ground at Panther's feet. Panther ran his fingers over the ram's-head motif on one of them and nodded.

"Good," he said. "Now, you can get up. Go home if you can make it, and don't forget what I told you. I'm not going to bother threatening you like I did Mokuu since you already heard it, but just… Just make the right decision."

"I'll think about what you said," Bear Fist said as he rose laboriously. "And what you've done. And what you've taken from me. I won't forget it. And one night in the future when the moon is full, you and I will meet again. Then and there, you'll learn what my decision is. I assure you now, you will not like what I have to tell you."

"We'll see," Panther said. "Now, start walking."

With as much pride and grace as he could summon, Bear Fist turned on his heel and walked away. In minutes, he was gone, swallowed up by the forest that had long ago swallowed up the ancient, forgotten city of Kementeer.

An hour before night fell, everyone left in Kementeer was ready at last to leave. The prisoners who'd been captured in months of Arczeckh raids all across Verdangate and Nishion had been freed and fed and taken care of by the Nishion soldiers. Panther had led groups of them around the city making sure that the Arczeckhi were actually gone. Panther even took a quick look around to make sure that Mokuu and Bear Fist weren't still lingering. By the time they were all satisfied of their safety and the prisoners' minor wounds had been treated with the materials on hand, the sun had sunk low in the sky behind the trees.

Panther and Rolan stood a little way off from the rest of the Nishion soldiers and the erstwhile captives. Rolan's foot, it turned out, hadn't been broken before, but only badly bruised. He was walking around fine on it now, even after days of hard riding on horseback. The wound across his forehead had healed up nicely too, though his left eye was completely useless to him now. He hid it behind a black leather patch. The mercenary fiddled with the edges of it as Panther tightened and readjusted the straps of the weapons he'd taken from Bear Fist.

"How do they feel?" Rolan asked.

"Heavy," Panther said. "Heavier than they look, anyway, but not so bad. It's a little like wearing a cestus and carrying a punch dagger in the same hand. I'm getting used to the feel of them."

"Good. I think we're all wrapped up here, then, all things taken into account. Are you ready to leave?"

"I am," Panther said. "But I think I'm going a different way than the rest of you."

"Oh," Rolan said. "It's time for that again, is it?"

"Afraid so."

"Are you certain you don't want to come back to Nishion City with us? I'm sure the royal family will change its mind if—"

Panther shook his head. "Don't worry about it. I was ready

to leave there anyway, remember? No sense going back there just to leave all over again."

"I suppose not. Plus, it seems as though you make everybody who's not me terribly uncomfortable."

"Also, there's that."

"So, where are you going to go? Or have you decided yet?"

"I've decided. I'm going back home."

"Nexus."

"That's right. I told Kellen before the attack that there's a lot of work there for someone like me to do."

"Undoubtedly. And I understand the authorities don't share the Realm's... religious prejudices."

"They don't," Panther said.

"Then I wish you the best of luck there, Panther. You'll be returning more a champion than you ever were when you left it, and I think Creation will be better for it."

"I hope so," Panther said. "Thank you, Rolan. For everything, now and before."

"And to you," Rolan said.

The mercenary held out a hand, and Panther shook it, careful not to gouge the man's forearm with the blade of his new weapon. Then, with nothing more to say, the two men parted company and walked away in separate directions. Rolan went back toward the soldiers of Nishion who were ready to lead the barbarians' captives the long way home. Panther headed south instead, angling toward the faraway bank of the Yellow River. He would turn west when he got there and follow the bank until he came to a settlement or a Guild port of call. From there, he would get on a boat and ride it as far as it would take him until he finally made it back to where his old life had started and ended. And when he got there, the divine and lasting work of his new life would begin in earnest.

And eventually, he would find out if what he'd told Bear Fist about redemption was really true or just his own wishful thinking.

Acknowledgments

Thanks go out again to my pal John Chambers, who knows *Exalted* better than almost everybody. Thanks also to Ken Cliffe and Phil Boulle for forestalling a complete mental breakdown by pushing back my deadlines when various werewolves jumped on my back.

And extra special thanks to Mike Lee, who stepped in to redline and develop this book when everybody's schedules went helter-skelter and out of whack, *then* got complicated too. After an impressive track record of freelance writing, Mike came on board as a full-time developer with *Demon: The Fallen*. Since then, he's always been there to take on any conceivable project this company can throw at him, and he's handled them with the grace and aplomb of a true professional. This book is one of Mike's last staff projects for White Wolf before he goes back to being a full time writer and seeking greener pastures. We're all going to miss his talent and insight.

About the Author

Carl Bowen has written novels, novellas and short stories for White Wolf's retired World of Darkness line, as well as helping usher in the new setting. He's also a copyeditor and sometime developer. *Pillar of the Sun* is his second novel for the *Exalted* setting (after *A Day Dark as Night*). In his spare time, he punches out scurrilous hooligans by the dozen.

Curious about other Crossroad Press books?
Stop by our site:
http://www.crossroadpress.com
We offer quality writing
in digital, audio, and print formats.